Life-Breath and the Truth

Life-Breath and the Truth

(The Real and the Delusory)

Kamala Narasimha
P.P.Giridhar

PARTRIDGE
A Penguin Random House Company

To order additional copies of this book, contact
Partridge India
000 800 10062 62
orders.india@partridgepublishing.com

www.partridgepublishing.com/india

Remarks by the Author of the Translation

The following remarks would sum up my idea of translation.
First of all, since natural languages are functions of a common biological infrastructure we humans share of cognitive faculties and sensory-motor abilities, we need to say that whatever is expressed in one natural language is necessarily subject to expression in another natural language, subject further of course to the constraints of interlinguistic transmission imposed by the nature of natural language.

One of such constraints is illustrated by the plural human third person pronoun *avaru* used by married Kannada women to refer to their husbands. *avaru* in this use is referentially singular but honorific. There is no way of replicating this in English, for English does not have a referentially singular and honorific third person pronoun. The pronoun *they* is necessarily referentially plural. One has to say *he* and add 'honorific' within brackets, which may be deemed klutzy. *gaLu* added to personal names and common nouns in Kannada indicates honour. Thus *shastrigaLu* (shastri-gaLu), *mantrigaLu* (minister-gaLu) are referentially singular but honorific. *gaLu* elsewhere marks plural number for nonhuman nouns in Kannada, while -(*a*) *ru* marks plural humans. I tried saying Mr Shastri, Mr Gowda and Shree Shastri, Shree Gowda in English translation, but neither seemed felicitous and then I switched to *the respectable Shastri* for *Shastri-gaLu,* and *the respectable Gowda* for *gowda-ru* which seemed okay. Kannada wives address their husbands simply as *rii* which is an honorific address term. Tamil wives say *ennange* 'what-honorific' which is indeed the parallel of the Kannada *rii.* There is no porting it to English even as any human can conceive this.

One holds on to *rii* and footnotes its meaning not because holding on to it amounts to resistance to colonization, as Rajiv Malhotra avers (see below), but because its parallels in other languages are oddly askew and this is the nature of natural language.

There is no elegant, nonklutzy and natural way of replicating in English the Urdu couplet

> aap ban gayii tum
> tum ban gayii tuu

you(most honorific) became you (less honorific)
you(less honorific) became you(least honorific=intimate)

English doesn't have a triadic second person pronoun paralleling the Urdu pronominal system of *tuu* 'you (sg)', *tum* 'you(sg, more honorific) and *aap* 'you (sg, most honorific).

Two reasons for saying that anything intelligible and anything expressed in one natural language is subject to being expressed in another language:

a. that humans are biologically and cognitively prewired identically and
b. sound and sense, the two sides of a linguistic expression, come from two totally and absolutely unrelated directions before coding took place.

Natural languages are genetically founded computationally configured culture-added technologies. Linguistic structure has nothing to do with culture in the sense that rules and regularities of grammar don't need reference to culture for explanation while the lexicon is embedded in, or motivated by, experiential reality.

The template, the motherboard comes from our genes while the words, the slot-fillers in the template come from society or experience. The rules and constraints governing lexical structure however are universal. For example, lexicalization is not a free-for-all. The material that can be encapsulated in a word is not arbitrary although it is admittedly surprisingly, but not totally unforeseeably, diverse. It is also conceded that the equation of the analytical or syntactic intralinguistic translations of lexicalisations is not full, as has been borne out, for example, by the now putative unequivalence of the lexical *kill* and the analytical *cause to die.*

Kate killed Kobo on Saturday.

as an equivalent of

Kate caused Kobe to die on Saturday.

is okay, but

Kate caused Kobe to die on Saturday by shooting him on Friday.

can not have as its equivalent

Kate killed Kobe on Saturday by shooting him on Friday.

where *kill* is NOT equivalent to *cause to die.* Or the lexical *accompany* and the analytical *go with. Go with* is intransitive while *accompany* is transitive etc.

The language-thought highway is admittedly a two-way street. It is true that the way a language casts general human cognition into its own lexical chase determines the way we look at the world because we speak that language. But since we humans are all identically wired, we need also to say that all linguistic meanings are quarried from the same cognitive bedrock, the same subsoil, and we know that there is cognition other than that expressed by natural language. This is subject to what epigenetic changes that can be brought about in language. Epigenetic effects, as opposed preformation, on natural language are as yet poorly understood. But whatever be the epigenetics of language, the heritable cognitive bedrock of humans cannot change so as to be unavailable to others. We know that thinking and consciousness are bigger sets than language. There may be areas of thinking not amenable for language and areas of human consciousness that may not be available for thinking.

The clay is the same for all of us, but the moldings and the forgings are different along lines that mark a language group as exclusive. A possible analogy of the alleged, but in my view, and in a deep substantial sense, pretty superficial, uniqueness of lexicalisations in languages is the human palm or tongue or the foot whose prints are unique to individuals, which we know is a great forensic help. The finger prints of even identical twins are uniquely different. Even though individual words, unlike linguistic structure, are socially motivated, they are, I submit, NOT unique to individual languages in the same sense as natural language, as a mode of thinking and creating mental worlds, is unique to man(there is no way a nonnatural language like an animal communication system can say "If opportunity is not knocking on your door, create a door!", or "Give me some milkless sugarless waterless coffee!" or "If I win in a race with my son, I lose!" or "I am you, you are me, what have done to each other?!" or "mere rang mei rangnevaali! (Hindi for 'the female who is going to meld in my colours')", "Sitting is the next smoking!") or consciousness is unique to man.

I am not sure if epigenetic effects on language affect the point that the material that linguistic meanings in diverse languages are quarried from is the same cognitive bedrock.

That words are NOT the concepts they symbolize, meaning they, the words are outside the ontologies of what they refer to, is possibly comparable to the idea that even man is NOT his nature or form, as argued by Deepak Chopra in a seminal article called The Future of Science and God (Speaking Tree 26th Oct 2014) as part of his suggestion that the universe, the brain and the body are manifestations of a universal consciousness, that they come from a common source, which is a possible argument for the existence of a single ulterior force.

It is clear that I am *not* my name and similarly I am *not* my caste, I am *not* my religion, I am *not* my language etc. and the sound sequence *tree* is *not* the concept or the empirical object of tree even in English, pace what the literary cognoscenti think. The linguistic word is an artificially arbitrarily constructed representation of the concept and the real-world object.

While syntax has nothing to do with culture so that we couldn't say SVO carries more English culture than SOV or a sentence like

Flinging out as it did from her mouth, it flabbergasted me.

is untranslatably English culture or NP-modifying relative clauses as in Kannada carry Kannada culture any more than sentence-modifying relative clauses carry English culture. At the same time we see that words like granny, mummy and daddy on the one hand and supper, lunch, dating on the other are enveloped in a culture. The thing to say here is that the lexical variants within the same language of the former viz grandmother(for granny), mother(for mummy) and father (for daddy) seem to be less culture-internal while the analytical variants of the latter namely midday meal(=lunch), night meal(=supper), a romantic outing(=dating) are incontestably culture-free in the sense that the locution *midday meal* is an expression made of sounds taken from a-receivable-by-all and produceable-by-all universal stock of sounds while the meaning is made from material which is human and hence universal so that its hard-to-contest adequacy of translation into any other natural language is a foregone possibility.

While the Hindi sentence

> mere rang mein rangneevaali
> i-gen colour in colour(vi)-prt-agnt(fem)

is for sure culturally coloured, we need to say we all share the cognitive fountain from which the cultural colouring springs. Which is to admit that the material out of which the culturally motivated lexical items are made we all share. Which is exactly why we can translate the above highly culturally coloured Hindi sentence as

> she who is to be melded (or meshed, merged or mingled or processed or woven or coloured or immixed or admixed or painted) in my colours

or whatever. That there is no translation of the above Hindi sentence either in Kannada or Angami or Gikuyu or Dyirbal (in terms of a cognition we all share) is unacceptable, just as that the word *dharma* is untranslatable is unacceptable.

paaru	peeT see	hai
Paaru-nom	belly from	be-prs

lit. Paaru is from stomach

"Paru is pregnant."

is a very Hindi expression to mean biological conception. That it is untranslatable is as unacceptable as to say the very English

Ferrina is in the family way.

is untranslatable. Neither of them has any hint of biological conceiving or pregnancy. As mentioned earlier, the idea that a particular idea has no existence apart from its linguistic expression is not right, although the ramifications of this need to be sorted out. (For example, how prelinguistic thought relates to this is a definite and significant question.) If this is true, that would mean that the linguistic expression is outside the ontology of the idea it expresses, which would naturally lead on to the absolute portability of any idea across language barriers. This will also put paid to the idea espoused by the literary cognoscenti that the expression itself becomes the referent in literary discourse.

In his recent HarperCollins book titled **Being Different** Rajiv Malhotra has a section called *Sanskrit Nontranslatables* in which he declares that certain Sanskrit words are not their putative or alleged equivalents in English. *dharma* for example is not religion, *atman* is not soul, *brahman* is not god and so on. I give below his exposition about *dharma* and *brahman*

Brahman comes from root word 'brih' means to expand. The all-expansive ultimate reality that creates all, lives in all and transcends all.	In Judaism, *god* was seen as Mount Sinai who is creator of universe
brahman is the cosmos and resides in all of us, unrealized as atman.	In Judeo-Christian sense *god* is separate from the universe.
brahman is not authoritative or punitive.	*god* is authoritative and punishes those who transgress HIS rules and those who do not follow HIS religion.
ishwara, brahman, devta and *bhagwan* all have different meanings and contexts of use.	They all cannot be replaced by *god* just like *uncle* does not necessarily mean chacha, mama etc.

Dharma comes from Sanskrit word 'dhri' which means 'that which upholds' or 'that without which nothing can stand' or "that which maintains stability and harmony of universe".	*Religion* is worship of divine that is separate from human, has religious institution/authority and governed. Religious rituals are based on events that happened some time in history. Hence all Abrahmic religions i.e., Judaism, Christianity and Islam are history-centric.
Dharma is conduct, duty, justice, morality, virtue, right and much more. Animals, Plants, Electrons have dharma but no Religion.	No such explanation for Religion. Also, Religion is only for humans.
Dharma is not LAW as law is authoritative.	Western religion believe GOD's law must be obeyed and hence non-followers must be converted or punished.

The first submission here is that the worlds of reference of lexical items across languages are not identical so that the English *soul* is not the Sanskrit *aatman*, *religion* is not *dharma* and *brahman* is not *god* and so on. This is not a big deal, as has been sought to be made out.

This askewness happens all the time across natural languages.

English has more than forty physical movement verbs, each including style, manner and intent of movement: *gallivant* in English means 'move looking for excitement' and *shuffle* means 'move without lifting legs very much' as opposed to *jog, run, walk* etc where you lift your legs fully. *sashay* is 'to walk casually' and *streak, amble, saunter, stroll, stride, stalk, strut* and so on mean 'move with some or other accompanying shade of meaning'. Many or most languages will not have single word equivalents for these. *vi* in Angami means 'be good', a two word expression in English. Examples can be multiplied in various less-known languages of the world.

The fact of the matter is that the word *dharma* includes in itself certain cognitive stuff which may not be the same as what its suspected equivalent in another language may include. People who say *dharma* is not an equivalent of the word 'religion' are right (but see below for a disclaimer). This is because languages lexicalise meanings in delightfully diverse, nonisomorphic ways. But the point is that to say that the word *dharma* has no translation in other natural languages and, to further suggest as Malhotra does, that

> "holding on to Sanskrit terms and thereby preserving the complete range of their meanings becomes a way of resisting colonization,"

Or that to translate the word *dharma* for example into other lanaguages is to colonise ourselves are way off target.

The word *dharma* is polysemic whose different meanings are pretty much sortable and externalisable in terms of its selectional affinities with the other constituents in the sentence. The 'range of meanings' that Malhotra says 'should be preserved' are sorted in terms of these selection affinities. Thus the word *dharma* in Kannada, for example, means 'righteousness' in a sentence like

> dharmaakke hedari badukidavaru naavu
> "We have lived, in deference to, and going by, righteousness"

It means 'morally obligatory duty' in a sentence like

> hettavaranna nooDikoLLoodu makkaLa dharma
> "Looking after parents is the children's morally obligatory duty."

It means 'natural property' in a sentence like

> meelinda keLakke hariyuvudu niirina dharma
> "to flow from a higher level to lower level is water's natural property"

It means 'charitable' in a locution like

> dharma chathra "charitable dwelling place"

In application forms, the word *dharma* means inexorably and exclusively 'religion' and nothing else, which only belies the thesis that *dharma* is not religion. One of the meanings of *dharma*, we are constrained then to say, is 'religion'. In

> dharma patni 'legally wedded wife'
> dharma-wife

dharma has a different but very definite meaning.

Cognitive legibility means translatability.

Whatever is externalisable is subject to translation. If one can externalise the various meanings of the word *dharma*, a translation of all these senses is very much on the cards. If you can externalize the various senses of the word *brahman*, all these senses are very much translatable. We seem to think that translation is word to word equivalence. That is not the way natural languages work, I'm afraid.

To declare for example that the verb *cu-vu* 'to marry (sbj: sg and fem)', for example, in Mao Naga, is not translatable because English or some other natural languages do not express it in a single word, like Mao Naga does, is laughable.

The Angami Naga verb *vi* 'be good' is another example which wouldn't have single- word translations in many natural languages. To say in other words that the English equivalents of these single-word expressions given above are not their *translations* doesn't make good sense, does it?

To say that English words like *date* (as in *Daisy is my today's date*), *lunch, dinner, brine* and so on and the Hindi *naana* and *daada* have no 'translations' in other languages because they would not be single words in other languages is not sustainable.

Is to hold on to the Hindi *daada* and *naana* themselves instead of their analytical English equivalents of *paternal grandfather* and *maternal grandfather* to resist colonization, as Malhotra has us believe?

Take the word *yoga*. What are we saying when we say it is more pregnant with meaning than a simple translatable meaning? The submission is the question of : can you externalize this pregnancy? or you can't? If one can't, it is cognitively illegible, which of course is surprising, in which case there is no longer any discussion. If on the other hand you can, then *what is the problem* is the question. It may be, like the word *dharma*, polysemic. We then need to sort the different individual meanings and render into other linguistic codes.

One meaning simply is 'physical exercise'. What is the mystery is again the question.

That there is some unfathomable mystery attached to some linguistic objects is a myth spread by some bigots, people who strike out on the path of rational enquiry armed with presystematic predialogue predebate prejudice. A rationalist, a real thinker is one who comes to the table with no predebate prejudice.

That there is more than one representation to some linguistic objects, more than one reading to some lexical objects and that words are open ended or nondiscrete in a certain way is true.

But otherwise that linguistic objects are mysterious is itself a monstrous mystery! As Deepak Chopra asserts in the article quoted above (The Future of God and Science, The Speaking Tree 26th Oct 2014), there is still some mystery about life and the universe in as much as questions like *when, how and why life began* (that appeared on planet earth four billion years ago - my addition. Giridhar) and *what is the nature and origin of the universe* (that began fourteen billion years ago) *and of human life and consciousness* (six million years ago when hominids separated from our arboreal ancestors) are still open questions. Such openness is what keeps the question of the existence of God open, says Chopra, which is why, reasons Chopra insightfully, militant atheists don't know what they are talking about.

I agree.

But such openness, I am afraid, is NOT the case with (the nature of, the scientific truths about, the design features of, and the internal structure and external function of) natural language (which may be fifty thousand years old).

Ideas like meanings are deferred, or can be deferred, that one can do anything and everything with natural language, that there is only interpretation and no definite meaning are parts of academic mythology, much like a cause-effect sequence denting and an appeasable, appealable, prayable, magical God is part of cultural mythology, much like the idea that linguistic creativity is an exclusive function of the writer rather than of the code or system and the idea that sound sequences themselves become their referents in literary cosmoses are parts of literary academic mythology.

We need also to say that, true as the idea that language does shape thought is, the cognitive bedrock material out of which this shaping takes place is essentially the same so that translation of this differently shaped thought cannot be thought impossible in principle. It is difficult to take the idea that some epigenetics is involved in grammatical gender, the way different languages cognise and organise the colour spectrum or the different orientations that languages have about space.

A word about my idea of art is in order since this novel quite fits into it although it does strain credulity and thus didn't quite sweep me off my feet. In the bargain the following paragraphs also place in perspective at least some of Kannada creative fiction. Not all of Kannada creative fiction fits into my idea of art.

I urge a healthy civilized debate and dialogue that this spell-out of my view of art could stimulate. A sizeable chunk of literary creation under the sun may not qualify to be art on this view of art. Quite a few Kannada novels certainly wouldn't be *art*.

More deductivist than inductive, more theoretical than empirical, this low-down on my view of art, argues that there has to be a natural adductive-abductive tension in art, which corresponds to how the world is and how you wished it was, or to the poetry of the soul and the prose of reality. There can be no such tension for example in sociology and cultural anthropology. Art is a magical carpet that wafts you away from mundanity and this-worldliness on to a heart-warming soul-lifting, soul-searching plane of, onto the infinity or divinity if you will, of human existence and being. This hallmark of art is the result of the adductive-abductive tension that runs through it.

The crux then is pieces that do nothing more than depict sordid irrational realities as they exist, doing nothing more about them are emphatically NOT art. This is a strict no-no for art.

How art can own something that reason disowns is the root question.

That novels like *sanskaara, tabbaliyu niinaade magane, dharmashree* among others in Kannada, and a humungous amount of what is dubbed 'creative literature' all over the world, does this. i.e it is simply incogitant replication of empirical reality, which renders them absolutely useless for mankind and the Kannadiga.

One needs intellectual crusaders in every society and not intellectually indigent efforts like these which further mislead the layman, pushing him up the ontological, epistemological moral and social garden path. Such efforts are not torch bearers of change in society.

They don't carry or create value. Such novels in Kannada as named above seem to be designed for Kannada society continuing to stagnate, stink, rot and regress as a casteist society.

That art and literature should by definition not be *mere* unadulterated realism might sound contrarian but here it is, the argument against every novel, everything that is big, bouncy and allegedly *artistic* that is intellectually indigent, lacking humanity and rationality.

Cut to the chase, the general point is essentialist and deductivist, and pretty simple, like all significant things in life are:

> Anything and everything one writes, paints, sculpts, sings
> need NOT be ipso facto art, much like anything anyone
> says need not constitute good sense.

Much like numbers don't, or the majority doesn't determine, truth, the fact that somebody has done what somebody in fact has, need NOT, ipso facto, mean anything, need NOT be significant, need NOT carry value. Rumi says there is an area for humans where there is no right or wrong and he would like to meet you there. True as this is, it is clear that in the business of social and individual living, there has to be a pretty strong sense of right and wrong both for breakthroughs in conceptual space, in science and technology and for social synergy and good. Otherwise there would be nothing like evil, good and bad, irrationality, immorality etc.

Every human behavior needs to fit into a template, a chase (as in letter-press printing technology), a procrustean bed. In their nature and character, these templates may be different for different arenas of human behaviour. The procrustean beds that grammars of natural languages are are different from the procrustean beds that artistic pieces are. The latter, for example, are admittedly freer (See below for 'distorted reality' in literature). But there is no denying that there is such a definable procrustean bed, however small. It is never a no-holds-barred free-for-all! It can NOT be. Science has this fool-proof way of consigning nonsense, material that doesn't conform to its procrustean bed, to the dustbin. Art in general and literature in particular, it seems, has no such systemic mechanism.

The following paragraphs elucidate what I think is the bottom line about art, its procrustean bed, its subsoil.
One could call it the art bed, analogous to river bed, seabed, garden bed etc.

Facts, experiential or imagined, are to art as food is to life.

Food is there for life, but life is not there for food. Life is something else. Its aim is not ingestion of food although, paradoxical as it may seem, life is, in an essential sense, a function of food. *Without food one doesn't survive and yet food is not life.* The same is exactly true of art. *Without facts art will not survive, and yet facts are not art.* Facts of life or of lived experience cannot be the aim of art although facts input into, and sustain art, pretty much like food inputs into, and sustains, life. Literature or art in general is partly a function of experiential facts and nonexperiential or imagined constructs. But this material from which art is made constitutes neither the output nor the goal of art, much like food, because of which the human body in fact exists and sustains, is neither the output nor the goal of life. Facts of life are thus, quite emphatically, not a sufficient condition of art, although they are possibly necessary.

If the hard empirical facts of lived experience are not the aim of art, *what is their role in art* is the question. Parallelly, if art is not a photograph or a photocopy or a mimeograph of life and reality, *what is it* is the question.

The role of reality in art is that of a scaffold, a paver, a service-renderer for something that per force follows the scaffolding and paving. Experiential facts are the source material, the pavement, the path-forgings. Facts only pave the way. Pavements are NEVER there for their own sake. They are there for people to walk on. Garden beds are there for something to grow on.

Seabeds and river beds form a footing that sources life. Art ought to source, give and nourish life like this. Empirical facts sort of found art, constitute the point of departure for art, get art going, relating art to life, preventing it from degenerating into didacticism, tendentiousness, discursiveness and sermonizing. Subtly interwoven into this level of scaffolding however would be and ought to be a level that transcends it, like in the sea shore event where the watcher is led to what he is led to by what he watches, mundane though the event very much is. As they say, to solve a problem we need to think at a level different from the level that the problem exists at. There are two such foundational levels in all literary creation, it seems to me. The essentially literary level is one that is different from the level at which the documentation of imagined or lived experience, the pavement exists. An accurate documentation of factual happenings in one's life wouldn't add up to literature, it seems to me. An imaginative weaving of these factual happenings wouldn't either. This nearly anybody can do. These two levels link in terms of what may be called distillation and an implicit bar-raising value-creating commentary.

What is it that the literary piece or any artistic piece distils the facts into, implicitly slides or eases the facts into, is the critical question in any art, it seems to me. Supposing there is an imaginative chronicling of this tale of Yazidis being enslaved by ISIS jihadists: very authentic and aesthetic tale. Why should one call this very accurate authentic archiving 'value-creating art'? Its being called art would be a function of what these facts distil into. At least make the description so touching as to give out a hint of its barbaricity.

Art, in my view, consists in such telling.

The pavement part is the mirror function of art while the distillation part is its lamp function. *All art is more lamp than mirror, it seems to me.* The mirroring is there for the lighting up, for the life-enhancing ennobling pointing up of things. In art the mirroring cannot be there for its own sake. It needs to make a hearteningly delightful difference to the reader at some level of her being without being preachy, without being tendentious, as does the sunset painting, adduced below from Hiriyanna.

What art does with empirical facts is what one looks for in any art. There is an anecdote that M. Hiriyanna relates in his book, Art Experience. On seeing the painting of a sunset the connoisseur remarks,

"I haven't seen a sunset like this in my life",

and the painter comes back with the following:

"Don't you wish to see one?!"

This exactly captures my idea of art.

How many Kannada novels, and how many Indian novels do this is a big question.

While the lighting up is both necessary and sufficient, the mirroring is possibly necessary without being sufficient. The lighting up could be in terms of cartooning, caricaturing, parodying and satirizing in emphatic terms. The artist is the flame in the mirror. The positive difference that we said art should make to the reader is in terms of the light of this flame.

Facts constitute the body of art while the soul that resides in this body is what I am arguing all art should have as their subsoil, something that is over and above this documentation or archiving.

One could indeed distort empirical, lived-experiential reality to achieve some aims but these aims, I submit, can never be in violation of the eternal human values of freedom, equity, justice. Dedalus Books in the UK for example has invented its own distinctive genre, which they term 'distorted reality', "where the bizarre, the unusual and the grotesque and the surreal meld in a kind of intellectual fiction". Man in fact has this pressing but natural urge of seeking novel ways of living and thinking. This is fine and welcome, but the point of the procrustean bed for art, as indeed for all human behavior, remains. Magical realism for example may or may not make sense. It is not necessary that all magical realism makes good sense, much like mere 'authentic' and 'aesthetic' depiction of undistorted reality may not make 'artistic' sense.

What with casteism, religionism, languagism, skin-colourism, patriarchy, slavery, umpteen blind beliefs, rackets and mafias, and inequities of all hues, most of the social ethoses under the sun may be described as 'sewers in spate'. Who would want these 'sewers in spate' to be replicated or represented in art as they are, depicting them 'in preplanned tours' like some Kannada writers have done? There are people it seems who would like that! At least I wouldn't.

I reject such 'literature', literature that endorses evil and irrationality, much like I reject all evil, all irrationality, all bloody-mindedness in real life: art by definition is NOT a photocopy or a photograph or a mimeograph of reality, much like a literary translation is NOT a photograph or a photocopy or a mimeograph of the previous text.

Art ought to stimulate the human mind and broaden its horizon and understanding in way that discursive discourse does not. How can a piece, doing nothing more than depicting for example a casteist society exactly as it is, stimulate me and broaden my understanding? This discussion is not for people who think art replicates reality like a photograph does.

Vis-à-vis their handling for instance of caste, most of Kannada creative fiction including the unjustifiably hyped **sanskaara** falls fatally short of qualifying to be called 'art'. See Giridhar 2015.

Things like caste, religion, dowry, patriarchy in India, kidnapped bride marriages in Kirgistan, head hunting in NE India, female genital mutilation(FGM) socially sanctioned in some thirty countries in the world including india, where Bohras practise it, child marriage, child labour, *leblouth* or *gavage*, the coercive practice in Mauritania the African nation of force feeding child brides to attain obesity, which is a desirable feature of brides in that society(Girl children are force fed as much as twenty litres of camel's milk and two kgs of millet everyday in Mauritania.) are empirical facts. One doesn't, at least i don't, expect art to depict these empirical facts as if they are the goal of art and leave them at that. The antilife Taliban opposes girl education, music, dance etc and even polio vaccination. Now, a literary piece endorsing such opposition can't rest back merely depicting an ethos that sanctions such practices. That would NOT be art. Art needs to do more. This design feature of art is more than clear to me.

I reject the idea that there is no 'design' feature or such a footing of the subsoil in art while reiterating that this design feature is not, and should not be confused with, *tendentiousness*, which is something we are all justifiably against in art, nor with, a classification of literature as philistine, promotional, philosophical and reflective literature, dubbing the kind of art I am espousing as 'reflective'. The only exception that i can think of where this question may not arise is light-veined literature or art of the kind that a film like *Irma La Duce* or Baby's Day Out exemplify, piquant comedies that entertain and exhilarate. But here also I don't expect unendorsable social categories and practices being endorsed. In other words, what I am arguing for overarches all art.

Mere depiction of facts as they empirically exist then is not the business of art, it seems to me. Quite a few Kannada novels do this, and quite culpably, in my view. Kannadigas need badly to rethink such literature as endorse things like caste, including a much hyped, much prescribed novel like *sanskaara*. I see that only someone like K.S Bhagvan has said something like this in the Kannada context. The communities that characters who are frowned upon in literature belong to, like Chandri, Padmavathi and Belli in *Sanskaara*, for example, must come out on to the streets to protest or litigate against the author.

Everyone whose community is demeaned must be able to do this: take the authors head on, or if they are believers in nonviolence, drag them to court.

That would be an infallible indication of the growth of the Kannada society. This is happening in Tamil literature, I'm told. One such literary piece, wherein some communities are demeaned, was taken off the university syllabus. Washermen have protested their demeaning in the Tamil film **Anegan**. If Indians endorse literature that endorses caste, all it means is that such admirers are also unabashed casteists or apologists for caste.

One needn't take casteists and caste-apologists seriously, much like we should not take seriously literature that shamelessly endorses and promotes social, moral and intellectual horrors like caste.

Casteists, religionists and languagists, i.e. people who believe in the supremacy of individual castes, religions and languages, and frown on others, belong to what may be called the 'mafia of the human soul'. These categories viz caste, religion etc are externally foisted, and hence eminently superficial, identity badges. They are not part of one's DNA. One's race, sex, colour etc are also outside man's ontology even though they are part of one's DNA. One doesn't *choose* to belong to any of these identity badges.

What art does with these facts is what one looks for in any art. There is an anecdote that M. Hiriyanna relates in his book, Art Experience. On

seeing the painting of a sunset the connoisseur remarks, "I haven't seen a sunset like this in my life", and the painter comes back with the following:
"Don't you wish to see one?!"

This exactly captures my idea of art.

Experience - lived or imagined - is admittedly the staple of art, but it can NEVER be the goal. Documentation and archiving of facts and, by implication, endorsing the evil irrational intellectually indigent empirical practices of society as a matter of course, is never the goal of any art. Many Kannada novels, including *sanskaara, tabbaliyu niinaade magane, dharmashree, vamsha vriksha* etc do precisely this, which is why it is difficult to see how they qualify to be dubbed *art*.

What we call such marks on paper is an interesting question.

There is something seriously wrong, I would say, with a society that accolades such creations. I would reject all such literature that endorses such an ontology-external social category like caste as a matter of course. I am befuddled, amused, saddened and pained by turns that the Kannada people seem to think otherwise.

It should be unacceptable to any thinking, rational, cognitive being.

Oppositions like mentalism-empiricism, deductivism-inductivism and 'poetry of the soul' and 'prose of reality' come into serious play everywhere including art.

My argument here is by the way orthogonal to standardly available prosaisms of *art for art's sake, authenticity, aestheticism, utopianism, realism and naturalism* and taxonomies and typologies of creative literaturelikereflective/ philistine/promotional/philosophical/entertaining literature and so on. The doctrine of Art for Art's sake says art need not trigger any conceptual breakthrough or motivate revolutionary transformational change in social space. Authenticity refers to faithfulness to empirical reality and aestheticism refers to beauty and elegance that transcends material reality and utilitarianism, to pleasing excellence of construction. In verbal art, does this aestheticism come from language or from nonlanguage? If it comes from nonlanguage, what is its nature? This view of art of mine impinges on the nature of this nonlanguage.

What I am arguing for here is true of the life-blood of all art.

The argument is that a certain subsoil, a certain substratum, a certain substructure underlies all art, much like a certain undercurrent, a certain subsoil runs through all of natural language.

When you stand on a beach, staring at the distant horizon across a humungous expanse of seawater, one forgets one's mundanity, one's materialistic utilitarian self-centred mindset, one's this-worldly woes. One is per force pushed to a different plane of one's being, to a different phase of one's consciousness. I have felt it when I listen to great music, see great sculpture, great painting, great dancing, see great human behavior and when I am with great people. You are unwittingly into a fresh consuming self-absorbed plane of being. Any sensitive human being gets life-enhancing intimations of an infinity that transcends life's mundanity, its temporality, its seedy sordid reality, much like an aging person gets increasingly unmistakable intimations of her mortality.

True art does that. True poetry does it. True creative fiction does it or if it doesn't do it, it ought to do it. True drama could do it. It takes you to a different, higher plane of existence, a serene sublime tranquil contemplative layer of consciousness, possibly not available to nonhuman primates. (Discursive discourse does it on a distinctly different plane.)

That is why we call it *art*.

It is clear as daylight that such an expansive mood cannot result from a depiction of things as they exist in society, however authentic and aesthetic may be the description. (Authenticity and aestheticity thus do not bear on my argument here.) This is because things in social spaces are often, and typically not, how they ought to be in a rational perspective. Most of them are dark irrational sordid things. Human societies are often 'sewers in spate'. When they are not sordidly irrational, the distillation part happens partially vacuously, but it still happens as in the case of the mundane and perfunctory sunset, about which there is nothing wrong or irrational. All art is a decisional act of intellectual accountability, social responsibility and moral acceptability. All art protects life and civilization like a construct called God presumably would. (This is, in a way, equating art with God!) This is a level distinctly and foundationally different from the level where one says art is NOT tendentious, didactic, propagandist or promotional. This is pretty much like the level where the head of a human or nonhuman primate family thinks well of all of his family members. All of the thinking and action that the head engages in in family spaces is built on, and is, indeed, a function of this level.

You deal with the world the way it is, and not the way you wished it was, they say. This dealing is by one who lives in the empirical world. Even the dealer in the empirical world often strives toward a world we all wish it was. Art is not empiricality although, as we said, it takes off from it. Art ought to bridge this chasm between the way the world is and the way you wished it was. Art is precisely the area of human behavior where there is a life-enhancing reasoned, if imagined and seemingly magical, thrust toward the way you wished the world was. Art in fact is one of the inhabitants of the space between the way the world is and the way you wished it was. All art is ever a move toward the higher, more sublime spaces that humans are capable of. In such a move one doesn't expect the baser phases of human consciousness like casteism, religionism, languagism and masculinism, child slavery and trafficking etc depicted only to be endorsed.

The following possibly apocryphal tale expresses best what I am at pains to press home:

> x and y are friends. Both live in their underground houses. x takes y home once. And y asks x: "You house is so very bright. How ?" To which x asks, "Why? Is your house not like this?" "No", replies y, "You come to my place!" x does call at y's home the following day. y is flabbergasted to see his own house brighter than it usually would be. ("It is because *you* are here!" y almost says!) This is because x is light and wherever he goes, it is always light.

> Artists are like x. wherever they go, they light up the readers' path.

Artists need to be positive life-enhancing symbols for mankind. They symbolise what is sublime in human consciousness.

By unraveling the inner significance of things they need to make others see the inner face of things that exist. As the redoubtable U.R. Ananthamurti said, the poet "makes the mundane look as if swilled out with the divine." Why should this apply only to sunsets, moonrises, flowers, mountains, dales and female anatomies? It behooves artistes to make social spaces also look 'as if swilled out with the divine'. This strain of thought is the natural flow of this definition of art.

I can't, no rational man can, think of artists perpetuating in their writings what ought not to be perpetuated in a social ethos. This, i.e. litterateurs perpetuating what ought not to be perpetuated, has happened time and again in Kannada fiction. A sizeable chunk of Kannada literature, especially fiction, is not *art* by this token. And Kannadigas seem to have lapped it up, and lapped it up culpably in my view, with reverential awe!

One needs to decide what such 'literature' is. See below for an input to such a decision.

The (rational) Kannadiga needs to pause, weigh, and consider this.

In his new book Art as Therapy, De Botton seeks to take the snob factor, the high-ground factor out of art. Art could celebrate everyday life. It can shore us up, slaying everything dark irrational and negative in our lives, making us feel less alone with the ornery melancholy stuff of life. Affording us hope and encouragement it can give us the ability to get on with life. These are possible only when art doesn't justify and endorse the sordidness obtaining in life.

When art itself is sick, as it indeed is when it justifies things like caste, religion, patriarchy, child labour, slavery etc in society, how can it be therapeutic? This is the burden of this argument about art.

As Stella Adler points out (TOI Speaking Tree 19th Oct 2014),

> *life beats you and crushes your soul but art reminds you that you have one.*

I haven't seen much of this reminding quality in Kannada creative fiction. What caste-endorsing Kannada literature (like *tabbaliyu niinaade magane dharmashree, sanskaara* and *coomana dudi*) that paints such irrational evil practices as they exist, literature that violates the ontological dignity of individuals by claiming to paint things as they are (it is Not clear why the dalit Chooma in the Kannada novel *coomana duDi* is denied conversion, for example), does is it culpably tells you such practices are indeed right, *which is exactly what one doesn't expect from art.* This is exactly the point.

It is NOT clear how the above named Kannada novels, given only as illustrative (not exhaustive) examples here, remind some human groups called 'castes' that they too have a soul, that they too have inner light like every human being on earth, that they are (also?) entitled to full ontological dignity.

One's conclusion then is that since a caste-ridden, patriarchy-ridden, slavery-ridden society is, for any healthy rationalist and rigorous thinker, a **sick** society, creative literature that mimics or mirrors such a society without being diagnostic and therapeutic about it is also for sure **sick** literature.

This *could* be true of a sizeable chunk of Kannada creative fiction as indeed of Indian creative fiction. The word 'creative' in the locution 'creative literature' does not merely refer to creating what does not exist, i.e it doesn't merely refer to imagined worlds, but to being creative conceptually, in the world of ideas, and linguistically as well. That the hearteningly refreshing quality of a literary conceptual cosmos is not quite comparable to the conceptual breakthroughs achieved in discursive discourse is of course true, so true that it goes without saying.
Rodda Vyasarao, who wrote Kannada's second novel *Chandramukhi's shock* (1900) has this to say:

> ...Unless there is a revolutionary change in the way Kannada
> novels are written, they are of no real use to Karnataka.
> (Rodda Vyasarao 1900, 2012:25)

Prophetic words! I have no idea, as I said earlier, what use novels such as *Sanskaara, Tabbaliyu Niinaade Magane, Dharmashree* and presumably a host of other Kannada novels have to the Kannadiga. That these may be or in fact are, *authentic* and *aesthetic* is NOT sufficient, as I argued above. Something more has to *inhere* in what is dubbed *art*. **Art is not an archival, incogitant and replicative documentation of empirical reality: there is a triangular relationship between art, empirical reality and human ontology.**

I have taken pains to elucidate this 'something more': a footing of a basic life-enhancing intellectual vitality, a scaffolding of a basic bar-raising civilization-protecting rational vibrancy, an inner current of a positive freedom-equity-justice vibe. A literary piece that endorses, as a matter of course, caste, religion, skin-colour, endorses man as against woman or patriarchy, slavery of any denomination, headhunting, bride-burning, pieces that endorse social constructs that are outside human ontology, it is clear, can neither be life-enhancing nor civilisation-protecting.

Such works cannot be called *art* in my view, and ought to be dust binned (by a rational society) without much ado, much like science dustbins nonsense. Note also that this also to do with how art relates to empirical reality and human ontology. The authors of such works have no idea of this triangular bond.

Note that Rodda Vyaasarao's statement came in 1900 and that the illustrative examples of novels adduced here came much later. It would have been curiously interesting to see whether Rodda would have been happy with the state of affairs now.

Another way of looking at art and literature, another way of saying the same thing is the following:

Truth, absolute or finite, is central to literature as it is to all cultural constructs, to all products of human consciousness. Honesty, absolute or finite, is central to literature as it is to all cultural constructs, to all products of human consciousness. Lived experience is central to literature as it is to all products of human consciousness. Totally magical, totally apocryphal imagination cannot be totally unconnected to the base of truth. Equally importantly, a basic intellectual perceptiveness is central to literature as it is to all products of human consciousness. A certain cerebral vitality that sifts through lived experience in terms of an intellectual strainer is central to literature as it is to all creative constructs of human consciousness. A certain imagined, if magically realised, rationality is central to creative literature, unlike for discursive literature, or to 'human' texts, as opposed to 'discursive' texts, as they may be called. As Dipankar Gupta said, "though intellectuals answer to no one, they are answerable to everyone." (Gupta 2011 from his article 'Neither King nor Philosopher' ToI August 30, 2011. p:12). All cultural constructs, all products of human consciousness should enhance, enrich, rejuvenate, augment, enliven, revitalise, refresh and nourish the reader's sense of being in one sense or another, it seems to me. They should rock you in a delectably deep state of absorption and engrossment, bringing an enlivened awareness to one's consciousness. A good piece of art including literature has you wake up to a fresh new day, as it were. It should seed one with the joussance of life in all its positivity even as it might and could legitimately picture the sordid ugliness and the seamy seedy realities of life, even as it makes one aware of the nature of the human condition. In fact a motive force of literature is to make one aware of the nature of one's condition. Any such piece of literature should incubate in your mind, grow in you and on you, swell in your mind before haunting it. One should emerge from a literary piece your mind on fire, as if from a dream, your soul touched and your sense of life and being redone for the better, revitalised, nourished and enhanced. One feels a sudden, if subtle, sense of growth, a sudden, if subtle, sense of delight and enrichment in the presence of great human beings. You feel your spirit lifted. So must be the case with good/ great pieces of creative literature, music, sculpture, painting, architecture and the performing arts.

Art in fact is a great life-giving, life-affirming, life-nourishing awareness tool, a tool that makes you upbeat about life. Anything that does otherwise is no art.

The internal rhetoric of a literary construct or any creative act for that matter consists in the terms it enshrines in terms of which one creatively negotiates with it. Many Kannada novels have that much less in terms of the terms the reader has in the piece for such creative negotiation with it. The reader's dialogue with the piece is stunted to that extent.

If the piece is founded on such grievous lacks, then the whole piece is worth next to nothing. The rational reader can in point of fact have no dialogue with such pieces.

That such literary pieces win awards is as much a comment on the award-dispensers, and on the nature of the discipline of literature as they are on the literary works, and the quality of the society these things happen in.

The key thing is pretty simple and that is that thought leaders in every human group need to have a vision of an 'expanding and unending future' for humanity of which Freedom, Equity and Justice are integral parts. I am afraid the typical Kannada writer, including the **otherwise** distinguished Ananthamurthys and Shivaram Karanthas, does not quite evince this. **The Kannadiga needs to realize this to prevent further damage to his psyche from 'creative' literature which misleads him**. Authors of works like **sanskaara** cannot be deemed thought leaders of their group. By upholding a social abomination like caste, a category that is socially irresponsible, morally outrageous and intellectually vacuous, such 'works of art' undoubtedly are also socially irresponsible, morally outrageous and intellectually vacuous pieces.

How are the authors of works like **sanskaara, tabbaliyu niinaade magane, dharmashree, vanshavriksha, kavalu** and **yaana** be torch-bearers of change for the Kannadiga?

While abominations like caste in social space pain and intrigue me, unsettle and upset me, befuddle me, caste as depicted in Kannada novels like **sanskaara, dharmashree, tabbaliyu niinaade magane, vanshavriksha, choomana duDi** amuses me.

It should amuse any thinker worth his salt.

So is the case with how woman is treated. How woman is treated in social space is also an abomination of our society and while it is upsetting and unsettling, how woman is treated in Kannada novels like **kavalu, sanskaara** and **yaana** amuses me!

It should amuse any thinker worth his salt.

The instant translation, titled The Drowners (The Real and the Delusory), of the Kannada novel *aapooshana* is delightfully different in that it doesn't depict, and endorse caste, as a matter of course. The translation, presumably rather than hopefully, captures an alien sensibility and makes it at home in English, which is what literary translation is all about. This translation is designed to be idiomatic and enduring, idiomaticity being related to transparency, which is a feature of what is called 'natural translation'.

The novel chronicles the life of a famous litterateur falling in love with a (Dalit) girl and later getting unwittingly tricked into self-destruction because of his own blind spots and vulnerabilities. Although the novel doesn't quite endorse caste as a matter of course like pieces like *sanskaara, dharmashree, tabbaliyu niinaade magane* and *choomana duDi* shamelessly and misleadingly do, because of which, I have argued elsewhere (Giridhar 2015), **they are by no stretch of imagination useful to the Kannadiga, to the Kannadigas' future**, it is regressive in that the female protagonist is made a theist from her original stand of atheism. Her standing before God, and outside the temple, to pray for a grant of her wishes is as inexplicably weak, it seems to me, as Praneshacharya's prayer at the dead of night at the Maruti temple in the alleged and irrationally hyped 'work of art' called *sanskaara*.

Grateful thanks are returned to E. Annamalai, Shreedevi Nair, Meti Mallikarjuna and Uma for listening to and for weighing in on my view of art, which only helped open the door, perspectivising, sharpening, and lucidifying my own thinking, to Ms Kamala Narasimha, the author of the original Kannada piece for prevailing upon me to English this Kannada novel after I had rendered another novel of hers, and finally to the highly professional Partridge India for offering to print, publish, and market what should, at least arguably, be a contribution to world literature.

References

Giridhar P.P. 2015 **(Literary) Art: An Interrogative Meditation**, accepted for oral presentation at the GSTF 4th Annual International Conference on Language, Linguistics and Literature. Singapore. June 8-9, 2015

Rajiv Malhotra 2014 **Being Different**. HarperCollins

Rodda 1900 **Chandramathi's Shock**.

FOREWORD
(U.R. Ananthamurthy)

As you have said yourself, Rajagopal is a self-important man of literature and an idealist. I don't feel he is a good literatteur. His feeling of self-importance is so intense, that he can love only himself. You refer to him in the plural, which is not right.

Ushe, the Dalit who loves this literary person is an intense woman and someone, who can love. You as a writer have written well about her. Jealousy, the ego of love, all these are life-forces. The reason that I read the entire novel with delight was because of Ushe's character. The core essence of the novel is the depiction of her feelings, her genuineness and her real ambition. She is not an idealist. She is human. She is the real protagonist.

Gopal cannot give up his self-importance. He is an idealist of the literary world too. However the failure of the literatteur to examine himself without self pity, evokes pain in others, because of his egocentric attitude, I can't consider him a literatteur. You know this too. But writing about such a self loving, self important figure in the honorific plural is not right.

Although you have narrative talent, there are occasions when you intrude in to the narrative. This is debilitating to the discerning reader. Every reader has his own views about caste and matters of love and one should not truncate the process of introspection happening within the reader to arrive at the truth. The author's opinion and voice must arise organically, through the actions of the characters.

I am criticizing you in the way I do, because I know that you have the art to write this way. This is only your second novel. The opinions that we perceive as truths are split with inner and outer forms. I don't see truth symbolically. Even if I may do, I don't display it. You are a courageous writer who has ventured to write about such things. A bold writer ought to write, without imposing anything on the reader. This is possible for you. I have both the confidence and the expectation that more good writings will come from you. That is why I am critical. But the characterization of Ushe and other female characters is quite intense and deep. I congratulate you for writing about a life of love and lust, with honesty.

THE EAST

Chapter One

"You will be bumped off sooner than later."

That in essence was all that the letter said. And this was enough of a kindling that ignited the distress of the mind, making it flame away. The body broke into a sweat before warming up. Efforts at shoring up on the way to easing up with some measure of comfort are coming to naught. It has been half an hour since this fear has consumed me. Death is not far removed from life. It is as natural and inevitable as it is near. But the body wouldn't be game for welcoming and embracing death. Who is it possible for to let life give itself up to death as naturally as one opens oneself up for, supports and shelters desires. Everything gets dramatically interesting with the feeling that there is still life. People do commit suicide driven by despair. But that is when everything gets unbearable. If everything in life is bearable, pleasant and pleasurable, no one would end one's life. But handling and managing life without any hassles, and with deep contentment, is not everyone's cup of tea. Death comes in multiple forms. What form would it take when it happens to me? Once that is decided, one would be free. But, if, certain of its coming, one waits at the door for death, the nature of fear would change. The density of fear might whittle away, and becoming aware, one might awaken. One could fortify and protect all the directions of passage that surround the body, but what if, before all this happens, death, suddenly, abruptly, enters the body? That alas is not in my hands. The more one thinks, the greater is the anxiety. Is it possible to still the mind under these circumstances? Who would write "You would be bumped off sooner than later" in jest? In case it is only a threat, they should say they did it for such and such reason(s). If they don't give out hints about the unexpressed reasons, what would one make of the letter? No matter how well one brings the mind under control, it suddenly pops up with anxious thoughts just like a dead body sits suddenly up. Could one fence in the mind and the soul and keep guard over them? One couldn't. But the body is always an open book. One could turn it over, crumple it and tear it off. Death is death, irrespective of whether I walk toward it or it walks toward me! Whatever the age, the effect of its blow is the same. It can't spare me because of my age. Some are young, some old. Young ones go even before the old ones, or the old ones may go before the young ones do. No one can say a word in remonstration. Death can hear no one's cries of pain. The people who posed the threat may themselves be into a conspiracy. It might well be an empty threat. Both fear and courage mingle. The mix gives out something new. This agitates and alarms the mind. The body breaks into a sweat, and then courage follows! As if I have found something to go by and the challenge of not losing it. In case one thinks of facing it, how much time do I have? Don't know. It may be five minutes, five days, five months or five years. There's no knowing. How do I know about the obligative debt I am under of this land? Nobody can stay back when everything is over. What work do I have? In any case I don't have to prove for any one about what pressure of work I have. I have thus no right not to open the door when death raps with the threat of murder. This is true. Why are such unnecessary thoughts pursuing me now like they are doing? All knowledge is being shed every moment. This mind is pretty much like this body. The body is pretty much like this mind. Is 'I' the body here? Or, is it the mind, or the soul? Where then am 'I'?

Yet this is the truth. I have the letter in my hand. It is an anonymous letter. How will I get killed? Why will I be killed? Does even a man in a respectable position like me get a death threat? This is pretty common for politicians. But if there is a murder threat for a writer, would humanitarianism have any value? Should I inform the police? What if I don't? If I do, they will probe who else but me. Let them if they so want. How much will they probe? They might investigate into my life, my career, and my confidential private life. But there would be no relation between one's very personal life and the murder threat. Yet we can't say that. One's very personal life may not pursue the high position I am holding. Highly personal life can only barely touch one's outer life.

But this is a murder threat. How has this occasion come about? Someone might have posed an empty threat. Someone might not have tolerated my ascendance. It could be an attempt to diminish my mental strength. This has nothing to do with the mind for me to think of drumming up courage to square

4

up to it. It is a plot of deception. I should prefer a complaint through my personal assistant. We could then wait and watch future developments.

I didn't get even a hint of this crisis. I didn't guess it. I used to pray to God at such difficult times till I became thirty years of age. I am already fifty eight, going on fifty nine. I am not a believer. But I do all poojes and other stuff at home. Whatever faith I did have in an invisible ulterior force has broken to pieces. Why did it happen? That this is what life has taught is the only answer to this question. That one shouldn't scorn the believers is something I keep in mind. I have always cooperated with my wife in her religious routines. To appeal to God to rescue me from this situation would amount to superstition. With the woman I loved growing apart and even with all that's materially possible being with it, the mind becomes a complex of insult, humiliation, disappointment, distress and anxiety, and languishing and sinking away as it did ever since I got married, I thought I found a beautiful small straw which I latched on to. I know that is unstable too. I never imagined I would be troubled by such a murder threat when the mind is enveloped by such restlessness of pain. I am feeling as if my legs and arms are being sliced away. I visited the loo a dozen times. Every time I came back, I touched the letter. And every time I touched the letter, I startled, burning with anger and anxiety.

Finding again the one you loved is not like being committed. That is an absurdity. Love, which had diminished and stunted my personality and which I lost had burned me up, casting its dark unseemly shadow on my life. Amidst the burnt up ruins of my life I have now got Usha. Whatever her age she is a girl. Both of us have savoured what we have lost. Words, wordlessness, anger, excitement, the flurry of agitation, love and lust at this age are all as pleasant as they are astonishing. Like cold water poured on withered arid land, this love has for the moment afforded me a wonderful experience. How attractive this has been, the love that has come without the string of familial responsibility attached to it!

In case I lose this, it would be as if life itself has vanished into thin air. The masculine stand that all the excitement, the manic passion, the beauty that she brings along with her is mine, the egoism of this is something I badly want for the moment. Only if one has this contented mindset could one work with any enthusiasm. Even when the woman i married is right in front of me, there is no haunting, no sensual longing, no rutting, no hungering, She would be somewhere away, what an irony! Usha! The frisson the name would send through my veins! I thrill with excited delight merely by remembering her. The sensation of her touch is something I never had in my life. I experienced the love of a woman long back. When i was thirty years of age, at the peak of youth there was this pull of youth and maturity. Now even after the passage of thirty years, there is the same effervescent exuberance and passion. But now life has matured out. None of us has any fear. The love used to evolve then only with anxiety. The anxiety of whether we would come together would often end in detachment between the two of us.

Everything is free now. Nothing is unclear. When there is clarity, there are no hurdles. There are no restrictions that come from the insistence to marry, or from issues of prestige and honour. It is only one year since I have got this delectable female company. That I won't be frustrated again has been my contented feeling of comfort. Ushe is already forty six, or forty seven. For some reason she hasn't married. She might in future. But she has herself told me she would not. "I have dedicated my life to the memory of your love," she coos.

But i am already sixty. How longer would the lust for life last in this body. Supposing some incident that mars my dignity happens? Let us not think of such a contingency. May not such a contingency arise! What if there is a threat to my position of honour and prestige, considering this is an immoral and socially uncommitted relationship? Such thoughts were destabilizing me, bruising and battering me.

The police inspector got the news of the death threat. Kalyan Singh was his name. He turned the letter over and over. After downing a couple of cups of coffee, he posed a blitz of questions:

"Do you suspect anyone?"

"When were you appointed the chairman of the Kannada Development Authority?"

"Did any others compete with you for the position?"

"Who?"

"Did any one of them threaten you?"

"Who was it who recommended your name for the position?"

"Is he still in power?"

"Which is your hometown?"

"Father?"

"Mother?"

"Family background? I am asking this because somebody might have done this intimidation because of personal jealousy."

"What is your wife doing?"

"What is the college in which you are working?"

6

"Why this threat for a good person like you, Sir? The letter has a woman's handwriting, there is no doubt at all."

Even when the enquiry got over, Kalyan Singh didn't go out. Rajagopal didn't want all this hassle of enquiry and investigation. He was the kind who found comfort and contentment, keeping to himself. But circumstances taught him to endure everything.

"We will detail a constable to be with you round the clock, Sir. He will come to your place at nine thirty in the morning. He would be with you right till you return home from office. On the days when you don't attend office, he will be on patrol at your house. Please cooperate."

Not that Kalyan Singh had any specially felt concern. He didn't. It was his perfunctory duty. But Rajagopal didn't want protection that eroded one's privacy. If one was engaged in work for most part of the day, one felt one needed some time for oneself. But at least till the present situation improved, he needed a bodyguard. The personal assistant was there for official work. He needed protection while outdoors. Although Rajagopal felt he didn't need anyone, he couldn't say as much. Besides, the Inspector was a sensitive person: he would ask a barrage of questions. All this was but formal security. He wouldn't get any protection with such measures. Would it be difficult to kill just because there was a constable keeping guard? One could kill when the constable went back to his house. How could he say all this to the Inspector? Would the Inspector understand?

Mortal fear and upbeat courage took turns in Rajagopala.

One had to pull the sheet of courage on to one's face and smile! The thought of sashaying over, standing by the window and surveying the world outside arose in his mind. He did amble over. But the anxiety of someone planting himself right behind his back and doing something to him shot down the idea. He wasted no time before walking right back and sitting down on the sofa. Attender Shivanna walked up and served him two cups of coffee. Rajagopal then closed his eyes with relaxed deliberation, thinking the truth might dawn on him if he closed his eyes and meditate. *Saraswathi has warmed to me,* he found himself saying to himself as he looked inward. *The emotionality and enthusiasm that I evince while interacting with Ushe are not possible for me with Saraswathi. But she has been steadfastly faithful with me. I have realised so many times that I may be cheating on Saraswathi with my affair with Ushe, but my egoistic inner self insists that I need Ushe's company. That can never be controlled. This feeling of guilt and remorse is washed away without a trace by the overpowering flood of the craving for the gratified contentment of physical union that this mad and furious love for Ushe cries out for.*

Why is the mind thinking these bonds when there is the threat of murder? Rajagopala found himself chewing some wordless cud. *There is a huge distance between love and death. It is at the same time close. Whenever we earn the love of someone, we threaten them with our own death to prove our love. Sometimes we die because of love. We win many a time and many a time we distance death, pulling victory near. That is, I have tasted victory with a woman, who is physically distant from me. I am fully living there with her although I am staying away from her. But staying and being near, and living with, another woman, I am as good as dead as a dodo.*

Rajagopal remembered what the Inspector had said. That it was the handwriting of a woman. *Who would do it? There is no such person in my circle. Someone could get it written by somebody. Such crimes are only got done. No one does it oneself. Doing them oneself makes it easier for being found out and getting caught.*

Even though he was hungry, Rajagopal didn't feel like eating. *Whatever it is, a constable has come to give me company,* Rajagopal told himself, continuing with his wordless meditation. *He accompanies me wherever I go: home, office, meetings or programmes, whatever. If I want protection I need to cooperate with him. What could he do, the poor chap! We have to wait and watch what this inspector does, having seen the letter. Is it anxiety, weariness or uneasy grief that is upon me? Why the heck did he come? What if he hadn't come now? What would have happened? I would have been much easier in my mind.*

By the time Rajagopal rose and got going with his work, a couple of journalists hemmed him in. Gopal didn't want any of this.

"I can't answer any of your posers," he said by way of a firm reply. "Who informed you about this? Please don't publish anything for now. That would delay nabbing the culprit. I have grown weary and disgusted. Please understand! When the atmosphere gets lighter, I will tell you myself."

Gopal did speak politely. But such sensational news is yummy food for journalists. The way one of the journalists there questioned Gopal was noticeable.

"Look here, Sir!" he said rather thickly. "Don't you understand? The government has changed. You were appointed for this organization at the instance of the Deputy Chief Minister of the previous government. You should have resigned by now. Don't you feel that way?"

While it did open up a new direction, the teaser flopped down with a thud without an answer in sight. Gopal made a false show of doing some serious reading. Sometimes you don't know whether to speak at all or even if you wanted to speak, what to speak. What would be the effect of the words spoken? What would be the meaning of silence? One may even know all this. But there is no point in blurting out something as the chairman against the government without any footing. Another thing is that a new thought had struck him only now. How could he react with alacrity to the situation? It may not be true. What is the point in speculating? Would someone threaten the chairman of an organisation? It might not be. Besides, the present government would have the authority to ask him to resign. But it hasn't. And it would be impolite to do so and no minister would do it. Litterateurs typically command respect and honour in society. Only rarely would writers behave like politicians. No one would respect such writers. Gopal didn't like to speak anything. Yet there was no ignoring of media persons. He simply stood there, his body language saying, "See, this is the way I am!"

"Say something, Sir!" insisted another journalist, perking up and diving into the conversation. "Or else, we may have to report only what we said just now."

When a journalist said this, Rajagopal had to per force say something. Gopal did say a few things. But he had to suppress some things that didn't quite brook suppression.

"Look! I am grateful for your sympathy," he bellyached. "but let us not publish such things under the current circumstances based merely on speculation. The police has taken possession of the letter. You ask the police about it. You publish only such things as the police says should be made public. Let us not make uncertain information public right now. You make the truth public after the investigation is complete. I can't answer your questions till then. You are saying the threat has come because I haven't resigned. No one would do that. What could the government do after all? I don't think that ministers, would, in the middle of their administrative work, have the energy and verve to do such things."

Would they refrain from reporting this in the media just because Rajagopal said such things? They would for sure report just as he said. Even if a tad embarrassing, the journalists prepared a little report without quite rejecting what Gopal said. Then treating them to a cup of coffee, Gopal sent them off after the usual courtesies.

In any case this incident was sure to appear in tomorrow's newspapers. What would happen next? Nobody knew. Would his villagers, his mother, younger sister and brothers not come to know? They would. This posed a little problem for Rajagopal. *Yet this is for real. It should square up to it. I should console mother. Mother is truly fond of me. Even though there are eleven other children, she has tremendous love for me.* The anxiety that she would feel wretched, seeing the news about her son, began to creep up his spine. He had decided not to let his wife know about this latest development. Now journalists themselves were reporting it!

In the meantime Udaya TV, e-TV and the state TV personnel got some information from Rajagopal. They didn't do any questioning though. They recorded just so much information as to telecast in the newshour for half a minute. Even then Rajagopal was at a loss what to say and do. *Why did the Inspector tell this to media people instead of keeping it under wraps? What is the need to attach so much importance to a mere threat letter? It should have been dustbinned. Why so much publicity for it now? How would the people receive this? How would writers and literature enthusiasts take to it?* These questions naturally popped up in Rajagopal. Rajagopal did get scared when he got the letter. But, now attacking him as they did one by one with unsettling force, thoughts and problems of various kinds frightened and alarmed him. While courage shored him up in one corner of his mind, a host of alarming hassles crowded another corner. *Would just one letter bring in its wake such a difficult situation*, he wondered.

Rajagopal sat down in his chair and even as he was recovering, members of other organizations appeared and began to express their own opinions, feelings and sympathies about what had befallen him. Everyone had some sort of anxiety, some sort of curiosity. Vijayamurthy, the Director of the Department of Kannada and Culture spoke for about half an hour. He held forth generally on how the present political situation impacted Academies and other academic organizations run by the government. But he didn't speak a word about how what he spoke had anything to do with the letter that Rajagopal had got. Then as he laid the cup on the table after downing the cup of coffee, he ended up saying something that compelled notice:

"Who were your rivals when you were appointed for the position that you hold? Does any of them have the backing of the present government? Think about this."

This afforded Gopal another hint.

But it didn't seem to him to be the reality. When he did land this position of the Chairmanship of the Kannada Authority, he had got it through the recommendation of the then Deputy Chief Minister. It was true that there were two other writers who were in contention. But that might not have any connection with the murder threat missive. Which writer would do such a thing? Shivalingaih and Raamalinge gowda were the shortlisted ones. *They are not the kind that would write such letters,* Gopal told himself. *But who would know what kind of venomous snake would be penned up in which anthill? Nobody would.*

Thankfully shaking hands with him, Rajagopal bade Vijayamurthy goodbye. He then sat back in the chair. The body felt heavy and the mind seemed to sink and shrink.

No matter what anyone says, the problem is mine, Gopal was into his aside over again. *It is only I who should muster courage. Whatever be the source of this situation, I need to face everything that comes along.*

It is only now after mastering several of my desires that I have had some reason for joy: the position of the chairmanship of the Kannada Development Authority. Some nameless love that had gone missing is back in my life at the age of fifty eight. This is all. Who could be the person who wrote this dreadful letter? The target could be the enviable position I hold, or my own self. Mine is the final say in the selection committee for bulk procurement of books for state libraries. Others don't utter a word about my opinion. Would they even so forge a plot like this? If so, who could it be? Or someone who is jealous of the position of chairmanship I hold might have done this.

Rajagopal did feel shored up by Kalyan Singh's visit. Feeling as if some kite had lifted death in its beak and had thrown it behind his back, he startled in fright. Bristling as it did with the turmoil of such thoughts and the restlessness of pain, his mind resembled a choppy sea. It was three o'clock. He asked the cop to go home for his midday meal before he opened the lunch box he had brought from home. He felt like retching. He then asked his personal assistant to be with him. The name of his personal assistant was Mallikarjuna swamy. He was a clever cunning man, the kind that sucked up to you with agreeably sweet words, and even as he fanned you with a golden fan, would, as if unwittingly, sock your face with it.

"Some scumbag has got this letter written just to spite you, Sir!" he minced. "Why do you worry? This must have been done with the purpose of making you resign. If you quail, they will further scare you. As it is, they spew venom at the very mention of Brahmins."

What he is saying is true. But how does one come to judgements about such people? In the matter of caste every one behaves in mod fashion. But caste does what it does deep inside. Ramalingegowda and the Shivalingaih the Dalit poet were my rivals it seems. But why this now? It is already one year since the appointment took place. True, the goverment has changed. Some people did say that we should resign from our positions once the Deputy Chief Minister demitted office. This kind of threat for that? What is wrong if we work for three years? I shouldn't fear if that is the case.

A new courage stepped into Rajagopal.

"Sir, won't you eat?" asked the constable in what was a voice of sympathy and respect, as he stepped in after returning from his midday meal. Gopal nodded agreement. The cop inquired about at what time in the morning he should report and at what time in the evening he could go back home. In sum he had to accompany Rajagopal wherever it was that he went. If he sat in his office he was to station himself outside, pacing the floor from that end to this, keeping watch over things. If someone came calling, he had to probe into who he was, whether he was known, or not known, to his boss etc. In case there was any doubt or suspicion he had to frisk him, his pockets and the waist belt etc. Once he had decided that this, i.e. keeping guard over someone, was his life, he had to consider it respectable and do it, irrespective of whether such work was easy or difficult, pleasant or unpleasant. The Police Inspector had given him some instructions when he left. His job was to write down the names and addresses of whoever came to meet the Chairman. His name was Hanumanthappa. Gopal found it easy, and made it a habit to call him Hanumanthu.

Hanumanthu was a natural and fluent talker. But he wouldn't talk unnecessarily. He was not the only one at the door. Shivanna, the Attender also used to sit on a chair outside Rajagopal's office. Attenders do the work having to do with routine office jobs like attending to their boss's work, taking away files, memos, instructions, correspondence with other government bodies, and mail to post offices, and organizing refreshment and beverages etc to visitors. But he sat outside Rajagopal's office, ever in attendance. That Hanumanthappa had been detailed to work with Rajagopal was a happy surprise for Shivanna. The work, position and dignity of their jobs was different, yet there was no dearth of friendship that went with talk and chatter. The twosome exchanged notes about their jobs and the style and manner of their work. While Hanumanthappa enquired about Shivanna's work in the manner of an investigator typical of the police, Shivanna would talk about the work of the Kannada Development Authority, the programmes, seminars, administration, the duties of the Chairman, his nature, and loyalty and about the visitors politely and in a dignified fashion. That too, in a voice not meant to be heard by the Chairman. They would engage in such talk only when Rajagopal was occupied with some visitor. When Rajagopal was alone inside, they would be busy with their own jobs. They hadn't so far seen either any hint of or the actual letter of threat to their boss. Only today had such a threat created an atmosphere of anxiety in the Kannada Bhavana, the building that housed these government departments like the Kannada Development Authority. What a great place of dignity this was! There was no room for such criminals in it.

This was Shivanna's opinion.

This was not untrue. But there was no denying that it was not fully true either. It was everyone's feeling that the Kannada Bhavana, which housed various academic government bodies, which was the treasure-house of art, culture, literature and language, had never ever got such a threatening letter. Not that it shouldn't happen. Even for Gopal it was a new experience. He was by no means a problematic personality. But the reality was that such a contingency had in fact arisen.

Constable Hanumanthappa had to go out for a smoke. But Shivanna couldn't be seen doing it. He was not to muck about, doing things like smoking. The Chairman didn't like such activities. When the cop walked out on such a mission, Shivanna sat there all by himself.

Rajagopal called him in.
"Don't talk unnecessarily with the cop!," he advised the Attender. "He is after all a policeman. He looks at everything with an investigating prying eye. It is not good to talk as if we know everything. Is that okay, Shivanna?"

Shivanna stood, his head bowed. *Did I talk about him?* Shivanna now went into a wordless huddle with himself. *What did I talk that I should not have which made him speak the way he is! It is really difficult to operate and navigate with these big shots.* When Shivanna walked out and sat on his chair, Hanumanthappa arrived and began pacing the floor from end to end in an orderly way. Exchanges between them abated. *Is everything over? No, it isn't.* Shivanna resumed his self-huddle. *There is something called* tomorrow. *The cop has to be here till the letter meets with some result. Where would he go?*

It was four o' clock, but Rajagopal couldn't bring himself to eat anything. Even home-cooked food didn't go down his system. He had neither the time nor the will to go out. Downbeat anxiety and a sick weariness, to boot. A pain that made him want nothing.
'Is this possible?' He asked himself. 'Would the Inspector find out who wrote the letter this very day?'
Keeping the day's mental pressure in mind, he sent for Mallikarjuna Swamy, his personal assistant. Handing Shivanna some papers and files to carry, the personal assistant walked straight to the Chairman's room.
"Don't worry, Sir!" he spoke some soothing words as he entered the room. "I will take the responsibility of organising next week's programme. You sign just these papers, go home and take some rest. I will attend to the rest."
Mallikarjuna Swamy got the boss's signature on some papers and arranged them systematically before quietly raising the issue.
"Do you suspect anyone of writing this letter, Sir?"

The poser astonished Rajagopal no end. *Just a while back,* Rajagopal found himself saying quietly to himself, *he said, "Some jerk has done this mischief, just to scare you, Sir. Don't waste time and thought on this!" The bloke is saying this now!*

Gopal simply bobbed his head without saying anything. A hangdog air on his face, he banged his hands on the two arms of the chair once before springing to his feet. His was anxiety that allowed no words to spill past his lips. Besides, his assistant's was this kind of question. He should have broached it right then. This was not a question that could soothe one. It was pretty pesky. It was a question asked simply to satisfy one's curiousity. As Gopal came down the steps, Hanumanthappa followed him and opened the car door. As Gopal sat on the driver's seat, the cop sat behind. This was inevitable. The Inspector had asked Gopal to take the cop wherever he went. Some other constable had been detailed to keep guard at night. After leaving Gopal back at his house, and carrying Gopal's things from the car and dropping them in the house, Hanumanthappa left saying, "I will come tomorrow morning, sir."

****

On reaching the house, Rajagopal walked straight into his room before losing himself in some study. Saraswathi, his wife didn't enquire about anything at all. She brewed some coffee and handing him a piping-hot cup of it, lit the lamp in the home-shrine. As she went out to kindle the lamp in the low earth-structure in which was a plant of holy basil, she was taken aback to see the police constable. Saraswathi was younger than Rajagopal by as many as ten years. She had done her M.A even before she got married. After husband came over and settled in Bengaluru, she had joined a local college as a temporary Lecturer. Yet she was quite a traditionalist when it came to doing worships and performing rites and rituals. She was from a traditionalist family.

When she returned, she asked her husband about the police vigil at the door. Rajagopal felt bewildered. Yet the reply was felicitous.

"That is in my honour."

That was all. A short curtailed reply. There is no asking back, or importunate probing, with husbands, is there? He had gotten hold of some book. Being all by oneself in a state of mind which didn't brook unfurling, cutting off all connection with the outside world and getting lost in a book was what Rajagopal was doing. It was like a *yoga*. It is only through good reads that one could detach oneself from the pressures and anxieties of this world. Rajagopal had thought this was indeed the sap of life. What would one feel but fear with a threat to life? It was difficult to get a disturbed distraught mind back under control. Saraswathi scanned husband's face, but no answer was there for the taking.

"Call him in and get him some coffee, Sarasu!"
She then called the constable in and made enquiries. He was to come every day for keeping vigil, he said. He was the security police. The same anxiety arose over again in Saraswathi. But the cop didn't divulge anything more. Saraswathi sashayed toward the kitchen.

Rajagopal had been quite at ease and at peace with himself before the letter entered the scene. He appreciated the value of that state of mind only now. It wasn't something one could chat with others about. One couldn't weep. If you felt scared, they would further frighten you. But one couldn't drum up courage and talk freely, feeling very emboldened either. *This constable, the inspector and this personal assistant of mine all bewilder me in one way or another, no one shares my anxiety. Terrorist menace has increased in Bengaluru. Who do I ask as to who is the man, why this threat and how to ask? Now there is the additional burden of the police on security duty with me! With him around there is no freedom at all. How do we ask him to sleep outside? How would he keep guard outside if he sleeps inside? Could we sleep, leaving him outside to keep watch? Sleep would now be far away from me. How would one sleep, when one is torn by doubts, depression and anxiety?*

Rajagopal had the habit of watching TV for the daily news. He didn't switch on the TV today. He didn't have the desire of seeing the news. Nor was there any need. *Some vanquished feeling has squelched me totally. It is amazing how such dark thoughts are battling inside an innocent mind. Who wants this power? I could live honourably in the village, looking after the little land and plantations we have in the lap of my mother and with my younger sisters and brothers and engaging myself in some or other writing. Whether such life was a rich or a poor one is not material. The thought of resigning comes to mind. But I shouldn't give the impression of having got scared. Saraswathi has got used to Bengaluru. She wouldn't come to the village, she says. City life is so very expensive. How would I be able to manage after I demit this office? Could I take money from her? If we retire to the village, she would squabble with mother and thus raise her blood sugar and blood pressure. Under the pressure of work she forgets every woe here in Bengaluru.*

He felt unbearably stressed. He would do with a peg of rum, he felt. Rajagopal took the rum bottle that was there in the almirah, taking care to see that his wife didn't see him do it, and took a glass of water along before pushing the door closed.

"Ri!.... come for your meal!" It was his wife who had called out.

Saraswathi prepared to place the meal on the dining table. Her husband didn't have any interest in anything. He sat before the plate, went through the motions of eating the meal before washing his hand and repairing into the room and sitting reading *Avarana*, the Kannada novel by Bhyrappa. Since he had drunk rum, the reading didn't move onward. The book he held in his hand was but a covering for the face. It was not like this yesterday. If the letter hadn't reached him, even today would have been pretty much like yesterday. *Which anthill does this snake belong to? It has come out and pounced upon me. When will I be free from this? Will the police let me be at peace? What to tell the wife? If it casts a chill on her, what do I do? Should I resign? Where do I go if I resign? That would be a great insult and humiliation, wouldn't it? She is observing me closely.*

What? He asked himself as the idea struck him that the threat may be because of some animosity created about the selection of books for awards by the organisation of which he was the chairman. *Is it possible to select books for awards without any yardsticks? Even if some book is not selected for the award, do they spew such venom? No,* he decided himself. *This i.e the murder threat is not because of selection of books for awards.*

This anger is for sure spurred by the jealousy about my position. The political situation has changed now. The Deputy Chief Minister who recommended my name for the position I hold has resigned. Maybe I should have resigned too following his resignation. That may be why this kind of fear is being created. It is fear everywhere, whether I am at home or outdoors. In the night this police

---

¹ *Rii* is an honorific address term for husbands, elders and strangers.

constable intrudes into my privacy and solitude. But whoever intends harming me will have to harm him as well. Let him be there for a couple of days. After that I will say I don't need him at night. Let the police be there only during daytime. Whatever form death takes, let it take. But because of me the police constable, his wife and children should not get into trouble....

Rajagopal drifted into sleep right on the chair after he closed his eyes keeping the book he was reading, by his face. After a while, he got up, walked over and slept on the cot. It was well over one hour since Saraswathi had nodded off. She didn't have all this anxiety and fear that Rajagopal was being torn by. She had a lot of respect for, and felt a lot of pride about, her husband. There was no question of talking back to him. She was aware that hers was a temporary job and that her husband meant everything to her.

Saraswathi never talked to her husband in the vein of exercising her rights. If she had talked more aggressively, Rajagopal might have ladled out his inner turmoil, who knows?! This was why the married journey of Rajagopal and Saraswathi seemed to be smooth sailing without any conflicts at all. Saraswathi might not have the experiential awareness of what this tormenting and pestering a wife meant so she could ask herself why he wasn't tormenting her, latching on to her, tagging her for physical intimacy and the primal act. Or, she might have thought, her husband might frown upon her, dubbing her a tomboy if she did so.

This feeling might have muted her.

If one thinks of her family at Madhugiri, one gets the chill. Thank God atleast I am away from all that scurry 'n scramble and hustle 'n bustle.

This afforded him a measure of solace. But although there wasn't deep down real happiness, could one rest satisfied with these amenities and social laurels that were his? You have a very physical body that eats not bland insipid things, but sharp peppery and pungent piquant stuff. And a mind that is aware, active and creative. Not that one doesn't want, like and need love, lust and enamourment. One does. But if one turns one's back on it, it is all renunciation and asceticism. Aren't there people who remain forever unmarried? There are. That is effortful restraint and forced subjugation of the senses. On such a site there wouldn't be man for woman and woman for man. No excitement and arousal at all. But here, with her husband that she loves being right in front of her, this woman acts like a chaste faithful wife, as if there has been an agreement of love and honour between them, an agreement that stipulates restraint of sensual appetite and mastery of the flesh. She didn't have the faintest doubt that her husband had loved another woman before their marriage and he had been frustrated there, and this was the reason why he had evinced no bodily hunger for her and why she had failed to tickle his sensual buds.

It was thirty years since they had married. That there had been no ups and downs and conflicts and squabbles indicates that she must be a dunce. In the meantime Gopal and Ushe were meeting like before in this very house. They are savouring love. All steamy moments of cuddling, coupling, caressing, hugging, kissing and petting that they indulge in as lovers were happening in the very house in which that ascetic of a woman went about as a smiling married woman, lighting lamps, smearing turmeric and vermilion on the wooden thresholds of doors. Her husband's steamy dance of love with his younger female companion, the *rasaliile* spread, like the smell of sprinkled sandalwood powder does, across the living hall, the *padasaale* and the bedroom. But she never got wind of this. She had immense trust in her husband. She believed her husband was indeed a man of supreme continence, which in point of fact was her experience with him.

What was more, sixty years was an advanced age. The idea is that people would not have great sexual drive at this age. Their wedding was a simple one. There was no dowry given or special treatment of the groom done with gifts etc. None was asked for. And her father wasn't financially sound enough to celebrate the wedding with lavish pomp and pageantry.

It was Gopal's mother who had hooked her to him with force. But his mother' word was Veda for Gopal. He was the eldest of the twelve children. While mother's affection was the highest for him among the children, every responsibility of the household was upon him. They owned some land and plantation n addition to a huge house at Madhugiri. Some of the land was sold off for the marriage of the girl children. What work did they have in the village-home? Sharade, the eldest of his younger sisters had retraced her steps back to her maternal home after being separated from her husband. She managed the household now. She couldn't behave aggressively at the husband's place. Saying that her husband's conduct wasn't right, she had returned to settle at her parents' place. There was no question of going back for her. She managed everything there now.

'Why should I go there?' Saraswathi reasoned to herself. 'Bengaluru is good and beautiful. Let him go there if he wants. He has this great affection for his younger sister. She teaches music at home. She is the one who performs the wedding and does the nursing motherhood of her younger sisters. She also sees to the education of her younger brothers. One of them is Srihari. He is a rogue. I for one want to hand him a hiding whenever I see him'.

'I wonder how she manages food, breakfast and stuff for fifteen persons, and the servants! He goes there once in a while and hands over money. Or else, how would she be able to tug the chariot of life. She even saves money out of what he gives them and dresses herself in a hip way. Even at the age of fifty, she looks very much a teenage girl'.

...These were the thoughts racing through Saraswathi's head.

One shortfall of this life was that Saraswathi didn't have any children even after thirty years of married life. Both Rajagopal and Saraswathi had this worry. But it is true that Rajagopal had found satisfaction and contentment in his own younger brothers. Saraswathi didn't take to this kindly. But being assertive and pushy with her husband, she figured, would amount to wrecking the high esteem she held her husband in and so kept mum and to herself.

****

Constable Hanumanthappa was present the following day. The one who kept watch in the night might have gone to sleep. Saying she had a class at 8 o'clock, Saraswathi went off. She had cooked breakfast and stuffed it into a hotbox. Gopal brewed coffee himself. Whenever wife was away, he even cooked his meals.

"Did you have your breakfast, fellow?"
"Yes I did, Sir! You eat your breakfast! If you tell me when it is that we are leaving for office, I will take out the car and park it here."
"Let us leave at 10.30. I have something to write."

There was a poem unfurling in him, seeking embodiment.

And lo! He did write it out, ever so smoothly and effortlessly, on a white sheet of paper, like one felicitously draws the ornamental *rangoli* designs in the front yards of houses. The grief, anxiety and fear that he had felt, and that had been efficiently dammed up since the previous night, assuming various forms and quietly beating time as in music, flowed right out. He wrote fast and furious, as if the words were gushing out like water through a breached tank outlet, an outburst that brooked no stopping!

Rajagopal's primary literary form was poetry. He had already pocketed several prestigious awards and honours including the Sahitya Akademi award. He had due contacts with political big guns. Otherwise how would the chairmanship of a huge government organization come his way? But he was not an evil or cunning personality.

One point is important here.

Bonding with politicians means enhancing one's own prestige by showing them the right way. And further to garner positions from them. Rajagopal was not an exception to this. He was close to the Deputy Chief Minister. And a close advisor to him. When the man was removed from the Deputy Chief Ministership, Rajagopal was the one who suggested organizing meetings throughout the state and this paved the way for the chairmanship that he ended up landing. In other words littérateurs are the backbones of politicians. If one writer advises the Congress party, another does it for BJP and a third for JD(S). When the party one advises comes to power, that writer stands to gain, the party favouring him for positions and honours. Rajagopal had landed the chairmanship like this. What would happen if, within one year of Rajagopal getting the chairmanship, he got a threat letter? Rajagopal was an important person in the academia. As an individual he was as soft and mild. His mild softness was in fact his attraction. He was suave in his speech. And he was good to look at, to boot, what with a chiselled face cut and a complexion that stood out in a crowd.

In real life however he had to endure a lot of hardship and pain. Disappointment and disinterest have become the main motif in his poetry. It wouldn't be wrong to say that Bendre and Adiga have influenced his poetry. He was politically connected only as part of his squaring up to modernity and not to do any politicking. But that there is a definite relation between literature and politics is true. Feeling downbeat and weepy is not all. One needs the outer world to be free of this low feeling. A booming boisterous laugh, the ultimate bonding experience, is possible only in the external world. How could one stay alive and grow if one maintains the same weepy face that you sport in family space in the outer world as well?

We don't know how Ushe drew him to her. It was right from her student days that he gravitated toward her in the way she looked at him, by her talk and the slew of questions that she posed as a student. When he was appointed as a lecturer at Tumakuru, Rajagopal was still a young greenhorn, with a moustache that was only beginning to sprout. It was not surprising that things had ignited between the two of them, he falling to her bait. To think ahead even in the tipsy ebullience of love is the mark of an educated man. But excessive attraction and emotionality create expectations. She was at the peak of youth; she was eighteen. And her teacher at twenty nine fizzed over with the hot blood of youth. Here one must talk about Ushe rather than about Rajagopal. He was very balanced, not given to extremes. He was intelligent. He didn't probe her caste. He had the long-term idea of letting her meet his mother and stepping into wedlock with her. But things didn't pan out the way he thought they would pan out.

He had tied the knot with Saraswathi.

And with it, life had diminished to the point of coming to a naught. He was not to find on this face the happiness that he saw in that face. One can't live out one's life, mingling with someone merely because one has married the person. This person that you have married is not the same as the one you loved. Both are for sure women! Yet one can't feel comfortable and at home with this woman at an age when you felt deep in your innards that that woman was your world. The words that you exchanged with her, her dulcet voice, the kisses that you exchanged, the moments when you held her hands, the touch that ignited fires in you, the walk that sent frissons zooming through your system, everything flashed across his memory screen before the screen went blank.

Life had become blank.

A teary darkness was what he found himself face to face with. This took Rajagopal deep into the past, to the day when his father shuffled off his mortal coil even before Gopal got married, the familial responsibilities that fell on his shoulders with an audibly heavy thud, and the pain of a married life that never really took off... Even amidst all these hardships, Rajagopal made life bearable.

Even if life made you feel down and out, you can't stop the business of living. To adjust to circumstances and determining to make something of whatever life you are leading is the hallmark of an intelligent being. In this compromised kind of life one might find comfort and contentment or might not. One might need to develop an outer phase and an inner phase to one's personality. One can't say everyone is happy and content in every way either. If one loses one thing, one develops a desire to get another. One might emerge a winner, an achiever with this intense inner struggle. Gopal gave up the ambition of his to get back what he had lost before accepting whatever came his way dispassionately.

Gopal ate his breakfast, washed his hand and was preparing to go to office. He wore only *jubba*s and *pyjama*s: he never wore anything more expensive. And those were either white or half white or almond coloured. He wore no other colour. He looked neat in that outfit. It was already ten thirty. How could he leave still later? There was an inauguration function of a book movement. The following day the new Deputy Chief Minister had called a meeting to discuss the culture festival to be conducted in the days to come. He had asked the chairmen of all Academies and Authorities to be present to discuss the modalities of celebrating the next State-Founding Day, the statehood-festival, the *rajyotsava* with great pomp and pageantry.

No matter how well he cleansed and did up his face, anxiety and fear were writ all over it. *Why this threat for me, and not for others? Okay, let us face it! When i go out for the meeting, I should leave this escort police right here at the office. No one should be told about it. If I take him to the meeting, everyone's attention would be riveted only on me. The police have said no one should know about this arrangement of security police for me. Even if someone comes to know, let us face it with courage. The one who has got me into this difficult situation might be one among them. We can't say for sure though. One of among them could be the culprit.*

Even while driving, sitting in the car, the mind thought along these very lines. He had got used to Bengaluru's traffic rules. The escort cop would sit on the back seat. Gopal didn't allow anyone to drive his car. He drove it himself. No matter which town he went out to from Bengaluru, he did the driving himself. His was very skillful driving.

It is difficult to drive when the mind is not at peace. But if he hired a driver now, he had to be paid his salary, which was something he ill-afforded. *The cost of living in Bengaluru is rather high. But if you are in the village, if you get ragi, rice etc just enough to last a year from the lands there, that would do. How would Sharade manage food for so many people and medicines for mother? The pension and the salary from his chairmanship are not enough for the two of us. The salary Saraswathi gets is just enough for her expenses and travel. The government bears my fuel expense and mobile charges. Still my money keeps flowing out like water. I am not corrupt enough to misuse and misappropriate government money. Those who are are looting the government money. But that is beyond people who are mild soft and kind in disposition.*

When he sat in his room some nameless dissatisfaction troubled and agitated Rajagopal. *I used to work so very smoothly and efficiently. But now there is some nameless hesitation, dawdling and indecision*, he ruminated. The personal assistant came over and got his signature for the papers of some programme. "There is the function where you inaugurate the book movement at four in the afternoon, Sir!" he said and left.

Rajagopal got some books having to do with the book movement function, mentally noted down some points before writing down some points. Speaking in public was something that came naturally to him. There was no need to strain himself or to labour. That said, it was not correct to speak for the heck of it, without any objective rigour either. To speak connecting what you are saying to the current scenario would be fine. Whatever be the mental stress that bugged one, that he had cultivated further the natural inclination and bent of mind to study had brought on some dignity and sheen to his personality. It was during this phase that his pains and woes had evaporated into a steady and composed state of mind. The activity of studying books and assimilating their content causes the glow of awareness and maturity that plays on one's face. The indirect satisfaction that he had got for now had made for even more beauty. We can say beauty at sixty is the solemnity that suits the age. Since he colored his hair, his was black hair even at sixty. The face glows on its own if the hair on the head is black. Although not fully and visibly lush, he had reasonably enough hair on the head. It was by no means scarce enough for the scalp to be visible. Yet it was rare for a hale and heartily full smile to fill the face. That kind of laugh would be like nectar. The ineffably deep satisfaction that the moments he spent with Ushe caused spread a highly contented smile on his face. The elegance of the intoxicated ecstasy of the smile that surfaces during those moments is different. But whether it was happiness or pain, it was the same for Rajagopal. He had this stoic attitude. He would once in a while flash a smile. That was all. That was his nature.

"Someone called Shivalingiah has come to see you, Sir. Shall i send him in?" asked the Attender, coming in.

Gopal felt a tad embarrassed. *There are restrictions even when some VIP comes along. But has Shivanna not seen Shivalingaih before? Shivalingaih is a Dalit poet. Why has he come now? What is there for him to talk to me about? He competed with me for the post last year. He is as well known and influential as me. But when I landed the position, he did feel jealous. Be it as it might, who knows why he has turned up now!*

"Come, Shivalingaih!" Gopal welcomed even as he motioned to him to take his seat. "It has been a long time since we met."

They chatted about the current political scenario, literature, books etc. before Shivalingiah, unable to contain his curiosity, did ask, "What is this, *guru*! Isn't this injustice to you! Who has posed this threat to a good pure soul, a *saatvika*, like you?"

The question that came instantly to Gopal's mind was "Who told you this?" But Gopal didn't let it tip over.

Instead he came up simply with, "Somebody has just threatened so I will resign. That is all."

"If it is just a threat, it would be okay, *guru*! Supposing this poses a danger to you?"

Why does he care? Gopal told himself finding himself deep in an inner monologue. *What has he to do with this? He is talking as if he knows everything. If you come to think about it, he also got his name recommended by a political leader. He could himself have been behind this! Someone would get this position after me. With no inclination and the sense to wait his turn, this man is deliberately poking at my thoughts. It would be good if I answer as if nothing has happened. If I show I am scared, he might further scare me. I needn't bother about the truth or falsity of my reply. I need to give him some reply, even if an evasive one.*

25

"Don't worry! We don't have to bother about the uncultured letters penned by these nonentities." Gopal snapped. "We can't grow if we do care for these things, can we? What will you have? Shall I get you some coffee, or tea? Or would you like some snacks?"

The formal courtesy of asking the visitor what he wanted to drink being duly completed, Gopal asked the Attender to get some tea, and was about to ask what else was the news when Shiavalingiah broke out with,

"We have the Deputy Chief Minister's meeting tomorrow, as you know. Be careful. The minister knows about this letter, it seems. He got it through the police. He might ask you about it."

Gopal began to break into a sweat.

He felt as if he sank down with someone pressing him down. It felt as if his heart missed a beat, and his breath ceased for a while. With some unease felt in the chest, Gopal's hand went inevitably up to his chest. He put his head down and set to thinking when, saying "What happened, *guru*?" Shivalingiah came round running. As if solacing him, he put his arm around Gopal and gave him the glass of water that was thereabouts for Gopal to drink.

"It's all right. Maybe I am under some undue pressure of work," Gopal gasped, recovering on his own and drumming up courage.

"In any case you consult and get checked up by a doctor. You shouldn't ignore it. This work and career are always there! They shouldn't come in the way of looking after your health, should they? Do you grow young day by day? As it is, you have suffered."

All he is saying is the truth of the moment. But it was true only on the surface. He would for sure have different thoughts deep inside. These people use the word guru, an intimate form of address and behave as if they are really concerned, but deep inside they would be really happy that such letter had indeed come, and that I am in an anxious fluster. He is not really my close friend. He has probably come to find out what my state is and whether I was contemplating resignation, and if he could grab that position. They talk something in public but would have totally different ideas inside. How would the Deputy Chief Minister come to know about this?. These filthy disgusting blighters would not leave one alone... They do the double work of rocking the cradle to lull the child to sleep and at the same time pinch the kid's bum! What could the Deputy Chief Minister possibly ask me? Such letters come as long as there are people burning with the fire of jealousy. I could give the same reply. If the body curls up, the mind awakens. And if the mind shrinks the body would awaken. Let this be! Let me fight it out!

"Wouldn't the Deputy Chief Minister have high opinion about, and respect for, people like us? He would!" Gopal now vented his thoughts. "Why should I be anxious? I don't care, Sivalingaiah! If there is a murder threat, the government should give us protection. Will it instead hold an undue inquiry? I indeed that is so, let it be! Thanks for your suggestion."

So saying, Gopal said goodbye to Shivalingiah.

Yet the huge arms of his apprehensions had cast their dark deep shadows across his mind. *The police might have brought it to the notice of the Deputy Chief Minister and to some highly placed officials so as to keep it under wraps. Some administrative strategies would be more important to them than confidentiality. The police transmit this through wireless. Now there is internet! It is confidential only in name but in effect it would be known to all!* This thought touched off an uneasy twinge in Gopal, bringing in its wake more unsettling tension. *Who should I beg for help? What is it that is still in my hands and what is it that has slipped out of my control? I need to steel myself to square up to this. One could attract both either softness or toughness. I should do it with toughness and turn that into my dignity. If Death that was to come several years later wants to come right away, why should I quail and jib? My death can not bring unbearable shock and danger to anyone very close to me, can it? I will cause some distress, that is all. I will not feel any pain the moment I die. Some pain when the actual killing takes place. Death will be instantaneous. Where will I be to see this temporal world's agony? But it should happen that those who wrote this threat letter and others who got it written and crave my devastation should come to feel envious of me. I could keep to myself, resigning my position and behave with proud self-importance. I could develop my writing and try new ways of writing. Why should I fall prey to these superficially nice but cunning creatures?*

A new glow appeared on Gopal's face.

Then surged up the promise of latching on to it for good. *I will win!* He told himself. *I shouldn't jib. I should not take this very seriously.* He stood

27

before the looking glass and brought himself to smile. A nameless feeling of a shoring promise seemed to zoom through him. *No moment is there for ever.* He was into his monologue with himself over again. *They keep moving. Change is like that. It is always there round the corner, ready to envelop you. Perhaps this moment will change, enhancing my mood.*

Gopal immersed in his read again.

****

Chapter Two

The fact that mobile phones don't make much noise when they vibrate is very convenient in a variety of senses. Gopal's heart would also vibrate along with the vibrating cellphone. Even at the fairly advanced age of fifty eight, feelings of love, attraction, pride, intensity and passion are all as true and real as the breaths we breathe in and out. The mind and body don't fail to horripilate at the two-syllabled wonder of "hello!", cooed as sweetly and softly as it could be. It was as if there were only these two in the whole of the cosmos: the books, the chair, table, fan and the police constable outside didn't exist!

"There was some news last night on TV channels. Is it true?"

"What is it?"

"Someone has threatened you with murder, is it true?"

"Whatever threat it may be, if you are with me, all this is trivial! When will we meet? It has been quite some time since we met. Will you show up tomorrow? Saraswathi leaves home around eight. I will ask the cop to come a little late."

"Aha! Look at you, saying this now! You haven't called me for so many days now. You don't have to worry. You could get so many women, which is why you forget to remember and call me. I won't come!"

"Ah, honey! Shall I rip open and show my heart to you, like Hanumantha did in the epic of Ramayana? Don't pester me at this age! I have had enough of this pining all these days. You come tomorrow!"

"Don't talk like they talk in your plays! I don't believe all this stuff. If what you are saying is true, you would have married me twenty five years back, wouldn't you? We are only trying to make possible what we don't get

29

at this age. If only we had married, everything would be ours. You married Saraswathi, thinking I am from a different caste, and under the convenient excuse that Saraswathi was the girl your mother wanted you to marry. You don't feel, no matter how much I suffer. The whole lot of you, Brahmins are like this, exploiting people, putting caste upfront!"

The words had poured out in deep frustration.

Gopal didn't speak. *Let her spill out all her grievance, I will talk afterwards,* he told himself. In fact it was only today that Usha had talked so much. It was around the year nineteen seventy five that he, letting go the teacherly feeling, fell in love with Usha, his student in Tumakuru. Since Gopal lived in Tumakuru in a rented house, she would visit him in the house on some pretext or another. Usha was an intense thinker, a great reasoner. But she never showed this prowess of hers before Gopal. She harboured a strange mix of anger and envy about Brahmins. Gopal was a lecturer in Kannada. He was straight-laced and mild in temperament. He was amazed into being smitten with her as much by her looks as by her piquantly mischievous conduct. She never broached caste with him. Her intention was different. Her agenda was to trap him in her manifesto of love, and giving him the intimacy of her bubbly youth, to trick him into a state of frustration. Gopal hadn't as yet married. He hadn't thought about the consequences of this intimacy either. But the story didn't pan out the way they thought it would. Usha, who had set out to cause frustration and disappointment in a Brahmin, was herself frustrated.

Gopal shouldered a huge family responsibility. His mother had twelve children. Gopal had six younger sisters and five younger brothers. With Father dying a premature death, the load of looking after the whole family fell bang on Gopal's head. Figuring that shuttling from and to Madhugiri would exhaust him, he had rented a house in Tumakuru. But now, having vacated the Tumakuru house, he had begun commuting between Madhugiri and Tumakuru. It took the hell out of Gopal, doing the father's obsequial rituals and the monthly afterdeath-routine, the *shraadda*. The education of his younger siblings and the managing of food etc for twenty people in the household every day was quite a task.

His father Nanjunda Rao worked in the law court in Madhugiri. He had made some property. He had bought some land and garden in

Shambhonahalli on the Hindupur road. He would grow some *ragi* and paddy on the land and managed this huge family. He was proud that his son was a Kannada lecturer. When, with father's demise, the huge responsibility of the family fell on his shoulders, Gopal was hardly twenty eight. Wouldn't this huge responsibility be a load on him? It would. He felt intense disappointment for so many days, remembering Usha. Even when he came to college, he couldn't talk to her. He was apprehensive of the embarrassment he would feel if people saw him talk to her. At this stage the thought of her caste hadn't crossed his mind. He hadn't tried to find out. Perhaps her intelligence, her attractive exterior, her skin-colour, the suaveness of her behaviour had led him to believe she was a Brahmin. He didn't make any efforts then though to find out her caste. Even now, twenty five years later, he hadn't. He hadn't the faintest idea of what her caste was. But this haunted Usha even now. Even now this thorn kept piercing her skin. It was only at the latest meeting that she had told him she hailed from a 'backward' caste and that she held a high position in the Backward Classes Protection Commission. In the intoxication of the intimacy that he had got after twenty five years, Gopal hadn't felt the need to rack his brains about, or splotch his mind getting to know, her caste.

She had come with the intention of cheating and frustrating him after wittingly loving him in her girlishness. But his gentle nonabrasive and benevolent nature had melted her heart. By the time the awareness that she, as his student, ought not to cheat on her guru arose in her, his mother had got to know from someone about the guru and the pupil warming to each other, and had decided on his marriage with Saraswathi without waiting for his approval. There was some palpable tension between the mother and the son because of some resistance to this from the son. Gopal held his mother in great respect. But he hadn't drummed up the courage to speak to mother about Usha. Life had sort of closed down, and he cried his eyes out, swallowing the grief all by himself. He never ever felt or got from Saraswati the kind of love and the steamy sexual excitement that he felt about Usha. Even Saraswathi never got the kind of lustful love she should in fact have got from him.

In the meantime, when Sharade, the first younger sister came back for good, separating from her husband, he had used a lot of his leave to shuttle between home, the court and her husband's place. She thereafter took on the responsibility of the household. She was now fifty four years of age. She saw to the education of her other siblings. Besides four younger sisters, she had married off one of the younger brothers as well. One jobless younger brother went about making speeches like an idealist even as he raised the matter of property, aspersing and berating Sharade with a liberal sprinkle of invectives. Warming to Gopal because of his intelligence and prudence, a minister had arranged a house for him in Bengaluru so Gopal could advise the minister about various issues having to do with the state. It was only now that he had landed the chairmanship of the Kannada Development Authority.

Over here, Usha hadn't married, and not being married, she had now enveloped Gopal cooing, 'I have spent my time and life in the remembrance of your love!'. Buoyant with this turn in his life, Rajgopal went about his daily life, feeling so full of vim and verve that he thought he could conquer the world, that the world was at his feet. The idea that she had stayed unmarried, waiting only for him, wafted him onto cloud nine, and it was as if his old age of fifty nine years gave way swiftly to the bubbly youth of twenty five years. This told on his body as well.

This was indeed the personal issue of one's body as well. This was in fact the reason why the Gopal couple was issueless. The acute disappointment that his marriage with Saraswathi had brought in fact revved up his mind so he scaled new heights of personal achievement. The poetry that he wrote during this time was the poetry of love, enamourment, sorrow and grief. It was true that the momentum and the rusticity of his language went down well with the Kannada literary world. What was more, he also received several prestigious awards including the Karnataka Sahitya Akademi award, the Central Sahitya Akademi awards. But the gratified joy that he had lost deep inside him no one had been able to dish out.

Usha had now completely occupied him. She was forty eight. Yet because she hadn't married, she thought she was still a girl of twenty five and so dressed like a girl of that age, wearing thin transparent sarees, wearing them in such a way as to keep the belly-button exposed, sporting lip stick, the eye-black, the black collyrium smeared around the lower part of her eyes, and flaunting the seductive swell of her bosom, and the curvaceous sculpture of her body like city slickers do. This was more than enough for Rajgopal.

"Is she the Ushe of yore?" he found himself quizzing himself.

He craved her physical intimacy, especially because he didn't have to commit himself to marrying her. The way he fell headlong into the pool of her love, lusting after her was amazing. Whoever would say that the fact that harking to the call of love of forty eight, the youth of sixty rained torrential love, wetting the soil was not right? Saraswathi was indeed a good-looking woman. But she never ever drew Gopal toward her. Gopal never ever poked her silence. He did touch her on so many nights, but it all seemed rigged up. But that even at that age, Ushe aroused him before affording such heavenly bliss was surprising and anxiety-inducing at the same time to both. The problem of youth that Gopal hadn't encountered before was now a problem. The way his tackle exuded sperms at that age had astonished him. He would make mental note of the day Ushe was to turn up at his place before taking enough preparatory measures. Why would he hold back the thirst of so many days? He had encouraged and emboldened himself, posing the question to himself of "If there is no problem, why defer gratification?" His younger sister had in any case taken up the responsibility of the household. *Even if i feel I am making a mistake, why engage in self-deception* was what he felt. *No one bothered about my joys and happiness! I fended for myself. If they now dub this 'immoral', how are they right?*

The person I feel love for is Ushe. The person the body responds to is her. I am by no means doing unjustly by Saraswathi, am i? In any case who would come to know about our affair? It is difficult for people in Bengaluru to look after their own affairs. Who would have the time to care for what happening in other lives, to keep track of who is visiting my house? Not even neighbours! Several people keep calling me at my home to get forewords written for their poem collections and to invite me for programmes and functions. Ushe is one among them, people would think.

But the threat of murder has hollowed him out. But can he forego the sensual delight of a woman's physical intimacy because of this fear? No, he can't, and, what is more, he shouldn't. The reply that he came up with to Ushe's question after a considerable while was as follows:

"Ushe! Don't you stab me with the question of caste. I hadn't known about your caste then. I am not probing you about your caste even now.

33

The circumstances of life made me behave the way I did. My mother has eleven children besides me. Father has been no more for a while. She felt the need of some support in the form of a daughter-in-law. It was she who decided on my marriage. Supposing I resisted it, what would have happened to the household? What about the future of the other children? Tell me! Love and affection are as much pain as they are pleasure. Understand this! I am already on the verge of sixty. No one can say for sure when life would stutter to a halt. We should take what comes to our lot and enjoy it. That is all that has remained now."

"No class now, Mr! I will come for sure at nine thirty tomorrow. I will be there for just ten minutes. I will have to go for a meeting."

"Don't bring your car tomorrow. Your car shouldn't be parked in front of my house. I will talk about the murder threat later. I am not in a position to talk about it with anyone. Okay then, see you!"

Gopal rose and shot a look at the doorway. The Attender was seated on his chair by the door. At a distance from his chair, the police constable was scouring the place about him with his eyes.

****

Initially she would come to him on the pretext of borrowing books. When she came, she would come fully decked, her cheeks smeared with fragrant talcum powder. Since her father was a government official, she would get money from him to spend on cosmetics like face powder, eyeliner, nail polish etc. She would play very suave, talking penetratively even as the words were spoken softly. "Youth is like this!" Rajgopal told himself, keeping mum. Teenage and youth are not very different. For the teacher who was thirty or thereabouts the company of a teenaged girl was a piquant tickle. Figuring that the girl was calling with books in her hands at his house for tuitions, neighbors never thought there could be something the matter. Yet it was embarrassing for Rajgopal. Nobody would take his behavior amiss. Which was why nobody bothered about her frequent visits. Nobody took it ill. Ushe's experiment, that is, her visits to her guru's abode got easy and smooth. Gopal's was a small rented house in KR extension. Ushe's was somewhere in a nook in Gandhinagara. She would visit him late in the evening. She brought him some snacks a couple of times. There was ingenuousness in her words, but this only masked what was afoot deep down. A secretive strategy that should not be used to play with youth was

34

at play. Her childlike words, the naughtiness and the maturity that she displayed at times drew Gopal to her. She got intimate with him, intimate enough, to talk not only about his lectures, but also about his looks and his desirably handsome face.

"The moment you enter the class, it is as if a bolt of lightning zooms through me!"

These words of his student darted across his being much like a bolt of lightning. She in fact called him 'lightning bolt'!

When she cooed and gushed, "Your smile is like a swing in a flower garden in full bloom!' Rajagopal was swept off his feet.

One day when she was doing her final B.A, she heard people talking about his transfer, and this shocked Ushe. She went to his place with a variety of snacks and a gift in the evening, but his house was locked. On enquiry, it was found that Gopal's father had passed on, that Gopal had gone away to Madhugiri for the death-rites, and that it could well be fifteen days before he returned. This further set Ushe back. Her plans went awry. She had thought she could trick the Brahmin and taint and impair his brahminhood with the show of her love for him, but now she herself lost out in her plan and this made her wish to seek his pardon. But Rajgopal was occupied in the death rites of his father. Each moment she spent now without him was an eon, she felt.

There was another doubt that bothered her.

That was, what if he got transferred to Bengaluru and went away. *There would be many students like me for him. I should see him atleast once and tell him that I can't live without him and that he should decline his transfer. But why would he listen to my words? Would he value my words?*

Ushe was battered and bruised thinking such thoughts for ten long days. She was at the moment reading Bhyrappa's novel, titled 'They grew apart ('*duura saridaru*')'. She wondered with some anxiety and apprehension, if, like the protagonists of that novel, she and Gopal would also hive off! She cried and cried, putting out her pain. But then she would find herself telling herself the following:

Chee! I haven't told him I love him, have I? Nor has he told me he loves me, has he? It is all my delusion. This being the case, why should we think we are separating? In case I now say I love him, how would he react? Having lost his father, he is woe-begone. What would he think if I broach things like love? But

35

on the other hand, supposing I don't do it right now, what if he is not available for my declaration of love?

Her heart emptied out and it was as if she no longer wanted to live. She didn't eat her food properly and this physically shriveled her up. She wouldn't attend college regularly. She would instead go stand in front of this and that temple and pray to God to grant her whatever she desired. She would swear her love and devotion for her teacher in front of Him, and commit vows to be carried out if God granted her wishes. Things like "Please let the God I adore come back to me!' she would pour forth. She had no use for the priest. She didn't go to the priest and ask for spreading her webbed hand over the salver of the wick lamp waved clockwise in front of the idol, the *mangalaarathi* and the holy consecrated water, the *thirtha* because that would mean narrating her tale of woes.

She was herself surprised by the change in her thoughts: she had long been an atheist but now she had taken recourse to God. In sum we can say her love for Rajgopal had brought about this change. She was now worried about how she looked: her hair remained uncombed and unkempt and her general appearance tousled.

After ten days she came over to the college, clothed in the recently washed worn-from-the-waist-down bottomwear of *langa* and slung-from-the-shoulder-down topwear of *daavani*, and her hair neatly combed and slicked up, and when she came, she was still in doubt as to whether Gopal was to turn up at the college that day. But she didn't find him. As it was, her face and mind had both been withered. They now went still worse. She waited for the college to give over for the day at three in the afternoon. She was on the point of leaving for home when lo and behold! there he was, appearing like a flash of lightning! Her heart beat pleasantly doubled and a solid ray of hope entered her mind in the thought of 'I can still live on planet earth'. He was not to be found ever since the morning. *Where did he materialise from* was the question that popped up. Oh God! She felt as buoyed up as to break into a rollicking dance. He was talking to his lecturer-colleagues. No hair on the head. He had a cap on. In fact it was difficult to recognize him. But Ushe did recognise him instantly. He didn't have any book in his hand. Was he on leave? Or was it his last day before the transfer took effect?

Ushe now felt a slight tremor in her heart. *Would he go away again? I should get talking right now.* But how? She had never talked to him within the college premises. You can't talk very intimately inside the college premises. Even as she thought on these lines, she strolled ever so slowly toward the group. Head bowed, she walked as if she was heading toward the library which was in that direction. Looking toward the group out of the corner of her eye, she pretended not to look, and by the time she turned her eyes back, her unspoken words fell into his heart. In the meanwhile, Guruprasad, another senior lecturer, who was part of the group, piped up suddenly and vehemently, his voice pitched rather high, "Usha! Don't you want your Kannada teacher? See, we have taken pains to see that his transfer was cancelled. Why should we lose such a good lecturer?"

The joy that Ushe felt deep in her innards left her speechless.

It was usual for lecturers to talk at length to B.A. final students. What Guruprasad meant was: "Don't you want his classes?" There was no other import. But Ushe gave Gopal a velvety killer-stare, a look that was as hearteningly soft as a flower and as uncompromisingly sharp and penetrative as an arrow. There played on Gopal's face a similar smile. There was in that look a mysterious ineffable creamed strain of kineticity. It was only those two who understood it. It was Usha who took up the word:

"Sir! Your book is with me!"

What in fact was meant was, 'Shall I come to your place to give the book back?' Only Rajagopal understood this import. He stumbled attempting to speak. He had to go to Madhugiri that day. He had plans to go straight to Madhugiri without going to his house in Tumakuru. But it was difficult to say this to Ushe in the presence of his colleagues.

"It is okay. You can bring it tomorrow, or whenever it suits you."

She took it to mean, "Come tomorrow!"

This was enough for her. She felt as if the whole world was in her hands. It was as if a dried up tank had filled to the brim. Going back home she ate in a hurry all that her mother had given her. Her father, who was a Harijan, worked in a government office. He had four children, three of them male and two female. She had a younger brother. Her mother was a cultured woman. She had raised the children rather well, keeping them clean and feeding them well and clothing them well.

Her father would often tell her that people at the workplace harassed and exploited him. He would narrate several anecdotes. Her father would come home exhausted from work and sleep off in the night, downing a peg or two of rum. *Government work is there just to carry on life. Exploitation happens there as well. It is not enough to give jobs and facilitate filling up of stomachs : social equality is necessary as well. This exploitation is always there.*

Swirling in Usha's noddle, such thoughts would bedevil her right through the night. There was some relief from such pesky thoughts when she came to attend college in the morning.

That day too she decked herself up in a special fashion: she washed her tresses that cascaded down to her knees after smearing them with oil, bunched and slicked them up, set jasmine flowers in them before, daydreaming that she coquetted about all over the room crooning, like actress Kalpana did in the Kannada film *Gandhinagara*, the lyric

the string of jasmine flowers you wear in your hair,
the love letter that I penned only for you

Then she spread her fresh locks all over her back, and imagining to herself Gopal breaking into K. S. Narasimha Swamy's song

The coal-black tresses sprawling all over the back
is like the descending in the distant hills
of the jet-black night!

on seeing the hirsute cascade on her smooth back and holding her from behind after brushing the hair aside on her back. Then she imaged Gopal as the hero of some other film, and as belting out

let the heavens fall, I won't let go of your hand
let the earth split open, I am ever yours!

which was another film song. Daydreaming and imagining things, Ushe thus rained on herself a profuse outpouring of love and romance.

Why call it imagination? It would remain merely as imagination if it had remained a desire that had grown beyond reality. What she was seeing now was just an infatuation called love, a kind of hunger. One can't say it wouldn't be true. When she went out in the evening, she had decked herself nicely. The two, for some reason, looked like strangers to each other. They didn't talk much. Although Gopal didn't have much hair on his head, he was attractive to her. Silence somehow seemed more bearable than a dialogue. Ushe's eyes glistened with moist emotion after a while. Taken unawares by the tears that had rolled down, Gopal took a surprised look at her.

"I feared you had been transferred," Ushe said sashaying over and holding his hand. "I can't live without you. I feel strongly I should be wherever you are. I can't for sure help this."

"You come live with me. In any case I need a maidservant who can cook, wash and iron my clothes! You fit the bill." There was a jocular strain in Gopal's words. Ushe burst out laughing, her laugh rippling the space around them.

"So then shall I stay back here with you, cooking for you?" she replied equally jocularly. "Will you eat what I cook? That would be my good fortune."

Gopal didn't know what to say in reply.

He sat mum. Even for him she was as attractive as he was for her. But a new awareness had awakened in him. That Ushe had spoken to him soothed Gopal, drowned as he was, in a pool of sorrow, frustration, and fatigue. He felt really delighted.

Getting closer, they exchanged their unspeakable thoughts and turmoils before, noticing that she had leaned on his chest, she quickly and bashfully got up. Gopal had held her hand firmly. She didn't summon the courage to crane her neck to look at him. But in Gopal took hold the ego-driven feeling of pulling her toward him and hugging her. Thinking that that would be the mark of his manhood, he pulled her toward himself with passionate force. The end that had covered her bosom of the upper overwear of *davani* that she had worn came undone, right into his hand. She grew still more confused before she turned toward the wall and covered her bosom.

Gopal felt he had done some wrong before he gave away her upper overwear of *davani* saying, "Wear it!" He then walked out and sat still, on the chair closing his eyes. *I don't know if what I am doing is right or wrong. It wouldn't be wrong if she comes of her own. But it would be wrong if I proceed further suo moto. Ugh! Something that ought not to have happened would have happened! She is still small, younger than me by a good twelve years. It is I who should advise her. How would it look if I do wrong? I have just come back performing father's obsequies. What if something untoward happens!* With such thoughts swirling in his head, Gopal sat wordlessly. But the male attitude of setting woman back effects changes in the body according to its requirements. Inner awareness and intellect should subdue this.

Gopal was surprised by the change that had taken place in him. *Oh, I didn't get to realise the moments when I touched her. How amazingly elegant and gracious is this thing called love! I want that light, that seductiveness over again! How to decline gratification that I never got to experience? I don't know why she is not coming out.* He sashayed quietly over to peek to see what she was doing in the room. She, a bundle of some kind of fear, bashfulness and an embarrassed kind of hesitancy, simply stood. Her eyes glistened with wet emotion. She walked quietly out. Looking at Gopal out of the corner of her eye, and saying, *"I will see you!"* she left, slipping on her footwear.

Her age is like that!

An age that thinks loving means drawing or pressing close to, and feeling nestled against the object of your love, doing something! And then in this process when lust makes you breathless, you withdraw as if shocked or something. You then run away without exposing your face, before regretting that something should have happened in the space - this time around, physical space - between you and your amour! And then you desire and prepare to inch quietly, snugly and hearteningly close to the object of your love. And then either draw still closer or simply clear out.

This experience was new to Gopal.

He tried to consciously dilatorily leisurely savour the moment when he unwittingly pulled her upper overwear. There was no delusion of any kind here. *Deciding whether it is pleasant or improper is upto one's mindset. It is an individual matter. Whether it is right or wrong would be complementary to future happenings of one's life. If it is felt to be true, that would complement one's desires. But if it is felt to be false, disappointment would be a foregone conclusion. During such moments one needs to use one's prudence and achieve equanimity. The chances then of things going awry are much less. It is as difficult as it is easy.*

Her figure, her elegant external form began to flash persistently across his memory screen. In any case touching her without being married wouldn't be proper, he told himself wordlessly. But the sneaking teaser of *what if he did touch* would at the same time persist. *Are there so many constraints on an exciting little gratification?* He wondered to himself. *She came on, on her own. What is the big deal; I could marry her in the days ahead... One* must *marry once you love somebody. There would be no meaning otherwise for love. That is the answer for the turmoil in my mind. But is love no more than this seduction?*

Gopal didn't get to sleep the whole night. Nor did he eat his night-meal. It was as if an active intense inflamed feeling had invaded his being, his body and mind. *Why did this happen today? What if, feeling alarmed, this girl had raised a hue and cry, and the neighbours rushed out of their homes and gathered in front of my house? Or, was it her ruse to do this just to splotch my image, to smear my fair name? When something new appeared in the thinking, both discretion and an analytical patience must have awakened in response to this kind of desire of mine. Or else, honour would go for a toss. It is hardly seventeen days since father passed on. Did this enamourment drive me out of the grief so very soon? Mourning is still on at home. It would take mother many days or even weeks to ease out of this period of grief. How do I look after the needs and requirements of food, clothing, studies and so on of twelve, thirteen kinsfolk that are in the household? There are going to be talks after the funereal period with uncles about matters of property. I need to pave the way of the future for my younger siblings. I need to see to the education of my younger brothers. That I have rented a house here is in itself a matter of considerable expenditure. The financial responsibility of the household fell right on my shoulders. Oh what kind of enamourment is this that has hemmed me in even in this mourning period when normal activities are suspended, the period of* sutaka?

****

He startled. It felt as if he had broken into a sweat in the dead of night. He woke up early in the morning, and decocting some coffee, drank the brew, and left for the college, eating some tiffin in Hotel Dwaraka on the way. Some kind of hesitancy and diffidence was what he felt. He spoke to no one. He kept solely to himself and to his work. Yet colleagues would enquire about his father's death, about his health, about his transfer that didn't take off and so on. He replied no more than what was absolutely needed. Ushe was nowhere to be seen. A kind of anxiety started creeping up his spine. *Why did she come home?* He found himself wondering to himself. *It was she who started it all. After entering, and spreading herself in, my spaces on her own, why is she bashful now, why is she jibbing at going the whole hog?*

On the one side, if there was some sound on the door or somewhere, there was this keen desire and sneaking hope that it was indeed she who had come! There was at the same time this fear and hesitancy on the other side. *Which of the two do I master?* When there was nothing happening, there was some kind of disappointment and frustration due to a miscarriage of expectations. While disappointment was one kind of frustration, it was some kind of serenity and ease of mind as well. It was not merely on that day but this combo of hesitation, desire, fear, disappointment, turmoil and frustration visited him for as long as fifteen days thereafter.

In the meanwhile he applied for leave for two days and went back home to perform father's death rite, the *tithi*. Even though Ushe did attend college, she didn't so much as look up to look at her teacher, her *guru*. She was somehow bashful and hesitant. Or was she feigning hesitancy and bashfulness? Her eyes, her heart and mind brimmed over with love. *How to let it come out? How to fufill this feeling?* were the posers that plagued her. Having done some touching, she had come away and sat down, shriveled up as a flower, crumpled up like a scrap of paper. This went on for quite a while, there being some barrier that had come and parked between the two that kept them from proceeding further. The two turned out to be challenges to each other. This eating into them, and unable either to contain the curiosity or to suppress it, the twosome wore away to pare down into half their weight.

****

To bring the mind this far from the barrier of love proved very difficult. Gopal got up and when, having walked over to the bathroom, he sprinkled some water onto his face, he felt easy in the mind. He looked out, wondering if Shivanna and the police constable had been listening in. But those two were occupied with their own jobs. When he felt relieved to realize that they hadn't overheard anything, he drank a bottle of water as he breathed a long sigh of serenity.

****

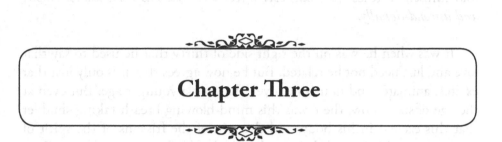

Chapter Three

He was to see the Deputy Chief Minister. *What is in store for me in the form of what he has to say?* He wondered. *What reply do I give if he asks me about the letter of threat?* He didn't want to feel bothered about this, but this topic came back to him over and over again. *How am I the cause of this? It has become pretty difficult for me to manage my own affairs. Things being the way they are, I have to reckon with these opposing provocations. The government does partiality even in money matters. It sanctions more funds to chairmen who it favours. And no funds at all to other chairmen. All we are left with in this conflicting situation is but the prestige that goes with the position of chairmanship. Whoever be the person, realising that all this is Kannada work, the government this government should be liberal enough to supply funds. But it wouldn't.*

As Gopal drove his car in this contentious and tense state of mind, a message flashed on his mobile phone. It was Ushe's message and it said, or rather, asked: 'What should I bring you?' She talks only in terms of messages at night. If Gopal is in the right mood, he replies. Otherwise he stays silent. Since Gopal was driving, he didn't answer. *Let her get angry. I would have a reason then to placate her. She would get angry and start to rage. She would rebuke me severely saying I was ignoring her. It is all right. She is in any case coming in the morning.* He told the cop to turn up a tad late.

Even while Gopal ate his night-meal, he wondered if she had got furious. *What if she doesn't show up? She could get really fiercely angry. What if she gets furious?* It was several days since he had seen her. He badly needed her physical intimacy. He felt as if his innards strengthened and as if a magical frisson swept his being. If just by her remembrance the body got stimulated, it would capitulate completely when she got physically close. *No lust,* he told himself wordlessly, *would ever affect love that has surrendered wholly and unconditionally.*

It was when he was on the right side of thirty that he used to say that love and lust need not be related. But he now agrees that it is only lust that excites, animates and nourishes love. That was a younger age. But even at the age of sixty, now, there was this mind-blowing breath-taking shudder that this excited in his body, and the rain of the frissons of the spirit of eroticism that his innards brimmed with that he felt drenched with. Even though he didn't quite want it, the memory of pulling her *davani* off came back to him, and he stopped eating the meal midway, washed his hand, got up and walked over to the bathroom before ambling off to the bedroom to sleep. Saraswathi was alarmed.

"Why! Did anything happen at the meeting or something?" she asked a barrage of questions with great solicitude as she followed him. "Was the *saru* not good? It didn't go well with the rice? Shall you cook something else and serve? Are you okay? Is there stomachache?"

"I am just tired. Nothing else is the matter. You go eat your meal!" he said before pulling the bed sheet over.

His mind went back some thirty years. Clothed as she was in the bottomwear of *langa* and a blouse, Ushe's beautiful form had back then made him expand and bloom, sent frissons of excitement through his bodily frame, and pushed him into a pleasant flux of agitation, making him want her over again. But pride and prestige had held him back.

****

One month had passed. The two lives had been distract and distraught, withdrawn from each other so as not even to talk or say 'hello' while passing each other by, but even as they sneaked quiet killer-looks out of the corners of their eyes at each other, they would walk about with self-respecting dignity and pride. Rajgopal was a judge at the sentiment-based song singing contest arranged by the Kannada Association in which twenty contestants participated. Ushe too had taken part. Gopal listened to her singing with his head bowed. Ushe wasn't terribly fair. She was more wheaten than white.

Not very tall but not too short either. Yet she was a stunner both in her looks and the sculpture of her figure. She gave musical voice to Bendre's timeless poem

> i am poor,
> so is he
> our love is our life,
> our life our love.
> that is what we brought
> to bear on that,
> and on this
> and on every potty little thing!

Swept off its feet, the audience broke into a boisterous raucous ovation. Gopal coloured up, blushing as red as a tomato. The boys had burst into a hearty bout of laughter because they had got wise to its import, and because it was she who was singing it. Gopal listened to it being sung, feeling some kind of embarrassment although he felt delighted deep inside that the poem had been crooned with him in mind. More marks accrued. Although she was not a great singer, she got the second prize because Gopal gave her more marks. She wreaked some wordless magic of the eyes on her guru.

She came by, the following day, carrying a box of sweets saying that was her birthday. Opening the door, Gopal stood back and aside, without saying anything. Draped as she was in a new saree, she looked full-blown, mature and majestic.

"Today is my birthday." She cooed ever so quietly. "Did I make a mistake by coming over?"

Gopal simply walked over to the living hall, after giving her a quiet wordless look of askance. He sat on the sofa there. She sat down too, at a distance.

"It is good, Sir!" she dimpled sweetly. "You look fabulous even when you get furious!"

This comment by Ushe sent ripples of cheerful buoyancy in the atmosphere.

"Why do you come to my place?" he asked, making it as direct as questions could get. "No other student has behaved with such familiarity and freedom with me. Tell me honestly. Why did you behave the way you did the other day? What is on your mind?"

The words of course popped out, straight and direct. But the thickness of his utterance had come about because he didn't want to proceed further in his relationship with her without making sure what was there in her mind although he was sure of what he wanted of it. Ushe was eager to say what she really had in mind. But the intense keenness to say it all made for a tremor in her heart.

"I like you, I love you. I feel like being with you always," she purred. "I felt scared the other day. I was anxious about what could happen. I also had this apprehension about what you would think. I felt the scare of my life the moment you held my hand. That was why I fled off, not quite figuring out things."

"Why did you come today?"

"Today is my birthday. I have come to give you sweets."

"If that is all there is to it, place it there and go!"

"That is all! I want to feed it to you. Shall I?"

Ushe placed in his mouth the coconut sweetmeat she had brought. Gopal held her hand before showing her a place close by to sit.

She had worn a saree for the first time in her life. She sat adjusting and readjusting the saree. She evinced now a deliberate desire to strut her beauty.

"What birthday gift shall I give you?" Gopal crowed.

"Give me whatever you want. I will preserve whatever you give till the end."

She had said this in some sort of alarm, as if she had decided that she wouldn't be with him for long. In our youth we fail many times to articulate what is in our minds, and so the truth goes unexpressed. But the desire to marry remains deep in the mind.

This happened with Ushe as well. Tripping she had ended up tweeting what she did. But Gopal didn't quite take it that way. He proceeded with the belief that he would be fully responsible for whatever happened:

"What shall I give you, tell me!" he asked, lifting her chin and looking expectantly into her eyes.

She was in no state of mind to reply.

When you find yourself physically as close as she did now to someone you feel emotionally close to, there is some sort of shuddering fear that something might come about, coupled with the intense irrepressible, if sneaking, desire that what should happen should indeed happen. Only her face, which was an expression of such a complex state of mind, and her body that was only longing for that very moment of physical intimacy, talked. Her mouth didn't.

This proved heady.

An inebriated Gopal lost no time in pulling her close to himself before he played an exhilarating game of *ookuli* [2] of kisses all over her body, from the forehead through her belly button and her middle right down to her toes. He in the process unwittingly threw to the winds the line between discretion and indiscretion, politeness and impoliteness, and propriety and impropriety. But that was all. He didn't go any further, thinking she might feel troubled and uneasy.

"Is the gift enough or would you like more?" he asked, holding her in a vice-like grip. As if closing down her body with both her hands, she shrunk her body and stood, as if meditating, as if in a trance. Unable to look at him from so close, she breathed ever so fast, her heart thumping away against her ribcage. Although her heartbeat and excitement signaling arousal did invite Gopal into a state of rut, he didn't proceed further. He lay wrapped, just keeping her, and savouring her presence, on his chest, thinking his sensual longing shouldn't advance without she agreeing. Sensing it was eight o' clock, he ran his fingers on her back ever so softly and slowly, awakening her while he said, "You leave now! People might take this amiss." She adjusted her tousled saree, slicking it back on. She didn't speak a word. Perhaps because of some distress or trouble in her mind or something, she didn't even raise her face.

He couldn't figure out her behavior.

Was what i did wrong? Or should i go ahead and fondle, neck and pet her? is she the type to take it like this? Had she been innocent and innocuous, she

---

2   This is a very expressive locution; **ookuLi** is a convivial frolicsome game played on
    festivals and weddings wherein a red liquid of various ingredients is playfully squirted
    on the participants.

would have felt a lot more pleasured just with this much of sensual play. She would have been as though the fragrance of triumphant delight had spread. Why is she silent? I have some fear even in this pleasure.

She adjusted her saree over again, and when she was leaving with a book pressed against her bosom, he asked, "If you feel you want my companionship, come again! If you feel this is wrong, don't! We won't go any further. Why are you silent?"

"Huun! Forget it! I won't come again." She bristled at Gopal. "This is enough for me. I feel exhausted. I have been unable to bear the load of just this gift. What if you do something else?"

She had gone red in the face by the time she spoke just what she had. Her heart beat doubled. Seeing this, Gopal felt he might capitulate. He quickly planted a kiss on her hand before sending her off.

****

Whether it is a disaster or a good event, whatever has fallen to my lot and the joy that has come with it are mine. Let us see what happens in the future. I could manage the household without any dent in my commitment to it. Mother has asked me to move back to our Madhugiri home for good, vacating the Tumakuru house. But I have got this bond of love just now. How to go away from honeyed romance? I could put up some excuse to mother. I can't travel daily from Madhugiri. There would always be power outages there at Madhugiri. That would hinder my studies. I could tell her this would affect my studies or some such reason. There can't be any marriage of men in the household for the next one year because of a death in the household. But there is no bar on girls getting married. That is called the 'give-away in marriage of a girl', the kanyadaana*(unmarried girl-give away(without any fees)). i should move in that direction for now. We should get Sharade, my younger sister married. She is already twenty four. I should never back off from this duty.*

Gopal repeatedly mulled these thoughts of familial responsibility and commitment. He remained wary of the possibility of he seeming to be indifferent to family matters in the intensity of his love and lust. So he reminded himself of it over and over again. *After the father's death, there would be nothing boding well for the future for the male members of the family. But what if the heat of love accosts you with a challenge, overriding this propitiousness and unpropitiousness thing? Would not this unfavorable element infect this? I need not rack my brains about it. Whatever has come about has come about. There is no undoing it. I could think about it after the one-year period. Ushe's studies for the graduate degree would be over soon. I can then broach marriage and get married.*

Rajagopal now felt easier in the mind. *I can reply in this fashion to whoever asks me about this. This is not something that takes away your honour. This is my wish.* The hesitance and fear left him. If you don't find an answer for such things, a persistent feeling of guilt would torment you.

From then on Gopal began to take his classes more seriously and efficiently. This surprised the students. They wondered how his involvement in the classes, his class-presence had improved and teaching efficiency had doubled. **Earth**, his collection of poems even won him a Sahitya Akademi award. Although he had suffered hardships in the family, he had found some success outside. There was this pain of father's death and the hardships and hassles that the death brought in its wake in the household on the one side and the magic that unraveled and activated the pleasant impulse of love in him on the other. The Sahitya Akademi award that he had earned perked him up now. A new fresh zest for life pulsed in his veins. All his students bustled about with great vim and verve at the felicitation ceremony organised for him right in Tumakuru. Ushe also hurried about with delighted zest. The happiness that she felt was not of one kind. She felt proud that she had won the heart of a sensitive poet. But the question of *will I get to marry* gave rise to fears and doubts. When they popped up, questions like *what was it that she had won* and *what was it that she had lost* would befuddle and unsettle her. She darted him a searching look in the middle of the programme. When he made eye contact for even for just a second, she felt a hot frisson coursing through her, and she hung her head. She used to, to begin with, argue so vehemently, posing questions like *why was it like that in the novel* and *why not like this* stumping her guru for an answer. She used to mock and laugh at some things saying they were superstitious. Gopal now smiled, seeing her fail. Narayana Murthi, the principal gave the felicitation address. Kannada lecturers accoladed the book. Some students sang some poems of his. Ushe didn't sing. She simply kept mum, enjoying the proceedings. Something that completely absorbed her made her silent and solemn. She sat in a nook, savouring and relishing the moments while she waited for his eye contact, and relishing it with great glee whenever it came forth.

****

The following day, as the day declined, dressed up in a saree, the saree end honourably covering her bosom, and, like before, with her full long lush hair cascading down up to her knees, she dropped by at the poet's place. She had a packet of sweets in her hand. Gopal stood stunned, looking at her elegant physical riches.

"Congratulations to the poet who won the Sahitya Akademi award. Please accept the sweets!"

"I don't want these sweets. Didn't I tell you not to come here?" he said in reply, a hint of mischief in his voice, as she stood poised to hand the sweets over, a trace of coquetry in her mien.

The import of these words quickly made the atmospherics hot. She remembered his words laying down when it was that she could come to him, and when it was that she should not. He had said she should go to his place only if she was interested in furthering their bond and should not, in case she felt it was all wrong. *What condition should I put forth now?* She asked herself breaking into a quiet dialogue with herself. *Shall I say we could proceed only if he was willing to marry me, not otherwise? But isn't it I myself in that case who stands to shrivel, sorrow and get sapless? How can I be without him? What if he forgets me after enchanting and mesmerizing me under his magical spell? How will i answer? How will I challenge him?*

Holding the packet of sweets in her hand, and caught in crosshairs, Ushe stood like a stone statue, gaping at him. On his part Gopal also stood watching her, trying to figure out what it was that she was thinking. Then as if he understood things, he stepped up, and taking the packet of sweets from her hand, fed her some sweets before eating some himself.

"Turn!" he said in agreeable animation, and as he turned her around, he saw the seductive splendour of her hair. He lifted the hair softly and subtly before kissing it.

Anger simmered in Ushe.

"Chee!" she said crossly. "You are kissing the hair! Stop it! You are now kissing the hair after asking me not to come to you! I don't want it. I am leaving."

When she was on the point of leaving, he grabbed hold of the hair and gripping and pulling her toward himself, he hugged her tight from behind her before showering a rain of kisses on her shoulders and back. Falling under the influence of, and being brought into subjection by, the smell of her body, he tightened the grip further before lifting her and carrying her into the room. Her saree had by then been mussed up.

The hot air of the earth and the rain of kisses from the skies mingled to ignite a fire that spread in gyres through their frames the moment he hardened in her pod. There was no knowing whether she was in him or he in her. With both getting thoroughly drenched in this magic, perfunctory mundane things like purity and impurity, the period of post death inactivity, the *sutaka* or no-*sutaka, tithi, karma, sanskaara* and so on wafted rapidly out of the window and into thin air, and the only reality that remained was this primal nakedness. That was the only savoury path to sweetness.

This was the only truth, the only reality.

It was as though the dry arid famished parched land of deprivation, desolation and bereftness filled to the brim by a sudden cloudburst. It was as though such an earth rejuvenated and acquired a new life in this flow and flux of lust. It was the new path, the new light, the new grace and elegance, the new birth. There is interminable meditation in this mantra. It felt as if there was a refreshing new charm, a breath-taking beauty that stirred and moved in them. It felt as if in the unique power of this nakedness, life, not in the least obligated to anything on the planet, bounced, got fertile and found full fulfillment, and then sprouted all over again. The two gave each other all they had. There was no room for the teacher-student bond here. That line being obliterated effectively, and egos vanishing without a trace, it was only passion, delight, pleasure, gratification and bliss all the way. A no-holds barred unfettered sense of exploration made the two desirably beautiful to each other in a primal sense. With every cell of their beings from top to toe horripilating with joy, who was the challenge to whom in this lesson and game of tasteful and juicy steamy passion, who was the student and who the teacher, and who was the surrendered and who the surrenderee?

Silence reigned around eight o'clock.

"You leave now! If you delay going, we may be in for trouble," Gopal suggested as he awoke her. Caught still in her hang-over of, the savory aftermath of, sensual fulfillment, she was not quite awake. She was not aware that she didn't have clothes on her body. She felt some untold feeling of great intensity surged up again and again. Gopal brushed her hair aside, and as he moved his fingers ever so softly on her cheeks and kissed them, he breathed, "Get up quickly, Usha! If someone comes over, the town would be abuzz with our news. Do you want me to be insulted?"

From cloud nine she slid right down to earth. It was her first sexual intercourse. It was the problem of a change in woman's body. Gopal didn't know. How would he know?

"Should I go?" asked Ushe of Gopal nestling her head on his shoulder. "I am exhausted."
"Impossible! You need to leave right away! Can you stay here?"

He got her up, and bunched and slicked up her hair, before he handed her the saree for her to wear. Hurrying her up, he handed her a bulky book for her to hold while he said, "Go covering your bosom with the saree-end, okay?"

After sending her off, he simply sat still on the chair for a long while. Then he walked into the bathroom, had a cold water bath, came back to tidy up the disheveled bed. The night-meal didn't go down his system; he didn't have the stomach to eat his meal. Thinking he could hand over the food to the servant maid in the morning, he drank a glass of water before turning in.

Some annoying anxiety troubled him.
What if someone had seen them? What if their encounter became the hot news of the town? What if things took a turn for the worse? Is this companionship as permanent as it is delight-giving? I don't know what came over her, poor girl! I didn't even make an effort to put her at ease. She was exhausted, she said. I could have handed her some money asking her to take an auto. She had brought sweets herself. I shouldn't leave her. I should inject courage into her saying I will marry her. She might otherwise think amiss.
When Gopal closed his eyes, thinking such rather tense thoughts, sleep came ever so slowly but ever so surely to him.

He didn't talk to anyone at the college.
The sneaking apprehension that somebody might have misunderstood his relation with Ushe had shut him up. When the principal himself sent for him, he walked over with some trepidation in his heart. The principal broached the sharp changes that had come about in his teaching style.

"Teachers should speak in the class only as loudly as is necessary," he suggested. "If you raise the pitch to make teaching very effective, you will have to double the speed of breathing. That would increase the pressure on the lungs. The heart may have difficulty in standing such strain. You should whittle down your zest and teach slowly, comfortably and well."

When the principal said this, Gopal felt relieved, as he said, "Thanks, Sir" *Why did this sudden change in my teaching happen? Where was this zest? Where was this voice?* he found himself asking himself.

He ambled back to the staff room smiling to himself. He felt a measure of comfort when he didn't find any hint of the knowledge of their encounter even among his colleagues.

In the meanwhile, he had to take leave for a week because he had to go home for father's third-month death ritual. *I should inform Ushe, she would get anxious, and disgusted and dispirited if she doesn't find me in the college,* he thought. *But I could talk only when she comes home. We don't talk in the college premises.* Just when he was thinking on these lines, Ushe came and, placing the book she had borrowed the other day in front of him, walked away. Gopal's heart skipped a beat before it melted away. He put the book away in the almirah. Ushe had kept a letter inside the book, which Gopal didn't notice. He didn't take the book home either. Nor did he inform her about his trip to Madhugiri. Gopal didn't rack his brains about this. It was important for him to worry about his younger sisters' future, and his younger brothers' education. The day after was his father's third month death-rite. The day following the death rite Sharade had to be shown to a groom-prospect. She had to be taken to Bengaluru for this. The groom was from the family of Venkata Rao, Gopal's mother's distant kinsman. Even if one sister got married this year, some burden would be off his shoulders. Not informing Ushe might disgust and dispirit her. *Let it be!* He found himself saying quietly to himself. *This would always be there : assuaging the anger and disgust of one's close friends.*

Gopal got on the bus to Madhugiri in the swirl of such thoughts.

****

"I will come by, tomorrow!" was what Ushe had written out in the slip of paper inside the book. The following day, thinking her beau would definitely read it, she gave her hair, like before, a thorough wash, and sprawling it out on her back, wore an old saree of her mother's, covering her bosom with the one-layered saree-end, saw that her clothes fitted her body snugly before making tracks for her guru's place. Seeing the door locked, she flew off the handle.

He has gone away even though I had given him the message on a paper slip, she thought before looking all around. The neighbours were all indoors. *I shouldn't enquire with anyone. If they take this amiss, it would be a disaster,* she told herself before, containing her frustration and sorrow, retraced her steps back home. *She, who had gone out saying she was going to a friend of hers, has come back early,* thought her mother before she told her : "Go get some ragi rains powdered in the machine, girl!. We will cook some ragi balls this evening." Ushe on her part took up the vessel of ragi grains, and walked away to the flour mill, the vessel of millets held in her armpit.

There were tears of disappointment and frustration glistening in her eyes. She however shored herself with the following unspoken words:

Did he deliberately keep me at a distance? Did he proceed further after getting to know about my caste? Or has he distanced me, having known it now? Can't figure this out. Why did he, who would always be at home, go away? If he has done this even after reading my message, this is done on purpose. There can be no doubt about it. I should not on my own talk to him or go to his place. Or even be visibly available to him on the college campus. If he wants, let him call me!

She was shocked not to find Gopal in the college the following day. *Whom to ask about his absence* was the question. She learnt that he was on leave. *But where has he gone? And why? Has he by any chance gone in connection with his marriage?* Ushe was all at sea. If she asked some other teacher, she feared, they might misunderstand. He was not found in the college on the second day either. The college seemed disgusting and dispiriting for her now. *Arre!,* she found herself wondering, *can I not live without him? Why is it that I am sinking, becoming less and less? What if, sometime in the future, what ought not to happen happens? I need to gather courage then. If one can't bear something, does one take one's own life?*

She felt deeply distraught, not seeing her lover the next day as well. Every day turned into an eon. It felt as if her eye sockets had sunk deeper. She got fever the next day and she was laid up. She went to the college only after four, five days. There lived a college friend of hers close by in the neighbourhood. She enquired with her about whether Gopal was attending college. When she replied he indeed had, her joy knew no bounds. With a newfound spring in them, her legs began to dance, itching to go see him. All her lack of spirit vanished into thin air. *Even if he distances me, I will go on my own to him*, she found herself saying to herself. She came round to the college, thinking of feigning some fake anger.

Gopal also had felt dispirited and disgusted the same way that she had. After conducting the postdeath ritual, he had gone over to Bengaluru for the bride-prospect seeing ceremonial in which Sharade had to be shown to the groom-to-be. The boy had agreed, and his consent had been conveyed. He was employed in a factory in Bengaluru with a four digit salary. He owned a house to boot. Sharade the bride had agreed too. The groom's folk were to come over for talks about the wedding the following month. Gopal would horripilate with great joy remembering Ushe in the meanwhile and would imagine things about his own meetings with Ushe. These imaginings would fill him with pleasure and joy from top to toe. There was only one difference. He felt the pangs of separation, knowing fully well everything. She on the contrary experienced the pain in great frustration and anxiety, not quite knowing the reality. Love means all this. There is nothing special about this. But if things pan out according to how we think, it is all right. But if things happen against what we think, trouble would be on the cards.

The moment Gopal stepped into the college after his leave of absence, he looked for his lady-love. As for her she had sat tight, shy, reserved and withdrawn in the classroom, not stirring out of it for any reason and clamming up completely. Whenever there was Gopal's class, she would sit unseen in a remote nook of the classroom. As soon as Gopal stepped into the class, her heart would thump wildly for a long fifteen minutes. She couldn't listen to the lecture, overflowing as her heart did with the great joy of seeing him for the first time after ten long days. Even if Gopal wanted to see her, he couldn't show his love in the open classroom. He was very disciplined. He looked at the first row, and then the second row. She was not to be seen. As he was into a spirited exposition of the love episode of Charudatta and Vasantasene of the play *Mrichha katika*, his eyes roved over to a corner of the room. Lo! She was there, head bowed, positioned so as not to be seen by anybody. Gopal felt as thrilled as if he got something he had lost. With this feeling of contentment, he taught the play with even more vim and even more renewed verve. The students sat thoroughly absorbed in his inspired teaching and when it ended, they clapped in a thunderous ovation.

Nobody noticed that Ushe was feeling bashful.

There is no telling where this attraction was! Would it leave you just because you sit, shy, reserved and timid in a remote corner? It wouldn't for sure. But I shouldn't submit so very soon, she thought to herself. *What about the fact of my going round to him all these days unsolicited? Why would he call me on his own? He never talks in the college. If I walk about without being seen by him or don't go round to him, the loss is mine! What to do? How long would this fake anger last?*

Ushe didn't know what to do, how to proceed further.

If anyone is to be worsted, or overcome it is me! He is after all a big shot. But why did he hug me the other day, forgetting the solemnity of his prestigious position? If he didn't want, or like me, would he do that? What kind of a desire is his? The aggression of planting kisses on the back, on the hair, on the waist, all over the terrain? Abba! This is what is meant by 'defeat'! Even when I say to myself I shouldn't lose, the same pull, the same attraction would take you compulsively right there! What if by chance he doesn't call me home? What if has gone to see some girl going on leave for such a long period?! What if he consents and marries?

Thoughts such as these that weighed in on the situation at hand didn't allow her to concentrate on other classes either throughout that day. The distress that was in her heart not finding voice, she was bewildered.

I should drum up the courage to walk with slow steps after the college gives over in the evening, she told herself. *Whatever happens, I should go round and ask him.* She strolled over to the library, got the borrowed book exchanged and was at the library doorway when Gopal showed up there. Bewildered, Ushe hung her head, faking humility, and this stirred up Gopal's heart. Unable not to be saying anything, Gopal tried to speak.

"You borrowed a novel from me the other day. Did you return it?" Ushe didn't quite make out the drift of his question.

"Yes, I did, that very day, Sir! You forgot!"

By replying, as she had, with a rather serious, if not disaffected or forbidding, mien, she disappointed her guru before, sweeping her upperwear of *davani*, she strode out as fast as the gushing water current in a flooded river sweeps everything away that is in its way. Giving himself a measure of solace, Gopal entered the library. But deep inside him brewed a compulsive preoccupation with her: this mindset in which she relentlessly, irresistibly and mercilessly engaged his thoughts defied description.

Then the inevitable blitz of questions took over: *why did she rush away like a tempest, without even speaking to me? Where is her house? I won't see her till the class I take tomorrow. Why did i fall into this fascinated captivation? However much and however long I long for her and crave her company, she is not available till tomorrow.*

As soon as he got home, he fuelled up on the wheaten chapathis and the dish of vegetables that mother had cooked and given him. He then had a nap, and getting up, sat with some books, preparing for the following day's classes at the college. Generally he cooked rice, the watery liquid dish of *saru, citranna, puliyoogare* and curd rice himself. A woman from a village nearby used to bring milk early in the morning. He would use the milk for brewing some coffee with the Nescafe coffee powder he had bought and kept at home, and curdle the rest of the milk into curds with which to cook whatever he wanted. He would snack on *idli, uppittu* and *puri* at Hotel Dwaraka.

He went to Madhugiri once a week. When he returned to his workplace from Madhugiri, Seethamma, his mother would prepare and hand him wheaten chapathis, enough to last a week, cook and give him a vegetable side dish just to last a day, and telling him to use the chutney powder the rest of the week, hand him a *paavu* of chutney powder, which would last the whole week. There were at home eleven little children. Besides seeing to the food and clothes of the kids, and the dish washing, Seethamma had to attend the courts about the property dispute. Her say was critical in the property dispute. She would go whenever there was a summons. This made mother hard and strong after father's death. When she went out, she would go, honorably covering her bosom with her saree end, and telling Sharade to look after the house. Mother would go even to the fields and garden to supervise. She had hired a family that she trusted to look after the garden at Akkiramapura. She would go to Shambhoonahalli once every two days.

Mother cooked food, made pickles and arranged fruits and milk, and curds for so many people. This huge task never deterred mother. This was one reason Gopal held mother in high respect. Gopal oftentimes compared mother to Nanjamma, a character in the Kannada novel *grihabhanga*. Whether it was something having to do with *madi*-purity, or the courts, or the fields and gardens or kitchen work, she managed everything with the same spirited self-confidence and dashing elegance of manner.

By the time, having eaten his meal and washed his hand and the eating plate, Gopal made some coffee and downed the brew, a rap on the door sounded. As he opened the door, who should be there but Ushe! She stood there, as tall as or along the length of, the door, and dressed up as swankily as the character of Alamelu in the film Nagarahaavu (=The Cobra), essayed by actor Arathi, wearing a *kanakambara* flower-coloured saree, her lush plaited hair descending upto her knees and a huge dab of vermilion powder at the centre of her forehead, enacting the lyric

Come, oh comely woman! Come, my lovely little star!

Who could say she belonged to a 'backward' class?[3] Nobody would. What kind of desire was it that filled her eyes? Her opinion was that equality was simply the love that she was achieving. But she didn't speak to anyone as loudly and aggressively as she used to. She feared the consequences if Gopal came to know about it and so had cut down on her talk.

Keeping the door ajar, Gopal walked in.

There was of course a nameless joy, but the thought that did the rounds in him was: 'She had run away from me in the morning. Don't I have self-respect and honour? If I allow some freedom, she would swagger, swank and strut around with great vanity!' This is what made him stand with his back to her. Besides, there lurked in his mind the sneaking feeling that if he saw her, he would melt away. She didn't quite know how to go about coping with the situation.

A deafening silence reigned for a while.

---

[3] This is another shibboleth Kannada writers suffer from, viz that some people are dismissible-looking.

She then sounded the bangles. She came over and stood right in front. He turned and stood with his back to her again. She shuffled over again to stand facing him.

"You asked me to give you the book. Show, show me the book that I returned!" she buzzed.

When Gopal walked in to fetch the book, she came there as well. Her heart kept beating wildly. That their hands were trembling both knew. She opened the book, took out the paper slip she had kept and saying, "Read this!", held it against his face for him to read.

"Look! I had to go for my father's ceremony. I couldn't inform you. Had you come?"

"Yes, I had." She bobbed her head.

Tears had filled her eyes. She had smeared turmeric powder over her face like Vaidik women do. Gopal didn't touch her. He simply kept glaring at her.

"Why do you look at me like that?" she flirted even as she covered her bosom and turned back to face the door. Her heart beat tripled.

"You look delightfully different today! I am wondering how much time you spend on decking and decorating yourself!"

"Do you look good if I have this dab on my forehead and if I fasten flowers on my hair like I have?"

"Everything is fine. One feels like just savouring it from a distance; Touch, one suspects, might mar and impair and destroy and defile it! There is a Kuvempu poem, you know:

you have become the prison of lofty splendor!
and i the prisoner, oh my lusty love!

The way you have decked up today is pretty much like what that poem says."

"Oh my poet Mr!, You would write a poem yourself, I thought. Instead you are quoting Kuvempu! Kuvempu is describing his love. You should write a special one for me."

"I will do that if you draw close."

59

Ushe drew slowly and quietly back. He took off the *Kanakamabara* flowers that she had in her hair, kissed the vermillion dab on her forehead, held her face, a full handful of it, before kissing it as well, touching her neck, making his delighted way to her cleavage and below, giving her memorably blissful heart-stopping moments that were to last a lifetime. It was like the big black humble bee finding its way into the heart of the *madhuvanti* flower and finding fulfillment. Lips found each other, getting into holy lustlock, licking, pressing and sucking. It was like tearing and throwing the sacred thread behind and away when the end of the death rite of *tithi* arrived... *prachanimite*, tip over a *uddarane*ful of water three times... *Rigvedajanya Shrii nanjunfraya Shatamah athaha putra Shrii Rajagopala Sharmaha, Jayasimha Sharmaha, Narayana Sharmaha, idam...*

As if all that got far and far away, and as that got away, it was as though this was the only truth, this big mantra is the declaration of the love, lust and rut, the abundant honey that the honeybee pours out. There is life in this fire-sacrifice. What with those shining eyes, those sparkling lips, that hardening tackle, he is the player of the veena of the heart. This is the moral, this is the principle, and wherefore is fear?

Every mantra poured into her as if it was done to smithereens as the two merged into a single cosmos, he the honey bee pouring the honey and she the receiver of honey. With the coquetry, the grandeur, the seductiveness, the swank, like the Mahamandali Rajeshwari that shines on the throne of emotions, stimulating and committing to this fire-sacrifice of love and lust, as they played it out in all its resplendently full and fulfilling glory, the soil, the earth, the site where this was played out achieved a happy state, good fortune and great felicity.

Bringing her an oven-hot cup of coffee, Gopal woke her up. He combed her hair and slicking it up, plaited it. He took up the saree that lay there before helping her to wear it as fast as they could. He wet a hanky, and wiping away the frayed edges of the smudged vermillion dab on her forehead with the dank hanky, tidied it. But her cheeks stayed oddly reddened. She struggled to put on the blouse. There was, besides, the bashfulness.

As she was on the point of leaving, he asked, "When will you come round again?"

She took the flowers that had been kept aside, and binding them in her hair at the back of the head, buzzed wordlessly off.

****

Gopal breathed a long sigh of relief when he realized that the two people detailed to serve him hadn't listened in. He called Mallikarjuna Swamy over to review the programmes that were to be done. He told him to dispatch invites and copies of the journal to the Chief Guests and resource persons for the Poets' Workshop. "The meeting with Deputy Chief Minster is at four o' clock, isn't it?" he asked handing him some files.

"Yes, Sir! You can go home and take some rest and return. Be careful at the meeting, Sir! You need to be careful, both while speaking and in the decisions taken. Don't give room for others. There is these days cruelty even among the big folks."

"Why do you say that? Do all chairmen of corporations and academies look that cruel to you? I don't think so. This deputy chief minister is a big question mark for me. Is he a casteist?"

"He belongs to a minority community. He is not very harmful. But who knows what snake is penned up in which anthill?"

Mallikarjun Swamy is the kind that doesn't admit or reveal things very easily and honestly. He is a fence-sitter. We should not continue any debate with such people. But what could we do? He is my personal assistant. Somehow the heart that is brimming over with love came under a murky cloud. Where did the self-confidence and courage that were mine minutes before disappear? How did I lose them? I decided that even if I resigned now, it was okay. Only if I think along those lines do I feel emboldened. And the thought that even if it means death, I should not resign injects loads of courage into me. But my bond with Ushe doesn't afford me much courage. Love could erase pain for a while. But it can not delay death. If you come to think of it, there is a close relation between love and death. Death doesn't mean the death of the body. The downfall of the mind is also the death of an intelligent human being. What is the phase of being I am at? What should identify myself as? Shall I give up love? Shall I resign? Shall I invite death and embrace death courageously? I feel strongly like letting out a huge scream! But one can't do that? One ought to control one's mind.

Gopal felt he was in a whirl. He drank up the bottle of water that was thereabouts before stepping up to the window and looking at the drivers of four-wheelers and two-wheelers that were moving about on JC road. *They drive their vehicles so very comfortably! But I am now feeling that I can't drive. This Shivalingaih has poured cinders into my head. Ushe's words fail before his words. Besides, there is this Mallikarjuna Swamy to reckon with. Neither of them speaks in a way that fills me with courage and confidence. No matter what, I should be calm and unruffled.* Gopal then didn't go back home. He got a meal from Kamat Hotel and eating it, got ready to go to the evening meeting.

****

It was six o'clock when the meeting ended.

It was already four thirty when the deputy CM got the meeting going. After speaking at length on the programmes celebrating the state's Golden Jubilee, he suggested setting up of a committee to forge the list of the state Founding-Day or the *Rajyotsava* awardees of that year. He assigned this responsibility to Rajagopal and the department of Kannada and Culture. Gopal agreed to it with great humility. He felt relieved that the DCM didn't broach and ask probing questions about, the letter threatening murder. A hearty smile lighting up his face, he paid his parting respects to the DCM by putting his joined palms at his chest before ambling back to the car. Every step that he took now oozed great self-confidence. *The minister has tasked me with a responsibility. He has liked my competence and nature. He doesn't seem to know that I have got this letter. This Shiavalingiah unnecessarily made me tense. Only greedy people are around me! Okay. This is enough for now!* When he was about to get into the car came the Minister's security guard to say, "Sir! The Minister wants you to see him tomorrow at five in the evening. He wants to talk to you about something. He will be there in his chambers in the Vidhan Sowdha." When he said this, Gopal's mind and self-confidence took a nosedive. *It is all right. I could resign if needed!* He slammed the car door shut before igniting the car engine.

Don't you get furious when you feel such heartening ease of mind giving way to pesky unease that quickly!

****

Chapter Four

Saraswathi got up early, finished her morning ablutions and worship in the home-shrine, and was cooking her husband some breakfast. The servant maid had said she would show up a tad late. Saraswathi had to leave for the college by eight o' clock. The college was quite near, in Rajaji Nagara second block. Just one stop by the city bus. You board the bus right in front of the house. She quickly made some chapathis and after stuffing them into a hot box, walked over to where Gopal was to ask if she had to serve breakfast to the cop as well. Gopal was still spell-bound, deep in his fine savoury delighting dreams.

"Shall I cook some breakfast for the policeman as well? I need to leave by eight."

Gopal deliberated for a while and, as he remembered he had told the cop to come a touch late and that Ushe was to turn up at home that day, submitted, "No need. I have asked him to turn up late. I will get him some tiffin, or I will myself cook something for him."

Saraswathi brought her husband some steaming-hot brew of coffee before she prepared to leave. Although she didn't clothe herself so as to flaunt the sculpture of her body, she wore quality sarees, draped honorably. (Read: leaving a lot, if not everything, to imagination.) Most of them were silk sarees. She was no fashionista. She didn't style up. Her hair had greyed, but she never coloured her hair, nor did she crop it. She did her routine of poojes and stuff with religious fervor. She didn't speak an extra word to her husband. She didn't take the liberty of even cracking jokes with him. Gopal was to take her out and buy her things she needed, wanted and desired. And he did that. Besides, with her own salary she would buy herself and for the household the things needed. She had this deeply deferentially held feeling that her husband was a great man and she shouldn't give him trouble.

Although Saraswathi used to dress herself, standing right beside her husband, there was nothing like he getting attracted, or he desiring her or teasing her about anything. That was not possible. Just plain indifference because of the feeling that all of it was mundane. There was no wild enthusiasm or intoxication. Even now his mind was thinking about the moments of Ushe's arrival, her words, the sharpness, the look of her eyes, the body parts and the gratified delight the next moments would bring him. He colored his moustache and the hair on the head, while he heated up both the body and the mind, thinking only about winning her, and imagining the possible ways of slaking the hunger of her irrepressible physical riches. Saraswathi knew he dyed his hair, which made him look like a boy. But she thought: *he wants to look young and good. That is his desire. Why should I take it otherwise?*

In fact Saraswathi was on the pudgy side. Her only mission in life was to cook yummy food, work hard, and to eat well. Gopal had a lot of internal strife, mental struggle. Struggle also in the family life. Yet he didn't look his age. He looked barely fifty.

After Saraswathi slipped on her footwear and went out, Gopal had a bath, and dressed up nicely. He ate his breakfast and sat waiting for the moments of Ushe's arrival. He had a book in front, but all his thoughts trained on how she came along after a long gap of thirty years and mated with him. That indeed was a wonder! Equally amazing was this bond. This love, which had originated somewhere and which went incognito for so many years, then took a rebirth, and rediscovered and reinvented itself. Where was this elegance, fineness and grace of life? It has created a whole new world. Had I not got her now, I would not have got the thrill, the frisson of the exciting pleasure that I have got. This new verve, this fine fine-grained delight!

Brushing the window curtains aside, he stood by the window, waiting keenly for her arrival. It was after everything had wound down that this life flowered all over again. *Is it really good on my part to crave her physical intimacy,* he found himself quizzing himself, *and behave as if I am the youth of those days?*

How stubborn mother was in putting her foot down to have me married to Saraswathi! She won. She had a word put in by some politician to get me transferred to Madhugiri. What kind of obstinacy it was?! The desire was to have her son right in front of her eyes. I lost the very will to live. Saraswathi married me with her qualification of a postgraduate degree. But she never made me feel she is my wife. Initially that was the feeling. Later realizing that life was only this much, I got transferred to Bengaluru after spending some years in Madhugiri. Bearing with Saraswathi because of life's inevitabilities, I learnt to face head-on and cope with its vicissitudes and hardships. After Sharade's marriage went on the rocks and the hardships we underwent as she returned to her maternal home, and with she herself taking charge of the household, my career in literature took birth.

Last year, barely two months after I took over as the chairman of the Book Authority, Ushe appeared all on a sudden with a phone call to me one day. She came home with a bouquet of flowers. Exuding an effusive "Congrats!" she sat on the chair opposite. None spoke for a while with time biding its time for the two of them. When she said, "I am the Special Officer in the Dalit Welfare Commission," I didn't find any changes in my perception of her although I had come to know some new piece of information. That he had come to know during the thirty year period. This was precisely why Mother insisted on marrying me off to Saraswathi. One doesn't know what question she will put! Otherwise had she married, would she come to me like this?

"What is your husband?"

Ushe burst out laughing. "When I am not married, how would I have a husband? Life didn't afford me an opportunity. Father went early. The responsibility of the household fell on me. I had done my M.A. They gave me my father's job. On promotion on the basis of reservation, they have appointed me as a Special Officer. How fair is to marry someone else after loving someone? It didn't seem okay to me. I have two younger sisters and a younger brother. I have helped set up their lives. They all lead good lives now. That is enough for me."

Ushe spoke rather fast. And it seemed she was giving vent to a suppressed pool of feelings. As she unspooled it, tears sluiced out of her eyes. *I didn't even have the qualification of wiping off her tears. What a sinner I have been! Whatever be her caste, once one loves somebody, it is one's duty to marry her. I wasn't able to do that. And then the sudden turn of events in life. What an excruciating pain this has been!*

"I beg your pardon for the mistake I made. But this won't afford you any solace. I have married. You haven't. That is the only difference. I haven't enjoyed any marital happiness. That perhaps is the punishment for me!"

Ushe enquired also about Saraswathi.

She was pretty much like before, like a girl. The same statuesque face. She has got fairer. The same style of wearing her saree, dinky and swish, wearing it in a way that fits tight and snug on her body so that her embon points dazzle your eyes. Tallish. Colored hair that had started to grey. A glibness of tongue. She has preserved the excellence of her bodily frame. Hair on her head is like before, visibly full, long and lush.

"Shall I leave? I have some work to attend to."
"Stay on for a while more!"

I took out the cold lime juice from inside the refrigerator and pouring it into a huge tumbler, handed it to her. She drank it and left. Her car is more expensive than mine. She is now financially well off. Positions such as the one she is occupying now you get only because of political influence. How did she wangle it? Is she in competition with me? The way she walked, straightening up attracted me, making me look at her over and over again. The loftily stylish manner in which she opened the car door, entered the car and sat down made me feel small.

Then after two days when I was the Chief Guest at a literary function Ushe appeared in the audience and this elated me. I had the satisfaction of getting back my personality which I had lost, and which I seem to have found just in her presence that day.

"Your speech was very good." she effused stepping up to me after the programme.

"Thanks" I stuttered before tagging, "Come home sometime!"

Ushe then didn't speak for a considerable while.

"Why should I come? What is there left now?" she said rather thickly, a spirit of resignation and renunciation in her voice.

A long pregnant silence lingered.

The answer I give now would facilitate her words that would follow. It couldn't be that I keep from speaking anything. But on the other hand my mind is not willing to lose her either. A light and simple reply tumbled in the end out of my mouth:

"One could see what is there if only you come. To say "What is there left now?" without coming over doesn't make sense, does it?"

Ushe darted a long piercing look at Gopal now.

That lingering look stabbed me! She is my student. But she is quite mature now. Her knowledge of the world would at least be like mine, if not more. I absorbed her look deep into me. Then without speaking another word, she ambled away toward her car in great style. She is forty eight, and yet she walks coquettishly moving and shaking her body parts. What is this? Even at her age, she walks moving and shaking her body parts! Her lush silken hair, which swung from this end to that as she walked, distracted Gopal. *I couldn't move out till she went near her car. Even after she got into the car, she must have noticed that I was still looking at her. So she is acting coquettish. Even now the same snug dress, the gait of walking with her bosom thrust out, but with some difference.* Gopal felt a lightning current of physical frisson whip through his bodily frame. He also felt a tremor deep in his innards. *This desire has made me have to look at her with such passionate intensity even after a long gap of thirty years. It has made me run after her in hot pursuit.*

Igniting the car engine, I followed her car. Wherever there was a traffic signal point I parked my car just behind hers. When you go from Ravindra Kalakshetra via Nripathunga road, you get a signal junction at Basaveswara Circle, you get another such junction near Swathi theatre if you move along Race Course road via Sheshadri puram. I had to turn left from there toward Malleshwaram Circle. Her car had parked just in front of mine. It was a thirty second traffic signal. Shall I ask her where her house is? But that wouldn't suit my position and prestige. I don't know her phone no either. She came to me on her own. She has now given no hint. Where does she go from here? Supposing I go behind her now? Sensual chase at this age?! She has already lost faith in me.

There's no telling how she will behave? What if she doesn't take kindly to my behavior? Gopal fell into some anxiously restless agitation. *Turning back, she kept looking at me through the glass window of the car. I on my part kept returning her gaze in the humble hope that she would understand me. There was no reaction from her. My heart missed a beat when the traffic signal flashed green, wondering where she would head. Supposing, God forbid, I miss her now, I would get to interact only when she spoke on her own. Her car suddenly headed off straight. Mine swerved left and drove toward Rajaji Nagara. I fell right into a waterless well of frustration over again: it was as if I had lost after getting what in fact was not gettable. I felt agitated because of acute anxiety. Is it possible to go chasing her car instead of returning home at eight in the night? A part of my mind said what I did was indeed right. How vain she is feeling because of her beauty! How about me? And my prestige? Am I any less? If she wants, she will come on her own. i should no longer stew in sorrow. I should achieve a tranquil state of mind on my own. That is life. If I wallow in anxiety nobody would come to my help. i have after all stayed away for so long. Why this attraction now? Why did the body waver and lose focus now? Is it that neither mind nor the body has matured. Is maturity desireless form? Or, Is it a gratified contented state of the body and the mind that have flowered and found fruition and fulfillment after experiencing love and lust?*

But have I not got these? Have I not attained maturity? Why did I follow her car in intense pursuit on seeing her puffed up body? Why did the vital me grow animated and quickened? This happened to me thirty years ago. Now at sixty, the body craves her! Chee! I need to forget this, it would be difficult otherwise.

When Saraswathi served the meal, I ate up the serving in barely five minutes, without looking to see what it was that she was serving. Saying, "What about you, Saru?" just to fulfill the requirement of talking to the wife, I walked into the bedroom to turn in. One talks to people one lives with, just because of (social) pressure. Those words don't come from the heart. Such talk happens only to prove to ourselves that we are all right, and in order to put out the pressure that has built up in ourselves by silence. Just to show how you are taking care of her, that you are a good human being, that you don't scold her, browbeat her, beat her or not even talk in a raised voice. Such talk is a self-declaration in confirmation of the idea that you are taking good care of her.

After a week Ushe called. My self-belief returned. I will talk with some indifference, *I thought. But such talk is beyond me. Her debt is on me. She is the one who spelt out the meaning of life and love for me. How could i be indifferent?*

"Yes, Usha!' I said ever so softly.

"Shall I bring you some snacks?" Her voice was as sweet and soft.

I didn't reply. What answer do I give if she poses such a question?

"You come if you want! Why this excuse of snacks?"

"No, no! Snacks are not an excuse. I want to bring you the snacks I have cooked myself. I make the sweet kesri baath very well. I will make it the way people at your home do! Shall I bring it?"

"All right. Do as you please!"

"What time shall I turn up?"

"Come after nine! I need to go for a meeting."

"Not if you hurry things up!"

"No, I won't! Come at quarter to nine!"

This exchange of words filled his heart to the brim. Yet there was some anxiety. Care should be taken to see that there was no trouble. Hopes sprouted and grew wings. *But why she is coming now? She, who had buzzed off, puffed up and swaggering. Will I cave in and capitulate if she appears with this saree draped like that! How do I manage the friction in my heart? Yes, I should! How I should conduct myself and how I should talk add up to my prestige, my dignity. I should gift her something. I should give away at least a couple of novels.* nela sampige(= *the land champaka flower) the collection of Kambara's plays would be a good gift. She will like it. Okay. I will give her that. I could go in the evening and buy it.*

Saraswathi left home pretty early the following morning. She had cooked and kept away on the dining table groundnut chutney, and rice rottis. *Forty five minutes after she left, the door bell sounded. I felt a nameless some sort of tremor. But I didn't let it show. Ushe pushed the door open before taking off her high-heeled footwear. Even without the chappals, she looked quite tall. There was a hotbox in her hand. I motioned to her to sit on the sofa. She sat for a long while, gaping at the floor below, not knowing what to say. I fixed her with my eyes. She had worn a rather thin saree. She had slicked up her hair, holding it together at places with clips, the lush shiny hair cascading well below her waist.*

Hair parted down the middle on the head. She had a large forehead. Her face smeared with a cream that suited it. The bottoms of her eyes smeared with eye-black, the black collyrium, and her lips with lip stick. Her belly button stared you in the face. Startled into the feeling that I shouldn't look at her body, I now shifted my gaze onto her face. She opened the hotbox, and holding the snack before me, handed me a spoon. Taking the spoon I tried to feed her.

"You eat!" she said softly and pleasantly, moving away.

"I will eat if you do!" I said by way of a reply.

"No, you eat. I will take away the hotbox. It should not remain here."

"Why?"

"What if your wife asks whose this box is?"

"You eat a spoonful! I will eat after you eat."

She moved away.

As she moved away, he tried to grab hold of her saree from behind. The way her body contorted and curved when he did that, there was at the same time a caving in and a captivation deep inside him. He inched close with the intent of feeding her. The heart beat a billion times. She shuffled away before standing leaning on the wall. When he took a spoonful and tried to place the content inside her mouth, she said, as she brushed his hand back, "You eat first! After you eat, you feed me a spoonful! You should not eat my leftover!!"

Her words were certainly right.

She had lipstick on her lips. If she ate first, that might attach to the spoon and he would have to eat the snack that would be mixed with her lipstick. Gopal took the hotbox, and emptying the content of the sweet wheaten grit dish of *kesari baath* into another box in the kitchen, giving it a rinse and putting a *rotti* and some chutney in it, brought it back to her. *Even when I gave the hotbox a swill, the rapid rise and fall of the compelling swell of her bosom haunted me. And when I got close to her, it returned over and over again, causing some anxious agitation in me. I was slow in coming out after swilling out the hotbox. She was trembling even when I handed her her hotbox.*

"Why? You seem to be quailing. What is the matter?" I asked, the tone of 'I-am-a-thief-myself-but-I-don't-trust-others!' in my voice. I didn't come back and take my seat after handing her the hotbox. I lingered on near her, exploring

70

her interior as if I had understood her situation. Her form and elegant beauty made me have to stay rooted, close to her.

"I will brew you some coffee. Sit!" She shook her head. "Why are you resentful? The other day you went away, without replying to my words."

"'If you come, we can see what there is for us', you said. I didn't quite figure that out."

The truth was that even he didn't understand it.

She blushed red. She looked girlish. Her body that had straightened stiff, thrust out and puffed up seemed in a restless sort of thirst: it was dancing a dance in which the emotion of love is mimically represented, as if to tease, beckon and challenge him. Her lips fluttered.

"You don't seem to have grown old. You look the same as you were thirty years ago!"

"That is because you look young. If I looked old, that would seem odd, wouldn't it?"

By that time the tears in her eyes had vanished, and a mischief had taken their place. As he advanced to wipe the tears in one eye, she grabbed his hand before kissing it. "Tell me now! What is the meaning of what you said the other day?"

He gave her a gaping look. "Even I didn't understand what I said. Tell me what you made of it!"

She placed his hands on her shoulder. His hand was still hot. She savoured that warmth. "I swear I have never looked upon any man like I am looking upon you!"

There was a meaning in her words that was sorting itself out. It was as if there was some teaching being done to an inner vitality. As if one got what one had lost. As if to say, "Hug me tight!"

I hugged her in a vice-like grip!

It was as though after a long drought, water had gushed now into the depths of the withered and parched drought-afflicted land, as if there was nectar poured into the heat, as if the whole creation had turned into a majestic entity of a colorfully festooned and decked up wedding-house, as if there was a flooding of milk and ghee, as if a dead body quickened into life, and standing up and holding a garland of flowers, wearing the headgear of gold coloured ornament of cloth, the baasinga *that grooms wear. Moving my hand slowly, dilatorily and deliberately over the honey-filled waist of the bride, threading smile against smile, lips and against lips, chest against breast, limb against limb, body against body, and struggling not to leave like the flower-casket carrying initiated mendicant renunciate, who has broken loose of the God of Death's rope, led her by the hand to the bedroom, made her naked as soon as I could, laid her down on the bed before showering a rain of kisses wherever I wanted. she grew aroused and hot. As if such a time would never come gain, she on her part cooperated fully, straightening and hardening me up, and invigorating my every nerve. The cells of my body came alive like the jog waterfalls that suddenly come alive once the rains begin to lash the catchment area. Her body stuck to mine like a leach and we never felt we should disengage. My age, achievement, caste, clan, principles, prestige, karma and so on blew away, out of the window. Feeling that this very moment was my moment of joy and fulfillment, I kept pressing my lips to her cheeks, lips, ears, breasts, navel, and into her middle.*

When she covered her face with both her hands, as she coyly said, "Enough! I need to leave now!" I felt like doing more and more. Unfurling her hair and moving my hands over it, unleashed an avalanche of kisses on her neck, nape and shoulders. She then pushed me back, and started to wear her clothes on by one. I combed her hair myself. She got ready. Her lipstick had smudged. She walked into the bathroom and gave her lips a rinse. Yet her lips were still red. I put my arms around her waist, and turning her face toward me, bit her lips rather hard.

"*Thoo!* Let go of me! You have become really naughty!" *She tried to release herself from my hold.*

"Who is the one who said, "I will give you sweets and snacks" and stood crying? And now who is doing the mischief, it is you!? Go away! If you don't want it, don't come here again!"

She turned toward me, and butting my body with hers, kissed my cheeks. "Let go! Let go! I will come again." When she said that, I drew away before I held her saree-end. She was receding from sight now and the scene of the way her lissome body swayed and curved as she moved away came back now, has etched deeply in my mind.

****

This was one year back.

Since then she has been coming off and on, storming my place like a hot tempest, talk, kiss and, with my member inside her middle, enjoy physical intimacy for about half an hour before strolling off. I don't ask her about anything else. She doesn't probe into my life. The love and lust and companionship I have found at this age seem natural to me, my exterior life and interior. That is the amazement here. People at this age become grandpas and dandle and frolic with their grandchildren. Why am I like this? One should accept what comes by. It is not possible to try to get what is not possible to get. When it is hot and muggy, one craves a cool balmy bracing breeze to waft by and touch you. Even in that heat, one could wipe one's body, wash the hanky and squeeze it dry. But when a gust of wind sails toward you no dunce would like to continue to be in the pesky heat. I have never ever talked roughly or indifferently to Saraswathi. I buy the household whatever it needs so she could be happy. I see that after Ushe's visit to my bedroom, there is nothing left behind as a residual telltale sign of her visit. If there is anything to be discarded I quickly dump such things in the dustbin. Till the time the day's discard is flung away, I would be a tad apprehensive. Nothing has fortunately happened till this day! One is for the mind, body and the soul, and the other for food, and daily life. I should pain no one. I have been talking a good deal more with Ushe from this year. That has afforded her some happiness. Whenever I go to help her out in household work she would say, "You go and read a book. I will do it myself." Husbands should not according to her do kitchen work. She cooks tasty stuff, all alone. I must eat it. Otherwise she, very concerned, would blitz me with a hundred questions; "Why? Is it not okay? Are you feeling all right? What is wrong?"

Gopal moved aside the window curtain and looked. At a distance, Ushe was coming, having just got off an autorickshaw. She wore a light rose coloured saree. Her silken hair had sprawled over her back. She was walking rather fast, swaying her waist. She would park the car somewhere, and from there take an auto. She couldn't do without the car. She didn't colour her lips these days. May be she did after she left Gopal's place.

"Who is it, who has written to you that you would be bumped off? I felt scared hearing it."

"Nothing will happen, don't worry. Someone has done it out of spite and jealousy. We shouldn't let such things bother us?" Gopal assured her, putting his arm around her shoulder and patting her. "What will you have, coffee, juice?"

"I don't want anything," she said, nestling her head on his chest, moving her hand over his cheeks, and hands, like one does with a child. She had tears in her eyes.

"Why are there tears in your eyes?" Gopal asked, startled to see the tears. "I said nothing is going to happen, didn't I? Don't waste time crying! Come along!"

Putting his hand around her waist, he then took her to an inner room. It was a long time since she had visited him. Gopal needed it. He stripped her to the buff, and did it to her, sometimes softly and sometimes fiercely, sometimes with soft love, and sometimes with fiercely aroused knife-edge lust. When he tried to catch her again with passionate intensity, she slid down the bedstead, holding the saree before walking away to the living hall. Holding the saree, he pulled her toward himself and when he let go of the saree, the way she panted as she moved away, strutting her stuff, swaying her embon points, his sensual longing and lustiness would increase a hundred-fold. He would rush forth and gratify her as fast and as much as she teased him. He would now become the bee and she the flower. The gratified pleasure that the two of them - the one who had assumed or put on the character of not wanting anything, the *soogi*, and the other the bon vivan, the *bhoogi* - didn't choose to take and enjoy sometime back, was theirs for the taking now and they grabbed it both hands! They didn't reckon with any hurdles. Determined to rise above hurdles, they were at this festival of sensual union like warriors who had declared an all out war.

Gopal hadn't as yet gotten over his aroused state even when Ushe put her saree back on, and bunched and slicked up her hair. Holding her hand and seating her by him, he lay down in her lap for five minutes. Getting up he handed her a glass of juice. He then seemed to remember something. He walked over and got some jasmine flowers from the refrigerator. "Wear it in your hair!" he cooed.

"You do it!" she flirted, turning and showing her back to him.

Gopal fastened the flowers in her hair before planting a robust kiss on her hair. Then on her back as well. Ushe startled over again. Since it was time for the cop to turn up, she turned to kiss him on his cheek, and saying, "I will come next week", left, slipping on her chappals.

An inspired Gopal sat down and penned a couple of poems about man-woman love as soon as she left. He had a meeting to attend in the afternoon and then a meeting with the Deputy Chief Minister in the evening at the Vidhana Sowdha, the seat of the state legislature. There now ran in his veins a verve and an indomitable will of conquering the whole world. So now there seemed no need to feel scared about what the Minister would say at the meeting. What after all would he say?

Supposing he asked, "Why did such a letter come?" why should I worry about what to say? Am i responsible for it? I should firm up my mind. i shouldn't quail! He took an envelope and wrote out the address of a daily newspaper, franked his seal and wrote down his signature. He was to give it to the cop to post it.

Rising he downed a cup of coffee, took out his dress and looked to see if it had been ironed. He decided to wear his suit for his meeting with the minister. So he took out the suit and by the time he made a trip to the washroom and came back, Hanumanthayya the cop arrived.

"You go post this envelope! I will be ready by the time you come back."

He hadn't told Saraswathi about this letter episode. *Because she would feel alarmed if she came to know of it,* he thought. *I should tell Hanumanthaih also not to divulge this to her. He might do it when he comes home in the evening.*

He tidied up the tousled bed, the erotic playground that he and Ushe had rolled and played about on. He put on his glasses, and when he saw a long strand of hair on the pillow, he took it and dustbinned it. He felt embarrassed to realise that he had torn it into small pieces. Gopal had always liked her long lush hair. Even now he believed that it was her glowing cascade of tresses that inspired his love and lust. He looked about, lest there was a tell-tale something. Saraswathi would come back from the college early in the afternoon. Supposing she saw something fishy, there would be a huge ruckus at home. There seemed some moist sticky spot on the bed. He changed the sheets, chucking the soiled bed sheet into the wash bin. *Saraswathi has never seen such sticky blobs on beds,* he told himself quietly.

Let her not see such pollution. Let her not sleep on the bed sheet that we had rolled and played about on.

This good feeling that he had of her helped him in seeing himself as a good person.

****

There would always be a good crowd milling about the *Vidhana Sowdha*. But today it was not that big. There would be people moving in front of the building housing the legislature, people who latched on to ministers to get transfers, jobs, other opportunities and what have you, personal assistants, relatives and other people close to them. Gopal parked the car inside the premises and walked to the Deputy Chief Minister's office. As he walked, several people paid their respects by putting their joined palms against their chests while saying, 'namaskaara!' and Gopal walked on, returning the greeting. As he moved into the minister's office, he told the cop to stay outside. There was a huge air-conditioned living hall. It was carpeted with a bright expensive rug. There were expensive luxury chairs for visitors to sit. Adjacent to this hall was another room. The door of this room was half-open. There was a liveried man standing at the door, regulating entry to the room.

"Please sit down, Sir!" he ejaculated as soon as he saw Gopal enter the hall. "The Minister told me you were to come. Somebody is talking something confidential with him. As soon as he is done, you can go in!"

There was already quite a crowd, waiting to see the minister. But Gopal got to learn from the Attendant that the minister was done seeing almost all and it was nearly time to shut down, log out and go home. Gopal stood thinking and looking around. *What arrogance these politicians have! They have the audacity to call us and keep us waiting.* This didn't look okay to Gopal. *I will see for another five minutes before leaving. Let him do what he will!,* he told himself without speaking even as his eyes trained on an oil painting of M. K. Gandhi on the wall. Then there was the sound of the minister's office door opening.

A woman stalked out briskly.

She wore large swanky sun glasses, heavy lipstick like film stars, a tinsel transparent light rose coloured saree, and a huge dab of vermilion on the centre of her forehead. Gopal only glimpsed her front, and when he saw her from behind, an electrifying current zoomed through him. Long lush mane cascaded down her back, below her lissome waist, swaying from side to side as she walked sinuously away. There were jasmine flowers fastened in her hair, decorating it. And those flowers he had set in her hair himself! The hair, which it was he who had moved his hands on, feeling it tenderly, savouring the touch, and kissed! *Isn't it Ushe? It is! Why has she come to see the minister? What showy gait she has! What swagger! What frippery! And she ambled away like a bolt of lightning, didn't she?! The tak-tak sound of her high-heeled chappals sailed over. He must be her personal assistant, he, who was outside and who joined her when she came out. He saw through the window rods the two talking and stalking away. Her office must be in this very building. Or the minster must have called her to talk about something.*

Gopal took his time to recover from the shock. When the man in uniform came to inform him that the minister was waiting for him, Gopal rose and went in.

The honorable minister seemed to be waiting for him.

"Come, Dr Rajagopal! I had heard of you. Today I get to see you."
He must be about my age. Only, I don't look my age! Gopal found himself saying to himself.

"What is it, Sir! You sent for me?"
"Nothing special! How is your work going on?"
"Everything is going on fine! No one had so far pointed a finger at my work. Why this question now?"
"Somebody has threatened you with death, i hear"
"Oh that! That is only to intimidate me because of jealousy, sir! There is no need to let it bother us."
"It would be fine, if it is only that. If it gets worse, what about your wife and children, tell me! Besides, you are an asset of our land."
"What do I do, sir? Fearing about anything is not my nature."
"You don't have to quail. But you can take precautions, can't you? There is increasing threat of terrorists in Bengaluru these days. There is this atmosphere of anxiety about what would happen where."
"Death will come sometime or the other to all. In case it arrives today itself, it is okay! Where would I flee, dreading it? It is not proper for people like me. I will fight."

"Some woman writer has written to the Home Minister complaining about you, I hear."

"Who, Sir? What has she written?"

"The complaint is you have misbehaved with her. You asked her to bring the book to your house, for selection of some award."

Gopal felt a sudden current of electricity flowing through his frame. *What kind of words are these from the deputy chief minister? About my behavior. About my character. My morality. It was as if the ground below my feet had caved in, splittng open and as if i was being inexorably sucked in... as if there was darkness all around and I couldn't see my way forward. How do I reply to him? What do I say? It was as if someone had lanced me with a spear. Who have I behaved like that with? I have only enjoyed physical intimacy with my love and with her consent. I have treated all others with utmost respect. I have never on my own asked anyone to come home. It does happen that whenever they need, people come on their own. Yet women don't. Which woman writer has done this? Or, is it all false? Is it an attempt to frame me? and if so who would I spit cinders on? If one has indeed done some wrong, one could agree. The one who is sitting in front is none other than the deputy chief minister of the land. Politicians take such charges as perfunctory things and they know how to hush up such things with the power of money. But what would the general public think if there is such slander about the literati. No one with any social conscience would act immorally. Really it is a conspiracy to dent my prestige and position. Who would stand to gain by smearing me with such charges? Why might they have done this? Is there a rule that a change of chairmanships of academic bodies is a must with a change of guard? Who has this pressing urge of doing this violence to us? I need to answer this charge. If you stay silent, they would think the charge is true.*

Then a voice that had been trampled deep inside came right out.

"Sir, look! I have not behaved like this with anyone. Whoever has written this must face me and talk to me. If the intention is to malign me, and remove me from my position, then tell me. I will certainly resign. I don't want such alms. A litterateur is a symbol of the society and the land. I am prepared to resign right here and now if you want to believe the words of a third party."

An agitated Gopal had spoken with a sharp certainty. *I hadn't thought such words could come out of my mouth! Not to speak of the deputy, let the chief minister himself come forth and question me.* He seemed to have arrived at the decision of *I should not live fearing anything or anyone. Although these people don't have anything grey in their heads, they, flaunting their money power, volunteer to touch the leftovers in others' plates. If you come to think of it, I have also reached this level because of a politician. That said, I don't dance to their beats.*

The minister took up the word.

"Look, Gopal! What you are saying is not right. Your words give the impression that it is we who have conspired against you. Please be patient. Did I ask you to resign? Take leave and relax for a few days. Your programmes could be deferred. Your position is your position after all this. Such allegations at this age and the murder threat tear at one's heart. I said what I did because of this."

"If I go on leave, people will believe that all this is true, Sir! For me my honour is more important now than death. If you hand over the letters I will try and find out who is after destroying my prestige and standing. The police is behind me. In case I go on leave, these people will come up with a hundred stories about me. One should swim, and if there are tides, face them and get ashore, and not opt to drown. If you are really interested in helping me, please persuade the Home Minister to somehow send you the letters. Or ask him to place them in police custody. Please trust me. That is all I am asking you."

The minister sat silent, for a long while, mulling while twirling the paper weight. Both he and Gopal had understood the heart of the matter. But *what to do next* was the question. The minister thought he had made a mistake by suggesting what he did to Gopal. Gopal too felt he had spoken a tad more than he should have. But still he felt satisfied that he had said the right things. It was already seven thirty. *Since darkness had fallen, the exchange should stop*, the two thought. The minister himself broke the silence.

"Okay. I will send those letters for an enquiry. Please pay attention to your health as also to the duties you are responsible for. *Namaskaara!*"

The minister rose before putting his joined palms against his chest in a parting greeting, the (non)redundantly used physical correlate of the verbal *namaskaara*. "Thanks, Sir," said Gopal before getting up and leaving the room before the minister did. He then scurried off to his car and without waiting for his driver, drove the car away. He didn't know how he drove the car and reached home. There was some burning and discomfort in his belly. He didn't feel like eating although he felt hungry. Didn't feel like drinking even though he felt thirsty.

The moment he got home, he shut himself up in in his room. He quickly changed before taking out the rum bottle that was in the cupboard. Saraswathi would always keep a pail of water in his room as soon as he reached home. He swigged up a *tambige*ful of rum, and sleep came to him, erasing all pain, and he lay down and nodded off. Saraswathi kept banging the door. But Gopal didn't hear anything. Saraswathi's anxiety reached the skies. She stewed, in great concern, in the idea that he, who had come home and shut himself up, hadn't opened the door even when it was meal time. She couldn't have scampered to neighbouring houses to tell them because her husband's name, a celebrity, would have been besmirched, if she did.

Just at that time, the cop on night patrol duty came over near the door. Emboldened, she told him about her husband. He also walked over and knocked on the door: "Sir, Sir!" As there was no reaction to this either, Saraswathi's anxiety tripled. She was all at sea. He never did this earlier: he never failed to respond, to open the door for so long. "Go scale the compound wall" she told the cop handing him a torch, "and, if there are no lights in the room, shine the torch and see!"

Neighbours who had by that time seen the cop climb the compound wall at the front walked over to their entrance door and stood watching the proceedings curiously. But not even one came forward to find out what was happening, let alone lend a helping hand. Nobody came out at nights. The house was near Navarang theatre in Rajaji Nagara. The road would be abuzz till ten in the night. But since it was the police that was doing this, nobody would keep from gaping at it.

The cop scaled the wall and moved the window aside. It was dark inside. He shone the torch in. Rajagopal seemed to be sleeping on the bedstead.

He watched Gopal closely. He appeared to be in sound sleep. "Don't worry, *amma*!" the cop assured Saraswathi. "He is in deep sleep. Maybe he was tired and has nodded off. You bolt the door and sleep!"

Saraswathi knew her husband. He never ever slept like this. How was it that he was doing this today? Did he sleep like a log, after getting drunk somewhere, and fearing the smell would give him away? She paced the living hall, thinking he might come out any minute and fretting herself to death with, *he could at least have eaten howsoever a little.*

She did this, fidgeting about in the living hall, right till 1 in the night before downing a glass of water and nodding off, laying out a floor mat on the floor, right there in the living hall. She didn't sleep on the sofa because that would trouble her back. She was used to this, coming as she did from a village. Poor woman! She had a husband only in name: she never experienced the sensual pleasures of marriage. All she got was the prestige and dignity of being the wife of so and so. Not all who get married get love. They get only family commitment. A wife, who is the distinguishing design feature of a family, would cook. That was her staple job. She felt sad and dejected that she didn't for some reason get any children. She gave up that worry after a few days. *If I had stayed back in the village after doing my M.A., I would not have got this salary!* She did her M.A. in Bengaluru University, staying in her uncle's. All she ever went to when in Bengaluru was the university campus and when not there, she would be back in the house. She had then come to Madhugiri. She didn't have any knowledge of the world. She confined herself to her own world. She would nowhere else get the satisfaction of being the wife of a big litterateur. Gopal never took her along whenever he went out. He didn't talk much either. But all that she got was enough, she would feel. She was a soul mate who never ever thought she was being done unjustly by, and who reposed enormous trust in her husband.

In fact she didn't even know that there was such a threat letter.

How would she understand his interior? Nor was she aware of the fact that Ushe and her husband met and made passionate love on a regular basis. But in case she did come to know of this there was certain to be a huge ruckus at home. Sometimes Saraswathi's words were sharp, sure and certain, brooking no counter. It was like, as they say in Kannada, breaking a stick into two discrete parts, with no two ways about it. She was mentally really tough and strong. How would a woman agree to these ways of the husband? Saraswathi's was a step ahead. *Only because of his vast learning and knowledge, he was not able to give her as much time, attention and love,* she thought, *as she would have liked. That was all there was to it. But deep inside he overflowed with love for me,* she thought! This feeling was what made her live life contentedly.

This, Saraswathi's argument, that is, was a strange one. Love is never the awareness and knowledge that lies under wraps. It has arms and legs. It is always on the move. If she didn't know there were things like throbbings, that was because of her feeling of contentment. If it was the case that she hadn't made her husband fall in love with her at some point of their married life, she must be a dunce! Had they had a child, Gopal and Ushe would now be grandparents. Does the fact that the love and lust hadn't borne fruit have any sense? Now while her husband was busy in his amatory romps with another woman, her position was fixed. If love fails, its disappointments and pressures should not render one of the partners useless. But this is what in fact happens. Even if it is not intentional, internal pressures squeeze them so that they reduce their spouses to naught. There is no difference here of man and woman. Even women are like this, but their way of showing it and sorting this out would be different and faster. Do or die is woman's way. They would adjust to their spouses. Or, they would sit on the special ornamented seat that brides sit on for prewedding ceremonies, the *hasemaNe* and wait hoping against hope till the symbolic marriage thread is tied around their necks, and then flee the scene, unable to stand the pressure. If they are patient, they would wait for a change of mindset. There would also be good cultured women, who think they should not do unjustly by their parents. There are for sure women, theorists of love, who think love and the lover is supreme. They would decide who is bad and who good. Here others' opinions would be like evanescent friendships that come into, and go out of, lives. There are also women who forget the men they loved, leave the disappointment behind, dump the husband before falling for some other man. The common belief is that sex is only with men they love. That emotional intimacy inspires physical intimacy for women. If that is not possible, physical intimacy would be only with men they marry. Now here is another project, another kind of bond. There is a new community arising of people who satisfy their hungers with abandon in the name of friendships forged according to their free will. Some say this is necessary to manage stress and pressure. A counter to this is: *haven't our ancestors grown up in a tradition? Didn't they have mental pressure?* But this has also a counter! : Not only our ancestors, but we have had such relationships from the times of Mahabharata and Ramayana. You observe it yourself. If you compare with those texts, many modern families have preserved our tradition and culture. How did Draupadi of the Mahabharata epic have a physical bond with five husbands? Why didn't she get any sexually transmitted disease?[4] There are people who ask such questions.

In sum, the truth was Saraswathi was not the heroine in this story. She didn't even have the second position. Seethamma, Rajagopal's mother or Sharade, his younger sister would fit that position. Saraswathi's was a negligible relationship for Gopal. But he had to live with her daily. He had to eat what she cooked daily. He had to wear clothes she washed. He had to sleep beside her daily like an inanimate object.

****

---

[4] This is trickier than the author of this novel would care to know! Nobody knows whether she got the disease or not. Does the author of the epic know? How would he know? This is also another example of the idea that everything that anybody, including literary artists, does need not *necessarily* and *inevitably* make good sense. It is also an example of some noticeably flimsy nonsolid klutzy aspects of 'literature'.

Chapter Five

Saraswati would get up at six in the morning. She would finish the cooking work, keep some coffee for the husband in the vacuum flask, put the breakfast away in the hotbox, and leave for the college. The college was close by. It was a private college. She didn't get a fat government salary. Yet Saraswathi always wore shiny silk sarees for the college. Her salary, meagre though it was, was enough for her. It was the husband who managed the household expenses. She spent only on her cosmetics and for decorative makeovers of the house. Gopal never probed her about finances. He phoned his sister regularly to ask about matters ranging from the expenditure at home, mother's health, her medicines, her food to provisions like rice, cereals, soap, salt and vegetables bought for the family before dishing out appropriate advice and suggestions. We don't know whether it was his nature or his habit or karma or whether it was his belief that for him Saraswathi, the wife was just a woman who cooked, washed dishes, mucked out the house and cleaned up clothes day after day after day.

It was quite late in the morning. Rajagopal hadn't woken up as yet. She as usual brewed coffee, cooked breakfast. She rapped on the door of her husband's room and, announcing, *"Rii*! I'm leaving for college!"* put on her footwear and left. Although Gopal had woken up, he didn't feel like coming out. Even if the anxiety had lessened with the overnight sleep, he didn't exactly feel lighter and easier in the mind. The moment he opened his eyes, the disquieting worry followed him.

Some woman has written a letter about me, it seems. I should rip her apart. Let me see the Home Minister today and assert that there should be a CBI enquiry. I should ask the Inspector what to do. Let me not quail. But today Ushe is coming home. Every time she was to come, Ushe caused some thrill and pleasant agitation in me. But today somehow I feel she should not turn up. Somebody could see her come to my place, and make it breaking news and smear my reputation. This would make disqualify to the post I occupy. Anyone can do anything. Politics has no mind of its own and no emotions. Politicians are always on their toes to expose people they don't like.

There would be decisions more of indiscretion and imprudence than of good sense. Tolerance and restraint have no meaning in politics. If their purpose is to depose me from my position by assassinating my character they might call my extramarital relationship with Ushe 'immoral' and go on to blackmail me. What do I do? I could ask her not to come today, and never again to meet henceforth. But if I did say that it I felt I stood to lose something important. But this is the reality, isn't it? If I have to survive I need self-belief and self-confidence, don't I? if one doesn't moral prestige, one wouldn't have courage. I need to control and restrain her at least for this. I should forget her at least for now. There is no other way forward. It would be really asking for trouble if you suppress individual desires. I am already fifty nine. Physical hunger at this age is in itself ridiculous. I should keep her at bay thinking I am unfortunate. But how would she restrain herself? As it is, she already jibes me about not marrying on the issue of caste. Let her do whatever she will. Keeping her at a distance is important; it is the need of the hour as well.

As he took a bath and dressed up, there came a phone call. It was a call from the police Investigating Officer Sundar. "Sir!' said the voice, "You had asked letters that someone wrote about you to be sent from the Home Ministry for investigation. You please take only those calls you deem absolutely necessary for you to answer. We will tap all your incoming calls with their numbers. This is inevitable for now. This is only the present situation. Once this sorts itself out, we will not have this restriction. Thanks."

Somehow the way the inspector spoke felt as if I was being stabbed. He on his part had only done his duty. But it felt to me as if a ferocious tiger had chased me no end. This woman, Ushe always keeps calling and chattering away. She doesn't understand these things. How does she react if I say, "Don't call me on the mobile!"? It is the same for me as well. My innards agitate if there is no call on a given day. At the least she would call at least once in the night. That would do for me. I would give back a missed call to her when she called. But now the situation had taken a turn that made her totally unwelcome and unwanted for me. Prestige seems important. If one asks one's mind, there is only one answer that would come forth. And that is that my prestige is way more important than Ushe, and love and lust with her. But then are the attraction, captivation, keenness of all these days false?

Why is the mind changing tack according to the situation? Would she stay silent? What if she divulges our affair to others? That would also dent my honour and prestige. She has said she never married. Maybe she does not have such fears. Taking that stance might be good for her honour and self-respect. As it is, our consciousness would first operate more on the factor of caste. Everything has been forgotten with the passage of thirty years. Why did she appear again now? Putting her at ease is a big problem. How amazingly strong is this attraction of mine for her? I will die over again: I will be deprived of her love. I will deceive myself for dignity, prestige and honour. Without her physical nearness and intimacy there is disappointment waiting for me. What to do? Nothing seems sorted out.

As Gopal ate his breakfast and was pouring coffee into the tumbler, the mobile rang. He knew that it was Ushe's. He remembered what the police had instructed him. *If they overhear us talking, they will suspect me.* He didn't take up the phone. The mobile stopped ringing after ten minutes. Having imbibed some coffee, he, feeling easy in the mind, sat on the sofa waiting for the police to turn up. Ushe herself appeared at the door. The moment she came in, she held his hand and with a show of great solicitude, and posing, "Who has given my love a death threat?" tried to provoke Gopal. Gopal rose, and backing away, sat down at a distance. He must have felt he would lose himself in her seductive attraction. Ushe felt alarmed too.

"Why? Why did you back away?"
"Let us not meet like this any longer." The police is recording my incoming calls. If they come to know about us, there will be trouble. Let us be away from each other for a while."

"How is that possible? Is it possible for you? I was feeling satisfied with a little love, feeling that a way forward had paved itself for the love that had been held back. How can one live if even this is barred? I won't live at all."

"Usha, understand this! You will also be there, living. And so will I be. We love each other. The bar at the moment is on physical intimacy. We can stay away like that, can't we? Let there not be the touch of lust. We will become small. This is the question of my honour."

"Say that! This question of your honour and prestige didn't exist before, right? Why now? Just because someone wrote a letter to you, you think and talk of honour, dignity and prestige! Which means only you have this dignity, prestige, and stuff, and I don't! All this is phony. When I came round sometime back, you were talking in your office to some woman for an eternity. I waited for a long time before buzzing off. You were so happy talking to her. I wanted to ask that very day who the woman was. I kept mum, thinking there should be no mistrust in matters of love. Without a family commitment for you anyone can walk into your life. I have now become someone you don't want. You will get some other woman. That is why you are putting it down to the police! You are saying they will tap my calls etc. I should believe this, shouldn't I? There is no difference between you and those politicians. They do what they do openly, declaring what they will do. You don't give any room for any communication or publicity. You said you will rip open your heart to show your love for me. Come on! Show! No such thing is possible for you. All this is theatrics."

"Usha! Stop it! This is the extent to which you have understood me. It is your stupidity if you think only because I spoke the way I did to somebody I look at such women like that! If someone talks about some book, we exchange ideas with civility. You said you saw me some day speaking to somebody. You should have come in. This suspicion is not good. You are the only woman I have looked at this way. If there is genuine love, one can do the loving from a distance. It could it seems do without this smear of lust. Besides, the circumstances prevailing now threaten to destroy my professional career and my mind. You are also doing the same! If you have any respect and regard for me, wish my good, wish me well from a distance. Love should always be prepared for any sacrifice for the wellbeing, the supreme good of the loved ones. Love that doesn't pose hurdles and silence that doesn't argue builds value."

"That means I shouldn't phone you. I should not get near. All you are saying is that we should not meet anymore, isn't it? How is that possible?"

"You can come round to the office. We can always talk there. But only about general things, not personal matters."

"Okay. No phoning up, no meeting, no talking. You can think I'm no longer alive for you. I will not live anymore."

"Usha! Usha!"

She strode away, crying and without closing the compound gate. Gopal had this gut-wrenching distress on one side and the anxiety about what people might think in case they saw Ushe making off, crying on the other. Since the two happened simultaneously, a strange weariness hemmed him in. *How to overcome this* was the question. He had decided at least on one thing: That he should distance Ushe. Whatever it was, she misunderstanding him was one thing while the possibility that she might talk ill of him with people, which might afford the people a wrong impression about him was another. *Nothing is putting me at ease. What is this karma!?*

It was ten minutes since she had left. Gopal downed a *tambige*ful of water. By that time his security guard came on. "Sir, Shall we go?"
Although Gopal mechanically nodded, there was no life in the nod. *Who wants this job? I can write and make a name! quite a few cognoscenti stay away from this politics and make a name. They don't get stuck in any sort of confusion. They lead tension-free and comfortable lives. Although there might be shortage of money, theirs would be trouble-free saintly lives that don't show this lack of money. But I don't have deep satisfaction. Although I own a house, and have achieved some significant standing in society, I am still seeking love at a personal level. Because I desired this position, this murder threat has happened. Such a letter no litterateur has got so far, they say. Life goes who knows where, seeking something. I now writhe, unable either to reach ashore or to stay somewhere. Poor woman, this Sharade, my younger sister! Since her husband was not all right, she came back to her maternal home and found*

fulfillment looking after her siblings. Always crooning, she manages rather well household work in the fields, study of her siblings, the work having to do with marriage and all. She never cribs. What a zest for life! Even now she goes over to the fields and washes clothes at the irrigation tube and puts them out to dry. She feeds mother. No other desire seems to have bothered her.

As for me, I enjoyed not one happiness, but two! Nothing is there in my hands now. I couldn't afford gratified delight even to my own wife who is right beside me. Shall i resign now and be all by myself? That would show my cowardice. If I proceed to fight, what if I lose even what I do have now?! Let me see, let things pan out the way they will. This injected some courage into Gopal. He took the car out of the garage before asking the cop over with a hand sign. Even as he was igniting the engine, the mobile rang. He took up the phone and pressed the key. It was a stern male voice. It was atremble.

"Sir, There is a bomb in your car!"

Gopal's heart leapt into his mouth. Not knowing what to do, a bewildered Gopal rushed out of the car before, showing the mobile call to the cop, he submitted, "See! They are saying there is a bomb in the car!"
"Who was it speaking, Sir! Was it male or female?"

"It was a male voice."
The cop first of all informed Inspector Kalyan Singh, "Come over immediately, sir! The car is right here. He has taken it out of the garage." The Inspector told the cop to get the car out on the road. The constable told this as well to Gopal. People surrounded the scene and stood watching. The Inspector brought along two constables for investigation.

As soon as he arrived, the Inspector examined the car. It was the new model of Maruti Suzuki. It had been bought only last year. There was no hint of the bomb anywhere. Concluding that it was a hoax threat, Kalyan Singh stepped up and assured Gopal, "There is no need to panic. They have simply threatened. That's all! Let me see from which number they have phoned you." He took the mobile from Gopal and called the number, but no one received it. It was a Rajaji nagara number. The call had come from very near. By the time the inspector gave the audience a piercing look and turned toward Gopal, an exhausted Gopal had gone in and flopped on the sofa, his hands on the head.

"Sir! Why feel sad and helpless? It is only a threat. There is for sure no bomb in the car. Why get tense?"

To relax because there is no bomb in the car one needs to be sure it won't happen again. Is there any guarantee? People might talk a hundred things when my car is being examined? How would others react when I myself am disgusted about myself?

"Scums! Frigging mother-fuckers! Why do they do such mean politics?" grumbled Gopal before he turned to the Inspector.

"This is not a question of tension, Sir! How long will the threat hover on me? More than the question of who would throw this threat is the question of whether this knife, bomb and pistol culture applies to someone like me. This threat is something I don't want. How and wherefrom is this voice posing murder threats and thereby unseating me come from? Why? And it is the anguish of knowing why, and yet not being able to express it. How many people would perish and be damaged with the planting of a bomb? What would people living next to me think? This is not a question or matter just of anxiety and fear. It is a question of my honour and self-respect. We hadn't told anyone about this. Now everything is out in the open. I opened the garage only now. How can someone plant a bomb in the car so quickly? Or we may think it was planted yesterday. It could be a warning that the next time around they will not make it a hoax."

"I don't know why, but you are speaking things that are not right. Please soothe yourself. Where has your wife gone?"

"She is a lecturer in a college. She left at eight in the morning. I haven't told her anything. Please don't let her know anything. That will grieve her deeply, poor soul!"

The Inspector cast a look around the house. He saw a string of double-jasmine flowers lying on the sofa. Looking closely at it, he exclaimed, "Sir! You said your wife left at eight. But this is lying here. It is eleven now. You let it lie here?"

Gopal was at a loss for an answer.

That was a flower string that Usha had tied onto her hair braid. Because Gopal liked it, she wore it whenever she came calling at his home. That had fallen accidentally now before she left the place. An answer came out tumbling : "No. She must have got the flower string for the God. She has forgotten it here.'"

"But there is no picture frame of God here on the wall above the sofa. And stuck to the double-jasmine flowers is a long strand of hair. These are flowers that have been worn once, not fresh ones. If your wife has left at eight, how can they be like this at eleven o' clock? Whose are these flowers, Sir?"

Gopal's heart was on his sleeve. His mind groped for a reply. *How do I reply? How many lies can you tell? My personality is sinking. I have already uttered whatever I had to utter.*

"Sir! These are flowers that my wife must have worn. Why do we suspect it? I think we don't need to dig deep."

"Does your wife have a mobile? Please give her number."

"She does use a mobile, but I don't have her number. We meet daily. I use the mobile only for official purposes. Not for personal use. That is why I haven't taken her number."

"Okay. Please give your mobile for a minute."

Gopal had to part with the mobile. That he handed it over as if in two minds as to whether to give or not to give created more doubt in the Inspector.

The Inspector scanned the missed call numbers. Seeing Ushe's number there, he asked, "Sir, You have answered this number yesterday, but not today. Who is this?"

"I was in the bathroom. You said I shouldn't talk much with anybody."

"Not me. It was the Investigating Officer who said that. The Home Minister has transferred the letters to police custody to facilitate investigation."

The Inspector handed the cell phone back to Gopal before chucking the flowers away. Gopal had broken into a profuse sweat. *What is this? Along with an enquiry into the death threat, there is an investigation into my honour! Somehow i feel I don't want these inquiries and investigations. The Police Inspector would for sure remember Ushe's number. He might call her to dig deeper. There is no telling what she might tell him. She is already cross with me! In case all this appears on TV and the media... all my honour, self-respect, prestige, position would all be reduced to smithereens. His heart started palpitating as panic gripped him. Did I want all this? I performed well for one full year. With the change of guard one disaster after another has pursued me...*

Where did I come by this woman, Ushe?! She has dragged me into the open and has had me stoned as it were after occupying me and stirring desire in my heart. I sat before the Inspector as if stripped naked. I should give him some reply. The inspector has taken this up. We can't now go back. It is as if I on my own have entangled myself in this.

"Sir, she is not a person you can suspect. She is only an acquaintance. Even my wife knows her."

"It is all right. I didn't ask you about her, did I? Shall I switch on the fan? You seem to be sweating a hell of a lot. Please take it easy and be comfortable. If you want, go to your office. It is up to you. Perhaps you can't really work today. Take some rest at home!"

The Inspector strode away, saying something to the constables. *There were now three constables at the house to guard me. One sentry at the car garage, one near the compound, and the third sentinel at the door. Even when I went out, there would be a cop as an escort. I was, in a manner of speaking, under house arrest! Somehow this disgusting weariness I could do without. These cops, this house, this polluted kind of atmosphere! I feel like fleeing all these. Should go back home to my native place. That might afford me some balmy bracing solace. I could that way pay attention to mother's health. This Inspector speaks rather sarcastically. Why would he need this number? My wife's number: he would ask her, "Did you wear a Jasmine flower string in your hair? Did you let it fall?" Why does he want all that? Why this work of poking his nose in our family matters? There may be hundreds of calls to me as the Chairman of the Development Authority. Why should one enquire into it? This is sure to appear in tomorrow's newspapers. Media people would come calling to blitz me with all sorts of questions. If they ask, who should I blame? Putting it down to present politics, I can't take jibes at anyone. All said and done, I can offer to resign. But what is important is how committed I would be to the talk of resignation. These people might have sent this threat just to induce my resignation: they would then grab the opportunity to occupy the position I am occupying now. I should not allow that to happen. I should fight. Even if the minister himself has done it, I should fight this out. I should give an open statement. If it appears in the newspapers, one would get to know the true colours of these ministers.*

This is certainly not about the selection of books for an award. Someone must have thought I should change to be in step with the changed political scenario. Shivalingaih, the Dalit poet said yesterday that the deputy Chief Minister had come to know of the murder threat. How did he come to know that the deputy Chief Minister had come to know it. He might be a part of this. In any case the government itself encourages such people. How does one live where pure fresh air does not blow?

A call from Mallikarjuna Swamy, the personal assistant came just then. "Sir! You are to come for a book release function. The function is at four in the afternoon. You leave home exactly at three, Sir. You can rest and relax till then. Inspector Kalyan Singh had called. He told me everything. Some sons-of-multiple-fathers are troubling you. Let it be. No need to worry about these jerks! You come leisurely, Sir!"

He spoke everything. There wasn't anything I could add! People talk like that, putting forth the problem and then suggesting a solution themselves. As if they are paragons of virtue, they say, "We have nothing to worry. Every hassle, every trouble only you have!" Their tone, their solicitude would be as put on as it can get. Everyone's would be a scheming cunning mindset. But they speak very delicately, nicely. Pain is extraordinary. But can't say what kind of distress would it be? Anyhow let me be here till three o' clock and see.

The book to be released had arrived yesterday itself.

A poem collection titled *Mallekaavu*. The poet was Ravindranath. Gopal liked the title. It was the name of a village, a small nondescript village on the road to Siddarabetta from Koratagere. Ravindra the poet hailed from the village. Every poem in the collection exuded rustic splendor. The word collocations were also very suggestively elegant, and were imbued with such magical skill as to turn the smell of cow urine and dung that come from the culture of the earth into sandalwood aroma. *As I read them,* Gopal reminisced, *my anxiety and distress seemed to wane away. There is no poetry greater than one that can banish one's woes. I should certainly go for this programme. I should share all of my experience.*

Gopal had nodded off, the poetry collection in hand. We don't know whether it was the impact of the drinks he had swigged the previous night or the mental stress, he didn't wake up even when it was three o' clock. Police constables were busy in their jobs. Whenever neighbours asked them the question, "Why security guards for a literary figure?" they would silently smile the question away. When somebody was importunate, they would tell him the actual reasons in a way that induced dread before ending with, "Why do you bother about the affairs of biggies?" Saraswathi returned home. When she stepped in, the phone was ringing. She answered it. It was from the personal assistant in the office of the Kannada Development Authority.

"Madam, Sir has a book release function to attend. Has he not left the house as yet? They are all waiting. Can you let me speak to him?"

"Okay. Call after five minutes."

Bustling about Saraswathi woke up her husband sleeping on the sofa before reminding him of the function. He quickly got up, had his wash, dressed himself up and as he tidied and spruced up his appearance, he said, "Saraswathi! Take care!" Signing to the escort cop, he walked to the garage, took the car out, and asking the cop to sit on the backseat, ignited the engine.

My husband never takes me along when he goes out, sighed Saraswathi to herself. *I too have desires and dreams, don't I? How does he write poems and stories without understanding this much?! All he writes is about love and lust, they say. But he has never conducted himself like that. Not even one day! Could one write this only with imagination? That is not possible at all. That would be like a flower without aroma. That said, can we believe that he didn't or doesn't love anyone except me? How mild is his personality! Somebody everyone likes! He has love for me deep inside. He always tells me so very softly to take care whenever he leaves home! He takes good care of me. What else do I need? He writes what it is not possible to say. If you have a husband you should have someone like him. If I had married a commoner where would I have got such a life and such honour?*

Saraswathi came in to concoct some coffee. The double-jasmine flower string that lay on the sofa drew her attention. She took it up and observed it. *How is this in here? Who had come here?* She was not the kind who would let go anything that lent itself to suspicion. Opening the house door, she asked the security cops as to who had come since morning. He told her about the visit of the Inspector, the bomb scare and the murder threat before that. Saraswathi's head swirled. Recovering she shuffled over up to the entrance door before sagging down there. It was as if on her, who had been dreaming, live cinders had rained. The policeman jogged up, to give her some water to drink.

"Didn't you know, madam!?" he asked.

Saraswathi nodded a "No!" even as her eyes welled tears. "No. I don't know. He didn't tell me! After he came home yesterday and shut himself in, it is only today that I got to see him. When I left this morning, he wasn't as yet awake."

"It is okay, madam! You make a vow to God. He will not let you down."

Telling her to close the door and get in, the cop walked away toward the compound gate. Saraswathi held the double-jasmine flower string in her hand, and looked it over. Thoughts raced in her head. There was in there a long strand of hair to boot. *I don't have even an iota of doubt about my husband. Why these thoughts then?*, She told herself chewing the cud. *Our servant maid comes after I leave home. Flowers must have fallen accidentally on the sofa. These cops say the Police inspector had come. There was no mention of any woman. So then this must be the maidservant's flowers.*

Then came inspector Kalyan Singh's call.

"Madam, you weren't there in the morning. I need to ask certain questions. Please answer correctly."

"At what time in the morning do you leave home normally?"

"At eight."

"When does Sir leave for his office?"

"Ten, or nine thirty."

"Would he be alone at home at that time?"

"No. There would be a lot of books around him. Even if I am around, he would always be reading and writing. Otherwise there would be the mobile you see!"

"Do you by the way have a mobile?"

"Yes, I do."

"Haven't you given that number to your husband?"

"No, I haven't, because that can't be given to any outsider. Certainly not to the police. It should be limited to our family members only. That is the reason why he didn't give it to you."

"You have let fall on the sofa the double-jasmine flowers fastened in your hair braid. I had to ask about your mobile because of that. But he said he doesn't know your number. That is why I had to ask you. There is nothing more to it."

"The double-jasmine string belongs to our servant maid. She is the one who sets those flowers in her hair. The string might have fallen on the sofa when she was scrubbing the floor below. Why should you phone me about it? You should, instead of probing into family matters, focus on detecting the crime and nabbing criminals. You shouldn't instead elaborate on the story of the double-jasmine string before me. There is no relation between that and the murder threat to my husband. Anything else you want to ask me?"

The Inspector never thought Saraswathi would talk the way she did. He had called to ask about something. Saraswathi was the one who had taken up the phone. *If I now ask who this Ushe is, she might answer as rudely. Why should I be curious? Usha might be a writer. I could ask Gopal himself. If I ask her, she seems hell-bent on aggressive defence rather than be concerned with her husband's security.*

"Sir, if you have anything more to ask, come home when he is around and quiz my husband. Why probe on phone for long? Shall I call off?"

"Where has Sir gone, madam?"

"For a book release function."

"All right. If and when there is a need, I will come and see you."

Saraswathi had talked the aggressive way she did, in order to defend something even while she suppressed a feeling she couldn't suppress.

Darkness enveloped her the moment she put down the phone. *Who has issued this murder threat? The security is for that. There has been only one cop so far. Now there are three!*

Besides, they have frightened us with the bomb scare. Why doesn't he tell me everything? That is why he slept off in the night out of dejection and distress.... Chee! I should have applied for leave and been with him consoling and soothing him. More than just food and beverages, some soothing words from the wife would have shored him up. Even now when I came home, he had gone into deep sleep. Only God knows, whether his is a neutral attitude of not bothering about such things or he is scared or he is really courageous. But one thing is certain. One can't say whatever happens to him will not affect me. It will certainly affect me. Either directly or indirectly. What can I do? Just because there is police standing guard one can't say there won't be an attempt to murder. A fear that was beyond our wildest imagination has suddenly sprung up and sat staring at us. What do I do? What is my role in this? What words do i have to soothe and put him at ease? For now this double jasmine string spurs me to ask him whose flowers these are, the moment he gets home. This being the situation, if I ask him about the bomb scare and the murder threat, that would relegate the double jasmine issue to the background. My first priority is to sort the suspicion created by these double jasmine flowers. But what has come to attention just now is this bomb issue. The inspector has told us about it. For him that is a big deal. If I inquire about the flowers first, I will become small. Let him come home first.

Saying to herself, "Let us tie up a bundle with contents in it dedicated to God and place it before Him and make a vow to Him. Let us also perform a wedding festivity for God Venkataramanaswamy of Madhugiri and at least wrap Goddess Dandina Maramma with a silk saree. In any case we are going to Madhugiri for father-in-law's postdeath ritual in the next fifteen days. We could perform these then. God would never let us down," Saraswathi placed a tied up bundle before the deity in the home-shrine.

There are so many temples in Bengaluru. Yet somehow there is only ostentation and pretence in those. One doesn't get any sense of divine devotion there. Temples have become commercial establishments like shops and malls. Priests pay more attention only if you place more money in the platter of the camphor flame that is waved in front of the deity and then offered to devotees, the mangalarathi. Only if you pay more are you given the edible that is placed before the deity first, sanctified and then offered to devotees as a mark of the inferiority of devotees vis-a-vis God, the prasaada. People who don't offer up money into the salver are not offered mangalaarathi even once, even if they circle the deity a thousand times in great devotion! This is the politics of the priests. Money is ahead, man and God are behind. Look at God Venkataramana Murthy in Madhugiri, so solemn- and majestic-looking. We don't have to stand and wait in serpentine queues. We could stand and have delightful eyefuls of the deity for as long as we want. You make vows any number of times and these vows would all be fulfilled, as they have so far been with us. Mother-in-law says the same thing: that seeing God Venkataramana Swamy of Madhugiri is pretty much like seeing the hallowed and fabled God Venkataramana Swamy of the hilly shrine at Thirupathi. Mother-in-law did go to Him for help when she had with problems with children. Let me not tell anyone about the death threat. I haven't switched on the TV for three days now. Even my husband hasn't ted doing it. The news would appear either in daily newspapers or on TV. What if they get to know then. Why this distress if in any case i am simply resigning? One feels like controlling the mind thinking that one doesn't have ease and comfort of mind if one pursues power and prestige. How does one have ease and comfort of mind even with these? Only power which talent begets and which is gotten without help from politics might facilitate ease and comfort of mind. The desires and temptations that i have strangle me. One can't decide what one doesn't want or does want for now. He knows everything.

Saraswathi got up and lit a lamp in front of the deity in the home shrine before paying her respects to Him by bringing her joined palms against her chest and sitting there for a considerable while, closing her eyes. The walls of the home-shrine were laid with huge tiles with God Venkataramana Swamy and there was also a three-foot long laminated picture of the deity. In front of the picture was a two-foot tall silver lamp of the olden times. She would always light it pouring ghee into it.

When Saraswathi sat before the deity, tears welled in her eye sockets. The fear of what if some disaster happened engulfed her even when God was in right in front. After staying put there for a while she came out, mucked out the husband's room, put the books in order, tidied up the sheets on the bed, put some of them out to wash and when she brewed some coffee and downed it, some sort of courage took hold of her. If one keeps oneself busy, one could overcome fear. You feel shored up. If one mopes, worry and anxiety augment.

****

"Some girl, a new poetess had come for the foreword of her new collection of poems. Those must be her flowers. Why do you bother?"

When her husband said this, Saraswathi chucked the string of double jasmine flowers away into the dustbin. If one nurses such doubts, it is difficult to live life. When word of the death threat came up, he ended his meal washed his hand and sat. No word came out of his mouth. Gopal clammed up about the topic of the murder threat. He knew that his wife would worry about it. It was natural for her be worried and alarmed. *I should give her a satisfactory and consoling kind of answer. She would feel alarmed otherwise. When no such ease of mind exists in me how could I console her? For now there is police protection. Mere keeping vigil would not be protection. They are all temporary. In case this is treat, or just a threat, one could threaten one's wife and achieve what one wants to achieve. There is no need to hide it from her. Let me tell her only what needs to be told. Not telling her would be a mistake. But how to tell is the question. How to tell this without inducing alarm or in a way that reassures her? Releasing a book and speaking about it fluently and relentlessly has to do with my heart's happiness. But this is an unbearable feeling. This is terror that one never dreamt of. Who is it that has this desire to wrench someone's heart standing at a distance?...*

Gopal rose and stood facing the window. Saraswathi washed vessels before putting them in a neat order, mopped the kitchen before emerging from it and sitting back on the sofa. She thought her husband would talk and she sat wondering with great curiosity what he would speak. It was not possible, like other wives, to torment her husband, importuning him about things. Gopal didn't expect such importunate behavior from her. She knew she should be dignified and solemn in front of her husband. She knew she shouldn't step beyond the limits of peace, forbearance and restraint. Gopal related to her everything. "That is why," he explained, "There is police standing guard by our house compound. There is no need to panic. This is only a ruse to make me resign, that is all. Let us face it without losing our restraint and courage. Just because a letter was written and just because there is a bomb scare, we need not think they would kill us. It would in fact be wrong to think so. Those who pose such threats would also have a sneaking fear of being nabbed. If worst comes to the worst, I can always resign and focus on my personal life and writing career. Why should we wane away, panicking and worrying about what would be our lot supposing this happens and supposing something else happens?"

"We have lived this far. Let us continue living like this, like ordinary people. I will ask the security police to be withdrawn for a few days. Let us see what happens. One should not flee the scene of life fearing death. We should face things and win. I haven't so far given anyone trouble nor pained anyone. Whatever you do destroys you. You be calm! You find your comfort and ease of mind in your poojes, prayers and worships. I will forget this anxiety, getting absorbed in my work. I don't like saluting and fawning on politicians. Let us see what they will do."

Husband's every word, which added value and optimism, penetrated Saraswathi. Yet sleep wouldn't come to her, however much she tried. The same thoughts haunted her. Anxiety that defied description bugged her. As she felt drowsy, she thought he saw some light moved to and fro outside the room she was sleeping in. It seemed as though the light moved around for a long time. It couldn't come in to the room crossing the window. It died out at last.

Saraswathi abruptly woke up. She had broken into a sweat. She touched her husband to feel him.
"What happened, Saru?"
Saraswathi nodded to say there was nothing the matter, and saying to herself it was all delusional, fell asleep again. *Do lamps have legs? How was it making a sound like human feet do? I saw only the lamp. I couldn't say who had held the lamp because when I woke up there was nothing to be seen. It was only a dream or a delusion. One shouldn't rack one's brains about such things. But on such occasions one tends to observe closely everything. The light of a lamp is a good sign. Something that was moving about outside the window couldn't find a way in. It died out because of the wind outside. This is indeed a sign of truth. It was as if the footfall was in a personality and as if the personality was the light. This light would be like real kindly light that leads us in people like a Gandhi, a Vivekananda or a Basavanna or an Ambedkar or a Mahavira or a Ramakrishna Paramahamsa. But that it had died out without coming in was remarkable. Would truth go way without entering our house as light?* At the dead of night such thoughts reared their heads in her head. *Sleep wouldn't come. My own husband has told me not to worry. I did switch on the lights to*

see but the window wasn't open. Ever since he received the letter of intimidation, Gopal always kept the doors and windows closed. Saraswathi downed a glass of water before lying down, and covering herself with the sheets, fell asleep.

****

Sometimes some desires pursue us even without our wanting them, and squeezing us no end, rob us of ease and peace of mind. Repairing our desires in such a way as to be content with whatever one has seems rare. Desiring something in one's mind and doing something else outside doesn't end up in contentment. If man gets whatever he desires, it only whets his appetite of more desires. Forgetting what he has in fact got, he desires other things. Even if it appeared I have rejected Ushe, the seductive spell she has cast on me continued somewhere deep in me. Where is her house? She said it was somewhere in Mahalaxmi layout. I never asked her. Both my mind and body desire her. But it is not possible for now. Can't speak to her on the cell phone. Can't meet her. She has carved memories all around me. I would have aged by the time I meet her next. Either the mind would shrink then or the body would no longer be keen. Fascination for Ushe is more powerful than this position, house, power, prestige and fame. This is a pleasurable disposition that doesn't know whether she is in my arms or me in hers. It is supreme pleasure that wouldn't be available anywhere else. The gratified delight that my union with her has afforded ever since her college days has inspired a lot of my poetry. It is she who has enlivened and animated my recent poetry. How to put that behind? I have given orders for this full sea to dry up. It is I who has asked her not to come and not talk to me. That was for my social position and prestige. Does that mean things like social position and prestige pose a challenge to our inner desires?

Many people take their wives along wherever they go like queens, happily showing to the world that they are as intimate as no other couple on the planet. They show that they obey their wives. Some are afraid. But such a display of intimacy and fascination never ever arose between me and Saraswathi. Had Ushe been in Saraswathi's position, i.e of my wife, I would perhaps have done it. Or my nature would have been just that. My fingers advanced several times to press Ushe's mobile number on my phone. What would happen if I did call her? The police have said they would tap my phone and record the conversation. It would be nothing short of disaster if they did overhear our dialogue. I even mulled deleting her number from my cell phone. But that would lead to a very difficult situation. It is becoming increasingly difficult to lead a life without her.

101

She felt so deeply hurt, going away with tears sluicing out of her eyes. I have behaved so very harshly. It, the separation, is becoming increasingly unbearable. Her memory haunts me at every step. Are such love and intimacy possible even at this age? I have begun losing interest in everything in life, much like boys, whose love is not requited, do.

One is the happening that ensued in the midst of the duties that I perform as the chairman of the Book Authority, and the other is the anxious situation of the death threat. The third is the void that the mind is moving toward, having lost love. The bodily hunger has long lessened. It was somewhere being assuaged. If, pinching myself, I cry that there is pain, who would listen to me? I have to find the answer myself. Patience is like a mother. Let me endure this pain. It has been more than a week. There hasn't even been a missed call from her: where did she disappear? As it is, she is short-tempered.

Maybe because he had taken a peg too many of rum, he felt drowsy, and, before long, was fast asleep.

Even though Saraswathi rapped on the entrance door for long, Gopal didn't wake up. Since Gopal had told them he didn't need them, the security police were not there either. Saraswathi felt a mix of distress and embarrassment. What would the onlookers think? Gopal had felt out of sorts and also because there wasn't much work in the office, he hadn't gone to work today. There was no rule that one had to attend the office without fail every day. Gopal had deferred the work that had to be attended to because of the death threat. Had there been no murder threat, there would be no pain, turmoil, embarrassment and insults, would there?

Saraswathi's distress increased. *What if husband had done something untoward? Ri... Ri.* So ululating, she knocked on the door. The people next door didn't talk much with her. Suresh, the neighbour came over to the compound wall before asking,

"Madam, you are rapping on the door. Is he in?"

"He must be fast asleep. That is why he is not opening the door," Saraswathi said by way of a reply even as she nodded in the affirmative.

"You call the phone number inside. He might wake up."

Saraswathi did as desired.

Yet Gopal didn't wake up. In the meanwhile shopkeepers from both sides of the house sashayed over to find out and to share her anxiety. As they exchanged notes, they came to know that he had a murder threat hovering over him. They said they hadn't seen Gopal since the morning. They hadn't in fact seen anyone anywhere near the house.

They walked right into the compound. They got anxious, hearing Saraswathi's words.

Does such a man get a death threat? He never talked in a raised voice. Poor fellow! Think of such a man being slapped with a death threat! What times are we living in? These are not the days for good people.

Saraswathi wept over again. They had taken care to see that the way they lived was not grist to the gossip mill. *Has he just slept off, Or, is there something more to this!...?*

Sarswathi had returned from college around four in the afternoon. It was now six, but the door had not been opened. Everyone walked over and banged on the door. Now many people from other neighbouring roads converged, crowding the compound of Gopal's house. Saraswathi was all at sea. Some had come out of curiousity while some had come over to put in a word of solace to Saraswathi. The police inspector had also arrived. People then only made room for the Inspector and didn't quite clear out.

The Inspector greeted Saraswathi with "*Namaskara*, madam!" before he also banged the door twice. He too called the landline inside. The ringing tone was heard outside but it didn't touch whoever was inside. As if their guesses were proving to be right, people were at a loss what to do. What to do next was the question. It was not proper to break the door open with no records to back such an action. The Inspector asked a constable to go round and look in through the window even as he handed him a torch. Walking over to the window and looking, the cop said, "Sir, the window seems to be bolted from inside."

"Madam! Was he for any reason disgusted or dispirited in the morning? What is the matter? What will you do? We can get the door broken. But you can't fix it. It is night time. How will you stay inside without the entrance door?"

"Ayyo! We should not break the door for just this. I will wait for a little longer. If things stay like this till tomorrow morning, we will see. We can then break the door open."

"Madam! Your husband it seems said he didn't need the security cops. You see when you were not around, we don't know who had come, and what happened. Supposing there is somebody else with your husband?"

"...."

"I will leave a cop here. You please don't go anywhere. Be here! There should be no trouble. It is possible that he is not inside, isn't it? He might have gone out, who knows."

Saraswathi too felt the same way and she wondered why this didn't strike her earlier. She had left the keys at home, and that was the key mistake. People now dispersed. Neighbour Suresh brought Saraswathi some coffee. More than the brew of coffee, Saraswathi needed to get inside. *Is her husband inside or not inside, what might have happened?* Such questions floated in her head and she never ever thought such a contingency would arise in her life. *Supposing people thought the wife of Chairman of the Kannada Book Authority was sitting outside the house like she was sitting! How odd and embarrassing! Chee... i did the wrong thing! I should never ever leave the keys behind...*

There was no sign of his being inside and it was nine in the night. The cop stood by the compound wall. *No matter where he has gone, he would always be back by this time in the night,* Saraswathi found herself saying wordlessly to herself. *Why did he do this tonight?* Saraswathi found herself in a state of agitated turmoil. *Supposing he is right inside! If so why is he not opening the door? There are no lights on inside. If he is inside and awake, would he not switch on the lights?* Even as her eyes glistened with tears, she wiped her face.

"Madam! Shall I give the Inspector the message?" The cop whispered into her ears. "He will come and get the door broken open."

Saraswathi nodded to mean "No" *The Inspector has said I should stay put here. How can I stay the whole night here? Where would I sleep? The cop would be around in case something happens in the night. But how can I sit like his through the night?* The heat in the mind doubled. *Should my husband bring me to this sorry pass?* Saraswathi had never in her married life got angry with her husband. But now she flew into a boiling rage. But the very next moment her heart stopped thinking of the possible disaster that might have happened. She now sat thinking of and praying to, the various Gods that she knew, and they were quite a few : God Venkataramana Swamy, God Narasimha of Devarayana Durga, the Little God of the village she was born and raised in, God Ranga of the Hillock, Fort Anjaneya, God Raghavendra Swamy of Mantralaya...

One notable thing is it was only Saraswathi who was interested in, and believed in and was devoted to, Gods. Gopal was an agnostic. He wouldn't say either that God existed or that He didn't. But he would never disrespect those that did believe in God. He always cooperated with her in her devotions to the Almighty. He never talked ill or light of believers, or charge them with neglecting their obligations, like some atheists do. He would maintain a serious mien. That was the case at home as well. He wouldn't back out when it came to doing poojas and other devotional rituals at home. He would bring his joined arms against his chest in obeisance and do the poojes with genuine devotion. But deep inside, he didn't believe in God. His wish was he shouldn't stand in the way of believers. He would religiously obey every word of mother's, believing as he did, in keeping his mother happy. He wanted to raise all his eleven siblings well. All of them however couldn't reach his level. One of his younger brothers was rather loose-ended, having done his M.A. but staying jobless, he would raise a din, asking for money and his share of parental property. So Gopal jibbed at going home to his village. Even when the death rites were being done, he kept the cooks at home in Madhugiri, and followed tradition only for the sake of the believers. He was happy that the memory of father brought them all together. Gopal liked this bonding very much. Sitting together with siblings and other relations and dining etc was something Gopal was immensely fond of. He desired that if his brothers, Shivaramu and Raghavendra got good jobs, they could help Sharade, their sister. If they joined a job anywhere in Bengaluru, they could think of their elder brother's house as shelter. But Saraswathi, Gopal's wife should adjust to them, shouldn't she? One of the brothers had done an M.A. and another, a B.Ed. To land jobs Vaidikas should have got good marks. The intelligent ones were cooperative with the sister in the hope that they would land some job. Even though Gopal believed in humanism, the feeling that he had saddled his sister with familial duties and responsibilities to migrate to Bengaluru for his own selfish ends oftentimes kept pricking him.

He could have remarried his sister off.

They had celebrated her first marriage so very pompously, spending so very much. He had been worried about how to manage the weddings of his other sisters. His father had made some property. But there were male children, weren't there? Gopal gave up his share of the property to let his sister take charge at home. She had studied up to tenth standard. Her worldly knowledge grew after she married and shunted about to public places like the court of law and so on. Teaching ritual repetitive recitation of the name of God Rama, the *Ramanama*, to people, she has resolved the ambiguities of life. She arranged for all her siblings to do their studies. She would go to the grooms' places herself, and taking care to see that everything was okay in their families, she would go ahead with the marriages of her sisters. Even when her sisters told her that they would on their own marry boys of their choice, she went to the grooms' places and talked the grooms' parents into a consensus before performing the wedding in a decent manner. It was a tad difficult when one of the sisters wanted to marry across caste. Yet an undaunted Sharade went about it, without denting either the sister's desire or the honour of the family. Now only one younger sister remained to be married. She was already twenty eight years old. They had seen a lot of boys but no liaison had clicked.

Saraswathi felt sleepy and she nodded off leaning against the wall.

Their curiosity of seeing what they wanted in fact to see not quite satisfied, the shopkeepers of the neighbourhood shut shop for the day. The street now wore a deserted look. It was 11 o' clock. Her stomach rumbled because of hunger and her mind pulsated, having to face a possible tragedy. There was no one in Bengaluru you could go to when in distress. There were some relatives somewhere in Jayanagara. But none you could expect succor from. His own colleagues stayed in far off places. If there was anything untoward, there would be a police case. And it would be headlines in tomorrow's newspapers. *In case he has gone out somewhere and comes back home late I should not talk to him,* decided Saraswathi. *Why would someone who would make his wife stand in the middle of the street in the dead of night need a family?*

After a long time, the sound of a plate falling sailed over from the kitchen. Saraswathi's body quaked. "What is the sound, madam?" asked the cop, looking toward the door. Rising all of a sudden Saraswathi looked

106

at the window of the living hall. She saw light through the opening of the window screen. Surprised, she banged on the door. The door opened.

It was lo and behold Rajagopal! "*Ri*, Why did you do this?" she asked, running to him, anxiety written all over her face. "What has happened to you? I have been waiting for you for the last four hours. You have slept inside. Why? Are you all right? Did somebody intimidate you? Why did you do this?"

Gopal took his wife in, and closed the door.

"I can understand your feelings of anxiety. I felt mentally tired. So I fell asleep. Don't blow this out of proportion. Be as if nothing has happened, okay? I may not have the ability to face and endure whatever you have to say. You can tell me all that tomorrow morning."

Understanding his wife's anxiety, Gopal served the meal of rice and *saru* to himself before asking her to excuse him for the mistake he had made. The way he was conducting himself, Saraswathi felt sorry for her husband. Her eyes glistened with tears as she felt for the small man that a celebrity of the land had been reduced to. She couldn't eat. She fed her husband the morsel that was there in her hand. While the two ate, no one spoke. Saraswathi remembered the cop standing outside. After their meal, she gave the plates a rinse before asking him over for his meal. He also felt very glad that things had turned out well. Inspector Kalyan Singh got to know the turn of events.

Today had taught Saraswathi an unforgettable lesson. When she walked in and lit the lamp in the home shrine, it was twelve o' clock.

****

Chapter Six

Security police guarded the Karnataka Bhavana. All the staff had come out. Against the background of the rumour that there was a bomb planted inside the Kannada Development Authority, the police had evicted every one and were investigating. Two lion-like dogs went sniffing the rooms. Chairmen of all the bodies had come out and sat in the hall. Gopal also sat, wordless. Everyone thought silence was discreet. Private anxiety-ridden thoughts raced in their heads. An anonymous call had said, "There is a bomb planted in the Kannada Development Authority. It will explode in half an hour." Hence the atmosphere of anxiety and fear. Everyone had respect for Gopal; some were jealous. Gopal's question was *What crime did I commit for me to be threatened like this?* Gopal didn't know the answer only when the question was asked in innocence. But he jolly well knew the answer when it was posed seriously.

Kalyan Singh searched all the rooms along with the Investigating Officer. Cops stood guard at the entrance of the Kannada Bhavana so that no one entered it. So people visiting the Kannada Sahitya Akademi, the Book Authority, the Development Authority, the Drama Akademi etc stood at the entrance wondering about the goings-on. Media people talked to Gopal about the bomb scare and were thrilled with the hot news. The police didn't let anyone near them. Only literature enthusiasts surrounded him. People were stunned as this was the first time it had happened in the Kannada academia. People were talking among themselves that they should protest against the government. But it was not proper to do it without any evidence. They were mulling protesting against the attack on literary figures.

Everyone had this good feeling of respect and honour for Gopal. Gopal was an honest and innocuous kind of man. The fact that there were threats to such a man meant that the new government was scheming to bring in a new chairman. This was the typical feeling among people. But Gopal didn't speak in favour of this position. He sat, saying wordlessly to himself, 'Come what may, I will not be cowed down. I won't blame anyone. I won't resign. There is police. They will protect me. Let the end come in whichever form it will. Let's see!'

So many of his fans called him on his mobile because they couldn't go in. Gopal himself gave them a measure of comfort telling them, "Nothing will happen, don't worry! Some miscreants have placed a bomb it seems. That will affect the neighboring rooms as well. That is why they are searching the other rooms as well. There is no need to panic. I am safe."

People milled on the streets right upto Ravindra Kalakshetra. When the TV crew started beaming the proceedings, there came a call to Gopal from Madhugiri. It was Gopal's mother speaking. "Come away my child!" she wailed as she wept away. "What you have earned is enough. Be in front of my eyes during my last days. You can be here, living modestly, eking out a living eating ragi balls or greens. Why live with bomb scares and murder threats? You tell your wife that there are no hassles here. Sharade is looking after everything. If Brahmins progress even a tad, they will pounce on them! The society has turned bad! But we want you. Come away! I am ever anxious for you there."

Gopal didn't know how to answer his mother. He hadn't so far told her anything about the bomb scare and the threat to his life. *But now the electronic media, E-TV channel, Kasthuri channels are shooting and beaming it live. Especially since they are doing it targeting my name, mother is concerned.* Gopal started crying too. He had broken down responding to mother's heart-wrenching call. He hadn't so far caved in. He had answered every question with remarkable courage. Whatever his celebrity status, he was ever the child to his mother. His mother must have heard on the phone the *sora sora* sounds of his sobs. *Since Gopal couldn't utter words, the pressure has expressed in tears in the eyes and the throat has choked,* she must have thought.

"Why, my child, are you crying! Don't cry! Chuck your resignation letter at them and come away! Drum up courage, my son! Sitting on the throne there doesn't make you big. Bigness is something different. Many have gone on to win the *Jnanapitha* award, writing in the wilderness of the woods and of villages, not writing in cosy AC rooms in the buzz of cosmopolitan cities. Where did people like Pampa, Valmiki, Vyasa and Kalidasa write?! Sitting in five-star hotels?! Desert that desire! Freedom from desire and fear is the only freedom! There is another younger sister waiting to get married. What if something happens to you! Wipe your eyes dry!"

Seethamma, Gopal's mother, grew strong and assertive only after her husband's death. This was mainly to set in order or repair the situation due to the loss of the property. She had raised the eldest son, Gopal with special care, realizing that he would have a significant role in seeing to the growth of the other eleven siblings. Gopal couldn't disobey mother's idea about his own marriage. She had protected and developed the fields and gardens in Shambhonalli, Koratagere and Akkirampura along with raising her children well. Fear was something she didn't seem to know. The family rolled on because Sharade had simulated mother's position. *How does mother know that people had got the Jnanapiitha award without holding power? She said that didn't require position and power. Who would give me more assurance? Maybe she thinks desire is per se wrong. In that case we would only be encouraging this dirty politics. Nothing that mother is saying is false.*

"*Amma*! Nothing will happen to me." Gopal now took up the word, a persuasive tone in his calm voice. "Don't worry. This is the handiwork of some cowards. If I encourage them by resigning, wouldn't that amount to capitulation to them? I am your son. Like you, I will face the situation head-on, with courage. Do you want me to be dubbed a chicken-hearted fellow because of your affection for me? If all this ends in disaster, people who are responsible for this will face the music. There is law and there is police. They will be punished. They also would have that fear. You be bold!"

I have said this to Saraswathi as well. Let us not lose control and restraint in any situation. You said some people who won the *Jnanapiitha* award were not in power. But that was during those bygone times. Times have changed. There is now an intimate relation between literature and power. This is the war now raging. You think for yourself. It is one year since I got this position. I will be at complete peace after two more years. No one will bother me then. I will, as you suggest, come to Madhugiri and be at both places. I will write at both places, here and there. You tell everyone over there: Sharade, Sahana, Sadhana, Sangita, Savitri, Jayasimha, Narayana, Sriramu, Shivaramu, Raghavendra and Susheela. No one need call me separately. Tell everyone nothing is going to happen to me, Okay? I don't speak to anyone these days. I spoke so much to you because it is my obligatory moral duty to solace, soothe and reassure you."

The emotional way in which Gopal spoke to his mother surprised the literati gathered there. *Is there such a big family behind Gopal?* They wondered. Who would in any case enquire about one's family background? A litterateur's personal life is hidden, like the fruit behind a tree's foliage. One gets one's experience only Could one get it on any other footing? It is certainly available for a trade off with money. This personal experience would later get recognised as universal truth and win popular approval. It has to do with everyone's life. Gopal felt embarrassed that everyone had overheard what he had spoken his mother. Yet he solaced himself with the belief that everyone would have a heart that probes such personal griefs and that it had come out spontaneously. Gopal had shown that no matter how big the son has grown to be, he is always, first and foremost, a son to his mother. People didn't take the fact that Gopal, so far wordless, had opened out with his mother otherwise. That they had understood him gave them a measure of comfort. This was the bigness that litterateurs ought to have. That was humanity and love.

Another world, apart from this, is that of creativity. That is the prologue to the expression of this love, affection, nature, creation, the natural rhythm and the feelings and ideas thereof. That is technique, maturity and fulfillment. It is the common belief that money, power, evil scheming and politics etc, which are different from this, wouldn't dominate the litterateur's mindset. Yes, one may agree superficially. But one can not agree that was the whole truth. Some get close to politicians, move with them. Get intimate, praise them to the skies to grind their own axes. If that politician loses his relevance, they fawn on other politicians. They tail those who had spat on them earlier. For politicians keeping literary figures close to themselves is a matter of prestige. Literary figures swagger, getting money, positions of authority and gifts from politicians.

But now the heat was on him, the litterateur.

Wiping his face with his hanky Gopal sat back wordless, as before. Balasubramania, a senior literary critic and Gopal's well-wisher parleyed with all present there before deciding to stage a protest the following day. He then went on to get a letter signed by all to be sent to the police inspector and the Chief Minister. He had a long discussion with the gathering of about forty people there about drafting the letter of the purpose of the proposed protest, saying he would prepare and get it ready by tomorrow and he wanted suggestions from the people there. A draft of a twenty-point agenda was prepared, stating what kind of security they would expect from the state, and pointing out the indifference the state had evinced about their security and so on. Balasubramania showed it to Gopal.

Having a look at it, Gopal wondered, rather cynically, whether that was of any use to deal with the present situation. But *they are all my ardent well wishers, I shouldn't dampen their enthusiasm*, he thought before, forcing a smile onto his face, he acknowledged, "I am grateful for your help, support and your trust. I will cooperate with you, in whatever you may do!"

The police scoured every room of the Kannada Bhavana right from the morning till about three in the afternoon. But there was no trace of the bomb. They deployed a bomb-detecting machine, and huge dogs. It could be a hoax scare. The call had been made from a coin-PCO. Who to ask who did the calling? This was how these coin telephone booths were being misused. One day they said the bomb was in Gopal's car and on another day they said it had been planted in Kannada Bhavana. If this happened for the third time, one couldn't think it a hoax because then it could be genuine! This, the smartness of terrorists, the police knew. That was why they didn't take their work lightly. Even if they showed some indifference or delay in other minor matters, there would not be a disaster. But one couldn't do that with bomb threats. This has to do, not with an individual, but a whole community of people. Who was behind this was the whole question now. Sundar, the Investigating Officer came down the steps talking to Kalyan Singh, the Police Inspector, saying there was a link between the bomb scare and the letter that Gopal had received.

"They might have got this letter written by somebody before posting it to the Minister. We have submitted those letters for enquiry. We will get to know some things before long. Let us not inform Gopal about this just now. I will speak to the Home Minister. I will seek his permission to deploy security police, not just at the entrance to Kannada Bhavana but in every nook of the building. That should be arranged at the soonest. We can't detail two cops at the entrance of the Kannada Development Authority and be done. Security is the urgency as of now!"

"If Gopal goes on leave for a few weeks, to his home town or somewhere, we won't have this trouble, will we?" said Kalyan Singh by way of a reaction.

The two stopped the walk down the steps.

Chewing the cud for a while, Sundar disagreed. "No, no! We can not ask Gopal to go on leave. He is a man of prestige and a man of his conscience. By asking him to go on leave, we are freeing the accused. You may know that even false threat is also a crime. Even if Gopal goes on leave, he has to come back, right? Even if he goes on leave on his own, that would wreck our job of nabbing the accused. Another point is if he goes home to his native village, terrorists will adopt a different strategy. They won't give up till their aim is fulfilled. Don't you think so? So let us give this up and take up investigation through some other sources. You interrogate his security and his office staff, his personal assistant. No one among them should go on leave during the course of the investigation. Even if they do, they should give strong reasons. Ask a cop to watch their movements twenty four hours. Even if somebody moves around the Development Authority suspiciously, ask him to detain him, make notes and let us know. No matter whose hand is there in this episode, we should get to him. No submitting to any pressure, political or otherwise. Thousands of such ministers come and go. Good people shouldn't undergo any trouble, okay?"

As Sundar and Kalyan Singh came down, Balasubramanyam and company gave Kalyan Singh the protest note as he said, "Give this to the Circle Police Inspector. The protest will be staged right here. We have said we won't stop till the Chief Minister himself comes over and meets us." The two officials exchanged looks.

"What is this protest for? What would the Chief Minister say? He would say this is injustice. This shouldn't have happened. But why do you think he wouldn't face such a situation? What you are doing would have some meaning if you declare who the protest is against. Such threats are not proper for literary figures. But it has happened! What to do? It is not proper to point fingers at ministers. So your protest is just against this incident. It is really of no use!"

So saying the Investigating Officer took a look at the text of the note given to him. The note asked government to take utmost precaution so such incidents do not recur. Handing the note to, and asking Kalyan Singh, to hand it over to Circle Inspector Kumar, Sundar got on to his jeep and left.

'Sir! We have done a thorough investigation. There is no hint of any bomb. You can now go to your room. We will see that Kannada Bhavana is given full security. Don't be scared. This is only a false alarm. Let me know about any person you suspect. You just give me missed call. I will be right with you."

Some six police personnel stood guard in front of the Kannada Bhavana. Two stood at the door with the bomb-detection gadget, frisking every visitor. Amidst all the din, the protest was staged too. Some fifty senior literati took part in the protest. Rajagopal couldn't participate. He had been appointed by the government. He sashayed over and sat in his chair at the Kannada Development Authority. The general understanding was that the government didn't quite care for such protests. The protest was but a symbolic event.

Kumar the Circle Inspector visited the site of the protest and asked his staff there to detail five cops at the site before leaving. He came back after a while and said, "The Chief Minister has gone over to Shivamogga on some work. You may present your grievance to the Deputy Chief Minister. He is going to be here just to see you people. You please sit in the shade. Your participation at such protest meetings is a question of the land's prestige and dignity. We feel embarrassed to stand watching people like you."

Sitting inside, Gopal observed what was happening outside. He felt pained deep inside, thinking of the distinguished people having to sit at the protest. The protest would do nothing more than warn the terrorists. Nothing else. One would also feel a bit emboldened. The whole thing had been telecast last night. There was no way of keeping it under wraps. *We should somehow get to know from Mallikarjuna Swamy if there were any from the literary circle close to any ministers*, thought Gopal to himself.

Pouring the water in the bottle into the glass, Gopal drank it. He then walked over to the corridor. All the programs of the Development Authority were deferred. All offices of the Kannada Bhavana were wrapped in anxiety.

While some said it was because of Gopal that such an atmosphere had been created, others said such intimidation was not proper for the academia. Like this Gopal was food for gossip for everyone. Amidst all this came a missed call from Ushe. Gopal didn't answer the call.

At times of anxiety such attraction recedes. No infatuation and fascination would stay after a long while. What remains is just the mind. Such shocks would be successful in repairing the imbalance of the mind and restoring equilibrium. But by that time the mind would have been battered and bruised. Would longing for love, standing in a vicious circle get you what is basically ungettable. If there is a no, it is all over. Let us see when things converge in time. I have been deprived of gratified pleasure in the end. Is gratified pleasure and happiness something that you get with her intimacy? Why did I think so? There is no answer to this question in my mind. He had lost only what was to be lost. *Now the same thoughts and the same suffering. This kind of pain and distress is making life dull and insipid. While the heat outside is of one kind, the one inside is another. What do I think about, being caught in the cleft stick?*

****

The Deputy Chief Minister arrived. Putting his joined palms together against his chest, he greeted every protestor before getting everyone introduced to himself and saying, "All of you please come in! We will talk, sitting in the hall." He took two hours, talking about the present episode, displaying his solicitude and love of humanity and ending with his suggestion that it was only Rajgopal who was probably responsible for the present pass. But the people present there didn't agree with the minister's assessment of the situation. "Rajgopal isn't that kind of a personality. The minister shouldn't place the blame at Gopal's door without any evidence to back it," they submitted. "He is an eminent person among Kannada litterateurs. If someone gives such a statement in this confused atmosphere, that would create room for misunderstanding."

We don't know what went through the minister's mind when people said what they said. "Tell me what I can do! The Home Minister has agreed to provide all kinds of security. Let us take precautionary measures so such incidents don't recur. But how does one know who will do what? Our positions are also subject to such threats some day. We can't say we will not be intimidated. One can't say this shouldn't happen to literary figures: that it has happened is true, isn't it? All right! We will from now on provide every security possible. You are all thinkers. Scholars. When you get honoured, you feel happy, and when there is trouble you blame us!"

After long talks, the minister left agreeing to some things. Rajgopal could apply for leave and go away to some tourist destination or to his native place or somewhere. Let the work of the Development Authority slow down. At least that way he could be away from death threats. His position wouldn't be in jeopardy because of this. Whatever may be the problem, he won't be replaced. We also hold him in great esteem. These words of the minister were like playing hide-and-seek in semi-darkness with eyes blindfolded. There is no credibility in what ministers speak. It has only the authority of power.

All the literary luminaries walked into Rajgopal's room. Their confidence-filled voices injected courage into Gopal. They also suggested to him that he could go over to his mother's place, and that that would reassure him, removing him, as it would, from the fear-filled scene of the murder threat. But none of this seemed correct to Gopal. Yet he treated them to some steaming hot brew of coffee before sending them off affectionately.

All this that has happened carries no meaning. The murder threat will hover and linger. Only I know this. Gopal found himself meditating about the happenings. *No minister can do anything about it. This is true of the police as well. They will do what they could. Some things are beyond anyone's control. They simply believe they are. But by way of taking precautions, the police can take some steps. What more can they do? One doesn't need a bomb to bump somebody off. There is no need of a bomb to do away with me. One could just intimidate. No matter how much I reassure myself, courage is sinking. I am about to be sixty. It is natural for me to feel that I have a life much bigger than this in the days ahead. But how? It is one year now since I experienced the happiness of landing the job of the Chairman of the Kannada Development Authority. I have felt a supremacy and dignity about the position. But now even that has been seriously dented. I don't feel just the threat of the words of "You will be murdered". I actually feel like I have been killed! Something inside me caved in. Is there something that can tamp my personality down so very deep? When none of this happened, how well and competently I was performing my duties! I feel my honour and dignity have taken a severe beating. Others are hassled because of me. Death threat for sure spells trouble. The police will guard me. But everyone is anxious about what would happen to these buildings in the event of a bomb explosion. No matter how high people hold you in esteem, if there is perceived trouble from you, the esteem that they hold you in will take some beating. As they suggested, I could indeed take leave and go over to my native place. But where is the guarantee that nothing would happen then?*

It was only Gopal who was getting these threats. If he was not there, there would neither be any threat nor anxiety. *So, what if they think removing me from the position I hold solves everything?* asked Gopal of himself. The situation was such that one couldn't say that that wasn't the case either. *How do I get out of this? When will i be free of this?* It was as if everything got murky and muddled. He couldn't see a path forward. He felt as if he was sinking.

"Sir!" called a voice just then.

It was Vasudhendra, the personal assistant to the Director of the Department of Kannada and Culture who stood at the door. He seemed to have come with the intent of saying something to Gopal.

"Hey, Mr Vasudhendra! Come in. Sit down! What is the news?"

Vasudhendra looked around.

Gopal had heard that he was a good man. He was the type that didn't talk unnecessarily. He had never come to Gopal to sit and talk with him. *There must be something the matter*, thought Gopal.

"Tell me! What is it?"

"Sir! It is the change at the helm that is the cause of this pain for you. Did you know?"

"Yes, I know. What could I do?"

"You have been nominated by the previous government. It seems you had rubbed the Deputy Chief Minister of that government against this government. You had given suggestions. You are the reason for pitting yourself against this government, they say. Are you?"

"That is not quite true. When somebody asks for suggestions, we should give, shouldn't we? Does that mean there should be such a death threat?"

"No. This death threat and the bomb scare have nothing to do with the minister. He can not stoop so low. But what I have come to tell you is something different. The Home Minister is asking the Chief Minister to replace you by some other littérateur. The Deputy Chief Minister also knows about this. They have discussed this confidentially. Satyamurthy, the Director of the Department of Kannada and Culture also knows about this. But please don't ask him about this. There is a conspiracy on even against him. The government is indifferent. But these troubles are not of his making."

"How do you say he is not responsible for these?"
"If there is an enquiry, and if one is caught, who would earn a bad name, tell me! Which party would be interested in incurring a bad name just for the position of the Chairmanship of the Development Authority?"

"Whose handiwork is this then?"
"We can't say whose it is. But the government is of course misusing it. One can use it as a reason for denying you things, can't one?"

His Personal Assistant Mallikarjuna Swamy, who was standing by the door, shuffled quietly in, and even as he said, "Sir, I am sorry I barged in, you seem to be talking about something!" stood as if ready to leave.
"Come in! Nothing special!" Gopal called him. He walked in, got some papers signed by Gopal before leaving right away.
Silence reigned for a while.
"Let's see what will happen, Vasudhendra!" Gopal piped up, breaking the silence. "Thanks for taking pains and the trouble of giving me the information."
"Sir, please keep this confidential. This man, Mallikarjun Swamy, comes in, overhears things and acts as if he hasn't overheard anything. It is such things that bring trouble!"
"....."
"Okay, Sir, I take leave!"
"Namsakaara!"

Gopal didn't get up from his chair. It wasn't the first time that Mallikarjuna Swamy had done that. Everyone would be curious to know about things that didn't concern them. But this bloke slyly makes it happen. And then shows it as if he means business. Vasudhendra is a delicate person. He must be around fifty years of age. He has been working here for the last twenty years. Very intelligent man. It is true that one can't deny or reject whatever he says. The minister may be unhappy with me for some reason. But would he do this because of that? Infamy is assured if he does that. Who else is doing this? Perhaps someone who is a rival to me is creating all this. But there is harmony, cooperation and synergy in literature. There is rebellion as well. But is terror a proper weapon for literary figures? A litterateur would certainly not do this. If a poet or litterateur has this cut throat eagerness, the world of Kannada belles letters has to hang its head in shame. Gopal submitted that this arena should not get to a position when it had to behead somebody on one's way to the throne. He sat all by himself.

"Sir, it is already seven. Won't you leave?" It was Mallikarjuna Swamy who'd broken his silence. "Shall I get you some coffee? You seem exhausted. You take some days' leave and go home to your mother or somewhere, Sir! That will take the load off your chest."
"I don't want coffee. Thanks! I will leave."

Gopal rose and left.
Poor fellow! thought Mallikarjuna Swamy. *What a great fellow Gopal is! His solemn gait has now shrunk. The dance of evil spirits seems to be on on his face.* Mallikarjuna Swamy tailed Gopal right up to the car before he handed Gopal the files as he breathed, "There is no much work tomorrow. Please take your time and come to the office leisurely. Don't get anxious, or sick and weary. Be lively and vibrant. Nothing will happen. I can say this much: it is only a threat. The bomb scare is only a hoax!" He left, getting his joined palms together against his chest in a parting greeting.
The security cop sat on the back seat. There were two cops on guard at home. But it was not necessary, felt Gopal. But what could be done? There was no other way for the present.

Saraswathi, who was waiting for her husband, didn't quite know why he was late. Gopal never used to tell his wife about such things. In his head right now were questions like why and who the person was and could be who was being recommended by the Home Minister. *Everyone would know. But this had been known only now. If i get to know, I could talk to him. Or*

119

else I can resign! I can prepare myself for things that might follow. Why should I torture the mind for this? Why should this spell trouble for others? My position would go still higher in that case. But if it indeed is true, I could talk to the Home Minister before giving a press statement and resign. I would that way have given body blow to the present government. Let me be free from all this. I will in any case get my pension. I could find fulfillment, doing some writing.

****

Chapter Seven

I will resign if things get disastrous.

This is what Gopal told everyone. *There is no other way. It is not proper to keep everyone on anxious tenterhooks because of me.* One week after he said this, the print media approached, and got a statement from, Gopal. *We need to toe the government's line. If it comes to it I will resign* was the stand Gopal took. This clearly was a fence-sitting stance. Gopal had a certain thing in mind when he took this stand. He felt light of being when he thought of the resignation, but he felt disgusted at the same time, it tearing at his heart. In the meantime the honourable Deputy Chief Minister himself called him to say, "Don't resign, Gopal! Let them do whatever they can! Don't let it scare you. We are there to back you." Gopal said no more than, "Okay, Sir!" *Let people write whatever they will,* he told himself wordlessly. *I will resign the moment I decide to.*

Gopal was now relaxed and happy after he arrived at this decision. He attended office. He talked to everybody smiling. In case somebody broached this to him, he would gloss over it, saying simply, "Why worry, now that I have decided to resign? Let them plant a bomb or stab me with a knife." Months have lapsed after he has said this. But he hadn't resigned. Nor had fresh threats come.

But the situation was tangibly tense.

The police security provided at the Kannada Bhavana was still in place. There was security at home and at the Development Authority. He had to endure it. He had to cooperate with the police. *The police is there for our protection. Life needs to adjust to everything and move ahead. Ever since I decided on resigning, I have never felt either anxious or scared. Nor has there been that zest for life since I gave up Ushe. That is, there is no anxiety, fear, enthusiasm or zest or passion of any kind. But how do we explain the smile playing on the face. Is it a higher state, overcoming everything in life? Is it a detached dispassionate state? This must be true. Mine is a state of renunciation that had transcended lust, greed and enamourment. It is important that I retain this deep intense feeling of renunciation.*

One has to lose something to get something. This, Saraswathi had also experienced. *If the husband's future and well-being are important, let him resign. We can make do with whatever we have without desiring more. We own a house. No spending on rent. There is no problem for leading a reasonable life. Gopal could pay more attention to his writing. The wisdom is in managing with whatever resources one has. If something untoward happens to him, what use is whatever money one has? Only my husband is important to me now.* She said as much: "If you feel like resigning, do it! You engage yourself in creative writing. Life will go on somehow."

But Gopal was only talking of resignation but deep inside he was thinking of many other things and venting them. *The Chairman is not all right. He talks of resigning but never tenders his resignation. With pressures mounting he must have gone mentally sick.* This was what Mallikarjuna Swamy said to other chairmen and to the Director of the Department of Kannada and Culture. This was the word doing the rounds now. The idea that the Chairman of the Kannada Development Authority had gone mad went viral. People believed that this might not be false. It was possible that the murder threat, the bomb scare, and a woman writer writing to the ministers assassinating his character and so on might have mentally wrecked him. Like this several tales about him took birth as days went by. This reached Saraswathi as well through the police. She on her part closely observed her husband's behavior.

Gopal would go out to attend his office saying he would resign. When asked on his return from office, he would change the topic, glossing over the matter. *My husband is hale and hearty. Nothing has happened to him. He never smiles at home. Would that mean he behaves differently at home and in the office? Isn't this wrong?* But it struck her after some thinking that everyone struggles to recover and be normal after experiencing shocks of the kind that he had gone through of late. *That must be the reason he was behaving the way he was behaving. How does he drive in this state of mind? He doesn't let others drive. We could have hired a driver. But we have to pay him! And have to follow him, which would take away our independence.*

Saraswathi also felt that *he could go on leave for a couple months to his native place. What can they do during that time? That would take away the disgust and weariness. What can these people really do? They pose only bogus threats. But negative mean thoughts create disaster for us.* She unbosomed her thoughts before her husband. "Go home to your village!" she suggested. "In any case you have to go for the postdeath ceremony of the father-in-law. You could stay there for a couple of months. Your mother would also feel happy and satisfied. You could also drill some sense into Srihari and arrange his marriage. This would be some sort of change for you. If there is some fraud here, publish it in the papers: let everyone see the injustice.'"

Her advice is all right, but I am afraid to go away suddenly leaving my position vacant. Gopal did some cud-chewing. *It doesn't seem right. As it is, they are creating all sorts of rumours. Later if they consider my leave as evidence to confirm me as mentally ill, there may not be much I can do. I should not create room for such injustice. If I talk to people smiling, they think I am really mentally sick. So let me put up a straight serious face!*

****

The smile disappeared.

It is difficult to reflect a relaxed mind on a serious face. It is indeed difficult to imagine one has a relaxed mind. The disconnect between the state of mind and the face! In sum he shouldn't leave work and so he kept attending office. He would go as an invited guest for book releasing functions. He would give talks wherever he went on the linkage between this ruthless and tyrannical terrorism, the literary realm and politics. Till the wounds of his mind were healed, he would perform, he thought, with great intensity, taking it as a great fight. People were scared to go to him now. His solemn face and personality would spark unease and fear in anyone. But literature enthusiasts would still treat him with great respect and reverence. Gopal too would respond to them cordially. But, loved or loathed, it was true Gopal became a rivet, a talking point in a sense for people around him. An attraction and a repulsion at the same time.

A terrible event came about in the meantime.

This further wounded and set Gopal back.

When one day Gopal was conversing with Chandrika, a member of the Development Authority in his room, Ushe rushed in like a gust of wind. All at sea, a rather sheepish Gopal welcomed her, as he showed her a chair to sit, "Come, Ms Usha!"

She had already got angry with him for talking to some woman. *If i am indifferent even now she will get furious,* thought Gopal *but that said, what do I talk to her in front of Chandrika? What would Chandrika think?* An embarrassing situation had been created. We don't know what went through Chandrika's mind. "Sir, you two talk! I will come back after five minutes," she suggested before leaving.

Gopal remained wordless.

The moment Chandrika went out, Ushe rained a shower of cinders on Gopal. "I should not talk to you. But other women can for any length of time. If I talk, you say the police is tapping your phone. You evade by lying, don't you? If you want something from us, you placate by saying you will break your chest open and show that my name is written in there in your heart. You call me sweetie, honey etc and now you publicise on TV about letter threats and bomb scares. Who was she that was sitting with you? Call her, I will ask her!"

"Usha! Speak softly. There is police and there is the attender. Listen to me! She is a member of our Development Authority. You shouldn't mistake her."

"That means you should respect such people, and cheat me! You men can behave like this with any number of women, can't you? And at your age! Everything seems okay for you."

"Don't blurt out whatever comes to your mind, Usha! Instead of solacing me, did you come here to demean me? You call me a debauchee! What if I call you the same? This is my office. I have a position and dignity. I am in a state of anxiety and shock. Don't fuel it! There is police, be careful!"

"If there is police, call them. i will tell everyone everything about you and your conduct. You asked a woman writer to go to your house with a book it seems. Calling us with endearments like honey, sweety etc like a poet, you fool us, don't you?"

Ushe's words were like a hammer bashing Gopal's head. Gopal flew off the handle. The two cops stationed outside scampered to the door. By the time Mallikarjuna Swamy also came over, Gopal had socked Ushe on her cheeks. Everyone looked on, shell-shocked.

"Rein in your tongue! I have never behaved like this with anyone. I will not talk with you either from now on. Chandrika! Please come here!"

Chandrika, who was sitting in the office of the Development Authority, came quietly over into the Chairman's room. She was wondering who this woman was, why the Chairman had smacked her and why they were talking the way they were talking. In the meanwhile everyone from the department of Kannada and Culture and other academies converged there.

"Have I ever behaved inappropriately with you? Please tell her!"

"Madam! i don't know who you are," spoke up Chandrika, mustering courage. "Rajagopal has never ever behaved inappropriately with any woman. He has behaved honorably with me as well. Somebody has hatched a conspiracy to frame him. This being the case, who are you, madam, to poke him like you did?"

Usha was wiping the tears sluicing out of her eye sockets. In the meantime the police constables came in.

"Madam! Please leave immediately," they said. "No need of unnecessary talk. If you talk more, we will have to call the inspector. There should be no such unpleasant incident here. They will subject it to inquiry." People got alert with the cops' words of caution.

Gopal heated up. Had he had an inkling that something like this would happen, he would have acted with restraint. What to reply if someone asked who she was? Coming into play, his discretion rescued him.

"Please leave without any more talk. People are doing all sorts of things to put me in the dock and get the position. Why do you put me to further trouble, imagining things? Policemen! Please take her out. Please! Don't come again with such things."

This raised Usha's hackles.

"Why should you tell the police to take me out? I will also say the same thing. I will move the court against you. Besides cheating a backward class woman, you have insulted me by rapping me on my cheeks in front of all. You are now asking the police to drag me out, aren't you? See if I don't have the same police do the same thing with you. I will slap an atrocity case on you, I swear!"

This had everyone there gaping.

Although everyone looked upon her as a devil on the scene of some planetary influence on the Kannada Development Authority, it was as if some secret was unfolding, some plot was unfurling and some inner pain jumped out with all its ferocity. Something that should not have happened had happened and from someone who shouldn't have done it. The police held her by her arms and took her out. People crowding the doorway gave way. "You scumbag!" Usha let rip, at the top of her lungs even as she went down the steps. "I will slap a court case against you and have you behind bars. How many more women will you wreck? He is a big literary figure, it seems. A chairman it seems! Slaps a woman, the jerk that he is! A tiger with a cow's face. These mother-fuckers trample the backward classes. We have to dance to their tunes."

For the listeners, this might create curiosity, surprise and some entertainment. Those who were downstairs began to rush up, attracted by this. The security police staff hemmed her in, and, seeing that she didn't utter so much as a cheep, took her up to the Ravindra Kalakshetra and left her there.

I don't know how many people saw this and how many overheard all this. Why did this happen? It was as if some venomous snake had crawled all over my body and my body was now an overflowing pool of poison. The head is feeling heavy and my vision is blurring. Things seemed to fall apart. The centre is unable to hold. It was as if the nerves had gone crooked. Rajagopal collapsed just where he stood. People around held him. As he sagged down, a call was made to Jayadeva Cardiology Hospital for an ambulance. A doctor came around and after checking him, declared, "There is no danger. There has been a mild heart attack. Call his house!"

Mallikarjuna Swamy immediately called Saraswathi's mobile to say,

"Don't panic, madam! We are all here! He is out of danger, so the doctor has said. Take your own time, coming."

He took Gopal to Jayadeva Hospital in the ambulance. The doctor there checked his plasma blood sugar levels, his B.P, and did an ECG test before putting him on drips to inject insulin to bring down the sugar levels. He was kept under observation. Gopal became conscious by the time these tests were done. The doctor warned him that he should not overthink, and that worrying would thwart their efforts, hiking the BP and sugar levels. And people like him should absorb such things in life.

Nothing that the doctor said registered.

Even though he didn't want to remember her words, and her unseemly high-pitched voice, they came back to him, over and over again, filling his ears like molten lead. *I should forget them! There is no other way. Or I should die. My honour and prestige will bite the dust. Will she really get me arrested? Will she slap a case against me? And if so, the chairmanship would be a wisp of my dreams! Ayyo! Oh Sin! where are you hunting me down from? For what and whose fury are you taking me as a sacrificial animal? What wrong did I do?*

Gopal screamed at the top of his lungs before he flung away the drip tubes. The doctor on duty, who was talking to Mallikarjuna Swamy outside the ICU came rushing in, and asking the nurse to hold Gopal tight, securing the drip tube with his fingers, and injecting some tranquillizer, let the insulin pass through. Rajagopal slept. Just then Saraswathi thudded up. Mallikarjuna Swamy related all that had happened.

"Who is she?" asked a curious Saraswathi.

"We don't know, madam! So many such people keep coming and keep blurting out crap! You pay attention to the chairman. There is every facility here. He may have to be here for a couple of days. There is no danger for now. But you should see that he doesn't get anxious and tense. After this you ask him to apply for a couple of months of leave on health grounds. Let him recover. He is anxious because she has threatened to sue him. Let her do whatever she will. We won't allow that. Sir should not come to the Development Authority for a few days. Life, and health, will be difficult if he gets tense, letting this haunt him. These drugs and injections curtail the brain, draining one of courage and spunk. Doctors would be on their toes to prescribe a hundred medicines for even small ailments, medicines which only take the sap out of you. They only make the disease disappear for now. You be courageous, madam! I will visit you daily. I have paid some advance to the hospital. They will settle the accounts when he is discharged. Madam, please don't jib if you want anything from me. Treat me as your own younger brother."

Saraswathi set to crying.

She had made vows to all and sundry gods for the sake of her husband. *But this had happened. Why did he allow the woman to speak? Why did she speak the way she did? Why did he slap her? Oh God! I don't figure out anything. She belongs to a backward class it seems. She will slap an atrocity case on him, it seems. Why did he bring these things on himself? He should have followed the saying,* Poor fellow, be much like what I keep you as! *Instead why did he bring upon himself the shrew roaming the streets?! What sin did I commit in which lifetime? I have no children. I could I thought look at husband's face in the absence of children and eke out a living, but Oh my Father! What misfortune You have got me into? I shouldn't inform this to anyone. Mother-in-law would panic. The police are there in any case guarding the house. I could apply for two days' leave and stay here. If Mallikarjuna Swamy could be here for an hour in the morning, I could go home and bring a couple of sarees for myself and a panche and jubba for him.*

She wiped her tears away. Coming out, she sat outside the ICU. "We have allotted a special ward for you, madam," submitted a doctor. "You can shift there."

"What special ward, doctor?!" she exclaimed. "When my husband is here, what do I do going there?"

The doctor had nothing to say to this. He asked her to get some medicines for the night before tagging, "Be bold! How does one manage if you get weak yourself?"

****

He would have to stay at the hospital, they had said, only for two days. But the stay, it turned out, was to last a week. This was because there were fluctuations in his blood sugar levels and the ECG. In the meanwhile the chairmen of all Authorities, Akademies, literature enthusiasts, his die-hard fans and others met Gopal to wish him speedy recovery and to reassure him. The words they spoke enabled Gopal to endure everything.

128

"Don't worry, Gopal! We are always there to support you. If someone has done this on purpose, you aren't responsible, are you? We don't even know who she is. She has come here to raise a stink. You can say someone has conspired to frame you. If you let that weaken you, they would target and further harass you."

Such words brought Gopal some superficial comfort. But deep inside truth would tend to heat and boil the heart.

Inspector Kalyan Singh visited the hospital in the meanwhile. Gopal related to him all that had happened. He asked the Inspector about this thing called 'atrocity' and how people moved the case about it. Kalyan Singh explained to him what it was, what could be the punishment if convicted, about the possibility of a bail, and the extent of penalty etc.

"Would that affect my position of chairmanship?"
"That depends on how the present government views it. If you feel bold enough to fight it, approaching a minister is what you should do."

Gopal didn't speak for a while.
The inspector himself then took up the word.
"Who is this Usha, Sir!? Why did she come here and behave the way she did? Please tell me the truth! If you are honest with the police, you will stand to gain. If not now, tell me when you recover. There is no problem."

Gopal kept mum.
He sat with his hands on his head. What to tell the Inspector? He couldn't say the truth. Nor could he afford not to. There was, besides, Saraswathi, beside him. Imagine him posing the question right in the hospital! *These police people are like this! If they have some suspicion, they would shoot questions then and there.* Sweat began surfacing on Gopal. Representatives of the inner turmoil and pain, sweat beads sat like pearls on his forehead.

"Okay, Sir! You can tell me later!" he said, putting an end to Gopal's misery. "I will see you later. You take some day of leave and go home, Sir! You can join duty after some days of real rest."
The inspector left.

But his poser began to bug Saraswati. No matter how many times she asked her husband, he evaded the issue by saying things like, "I don't know. It seems someone has conspired to unleash her on me!"

We can't say how true and how false this reply sounded to Saraswathi. But she reduced to silence, not being keen to poke her husband again and again. In fact she didn't really want to probe it. She had done the asking only because the police inspector had asked such a question. It was not known whether her curiousity was satisfied or not, but she kept silent, saying to herself that his recovery, discharge from the hospital and return home was all that was needed.

****

Usha, who had threatened to slap an atrocity case on him, didn't carry out her threat. She in fact felt disgusted with her own behavior. She felt ashamed that her words had led to a near-disaster. When she learnt Gopal had suffered a mild heart attack, she thought better of even talking to him, let alone moving the court against him. This made Gopal heave a sigh of relief. *But so many people were witness to the scene of that day. How many people do I answer? Let me know go home to the village on the excuse of health. Saraswathi would be here shuttling to and fro. The police would be here in any case watching over the house. I would be that way paying attention to mother's health. I have no particularly pressing work here. The Deputy Chief Minister had assigned some work the other day. I could ask him to let me do it after i come back from leave.*

I still have two years of this chairmanship. People have already kicked up so much jealousy-driven ruckus. How would they bear two more years? If I resign now it would amount to total defeat. It would amount to an admission of my moral disqualification. Why did Ushe do this? Her very name sets my body boiling. Poor Saraswathi! She has been taking good care of me, taking leave of absence from work. She feeds me oven-hot food and hot water. She washes my clothes, bathes me daily, keeps other things like bedspreads, bedsheets etc neat and clean. She has this love of the husband. I never tried to placate her. That kind of sensitivity, of love, affection, concern, bashfulness vis-a-vis her I never felt. An unwritten agreement of this kind has underlain our equation. This is the reality. I should let my mind adjust to this. There is no room for any other feeling. With Ushe now it is like a stick broken unambiguously into two. She would now be on the other side of the wall that has arisen between us. I should never ever have any soft corner for her. She is, besides, my student. Is that the kind of respect that one gives one's teacher? What words! "I will slap a case against you! "You scumbag, with not a whit of honour and respect!", "How many women he must have cheated!"...

Oh God! To recall what she spoke would be to fill oneself with venom! I had so much emotional attachment to her. I had loved her so very much! Is there an unseen hand at work? Why did she do this to me? Even if I don't reveal the nature of our relationship, she herself might! What if she does?! The possibility gives me the shivers. Kalyan Singh might enquire about her workplace. What would she say? And my honour would go for a toss! I should tell the inspector that I don't know who she is! I could also say she was my student. We loved each other and since a marriage was not possible, she is now blackmailing me. In case they get some information of her whereabouts, she might say a lot of things about me. So it is better I say I don't know her. But what if the inspector gets to know he would deride me saying I lied. I would become small whether or not I tell the truth. The best way out is to avoid answering any queries.

And what do I tell my office staff, the computer madam, clerks, committee members of other academies, chairmen, workers, literature enthusiasts? What if they come to know we had an affair? Wouldn't they demean me, degrade and debase me? I hadn't got to meet Ushe for a long time. It was recently i got to meet her. She didn't marry, she said. I believed everything. Now things have panned out the way they have! Who would believe this if you told anyone this? They would blame only me. People would only say that one should guard one's character, the prestige and honour of the position one is holding and not hold someone who one doesn't recognize responsible. But I was wrapped in her love, wasn't I? That is not untrue. I never felt it was wrong. But now it is chasing me down like a ghost.

Facing the reality has in itself become a big challenge now. How could I now go about with my head held high and with my prestige and dignity intact? What if she divulges the nature of our relationship with someone? That would mean death even while being alive. I shouldn't have got close to her again. She hasn't moved the court for now. But what if they dig out details of who she is etc? There are now new technologies of polygraph, lie-detection test etc. I would be caught if that happens, wouldn't I? I shouldn't for the life of me give out hints of details *about her. I quailed at the bomb scare so far. Oh a new heart-wrenching fear has begun to tear at me. But there were others who would share this anxiety created by the bomb scare. This fresh fear is something I can't unbosom to anyone. It is burning my insides. My love and the bodily forms of lust burned fiercely for some time during the evening of my life, and now are hunting me down. It is only now that I realise that this is all there is to it. Did she come to love, or swallow me up. My state is neither this side nor that, neither fully living nor fully dead. I don't even have the strength to say it is false. While it would be one kind of falsehood if I say I don't know who she is, to say somebody has made her frame me would be another. Because she is possessive about me Ushe has flown off the handle. Woman always exercises her right that her lover should not even smile at another woman, let alone talk with her. Ushe is no exception. She has done what she has because of her love for me. But this is excessive emotionality. Shouldn't she be serious and dignified? Shouldn't be aware of my position and prestige? Why did she speak such harsh agitated words? It wasn't necessary at all to scream the way she did.*

Every morning as he wakes up, the same problem presents itself before him. Saraswathi has begun to go to her college. Rajgopal hasn't as yet applied for leave. But he hasn't been attending office either. Mallikarjun Swamy has been coming home with any mail he might have and getting his signature on official documents. Whenever he came home, Gopal would ask, even if hesitantly, "Who is she? Did she come again?"

"No, Sir!" he would reply. "She hasn't come again. But people in other akademies and in the department of Culture are talking all sorts of things. Suspicious tales have sprung up about her. But you don't worry, Sir! Instead of responding helpfully to such situations, these people fuel the fire. Why did she speak the way she did, sir? Maybe someone has sent her to frame you, and bring you a bad name, isn't that so?"

"Yes. I also feel the same way."

If only others assume this! Gopal said to himself. *I could then escape. Mallikarjuna Swamy is saying people are taking all sorts of things. What are they talking?*

Gopal couldn't keep from asking, "What are the others talking?"

"They are saying some woman writer has sent a letter to the minister about you. The woman may be this woman, they were saying. Don't worry,

Sir! The longer it is heated, the brighter would gold shine. You will have good times, Sir! People who have done heinous things go about as if nothing has happened. Why should you worry, you are such a great man?"

Gopal would feel emboldened the moment Mallikarjun Swamy spoke those words. He would feel a measure of cold comfort. But when he was all by himself, he would feel desolate, with Ushe appearing before him in a hallucination and laughing a hideous laugh. It would be as if a huge wave lashed the shore and he was flown away. *The mind which didn't feel scared by murder threats and bomb scares is quailing because of her! This anxiety caused by her is more penetrative than the bomb and murder threats. So much so that I am getting increasingly weak. She said I was a cheat, a tiger with a cow's mask. It is as if my whole personality is sinking. Do i deserve such descriptions?*

No matter how talented man may be and no matter how many awards and hon ours he has won, he becomes a midget in this matter. It is as if a snake has bitten you. If only I overcome this somehow! I shouldn't get into such things ever again. Let her do whatever she will. I shouldn't act in haste. I should keep to myself. No anger, no speaking any words. Let me neither invite such things nor give them up. If you step on live cinders and then dip your leg in cold water, there are bound to be blisters. It would be more than okay if I get back to attending the Development Authority office like before. I will have won my battle.

Many people wrongly construed Rajgopal's situation. Some sympathized with him. In his absence there was hushed talk at the office about the whole episode. For the woman to speak so demeaningly about him, there must have been something the matter between him and her, they thought. Otherwise why would he ask her to go away instead of asking the police to arrest her. Why should he have collapsed? All biggies are like this: live cinders camouflaged in ash.

He was in this way the butt of small disparaging talk. Not that had Gopal started attending office, they wouldn't have slandered him. But the fact that he took leave only served to loosen tongues.

****

Chapter Eight

Ushe's house was in the Mahalaxmi Extension. It was quite a big house for her, who lived alone. She had successfully performed all life responsibilities. With the funds she had saved, she had bought a site and built a house there within two years of her migration to Bengaluru. It was now ten years. Her younger brothers and sisters kept visiting her along with their families. But in the end she was all by herself.

Today she somehow didn't feel like getting up: she felt so totally out of sorts. She had in some form got back the love she had lost thirty years back. She felt so animated and energetic that she would put on a variety of blingy sarees. She would smear her cheeks with a variety of talcum powder and snow. She worked daily on gadgets that kept her slim and svelte. She would visit beauty parlours to maintain her long and shiny tresses, polishing them. When she went out to visit her lover, she would have an expensive facial, have her eye lashes and eye brows trimmed and beautified, have a vigorous workout, tying a waist band around her waist so she looked young and seductive. This she used to do even before she came by Gopal. Now these body exercises of preventive maintenance augmented. She would exercise restraint even in the food intake. But her balloon had burst. Not that Gopal had asked her not to go to him. But the snake of some sneaking doubt had entered her head and was wagging its raised hood. She never regretted the fact she never married while he did. She indeed thought the gratified happiness she got with him was her fortune. But this was different from that. *That I loved such a gentleman and he in turn loved me was the only pride that was to stay in life*, thought she. But there are no witnesses to such a relationship. Gopal never allowed her to take photographs of them together even on her cell phone. Love was only for love. The only thing that brought her comfort was the belief that none would give the other any trouble or discomfort. Nobody would agree to things like photographs, evidence, horoscope, caste and stuff. In the bygone times people would deride people with descriptions like 'keep', 'concubine' etc. The practice exists even today. People would do that if it is for outward display, with the two moving regally about, sitting by each other in swanky cars. They think this way of doing it unseen will not cause the use of the same word. But by the time they realize that this is indeed that, the end would have arrived.

This is now Ushe's worry. It was not as if someone described her like that. *Even if someone describes me as a keep or a prostitute, let them! Would not that be true even of him? It would. Is the word only for women? Would nobody say 'the keep' of a man? What is the hassle? Would the society approve if I marry him now? Would Gopal agree? In case Saraswathi says yes, that would amount to gross disrespect. It would be amount to being dead even while being live.* So it was several days since she gave this up.

This is my lot, she told herself before resting, feeling resigned to it. An odd thing that had happened fifteen days back however kept haunting her.

Ushe had been invited to speak on woman's problems on a Dalit platform in Ravindra kalakshetra. A minister was to take part. She had called her lover over. She was not a famous person like Gopal was. But Gopal had declined her invitation, saying, "I never attend programmes of which I am not an invited guest and which are designed for politicians. I would like to be behind the political screen. I don't like fanning them." This did dampen Ushe, but it was after all love, wasn't it? One should adjust oneself. She didn't force him. *But would not he come at least for my sake* was the question. This didn't end here.

An odd reverse poked and dented her self-respect.

The function at the Ravindra Kalakshetra had been slated for five o' clock in the evening. A street play on the exploitation of Dalit women had been arranged before that in front of Ravindra Kalakshetra. The guests, invitees and the audience were to watch the play before moving in for the formal function. One of the invitee guests was Ushe. The Deputy Chief Minister was the Chief Guest. Shivalingiah, the Dalit poet was to inaugurate it. Ushe was to speak on the exploitation of Dalit women. Some

Dalit leaders were watching the street play standing in the front row. Ushe's thoughts would revolve around Gopal. No matter where she was, no matter what she happened to be doing, the thought of him occupied her sensitive mind. There was an interval of two minutes after half the play had been staged. Behind the crowd of onlookers, there was a passageway left vacant, sufficient for a car to drive through, which led to the Kannada Bhavana. Just at that moment a swank red car drove fast towards the Kannada Bhavana. A woman drove it. She looked delightfully compelling. Ushe looked out of the corners of her eyes. The woman was talking, happily smiling with whoever was sitting beside her. When Ushe realised who it was that the driving woman was talking to, she felt as if a thousand scorpions stung her all at once!

It was, hold your breath, Rajagopal!

He was smiling too. Declaring his love to Ushe, Gopal had affirmed a thousand times, "I will prise open my heart and show you my love! Only you are there, none else!" But now the same man was chatting up some woman after declining her invite to attend her programme. Was it a dream, she wondered. Was it really Rajagopal? *May be it was somebody else?* She moved her eyes again at him. *Yes, it is Gopal! Gopal, who wore a cream coloured suit, looked handsome. It is Gopal, my life, my everything! Shall I run and ask him why he was moving with her? But in the eyes of society, what is his status and what is mine? Am I his wife? No, I am not. But who is she? What right does she have to talk to him smiling the way she was.* There was a fierce dance in Ushe's innards of boiling lava! Turmoil. Pain. Ushe couldn't stand there. She was curious to know who she was. She struggled to bring that keen curiosity under control. Her imagination ran riot. *Didn't he come to listen to my speech? He is coming back from somewhere.* The next scenes blurred. She didn't see anything. *I shouldn't worry about this for now. I should speak, as per the programme. If I don't speak well at the function, I will be the butt of ridicule. But why did Gopal do this? Who is she? How could he behave with her the way he was? Even if he did, who would come to know? If that is not the case why would a serious minded man like him go about in a car with a woman chatting like that? He tells me, "Don't come here in your car. Come walking! People would note down your car number and find us out." But now is it okay to travel sitting right by the side of a woman! But I haven't ruled this is wrong and that is right. I don't have that kind of familiarity and freedom with him, do I? Nothing more than some love and some bodily gratification.* Except for this, if one came to think of it, she had nothing to do with him: she couldn't ask questions like why he was going wherever he was going, why he was seeing such and such a woman, why he was talking to such and such a person and say things like he should put up a solemn knotted face with others etc. it was not possible either to expect such things or to be stubborn about such things. In case she grew obstinate, the relationship would weaken. Or even if you were telling the truth, it would look like falsehood. Or he would reply with, "I may talk without any reason. You ought not to mistake it even if talk with some people." There was no evidence for any improper behavior. It was not possible for Ushe to pursue such things either. Who was she? Why did she bring him in her car? Where was his car? She looked like a Brahmin woman. It wasn't for sure Saraswathi. Saraswathi was not that advanced. She never went to any programme with Gopal.

As her speech ended, she walked over to the Deputy Chief Minister and said she had an urgent case to attend to, so she had to leave immediately and she might be excused. "Okay, you can leave," said the minister. "There is no problem." When Ushe came out, it was six thirty. People around were talking among themselves that there was another programme going on in the adjacent Nayana Auditorium. Ushe's thoughts were all riveted on the Kannada Bhavana. As she passed that by, she noticed a seminar going on in Nayana Auditorium. Ushe quietly walked in. She sat in a chair on the last row. There were not many spectators. Gopal didn't notice Ushe entering. He sat on the platform, dignified and solemn. Ushe did notice he was looking at someone among the audience and smiling. She waited for him to smile again to find out who it was that he was smiling at. When everyone laughed, Gopal smiled too, looking at the person in the audience, and when Ushe took a look at the person he was smiling at, a blazing fire broke out in her! It was the same beauty who had driven him in a car. Ushe could see only one half of her face. Her back was a wide sieving pan, completely naked. Hers was a snow-white complexion. Her cheeks would noticeably dimple when she smiled. She had a lashing sharp seductive smile. Why was Gopal smiling, looking at her. What was the fascination? *These men are like that, chasing women who are attractive!* Ushe compared her looks with the woman's. Ushe was old. The woman might be younger. Maybe that was why Gopal was after her. Or the woman was after him. What a mysterious smile it was! They seemed to be smiling, hiding a secret only those two knew. Their every smile fed poison to Ushe. Her innards brimmed with grief. If the person you have mated with is after another person, you feel dejected and depressed. She had to arrive at some decision. Or she should forget everything and leave. But why should she leave? *Has he not loved and mated with me? That would suffice; One is the witness of the conscience to the other! Why should he smile like that? Has he at anytime smiled like that along with me? It simply is lust. And how discriminating! We after all lag behind. He prefers his own caste folk.* Ushe's thoughts thus turned to caste. Helplessness on one side, and turmoil and pain on the other. *Or it may not be sensual love. It could be exchange of ideas on academic topics during which he may have smiled humorously. Why am I suspecting things so very soon. Maybe noticing me seated here he might be smiling at me, for all we know. No, no! He never smiles like that at me, and in public he doesn't do much talking and smiling with me.*

Ushe didn't let go of her suspicion. There were two women seated a few seats away. Determined to do something, she moved to take the seat right beside them before asking, "Madam! Who is she who is sitting in the front row? The one who is fair! Do you know?"

"She is Dr Mangal;a Deshpande," said one of the women after sizing up Ushe, looking at her from top to toe. "She is a Professor at Bangalore University. She was Dr Rajgopal's Ph.D student."

This sank Ushe.

All her doubts were dispelled. It was very insulting. Disbelief gored her. She had heard Ph.D guides sexually exploited their students. *Who would say no to a beautiful woman seeking PhD guidance? Does Deshpande, her surname indicate her husband or father? Whatever it is she has spent a lot of time with my lover. I have been meeting him once or twice a week only for the last one year. She has already finished her doctorate. That means he is not guiding her now. They have come, sitting together in a car. Where did they come from? And why together? Or even before these thirty years did Gopal tell her he liked her before trapping her and enjoying her physical intimacy!!!...* Ushe quaked. Thoughts of various hues began to race in her head. *An agitated state is what complements such abductive thoughts. But not all this may be wrong. Not all is true. He might justify what is happening. What am I to him? I am not his wife. He plays the part of a lover boy so very naturally. He is so very lustful even at this age. Imagine what he could have been when he was a young professor at the University. He has become the chairman of the Development Authority only recently. He has guided so many Ph.D students. He has also written forewords to so many books written by women writers. Has no one been at the receiving end of his desires? Why is this not possible? I trust because I want, need and like it. He would say the same thing; "Look! Come to me only if you trust me! Not otherwise!" Does he not feel the distress I feel? He never presents you any gifts. It looks as if I went to him because of my craze. The smile that he smiles along with her has stabbed me! You feel loony! The intense pain of a stab. The body and mind that went gung-ho at his very sight is now shrinking away.*

When Gopal's turn to speak came, he signed from the stage to the woman seated below. She rose quietly, and adjusting her saree-end covering her bosom, and letting her saree fall right upto the floor, coquetted her way up. She went and showed Gopal something from a book she took along. Her lips nearly touched his ears when she spoke to him. On his part Gopal took the book before he took a thankfully appreciative look at her face. Ushe was surprised. *What is this*, she wondered. *He never talked to me in an open-minded way when outdoors. Now before biggies, he opens out to her, talking and laughing. That means there is a difference between this woman and me. What is this difference? How does one find out? Is there indeed a need to find out? I never talked to him with mistrust. I couldn't speak a word extra. In fact in the presence of love there should be no other topics. But what if suspicion hovers in front of love? I should speak out. Let me wait for a few days. It would be wrong to ask him right away. For how many days could I endure this? And how? Does everyone who talks smiling love you? Do they lust after you? He didn't tell me he had such a programme today. Why didn't he? Is there any relationship between that and this suspicion of mine? Why this pain?*

Why did I come to this programme? Why did I, who adorned a high position as the Chief Guest in another function, come and sit here as a nonentity. But in case I didn't come here I would not have seen Gopal laughing and talking with another woman. There would have been no suspicion. But even if I wasn't around, they would for sure be smiling and talking like they are. At least I noticed one truth. But in case it is a truth, I am as good as dead. In case it is false, I should not go in future to such programmes. With such a trauma it is difficult to remain alive.

Ushe rose, adjusting her saree-end covering her bosom, before she sat back, seeing Gopal walk over to the mike to give his speech. She came to know about the nature of this function only when she listened to Gopal speak. It was a discussion about a book. The author of that book was

Mangala Deshpande. That was why she was swaggering and strutting like that. The title of the book had been written on the screen stuck on the wall behind. It was 'Ankura - A discussion'. When Gopal spoke, he addressed only her. He was saying Mangala Deshpande had left a stamp of newness in the world of women writers. That he was really proud and happy that he was her Ph.D guide. When the programme got over, a sneaking desire pinched Ushe, making her think whether she should meet Gopal. *Shall I offer to take him in my car? What would he say in response? What if he wasn't available for me to speak? What if something that pains even more happened? Shall I leave? He would surely get to see me now. Even if I don't speak, it would be okay, but if I don't at least smile, he would take it amiss. But he is wrapped in the rainbow colours of her smiling presence. How would he take this approach of mine? If by chance the suspicion that I felt turns out to be true, that would surely show on his face. Would he remain unannoyed? He may not talk properly with me, he might express embarrassment.* She made bold to walk over and call him even if he wasn't available all for herself.

Toward the end of the programme, Mangala Deshpande went up, to the dais, to be part of a group photograph of the participants of the programme. She stood right beside Gopal. No one misunderstood this gesture of hers. She was a tad pudgy, and a tad younger than Ushe. But at such times, nothing matters to women except the suspicion they feel. The fire of excited agitation burned even more fiercely in Ushe. She felt her head whirl. Bearing the discomfort, she came out. She stood gape-jawed, looking at the happenings from a distance. Guests trooped out, and getting into their cars, went off. It wasn't a big audience. It also disappeared in no time. Speaking to some of his close associates, Gopal kept looking at his watch. We don't know whether he noticed Ushe there. But her inferno of love wouldn't abate. An envious desire of asking her lover and taking him away in her own car gained momentum in her. Even as she waited nervously, she stepped up, not letting her jarred nerves show. Gopal felt embarrassed and alarmed at the same time.

"Greetings, Sir! Shall I drop you at your house in my car?"

Gopal didn't know what to say. It was totally unexpected. The one who he was speaking to gawked at Ushe. Nobody knew her. Gopal's face knotted up a touch.

"No! Thanks," he replied as fast. "Why trouble you?"

Ushe couldn't have pressed the issue further. But his refusal added up to an insult. A hot mix of affront, deception and disappointment hissed away inside her. Unable to do anything about it, she only gawked at him. This he also recognized. He had at their last meeting kissed her hair before sending her off. *What has happened now*, she wondered. Was it that he couldn't speak to her when in public like he did when they were alone together? Darting him a look of exasperation she went past him. *I have had enough of his friendship*, she told herself. Even as she walked toward her car, reining in her desires and thinking of how to teach him a lesson, a car drove past her. It was the same red car. Dr Mangala was driving it. Gopal sat beside her like before. The car was moving rather slowly when it went past her. When Ushe shot a look at him, Gopal looked at her rather helplessly. Her eyes were shooting live cinders. As she reached home, she swallowed a few sleeping pills and slept off. Her thoughts, heated and chaotic, raced every which way. These sleeping pills help regulate and tranquillize you. Ushe kept some handy for her. But she rarely swallowed them. In fact, there had arisen during the last one year no occasion to take them. She was always happy. She had never doubted Gopal's love for her. Now, you see, this has happened. One could shed it if you were sure it indeed was it. But it was not known whether it was true or not true. One couldn't lose sleep in this turmoil for one couldn't go to office getting up the following morning. There was a special case the following day. One couldn't say it directly. *Whatever it is, let me be calm,* she told herself wordlessly. This relaxing thought crossed her mind only when she began to doze off after popping the pills.

But that she hid away at home applying for three days' leave had nothing to do with the state of her love. One thing was clear here. This, the episode of the function at Ravindra Kalakshetra, had come about fifteen days ago. After that she had interacted with Gopal as if nothing had happened and made rather vigorous love to boot. She had even had him fasten jasmine flowers in her hair. She didn't even ask him why he did what he had at that function. Questions like who she was, what the relationship between him and her was etc. She had acted as if she had let it pass. This was because Gopal hadn't really noticed her arrival at the scene of the programme and she getting distressed. So she shouldn't grill him about anything, and analyze her situation for him. She thought she had arrived at some decision of not having him beg her pardon even if he wanted on his own to beg her pardon. She learnt deep inside her to suppress such matters.

That meant that that she had got sick and weary was not because of Gopal's companionship with the other woman. She had called her lover's mobile several times yesterday. But he hadn't picked them up. She called again this morning. He didn't take it up even then. She called again in the afternoon. But there was no reply. When she called at five in the evening, Gopal responded with no more than an uninterested 'hello!' There was neither vim nor verve in the voice. Earlier, he used to exclaim, "Hi sweetie!, honey! It has been so long since we met. When will you come?" His disinterested voice disappointed and insulted Ushe now. In fact it completely deflated her. She didn't want to show her disappointment though.

"I thought of coming to your house. Shall I?"

There was silence for a noticeably long-drawn time.

"There is a programme tomorrow. I need to leave early."

This really shocked Ushe. *Why is my friend, who used to be on his toes to receive me and chat me up, is replying like this!* It looked as though flowers in bloom in the courtyard had burnt to emit a jarring burnt up smell. Earlier when he talked, his words would spread the soul-warming smell of fresh jasmine flowers. *What happened now? Why is he responding like this? If somebody has sent him a threat letter, why distance me?*

"No. I must see you tomorrow."

"Ushe! My situation is getting increasingly difficult." The reply was still pungent. "I can't speak to anyone like I used to. Leave me alone for some time. Let things cool off."

Ushe was all at sea.

Whenever Gopal resisted her approach, her suspicion would increase as did her feeling of being insulted. He used to declare he could overcome anything with her companionship and intimacy. But he was saying this now!

"I will come to your place tomorrow," Ushe put her foot down. "Just for five minutes please." But hers was a beggar's submissive and spineless voice. "Okay,." Gopal agreed, dispassionately. "You don't understand. Just five minutes, okay? You could come at nine."

Then the mobile disconnected without warning.

This was like getting invited for a dinner after begging to be invited!

Usha felt as though she had been slapped on the face. Her face went pale. *Why should I feel obliged to him? Should I beg him for favours now after he has looted my riches? Whatever the situation in life, should he talk to me like that? He is talking as if he has something to hide. Some kind of crack in the relationship is there to be seen, did we need it? I had seen greenery after a long period of drought. it It is only now that I breathed with comfort. Soaring desires. And pearls rained and kisses had poured like lashing rain. The sweet dream of that poetic mind. I had the good fortune of fragrant fresh flowers being plucked and fastened in my hair. Where was this venomous little snake in those soul-warming jasmines? No matter how long I thought of the correctness of my stand, my thoughts continued in that vein.* If this disappointment turned two-faced and the situation didn't allow it to disappear, it was a scene that tested her endurance. The more she thought of the insult, denigration, the pressure and the pain of having lost something this entailed, the more she was worried.

No solution seemed in sight.

Shall I go to him tomorrow or not? She spent two days deciding this. The leave ended. She had applied for leave, unable to go to work in this aggrieved state of mind. She had to go to work as usual. *No one could solace anyone. Gopal seems to be stewing in his own grief. Maybe I shouldn't have pained him the way I did. But putting forward this excuse what if he began another game with that woman? Men are experts at this game of cheating. But don't women cheat?*

Ushe needs to put this question to herself and find an answer looking deep within. Wasn't her plan of disappointing him, wrecking his brahminhood after trapping her own teacher in her net of love in what apparently was girlishness an act of cheating? It was. But fortunately she softened and mellowed when she lost herself in the power of that love. But the stance she had taken as regards caste didn't last long. She fell all over him because he was a brahmin and then induced love in him as well. After both were truly and well in love, she had forgotten about caste. She made him also relegate caste to the background. She would talk so very delicately that the issue of caste never came up. She would talk about her parents, and not take names or talk about the situation of the family. She would grab money from her father after talking to him aggressively and buy nail polish, bangles, sarees and stuff. Her younger sisters and her younger brother lived like very ordinary persons. After father's death she of course landed a government

143

job. So many persons from her own community then came forward to marry her. *But I have loved and mated with a Brahmin. If I marry at all I should marry only someone like Gopal. I deserve that.* The arrogance of a self-important question like *Do persons from my community deserve to marry me* developed in her. It looks like arrogance when it becomes outer show. But deep inside there is always this turmoil. She wore this shackle herself. Her mind told her she had risen higher than her own folk and that she shouldn't touch them. She had thus distanced her own people. She would scold her own siblings about the way they dressed, about the way they ate, the way they talked etc. She had thus become a bad character in their eyes.

People often think that it would suffice if they come up in life and even if others lag behind and this would amount to equality. She was no exception. Big officers, litterateurs, and ministers would behave like 'backward castes', demeaning other castes, screaming 'equality', 'equality' till they move up themselves. And then they would not even sniff their own folk. A cobbler grinds away his life mending footwear. Scavengers and night soil carriers do it, breathing in the foul smell of shit till they breathe their last. Pig-catchers catch, kill and sell pigs. Members of 'backward' castes act as if they were never born in that community. No one does the job of providing release and freedom from such mindsets. People ranging from priests to government officials look down upon other castes. Unparliamentary four-letter words these people use for people from their own communities. Where is equality here? Is one man's progress among a hundred people equality? Equality is when everyone comes up in life.

When this complexity of communality assumed some maturity, this pain haunted Ushe rather acutely. She was an untouchable. That Gopal also had kept her at an untouchable distance did bug her initially. Not that it didn't now. That she had got a good job has considerably lessened that pain. She had besides the responsibility of educating her younger siblings. She had to take them along whenever she was transferred. As if to prove they were lesser than no one, she had got her younger sisters educated, before marrying them off. She never let up on educating her younger brother, beating him if necessary and got him to score good marks, before getting him some position in life. This was the heat of life. By the time all this pressure and heat subsided to let life flow smoothly, she hadn't yet married. One couldn't say she wanted, needed and liked love, but didn't feel like marrying. Her mother had told her several times to get married and only then would she get some happiness in life. Ushe didn't bother about this advice. Whenever mother broached marriage, she would say something in reply, suppressing her conflicts inside. She thought she was always different from those people. None of them was her equal. She was related to the other castes, and not to her own people. *Besides I look different from them, which is why other castes like her, touched her and mated with her,* she thought. She thought only this much. She would keep the rest away, or pretend as if she had forgotten it, feeling proud to herself and enjoying its pleasure. The pain which would be hers after all this was something that tore at her heart, taking the hell out of her. Not only that. Her delusion that she belonged to an upper class made her mental life miserable. She lost her meals of a year for the sake of a single meal. Several highly placed officials volunteered to marry her. But none of them appeared to be good-looking to her. She alone was beautiful and her beauty was not easy to come by even among Brahmin women, she would think. They had also endorsed her opinion. *Then why should I play second fiddle to or care for, my own people,* she convinced herself. This delusion of hers had kept her aloof till the very end. She bought whatever she wanted and ate whatever she felt like. T.V, fridge, washing machine, interior decoration and all such things that a huge house like hers required and to cap it all, a car! This was how she grew up. When everything was over, she had got this gratified pleasure of love! Life had become sweet like honey with Rajgopal becoming her intimate companion. This life was flowering now. It was yielding fruit. It brimmed with sweet honey. The sea that had looked desolate at one time was now overflowing with foam-flecked water. But a curse now!

Ushe had lain on the floor on her belly under the whirling fan overhead for quite a while. She didn't want either a bed or a pillow. Not even floor mat. The cold floor would assuage the heat flaming within. The servant maid would daily sweep and mop the floor. What else could Ushe do? She could eat her meal. She could weep. She wouldn't go out. She would at times go for a walk early in the morning, dressed up in cuudi and daara. For a couple of kilometers. She didn't want even that for the last couple of days. Why should she mortify her body, for whose sake? We wouldn't know how Gopal was going to talk to her tomorrow, how he would behave with her. She had asked him repeatedly and got his permission for her visit to his house. There was not much enthusiasm about it now. Earlier, tremendous happiness would rush in whenever a visit to him was on the cards. But now there was some sort of desolation and complete lack of vim. It was as though the elegant beauty of her face had been wrenched away. The face seemed dead even while being alive. She hadn't seen herself in the mirror for several days now. Even if she mustered some courage to get on, memories would chase her down, opening layer by layer before her. Memories would tighten her being. They would play obstinate before, as the tragic heroine of disappointment, frustration and fury, she would present herself before her. She would then do the solacing herself. *There is something called tomorrow, let us see!* she assured herself in a wordless aside before getting up and downing a cup of steaming coffee. She would try not to worry, closing her eyes. But no matter how well she tried not to slip into that cesspool of frustration and dejection, she would for sure slide again into it. After a few moments of this rise, the same scenes of Gopal and Mangala Deshpande laughing merrily, sitting cosily together in the car would flash compulsively on her memory screen. Ushe gave her head a vigorous shake before covering her face with both hands so as not to cry, and wiping her face. *I am going to Gopal's place tomorrow, I should deck and decorate myself well enough so as to look better than before. I should look dishier and more desirable than Mangala! I can get the hair coloured and massaged and get a facial done so the face glittered.* So she got up bracing herself and filling her legs with strength. Her head seemed to whirl. She hadn't eaten, she realized. She walked over to the kitchen. The servant maid had washed the dishes. Ushe generally didn't go to hotels for food. She would get something cooked at home and eat. When in office she would often eat getting food packed from hotels. She now took a fistful of ragi flour, mix some chopped onion, took out coriander leaves from the refrigerator and chopped them up, and mixing them as well patted out rottis before putting them on the large pan. Then she kindled the gas stove and cooked the rottis on it. When the rottis got ready, she took out some curds from the fridge and ate the rottis along with the curds. This was all for breakfast. Rice she seldom cooked at home. She would make snacks like rottis, chapatis, and doses at home for breakfast and get some food from some hotel for her midday meal. As for the night meal, she would make do with so fruit, juice and milk. One notable point was that she had given up eating meat years back. Here also her inner light had projected itself. After her mother's death she never touched meat. Whenever her younger sisters came home, she would cook rice, vegetable dishes, saru and the sweet liquid dish of payasa herself and serve on plantain leaves. Or she would treat them to meals in a good hotel. Although younger sisters had the desire to eat meat, they wouldn't say anything because of the elder sister's mindset. They often came home during the holidays. Her younger brother had good job too. He would be always guided by his elder sister. He didn't have the desire of eating meat, much like her. That was also because of her influence on him. When she got free of family responsibilities, with all younger sisters getting married, and the younger brother being the sole resident at home along with her, meat became totally taboo. Some inner attitude had inclined her to this commitment. The younger brother had also thought that was the right thing and had habituated his body to it. Now even when he had got married and hived off, meat continued to be out of bounds. He had told his wife as well. "You can get meat cooked at your mother's place whenever you go there. I will not have it", he had told her. She, who was an incorrigible meat-eater, didn't take kindly to his words and she felt like retching. She would often squabble with him about this. When he went to office, she would go out and eat a meal of chicken curry and mutton head. He would never get to know this!

Ushe changed the saree and checked to see if there was change in her purse. She locked the house door. When she took the car out, and was on the verge of opening the compound gate, memories of Gopal came flooding : *Will he hug me tomorrow like before? Will he talk to me with genuine love? What is this? Such turmoil even at this age!* Her periods had begun to stop. The monthly cycle wasn't happening as regularly as before. *I am decking myself out in a coy and flirtatious fashion, like teen aged girls! Chee No, I need not go to beauty parlors. Let me go to see Gopal just like this, undecorated and unadorned. Why would one need this outward elegance when there is genuine love? I should put this question to myself again. Does desire spring only when there is outward elegance? Sometimes the mind says 'yes' and sometimes 'no'. What kind of argumentation is this? Supposing I didn't look attractive to Gopal, how would he get attracted at this age? That means there is only bodily attraction and not love! I am steeped in an illusion. He might not have touched me, had I looked aged.*

Without opening the gate Ushe left the car inside the compound, opened the house entrance door before she sat on the swing in the huge front entrance hall. Using her leg as the lever, she pushed herself into a swinging motion. The same memories. *Is there deception in Gopal's smile and love?*

Does he behave like this with any others? He could do this with many others, and after enjoying them, tuning in to their desires, could simply abandon them! But we are talking about Rajagopal, damn it! He is such a big luminary in the Kannada world. But what if women come on their own?! That is not possible, is it? This is a moral question. No. this is not possible. Gopal is not that kind of a person. Something in me is screaming it. But there is desire which is beyond this. A thirst, a hunger, which is deeply embedded in us. What if I pose all these questions back to myself? How deserving am I? Have I married him? I have got this right on my own initiative. She is someone I don't know!, *Gopal might well say. He might talk like that if a situation that dents his position of prestige and power arises. Such a situation has in fact come up. There is no doubt there might yet come up another such situation. Is this all to love? There was an insult thirty years ago. Another such humiliating insult now. And along with it a realisation of selfish interests. But I shouldn't take a hurried decision. I have faced so many daunting situations. Let me bear it. We are meeting in any case tomorrow. Let me ask him. If we want, let us meet and mate again. Otherwise let us not. If it is the case that this is all there is to him, the esteem I hold him in goes down. Let me not grieve and sorrow. Let me think I decorate myself for my own sake. I have some position in society. Besides if one doesn't groom and deck oneself, people would consider you stupid. Why did I, who was about to leave for the beauty parlour, stop? The mind that wants to do something needs the inspiration of tomorrow. Okay. Be it as it may. Gopal hasn't promised to give my life a new meaning. He has mated with me even after the incident of that day. He has kissed my tresses. I didn't broach Mangala thinking I shouldn't be the one to initiate a probe. If did would it for the physical gratification I get? Or would it be with the intention of not denting his position and prestige? Why was I so dumb as not to ask this question the other day? Another reason is that since Gopal had got this letter of a murder threat, I thought of behaving normally as probing would further weary him. I am disgusted that he spoke the other day without any enthusiasm. Why should i take it amiss?*

With such thoughts whirling in her head, Ushe drove her car toward the beauty parlour in Malleshwaram.

****

Chapter Nine

"How can you all of a sudden resign? It is important for a literatteur to have the administrative skill of facing any situation that he may come by. What reason would you adduce for your resignation? If it is about health, you take two months' leave. There is no problem. Don't say later that it was because of me that all this happened. As the chairman of the Development Authority, do you need to make a mountain of this molehill? And this happens only with you. What about the chairmen of other academies? It doesn't happen with them, right? Did you have to let it go up to the Home Minister, tell me! This is resignation, Mr! Not something you doodle on a piece of paper with your pen!"

"Sir! I have a personality too. You don't have to give me this official power saying that politics is somehow bigger than literature. Did you call me to talk only this? I have never mentioned your name anywhere. I don't know it either. You are only saying it now. Actually I am resigning for my own sake, for my peace of mind, so that people are not put to trouble. I didn't know you were the reason for this. Why would other ministers ask you? I don't know. Why are you throwing your confusion on me? You get whoever you want."

"You are putting the blame on us?!, Mr Gopal!" rejoined the minister. "You are talking like this, keeping a host of mistakes in your own self. Do you know there are so many allegations against you? Yet assuming that we should not ignore literatteurs, and that you are a good person, we are asking you not to resign. Yet you are at your arrogant best."

"What allegations, Sir?"

"Who is that woman writer who has written against you? You told her to go and see you at your home, it seems. You tell all women who come to your Develoment Authority to call at your place, do you? Besides, who was the woman who raised a stink at your office the other day? Why did you slap her? She really demeaned you, they say. We get to know these things quickly. We could have sacked you. But we thought better of it."

"Sir! These are things people have created to frame me. This is the strategy some vermins have come up wth so that things you are saying now could come from your mouth. There is no need for you to call me to talk to me like this. I am resigning precisely because this dirty politics is not for me. I am not able to think differently about such things."

Gopal got up and readied to leave after joining his palms against his chest in farewell greeting. The minister himself then stopped Gopal from leaving as he said, "Look. What has happened has shappened. Our police has already provided you protection. It will continue. You can take three months' leave, not just two months'. Someone else will take charge of your work. Let not things get into a muddle because of this. The Deputy Chief Minister was not happy that literatteurs went on a protest two months back. Let us not create another hassle now. One and a half years more for you. Why create problems?"

"Okay, Sir! Let us see! I will apply for leave for now. I will join, provided my health and the prevailing circumstances suit it. I will come whenever I like. You do whatever you will. Your likes and dislikes are not important for me."

"Would that mean you don't require our recommendations and facilities?"

"No, sir! Certainly not!"

"This is impertinence!"

"I have been pained a considerable lot, Sir! You will not understand it. You are a minister. Your anxieties are different. We live like ordinary beings. We also have a social life, Sir! Don't mistake me. I am ever grateful to you for your liberal ways and concern for me. Namaskaara!"

Gopal strode out of the Home Minister's office with the satisfied ego of a general who had just won a huge battle. *I don't want any of this prison-house. These blokes are jerks who would lick your feet whenever it suits them or kick you out of sight when it doesn't suit them. Third rate politics is what they do. Now they want to fawn on me, holding my feet. It is going to bring their party a bad name, it seems. Not an iota of sense they have in their noddles. They think literatteurs are puppets they can control. They can't govern the state properly for five years, and they want to teach me administration! They deploy police to nab thieves. To nab these mother-fuckers we need to appoint huge commissions! Let them make anyone the chairman. Let them go to hell! Thoo! To hell with their company.*

Rajagopal let flow a river of cuss words on them, got into his car and driving it at the maximum permissible speed, reached home. "Don't come here to give me protection from tomorrow! Tell your Inspector!" he told the police standing guard at the entrance.

He then quietly got into his room, and sat, a book before him.

Saraswathi lit the lamp in the home-shrine, and was surprised with her husband's ways. She placed a cup of coffee before him. He didn't speak.

"The minister had called you. What happened?"

"..."

"Did you say to him that you would resign? What did he say?"

"What would he say? "Don't resign now, That would bring the party a bad name", they are saying. They blurt out whatever comes to their tongues."

"Do whatever you want, I will apply for leave now. If I feel like, I will come back. You feel free to do whatever you want, I said."

"You did the right thing. We can be at peace atleast in future. I have made vows to God... Let us go home to our village and do the wedding festivities of God Venkataramana Swamy, dress Goddess Madhugiri Maramma in a gorgeous saree. I will stay there for a month and return. You can come later, it is okay."

"What are you saying? Will you be alone?"

"I will. I have the support of God. I don't feel scared. Who will do anything to me? Only people like you are subject to such threats."

Although Gopal's wife's words were innocent, they were mysterious. She used to be cool and collected. She was like that even now. She was a gutsy woman.

"Okay. When will you apply for leave? Let us leave together. Do all your poojes, and divine festivities to your heart's content. If you need any money, let me know. I will go to the bank tomorrow and draw money."

"No, Since it is I who has made vows, I will perform them with my money."

"Were not the vows made for me?"

"It is okay. There would be some or other expenditure in the village. There would also be father-in-law's postdeath ceremony. Some money would be required toward mother's health. And would you not gift everyone something or other? We are going after a long time. We can also go to Devarayana Durga and Goravanahalli. Your younger aunt and your maternal aunt are there in Shira. When we go to see them, we should take something as a gift. Can we go empty-handed? Sharade had phoned us, you remember? Some boy had come to see Sadhana. They might ask for something for the marriage. You pay attention to that. She was saying there was no money except the house to spend for the marriage. Maybe she meant this time it is you who has to bear the brunt."

"*Abba*! What are you doing: you are speaking so many things all at once! You have put forward a long list of items of expenditure. I don't have that kind of money. I might have twenty or thirty thousand. Can one perform a wedding with that?"

"You are already sitting as if a huge rock has fallen bang on your head! Let us leave everything to God. Let us first of all leave the air of Bengaluru behind and move out."

That her husband had spoken so much was her good fortune, thought Saraswathi. She walked across to the kitchen after putting joined palms against her chest in deference to the deity in the home-shrine. She was thinking of cooking something really yummy. Along with rice, the side dish of beans, and some watery *tili saaru*, she also cooked some chapattis and served her husband with great vim.

"You also sit and eat with me, Saru! We can serve us." Her joy knew no bounds when her husband said what he had.

"You eat! I will eat later," she replied animatedly before she washed the plate her husband had eaten from. She ate, serving herself, washed all dishes and tidied up the scene before, humming some song of Purandara Dasa, she went on to tidy up the bedsheets on the bed. She then went out to see if there was police and if they were there, to see to their meal. They had already gone out to some hotel or somewhere.

"Saraswathi! I have asked them not to come from tomorrow. Why should they? Do you think they are needed?"

"Yes, indeed! We are not going to be here. Who would guard the house?"

"The police are there for my protection, not to stand guard over the house. If I am not there, they are not likely to be here. Don't worry! I will arrange for something. Rangaswami my attender's house is closeby. We can ask him to sleep here at night. Don't worry! You sleep!"

Husband and wife slept a sound serene sleep for the first time after so many days of anxiety and turmoil. Rajgopal in point of fact came home huffing and puffing. But the moment his wife broached going home to their village, the idea that they were going to a world of innocence, his mood changed. That he said he would resign seemed proper to her also boosted his morale. Whether what happened was for good or worse, that he had escaped a threat to his life and that he was to go home seeking peace of mind relieved him. *Have had enough of this fame and prestige. Life is far more important. Let me live with my near and dear ones, with all their trials and hardships. Evn if it means hardship and loss, let me get away from this scene.*

In the meantime even though Ushe's memories came bounding into him, his mind cast her away as a dispensable discard. He went to the bank the following day. An obedient compliant Rangaswamy said, "You go, Sir! Even if I can't, I will have my son sleep at your place." He gave a note to the police Inspector saying since he would be out of station, there was no need of any police protection.

"Shall I send a constable along? Or you can tell the police at Madhugiri. They will arrange."

Rajgopal declined the offer. "There is no question of fear and terror in the village I was born and raised in. You also visit our place! My wife is keen on doing the wedding festivities of the deity there. You would that way have visited our place. There is as you know this single-rock hill in Madhugiri, the only of its kind in the whole of Asia. You could climb it."

"I need to tell you some things." The inspector began as he shook hands wth Gopal. "The threat letter to you and the letter written to the minister have the same handwriting. A woman's handwriting. It has been done by one and the same person. And this bomb scare is a hoax. I suggest that you shouldn't get anxious and tense. Not that there is no man's hand in this. According to informed sources, it is not done for power. Someone close to you may have done this to intimidate you. So you be calm and relaxed!"

Rajagopal felt really relieved and relaxed.

"Thanks, sir! I will never ever forget your cooperation in these trying times. But fears, anxieties, and joys and sorrows don't come giving us prior notice. They come suo moto, on their own. They go away on their own. Nothing is in our hands."

'You are after all a poet. You speak loading words with a lot of meaning! Good luck!"

Gopal readied his own car for the morrow's journey, telling his wife as much.

A new journey began.

****

THE WEST

Chapter Ten

Bengaluru's cement, stone and box-like buildings rose sky high, making the man who created these glorious structures seem like a midget. Does man even once think : what if these high-rises collapse for some reason!? Urbanisation doesn't mean only factories, industries and sales. These huge gargantuan buildings also are the bases of commercialisation. One could pack the population of a whole taluk in one apartment complex. There would be the facilities of a whole town there: hospital, school, market, tailors, and so on. What else would one need? But is this all there is to life? If you want outside contact, there would be a watchman standing at the door. He would be there, standing guard even if you are late coming home at night. Getting caught in Bengaluru's traffic snarls is a daily happening. No matter what happens, whether a life is at stake or whatever, nothing could be done about traffc jams! In such a scenario we have such houses, with their own restrictions!

Nothing could be done! Life does change according to times. It is inevitable. They have developed the ability to progress according to one's free will even within these regulatory matrices. You would get an answer to modernity even when it exerts pressure on you. They go forward making what they get their own. Even if this great city life appears mechanical, it is true to say that it has provided a way of life to many. So it won't do to look at one section of the population. We need to look at all. One can give a meaningful definition to Bengaluru only when you look at people of all sections and at various phases.

When Dr Rajagopal and Saraswathi stood at the eighth milestone traffic signal, some thought that was beyond words was at work in both. Gopal had stopped driving for the last one month, and it is only now that he was driving long distance. Even if he felt tired, he had learnt to manage.

They drove to Tumakuru from Dabaspet on their way to Madhugiri. They felt a measure of comfort, sipping a cup of coffee at Tumakuru. The mere thought that they were going home to Madhugiri leaving behind the commercialised atmosphere of Bengaluru was in itself delighting. That all this was theirs was the source of one's attachment. The hotels, the friends, the houses that you got to see on the way were exhilarating. During childhood, making a trip to Tumakuru was in itself a huge achievement. Tumakuru had changed now. When he travelled to Madhugiri from Bengaluru, he would come via Tumakuru. Somehow today the town seemed all the more beautiful. Gopal drove the car rather slowly upto Gollahalli, through Antarsanhalli, Yallapura, Arakere, Amalapura, Sitekal pallya, Holatalu, and Beladhara. It was a track relatively free of traffic. One or two buses, autos and two wheelers was all you would face. No anxiety driving. When you saw the hills around, thoughts such as how far would those hills be from the road, were there roads to go there, were there people living there etc. would cross your mind. As if as an answer to such thoughts, there came into sight a woman on the hills grazing sheep. Saraswati wondered how the woman scaled the hill. If you come to think of it, village women climb hills rather effortlessly. They dive into wells and ponds and swim. Some of their skills city women don't have. Since they eat more ragi than rice, they stay slim of build. This was why it was easy for them to climb hills and hillocks and to do things like swimming. In cities and towns one gets to sport a paunch even if one eats only a little rice.

Since it had rained, the countryside looked swilled out and freshened out with rain. The scene of pits and rivulets flowing with foam-flecked water was very delighting. Peanut seeds had been sown. As they were sprouting, the seedlings emerging out of these seeds in rows presented a picture of vibrant life and vitality. Those little beings were to become food tomorrow for humanity as they grow big. They would then go back to the soil. In a similar way the ragi crop had grown to some height, and these little stalks stood out with their greenery against the background of the brown soil underneath. The crops of the paddy fields adjacent to the Brahmin neighbourhood, the *agrahara* looked like squarish, triangular and rectangular green mats from a distance. Some women were weeding the field around the peanut plants. They looked away at the slow-moving car. There is a backdrop to this *agrahara* being named Jetti agrahara. Since the village was populated by a lot of wrestlers, jetties in Kannada the adjective *jetti* 'wrestler' had tagged on to the name of the village. Less than a furlong from here is another village. Then you come by Koratagere in two minutes' drive. What a variety of villages! What greenery! Life is very peaceful in these parts, affording peace of mind. Those who see this scene feel that one could lead tension-free lives here. But you would come to know the hard and seamy inner truths of the place, the difficulties and hardships, if you ask the farmers living here. Not even getting what they invest, they struggle for a day's meal. They only grow things. What they get when the grain they grow ends up in the market is anybody's guess. Only for a few is this profitable. The rest eke out a miserable life. Gopal stood for a while looking at the hills around, the green crops, and the flowing brawling waters. On the road to Gauribidanuru near Holavanahalli was Akkiramapura and near Akkiramapura was our garden. When Gopal told Saraswathi that there was such a beautiful atmosphere there as well, Saraswathi said she knew about it. When he told her, they could go there sometime, she nodded yes.

The car moved slowly up to Beladhara.

The hills and hillocks all around, brawling stony brooks, swinging *honge* and coconut trees and a variety of green flora beckoned them. It was as if the heavens were within their hand-reach. If the land of yellow sunflowers was on the one side, on the other side was the Gollahalli tank. They stopped the car to take deep eyefuls of the beauty of the sunflower fields. Saraswathi offered a coconut to God Anjaneya swami of Gollahalli. Some undefinable joy inside. She walked over to her husband as if as a newly married bride.

"Look! there is a tank surrounding this temple," Gopal said to Saraswathi, pointing to something at a distance. "There is a stone-and-mud structure housing a basil plant right in the middle. How is that possible? It is lovely, isn't it?"

"Okay. How have they built that structure?"

"I don't know. Don't worry! But it's so very meaningful, isn't it?"

Before they reached Koratagere, they saw the lovely scene of the tank weir being breached. Parking the car they got down. People were talking merrily among themselves about the tank weir.

"The tank is very small. Just a little downpour and the weir gives way!" they were chattering away rather sarcastically.

Whatever it was, husband and wife thrilled to see the foaming little cascade of water!

All the way from Koratagere to Tumbadi, it looked as though the fields filled with greenery, and the majestic hills and hillocks around beckoned them with great love and solicitude. How calm and peaceful! The plantain trees, the coconut and areanut palms filled their hearts even as he thrilled with the feeling his village was nearing. The fort at Chennarayanadurga, which was at a distance of two or three miles, attracted their attention.

Madhugiri hove into sight.

The Madhugiri hill was like a crown to Madhugiri. Just as they traversed one kilometre from Dasarahalli, their hearts and eyes both filled up. Much like a keen mother looks forward to her child's arrival, the Madhugiri hills welcomed them!

Dasarahalli was situated beyond Tumbadi. Just a short distance from there, there was a small pond filled with lotuses. Some of them were full blown flowers while others were still buds. It was good to to look at. People like us couldn't pluck them. The pond was a sink of filth. If you stepped in, you were bound to slip and fall. We should see God in simply looking. The couple spent some time looking at the elegant beauty of the lotuses and chatting about it. Madhugiri Hill compelled attention even from that distance.

It was a majestic and splendid single-rock hill, the biggest in Asia.

The people of Madhugiri might not themselves have known its importance. It hadn't got the dignity and justice due to it. The government hadn't paid it as much attention to it as it ought to have. Was it a small matter that it was the biggest monolithic hill not just in India but in the whole of Asia? There was nothing near the hill to show that it was an important landmark. Only the people who lived closeby enjoyed its grandeur. *The government is playing hide and seek in protecting and promoting such a natural wonder,* says Gopal rather thickly. Gopal had great attachment to it because it was his birth place. But if you were to move forward in life, Bengaluru became important. It was, besides, the state capital, a literary and cultural hub. Gopal had thus migrated to Bengaluru for inevitable reasons.

"No matter where I am, never will I forget Madhugiri!"

Thus spoke Masti Venkatesh Iyengar, who was once the Assistant Commissioner at Madhugiri. The town had changed a tad now. But yet it had retained its old world charm. The town was like a big family, every household being a spoke in a huge wheel. *This is what I felt in my childhood. Now, when I have grown up, the only place that I go to when I go out are the fields. That too, along with Sharada. There is a house, an ancient homestead at Akkirampura. There are besides my friends there. But it is difficult now to get together like in olden times. Although it is a small simple town, residents believe the politics of the whole world happens only here!*

When the car pulled up in front of the house, everyone, all his younger brothers and sisters, came running, exclaiming, *annayya*! before grabbing and hugging him. Their house was well outside the town, on the Shira road near Siddapura, near their garden. It was an ancient house, built so it could be near the land and the fields. Mother had a huge emotional attachment to the house. Sharada had got it renovated to suit modern requirements. Such a huge construction in towns would have fetched a rent that a charitable choultry would fetch. The site area of the house was one acre. It had been built by grandpa. Father used to say when the property was distributed, father had got the house as his share. Father had two younger brothers. Grandpa had passed down sufficient fields and land to them as well. But they had sold their share off and invested in their business. Younger uncles were there in Madhugiri. One of the younger uncles was no more, but his widow was around. They were all reasonably off. Trials and tribulations are always there in every household. It was a family interested in the tradition of madi-purity and stuff. More of it in the younger uncle's household. Some odd reverses and abominations raised their heads on and off.

Every sibling waited with bated breath for the arrival of their elder brother. The affection they evinced overwhelmed Rajagopal and Saraswathi. Mother was shouting from somewhere inside. She was not able to move properly, her legs not being fully normal. She just about managed to sit and lie down. Sharada had a toilet built inside her room. Mother would visit the

161

loo and come back and lie down. But her mouth was fully functional, her shouts ripping the roof off. She would monitor the household affairs from where she lay. She had the dignified authority, necessary to rule. She had at the same time enormous love and affection for all her children.

"*Le* Sharada!" she shouted now. "Get the salver of the glowing wick lamp with vermilion water in it and wave it in front of both. My son has returned having conquered death."

Sharade stood holding the salver at the door. Seeing her elder brother, Sharade couldn't contain her sorrow. Tears sluiced out.

"Ee! What is it? You shouldn't cry when waving the platter of the glowing wick-lamp. Sahana, Savitri! You do the waving! Sharade has enormous love for her elder brother. So she is overwhelmed by his very sight. You do it!"

Recovering, and wiping her tears away, and asking Sahana to join her, Sharade did the waving of the platter of the glowing wick-lamp and asked her elder brother and sister-in-law to enter the house before walking out and spilling the vermilion wash outside. Gopal then walked straight to where mother lay.

"How are you, mother?" he asked.

Sitamma's dammed up sorrow breached and, holding her son, she cried her eyes out.

"What even if something happens to me? You are the ones who need to live and live well. What is the use of this creature living if you are in danger? Forget about us! How are you now, tell us! You were hospitalized, we heard. You wife never informed us, you see! Why do you care?"

"*Chee*! It is not like that! We thought you shouldn't unnecessarily worry. If we were in real difficulty, we would certainly have informed you people. I will be here, you see now, for a good two months. You look after me however much you want!"

Gopal moved his hand ever so affectionately, holding mother's hand. He wiped her tears away. "You shouldn't cry like this. Am I the only son for you? There are five others, see!"

"Whatever it is, Mother has a soft corner for you. She would give up her life for your life. The love the eldest son gets is a tad higher."

Sitamma got furious hearing these words.

"Have I treated you any less?" she said rather thickly. "He has given up his biological mother to become the son of the land. I only have some special respect for him, that is all! Besides, some jealous jerks have harassed him, threatened to kill him. Would not mother feel the pain?"

"That is all over, *amma*! Why talk about it now?"

Gopal too respected and loved his mother pretty much. It was only the situation that took them apart. But whenever he came home, he would spend most of the time with mother. He was ambitious. When the area legislator became the deputy chief minister, he became his intimate loyalist and went to Bengaluru. He landed several awards, and he won fame and name. Had Sharade not borne the responsibility of such a big family, it would have been impossible for him to step out of home and achieve what he in fact had. So he was sometimes haunted by a guilty feeling toward Sharade. But what could be done now? Things had happened. Of the five sons, one had got married and had two children: one boy and one girl. One younger brother was employed in a cooperative bank in Tumakuru. He commuted daily. He was planning to hive off after getting married. Another younger brother was Srihari. He had done his M.A. but being jobless, he would engage in idle rough useless negative talk and simply potter about. He had of late joined a naxalite group it seemed. Why did he become that? He would always hurl abuses at politicians, and would lie on the open front veranda of the house drunk. This saddened Gopal. Srihari was already forty, which was why Sharade hadn't married him off. Raghavendra and Shivaramu were hunting for jobs. Jobs were not easy to come by. One of them was twenty six and the other twenty four. Among the girls only Sadhana was there to be got married. She was twenty eight. Behind Sharade were five younger sisters and five younger brothers. Sharade had got four of them married. She had got one younger brother married, some eight years ago. He was two years older than Srihari. And younger than him were two girls : Susheela and Savitri. Having been married, they had high-school going children. Everything was Sharade's responsibility. Sahana had got married only two years back. Elder to Sahana was Sangeetha. She had chosen her boy and married so that groom-hunting had been averted. Even in her case Sharade went off to the groom's place, saw the boy and talked to his folk before the wedding. Younger uncle targetted her for this.

Somehow Sharade was never afraid of anything. Going right ahead doing what seemed right to her, passing by the world, she was herself to her own world. Her kind of life had made her stand up for herself. But, although she was the eldest, she looked pretty much like the youngest child. Even though her younger sisters had got obese and got to the stage of being grandmas, that the fifty one year old Sharade looked girlish was amazing. Her everyday vibes brimmed with meticulous hard work. She never sat idle. She would go work in the fields, the land and the garden. She would wash mother's clothes, muck out her urine and stools and stuff. She was the one who saw to life-ceremonies like the thread-investing ceremony, weddings and so on. Once, Savitri's labour throes started at home and Sharade did the abortion herself right at home before getting a lady doctor home. The lady doctor took her to task before admitting, "You are really solid, woman! But pardon me saying this, What if something goes wrong?"

Among these twelve children while Rajagopal's ways were one kind, Sharade's were completely different. The rest, the younger children made an ordinary group. But Srihari's was a separate case. If there was a problem it would be of his making. Nobody else but him talked negative unproductive bloodyminded things. At home it was either Sitamma's voice or Sharade's that held sway. Sharade had studied only upto tenth standard. She didn't let up till her younger sisters studied to become graduates. She wielded the cane to correct and get her younger brothers educated. She herself washed their clothes, taking them to the fields and putting them out to dry at home.

She has also changed now. She has bought a washing machine. But she likes to wash with the canal waters in their fields. Only when the clothes to be washed are one too many does she use the washing machine. Every younger brother has his own room. There are ten rooms in the house, each room like a little house in itself. Grandpa has built it so everyone would live together. Maybe Gopal's grandpa handed down the house to Gopal's father because Gopal's father had as many as twelve children. Sharade has furnished each room with a study table and stuff. She has modernized the bathroom. She has seen to 24 hours' water supply at home from the garden well. That one should live well within one's means is her argument.

Younger uncle did try to gain possession of the house after Gopal's father passed on. Gopal back then didn't easily reject uncle's words. There was a time when he thought his younger uncle was like his own father. But

Sitamma did change her son's thinking, forewarning him, "Be on the alert, son! You shouldn't blindly follow them."

After Sharade's marriage broke down, the relationship between Gopal and his younger uncle weakened. Since it was younger uncle who was responsible for Sharade's groom and marriage, younger uncle didn't come forward to take up any responsibility of the household. Sharade herself became the boon for the house. Getting a divorce from her husband with her elder brother's help within a year of married life, she became the pillar of strength of her maternal household. She was just twenty three years old. Within a year after this event, Gopal got married. So her mother's place became Sharade's field of work.

The young ones chatted sitting by Sitamma, the ancient woman.

When Sharade said, "Come everyone! We will have our meal and talk," they trooped into the middle room. Sharade served Sitamma her meal on her bedstead before placing a *tambige* of water by it. Sitamma couldn't sit on the floor. Eating plates were placed on the floor in the middle room. In all sixteen persons, including Susheela and Savitri and their children, ate their meals. Gopal and Saraswathi were delighted at the prospect of members of their family eating together. Pleased herself, Saraswathi also did the serving. It was Sharade who had cooked. She did the cooking in ten minutes whatever the number of persons who were to eat. Now there was liquid petroleum gas. She had bought large vessels for cooking. Besides going to the weekly shandy to buy vegetables and stuff, she was growing in her kitchen garden several vegetables like ashgourd, ridge gourd, cucumber, pumpkin, bitter gourd and snake gourd etc. She grew so much of these that she even gave the surplus away to others.

The desire to afford a good life to her children was of course right. But the thought that Srihari had turned out the way he had bothered Sitamma. She had taken great pains for his sake. The fact that he had, in spite of it, gone up the wrong path was hard to take. This pricked Sitamma like a thorn. She came to lament that even when she felt a measure of relief with Sharade shouldering all family responsibilities so ably, one of her own sons had become a thorn in the family's flesh.

"Sharade! Where is Srihari?" Gopal did ask.

"We don't count on him, *anna*! You eat your meal now. We will talk later. Come everyone! Mother has finished her meal. I will serve everyone." Saraswathi also helped her. Especially for her elder brother, Sharade had got through Sakamma, the servant, beans from the fields, got them peeled and soaking, softening and squeezing the pulp out, made a *huli* of them. A mouth watering spread of raw, uncooked salad, the *koosambari* of green gram and bengal gram, the sweet liquid dish of poppy seed *payasa*, ridge gourd *bajji,* coconut chutney, lemon *chitranna* and a pumpkin side dish was there to be had.

Sharade would cook and put up such a spread in front of them at every programme at home. Mother would also, in the bygone days, get them all together on festive occasions and cook such delicious delights and serve them with deep affection. Supposing some didn't eat, she would make them eat even if it meant spanking them. They had all become adults now. They had their own family hassles. Since everyone had been asked to come, everyone had turned up. Except younger brothers and those who were working in Tumakuru, all married girls would leave immediately after this. Sadhana, who had only recently married, would stay back. The married younger brother had hived off. His wife somehow didn't like Sharade's ways. But Sharade was not one to crib about this. She was mentally primed for any hardships. She had painstakingly paved a way for all girl children. It wasn't possible for younger brothers to keep such a hardy woman out of the scheme of things. So he had planned to separate after the wedding. He never ignored his elder sister's words though. But he had to do justly by his wife, hadn't he? Because his dear elder brother was to come, he had come. His wife had turned up too.

****

Sharade laid out mats all over on the floor in the living hall for everyone to sleep. Gopal sat on the divan there and kept enquiring about his younger sisters and their families. Sharade was emptying the vessels and putting them out for a wash. Narayan, who had two children, sat by, asking about life in Bengaluru. For Gopal it was as if that was the day that had brought him the most satisfaction in all his life.

Gopal had started feeling for his younger sister because he had left behind a family as big as a ship for her to tend. "Come, Sharade! Come and sit by me and talk. Don't be always working!" He had her sit by his side before he addressed all:

"Look! Do you know why Sharade still looks girlish?"

"Anna!" Sadhana it was who got up and submitted, "These people slept off as soon as they ate their meals. But *akka* is not life that. She is always working. That is the secret of her eternal youth."

The married elder sisters got up and gave her a playfully envious punch.

Spending time like this chatting and joking, they didn't know how time passed. When the girl children readied to leave, Sitamma came effortfully hobbling into the living hall. Sharade ran up, got a chair from somewhere and had Sitamma sit.

"Don't go today. You can go to the Venkatramana swamy temple today and leave tomorrow."

Mother's suggestion sounded right to everyone.

They phoned their husbands. Savitri lived in Shira, Susheela in Mysore, Sangita right here, in Madhugiri and Sahana in Davanagere. They felt good that they could be with their mother atleast for another day. Savitri and Susheela's children were playing in the courtyard. The living hall itself was as big as a playing ground. It had an ancient swing and four majestic pillars. Even when everybody slept there, only one fourth of it would have been used. The doors were also equally majestic, so big and heavy that three or four persons had to push them to close them. Huge rafters. How many people would have the good fortune of living in such houses? In cities they feel fortunate even if they get some poky little space to live in! Gopal's mother must have felt fortunate to be able to live in such a splendid house! It must have looked like a palace to her. This was the reason for her enormous affection for the house. Her lust for life was also a pride about life, pretty much like the pride about the house.

"Yes, *atte*!" Saraswathi chimed in. "I have made a vow to God Venkataramana swamy of performing the Divine Wedding Festivities. Tell me about a good day from the almanac. I will talk to the priest when we go to the temple in the evening." Sitamma took the astronomical calendar, and having had a look into the yearly calendar of lunar days, solar days and asterisms, said, "The coming Sunday is the thirteenth day of the lunar fortnight of the Kartika month. That is a good day."

Every one agreed to come to Madhugiri that day. Saraswathi chatted away hilariously decreeing who had to do what that day. "Atleast because of this Sadhana's marriage would be fixed, let's hope," butted in Sitamma, a desperate earnestness written all over her voice. "You people leave. Have a wash and a cup of coffee before leaving!"

Only Sharade stayed back at home.

One reason why she stayed back was to give mother some company. The other reason was to cook for the night meal. No matter how Gopal insisted, she didn't agree to accompany the visiting kin to the temple. Saying, "You people go! Madhugiri is not new to me!" she brought a large circular edged brass dish with twenty steel tumblers and a kettle of coffee in it and distributed the drink. Sharade's immoderate politeness didn't seem okay for Gopal. Lest his other younger sisters took umbrage, feeling bad and descriminated against, he successfully contained a rapidly rising urge to go public about it. Sitamma called the priest to inform him of the visit.

It was Srinivasa Bhat who was doing the daily pujas at the temple. For him the position of the chairmanship of the Kannada Development Authority was indeed a big post. He decorated the deity a tad more today. In fact Gopal didn't quite believe in these worship and Divine Wedding rituals. But he respected those who did. All of them walked their way to the temple around six in the evening. Only Gopal came in the car. Saraswathi too walked along with her younger sisters-in-law. Not that Gopal couldn't walk. He did have this hesitant, abashed, reserved, cowering kind of nature. His was a different status outside. He brought Narayana and his children in his car. The temple was full of only this family. The priest did a homage and worship, the *archane* to the deity in the name of all others and a special pooje in the name of Gopal. Unmatched joy enveloped Saraswathi. She stood, in reverential awe in front of the deity, her joined palms placed against her chest. Her husband also stood watching the proceedings, a contented satisfied expression showing on his face. It was a huge idol. And what a lovely figure it was! There was no doubt that even an atheist would get attracted by it. The tower of this temple was an attraction in itself. These two pyramidical towers, those of Malleshwara Swamy temple and the Venkataramana Swamy temple, stood out in the whole of the town. They were like crowning domes, the rounded pinnacles, which you find on top of temples, for the whole town.

These famous fabled temples had a history of four hundred years, no less. There were rooms right above the sanctum sanctorum of this temple. Rituals for the God used to be done on Navaratri festivals. Special homages used to be performed on the days of the eleventh days of the waning and waxing of the moon. But since devotees didn't donate much money, there wasn't much improvement in the temple. And if the temple was modernized, there would be no room for real *bhakti*. There was commercialisation now in Bengaluru of the business of renovating and protecting temples. Even *bhakti* had been globalised. Some people were unable to stand the globalization of *bhakti*. There seemed to be competition even in what God expected from his devotees. The poor looked inferior with these discriminations.

This didn't look right to Gopal.

Whatever be his caste, if it was a minister or an MLA, the priest would take him upto the sanctum. But, if it was a poor man, even if of the same caste, they would leave him behind at the place where footwear was kept. Gopal had to face many such sickening situations. But now at a time when his wife talked about the Divine Wedding festivities, Gopal had to intervene. It was decided the Divine Wedding festivitiy would be held the following Sunday. About hundred fifty people would get together for the meal that day.

"You should take care of the meal. We look after only the worship and homage part," submitted the priest.

"Is it possible to serve the beggars and the poor that day?" asked Gopal.

The priest felt more wretched than angry.

Saraswathi took a look at her husband's face, wondering why he was suggesting what he was suggesting.

"How is that possible, Sir?" the priest submitted, sounding very concerned. "They will dirty the whole place. What would people say? How could i say no when you ask such a question?"

"We will muck out the place after the meal. If I have this done, other people would follow this precedent. That is not wrong. We should fill the bellies of hungry people."

Saraswathi, who had been listening to husband's words, got furious.

"Ri! Instead of suggesting that we could call kinsfolk or some Brahmins, you are talking about ideals?!"

"Hee! We will call them and these people as well. Let some beggars come and eat! If we distribute handouts among slum-dwellers, they will for sure come and eat."

Hearing their elder brother speak the way he did, his younger brothers only thought their brother was a great man only because of such thoughts. But everyone knew it was not really possible.

But Gopal didn't stem the flow of his thoughts.
"Look, respectable priest! We could serve our relatives in the kitchen. We can serve the poor and the beggarly in the temple precincts. I will get the place cleaned and tidied up, okay?"

The priest agreed.
It sounded right to Saraswathi as well. Something disastrous was about to happen, she had thought. That her husband himself had shown the way had brought her a measure of satisfaction. The priest himself decided on and arranged for the cook for them. Saraswathi returned home with the satisfied feeling that more than three fourths of the work had been accomplished.

Chapter Eleven

The foam-flecked sea waves hit the legs so one feels that the ground below the feet is sinking away. But one has to keep the feet firmly planted to the ground below. Or one would go down into the waters. Once you stand firm, you feel like staying like that for a long time. You feel like going farther and farther away into the waters. Once waves lash you, you stop, you feel like holding onto something. But there is no anchor to hold on to. If you lose heart and panick, you fall right into the waters. Yet you need to pause and stand firm. How thrilling it is when the waves lash you as high as your neck! It would be as if you become one with the waters, as if all your woes melted in those waters. See! Another of those gigantic waves is coming at you! What intense rush! One must face it. It would be a great experience! *Arre*! As the wave nears you, its height reduces! Does it lose out to the pull of the ground. Or, do men get afraid and move toward the ground?

You don't tire, no matter how long you play this game!

Yet what work does one have once darkness sets in? People come to this beach only to watch the sun set. That is a piquant experience. The setting sun looks like a crowning glory of the moving swell of the sea waters. One must agree that that is all there is to this world. A sea bristling with waves, and wherever you cast your eyes, you see the aggressively delightful play of the waters. Against the crimson sky in the distance the sun is itself like a bob of vermilion powder. The sun seems to slide in a seamless downward movement without waiting for anybody's permission or command nor acceding to anybody's request to wait for a little while longer, much like guests who leave as if under pressure of some other work, like a hero getting

171

down from a chariot : his elegance is peerlessly unique. He is a truth-seeker who wants to follow some inscrutable truth of the planet like a rule. Everyone, for whose life on the planet he is the source, believes no matter what, he will come back day after day, week after week, and month and year after month and year. Yet there is disappointment for a moment. There is a tomorrow only for him. No human believes there is a tomorrow for him, as he may be no more tomorrow. But wherever we go, there would always be a sun. We can't see him the same way, in the same shape everywhere. While he presents a commanding picture of a boiling volcano elsewhere, here, a picture of pleasant cool, he bends over for the beauty of the sea, morphing his menacingly fierce form into a child-like innocence, disappearing like a child does into his mother's lap, looking sometimes like a lover filling you with the pangs of separation and sometimes like an orphan declaring his orphanness. The magical entity who, very much the vermilion dab on the forehead of the Ganga, lays out a bed in the hearts of spectators who decide on the moment they have perceived with their own minds and wait before he disappears. Only those who have found this magical being should tell us what they saw here.

Most of them are tourists. Some are foreigners. They are of late valued highly. They lack clothes, not money. They knock about shamelessly semi naked, slinging on their backs bags that contain their necessities, eat something that doesn't fill bellies, paying as much as is demanded, drink, enjoy themselves. And women go about, flaunting and shaking their embon points, compelling the attention of passers-by. They become yummy food for Indian eyes. For those who have come here to enjoy and appreciate the roar of the sea and the beautiful sunset, these foreigners might turn out to be spoilsports. For some they might be the inspiration to deck and decorate themselves even more. You look at any beach of the district of Dakshina Kannada, these foreigners rule the roost, lying endlessly where they lie and pottering about endlessly where they potter about. A smile playing permanently on their faces, they make the onlookers deeply envious. Young or teen ager boys satisfy their itch, feasting their eyes on their seductive physical riches. Some of these indoAnglians have struck roots in our land. The law of the land of course allows it. Haven't Indians gone abroad and settled there? But Indians have gone abroad only for higher studies and work. That in fact is a matter of pride for the country. But the fact that these foreigners live here their bohemian lives, without any discipline makes protection of social health a difficult proposition.

Around six thirty the sun reached his goal, disappearing and leaving an ever so small opening for light to pass through. Darkness began to fall and visitors began to move toward their vehicles. Many people went off. As darkness closed in, the roar of the sea increased. The lashings of the sea waters, sounding as if they are furious and crazy, are a permanent feature of the lives of these rocks, the huge sand dunes and for sea creatures like mushrooms and other plants. Little crabs would leap along with the crashing waves, and once they land on the shore, they would try to hide away in the sand dunes when another billowing wave would land depositing some more conch-shells, some more worms, some more oyster shells. In some of these shells, the worms would still be alive. Plainspeople feel they can make handicraft items out of a selection of these shells when back home. They bring these shells home. Some make some art out of them while some chuck them away in a nook. Some others display these to visitors at home. The sea has become an integral part of the lives of the Dakshina Kannada people. In case the roar of the sea is not heard for some time in the night, they rush toward the sea, fearing some disaster had come about like the earth has stopped rotating or something. For fishermen of course there is no life without the sea. It does happen that they catch a variety of shining fish and filling them with salt, would transport them through the very same sea. They also dry the fish and export them. There are organizations and movements of these fisherfolk. The fishing industry has grown into a huge thriving industry. Since this is the case in Karavara, Malpe, Mangaluru and Kundapura, it has become the source of their daily food for common people. For them sea is as dear and as bhakti-inspiring as land.

Ushe selected some shells, and stretching her legs on the sand, trained her eyes on the setting sun. The more you saw this sea which incorporates life's disasters in its waves, the more you crave to see it. There is some quest in this unique, miraculous power. We struggle to see God. We end up some where in our search. This enormous, tremendous and unique grandeur, the enchanting beauty has grown beyond the combo of land and sea into a surrounding enclosure, standing out as if there is no room for any worry. This, this thing called 'sea', is the music of infinity that beggars description.

She had come to the sea seeking a release from all her woes. There is a gigantic force awakening inside her that can rise above everything as long as there is the sea in front. An enormous power is crystallizing inside, something that didn't happen, standing in front of God Krishna. A clear humanity is waking up. A supreme joy of rising above a hundred hassles. The feeling that has forged with the touch of water and earth is solidifying in the heart. But it is not permanent. The mind becomes a dung hill over again if the sea gets away from one even for a moment. The same old memories, the same old insults, words, oppositions return to bug you, no matter how you hold them back. Even in the presence of the splendor of the waters in front, the same suffering overtakes you.

The mind doesn't need to be educated about what to rise beyond and what to seek shelter and support in. It survives on its own. It loses on its own. But no matter where you stand, this pain is unavoidable. There is the distance of the elephant and the goat between the salt of tears and the salt of sea water. Whether you stand on the the mountain or dive deep in to the waters, it is all the same. The pull of mundane life is inevitable. All these seem euphemeral. When after the incident the other day I felt shaken, unable to argue the rights and wrongs, I had to try to bring life back on track, applying for twenty days' leave on medical grounds.

Taking younger sisters and their children along, she had gone on a week-long excursion to theses palces in a hired Ambassador car. They had a delightful eyeful of the Jog falls yesterday and reached Udupi only this morning. They had checked into a hotel, and freshening up, had come to the beach now. Buying the children whatever they wanted, the younger sisters were playing with their children, leaving the elder sister all to herself.

Their sister liked to be all alone at times.

Not that she had frowned upon her younger sisters. She would keep to herself and to her work. She had forgotten that there was another world, that of marriage, children and family. Besides, she was educated. The sisters were by no means equal to her. She had found happiness in being single. She has a good position, is good looking. The younger sisters did not stand out in looks. She was the one who had shown them the path after father's death. How was it possible for the younger sisters, who thought this way, to understand the pain behind Ushe's deep silence? After spending a considerable amount time on the seashore, they, even if unwillingly, got on the car. Ushe sat by the driver. Along with their children, the two younger sisters sat on the backseat.

Parking the car in a narrow alleyway, they came to have a *darshana* of God Krishna of Udupi in the Krishna *matha*. It was already nine clock in the night, and the temple people were about to wind up. Standing in the file of darshana-seekers, they had a glimpse of the God through an opening. It was a highly satisfying experience. Ushe was not one to be after God, to pester Him, asking Him to do her this favour and to grant her that boon etc. But her current situation and state of the mind had made her bow before Him. She had spoken unspeakable things to him the other day. Now the disappointment of not having the face to face him, which threatened to swallow her up, had wrapped her up. She was doing justly by herself for her behaviour of that day. It might be the case that Gopal was not what she thought he was. She might have misunderstood him herself. In case it was her fault, it was not at all possible to face and talk to him. What a shocking blow! It felt as if the body had been poisoned. How could she stand it? What use was it standing before whatever God, folding your hands in obeisance? In case this mistake of mine is not pardonable, where would I again get that lover, and the sensual joy that he afforded me? This anxious thought assailed her relentlessly, sinking and dwarfing her. Besides this, some other irredeemable feeling of criminal guilt was trampling her. Along with this, when some of Rajagopal's behavior and when her doubts returned to haunt her, she felt excruciating headache, she felt so tensely agitated that she felt like shouting at the top of her lungs that it was injustice.

She had found a way of getting this agitation under control. Whenever these doubts bothered her, she tried to distance herself from them, helping still the mind.

But such a situation would be temporary. This peacefulness might last ten or fifteen minutes, and then the same agitation and the same painful turmoil. This had reduced Ushe to half her size. Polarities like truth-untruth, justice-injustice, doubt-pride, love-hate assailed her thoughts, giving rise to extreme mindsets. She hadn't coloured her hair, hadn't put on any cosmetics on lips and cheeks. *Why do I need these? Why should I look good? Who should I live for?* This had resulted in some kind of renunciation. When the thought that it could be because of caste that she had been subject to humiliation and demeaning crossed her mind, she got even more depressed. How was it that he would grab and hug me? *How was it that he fondled me, holding and pulling me by my hair? The way he occupied my body was amazing! Did these things really happen? Then how did he change like he has? Why this crack in the relationship? Why did I turn so fierce and cruel?* The more she thought about this, the more muddled did the mind become. The bond that had gone missing had come back after thirty years. Hadn't caste entered the scene of doubts, insults and status and positions? Who would answer this poser? Who had to give himself/herself the answer? *Gopal is now in the hospital after suffering a heart attack. I have lost my right to see him. There is no question of meeting him, is there? It would suffice if his office staff doesn't get to know who I am! If it is known that I am an Officer in the Backward Classes Protection Commission, things might get worse. It would be big news in the media.*

This matter forunately ended right there. It was becoming difficult to assume a different form digesting it. Thinking better of fighting a legal battle, she chose to stay away from such things. Not controlling the mind before things came to a head was the root cause of all this. *Let some days pass. The crack might not heal. But the pain might subside. Are this separation and weary disgust permanent? The relationship will not for sure take a form different from this. I should firm up the mind, deciding how I want to live. Is this possible? I hadn't a year ago thought that I would live like this. I was then all to myself, unaware that such delighting gratification was there to be had. And when I did get it, I took it with amazed joy. No matter how many years pass, love returns as a seeker, may be because of the debt of protecting the belief and trust or because of the fascinated gravitational pull between the two persons. But why did this happen at all? Did it break down because of me? Why did I express such fury the other day? I could have borne it with patience. How did this thing called tolerance lose it meaning in me? I am mild and tolerant most of the time. I shouldn't have talked to the Home Minister. It was a mistake. The minister's words have created this situation. Where is the solution for this? How did all these come about : this politically charged situation, my dubious condition, and on the other side how Gopal, Mangala Deshpande and her smile put paid to my joyously contented existence and Gopal's indifference. Since there was a severe blow to the deep love that I had about him, he is now in a hospital. This evil behavior of mine almost killed a life, didn't it?*

Ushe woke up at four in the morning. The same thought crossed her mind again. It was as if she wanted to search and find out where she was. Ushe got up and stood by the window. It was silent and still, except for a coffee or a tea stall here and there. The pyramidical tower of the Krishna temple stood out from a distance. *I have done a darshana of God Krishna last night. But the experience that I am feeling now and the direct experience that I got last night are different. The Kanaka tower that leans on the Krishna temple tower grabs your attention and stills you. How did Kanakadasa, hailing from a backward community get so close to God! He is the great soul who, rising above these Vaidik egos, showed only bhakti matters. It is amazing how he rose above these worldly equations and didn't even ask God for any favours. Why is it that we don't go beyond our feelings?* She felt the satisfying comfort of some light enveloping her. *But it is rather difficult to hold on to this state. Kanaka is a great example of* bhakti *holding its own against the clear truth of God. Udupi is a good example of the glory of these two forces coexisting. This in fact is the vibrancy of Udupi. One has a hundred things to learn in life. Man's weakness is the lack of effort to learn. Not everyone can become a Kanaka, which is why he is considered great among the Dasa saint-poets.* Some emotionality enveloping Ushe, she stood with her joined palms against her chest in reverential salutation in front of God for a long while. She then rubbed her face with her palm. Ushe walked back and lay down but the Kanaka tower lingered on in her memory screen long after it had been seen.

****

They had a sanctified sighting of, or *darshana* of the God in Shringeri and after the night meal stayed overnight there as well. Their minds got full with the *darshana* of Goddess Sharadambe. *What lovely form! The form of the mother, which helps understand the woman in the large sense.* An emotional upsurge to ladle out all of one's woes came leaping up in Ushe. She offered a saree and a puje to Goddess Sharada. One thing is important here. There was no occasion to broach caste here. Ushe didn't make any room for such a thing. One keeps aside law, struggle, strife and revolution and goes about doing one's travel, *darshana*s and worships and eats the meal at the temple if available or else eats at the hotel and moves on. After a day's stay at Sringeri, they left for Horanadu. *The picturesque hilly terrain gave us a memorable experience.* No matter which beautiful place you went to in the world, this kind of sight was hard to come by, it seemed to them. The curves, the hair pin bends, the brawling bouncing little water falls by the roadside, the huge trees and the delightful greenery in the deep dales took away their breaths. But they didn't fail to feel that this natural scenery was as beautiful and amazing as it was perilous. Even at the slightest curve on the road, the vehicle coming opposite you, has to give you prior warning. Otherwise danger would be lurking round the corner. If you get absent-minded, you are bound to plunge into the ravine. But the local folk say, "God who people come seeking doesn't, can not, let them down. Such an event hasn't happened anywhere here![5]" Such talk increases the belief and devotion that devotees have. Importantly, drivers need to be extra cautious.

When Horanadu was a little distance away, the track didn't feel smooth. Because of torrential rains, the river was in spate and the home stretch to Horanadu was dotted with pits overflowing with rain water. There was one stream running right through the road. All at sea, reversing the car, they parked the car by a roadside tea stall. On enquiry the tea stall owner said there was a wooded detour to Horanadu from that point. It might take an hour to get to Horanadu by that track. Ushe sought the opinion of her younger sisters. To proceed or not to proceed was the question. By the time they reached Horanadu, it would be night, and going to Dharmastala from there would be dauntingly difficult. But returning home without seeing these places would not be right either. She talked things over with the sisters. *No matter what, they should go ahead* was the advice. Ushe felt a measure of comfort. "Be careful about children. This is the hilly ghat section. There might be vomiting. Keep the pills, biscuits, water etc, things that are needed for night travel, ready just in case", she advised. In the meantime, the driver butted in with, "Let us go! One more day wouldn't make a difference!" Ushe didn't like this intervention. But it was he who was doing the driving. It was his car. He had to take precautions. So it was his take as well. Travellers exerting pressure didn't seem right to Ushe. It was already one thirty in the afternoon. "Get in! get in!" she goaded her kin. "We can decide after reaching there."

This pleased the younger sisters.

****

Forlorn and desolate woods surrounded the travellers.

Pouring rain, and a long winding little track, looking like the parting of hair in the middle of the head, ran in front of them as if it was driving

---

[5] This is one theoretical problem with literatue as a discipline. How does the author know? How do the people know? If the argument is that the author is only blindly repeating what the rabble believes in, then the counter is that the author has no business to merely replicate irrationalities and abominations abounding in social space. See Giridhar 2015. The onus is on the author to lead the people!

into a mystery, into an unknown, unknowable secret. The car was moving. Branches and boughs of trees all around within handshaking distance, flowers they had never in their lives set their eyes on, leaves that looked like flowers, and twilight was in sight. The sight of water flowing on flat land for a while and then leaping down as a fall before it again brawled along thrilled the kids as much as the adults. Kids stuck their hands out and felt the rain. At one point Ushe stopped the car and took the kids out to the leaping gush of water by the roadside. They played, frollicked with the flowing gushing waters. The rain stopped for a while. The surprising thing was even if it rained, there was no hint of cold weather. In our plainlands, even if it rained a tad, people would cover themselves with sheets and blankets saying it is biting cold. Rains are an integral part of people's lives in these parts. In case the pouring rain pauses even for a while, they think a catastrophe is about to befall them!

Ushe, who got into the car along with the children, asked the driver to start the engine. Much as the driver tried, the engine wouldn't start. The driver got down and checked. One of the tyres had punctured. "I will get it ready in half an hour, madam! You go around and while away time, enjoying the scenery!" piped the driver before he got going with fixing the problem. Pangs of hunger rumbled in everyone's belly. It was a place where nothing was available to eat. The site was a spectacularly beautiful sight. But there was no place to sit and savour it. There were some stones by the waterfall, but because there was green algae slime, it was slippery. Forget about sitting, you couldn't even stand by the roadside. Cars, buses and trucks would be all the time zooming past. In the end the driver suggested, "You take some vehicle from here, have a darshana of the deity, eat your meal and be there! I will get this fixed and come over there. We will then think about what to do." This seemed right. They waved down a private bus named Annapoorneshwari and reached Horanadu.

As they reached the temple town, the temple cooks had their shout going of, "You come and have your meal! This is going to be the last row of eaters. We are winding down. We will after this have the great ceremony of waving the burning lamp for the deity, the *mahamangalaarati.*" The question of whether to eat before having a sanctified sight, or darshana, of the God and offering a pooje reared its head. When they saw the alighting passengers stand in the queue for meals, they did the same too. What if they missed out on meals? It was already three o'clock. The kids were hungry.

Then there was this talk heard from one of the passengers that this indeed was the right thing to do. It was only after the devotees ate their meal that the ceremony of waving the burning lamp to Goddess Annapoorneshwari took place in Horanadu. While the ambient natural beauty of Horanadu overwhelms you, the treatment the cooks and other temple people mete out to devotees is no less remarkable, welcoming them with loving respect and serving bellyfuls without sulking and fretting.

Ushe donated a thousand rupees to the food-donation fund after she and her kinsfolk ate the temple meal of the sweet liquid dish of *paayasa*, had a homage to the deity done in the name of the kids and had a sanctified sighting of, or darshana of, the deity. She now felt easier in the mind. When they emerged from the temple, the mind-blowing nature scenery of the deeply wooded Malenadu region of Kannada Nadu surrounding the temple bowled them over. Their legs wouldn't come out. Younger sisters went away to buy their children playthings, toys, rings and necklaces. Ushe sat mulling something on the stone slab of the temple courtyard even as she savoured the natural splendor around her. Eyes fed pleasant things to the outer mind. The heat of the inner mind kept startling, searching for what could feed it contentment and peace of mind. To ask God to provide solutions to such psychic pain would be childish. *That is not for adults like me. I entered the scene of a family and tried to fnd solace in the cracks I made there. Goddess Annapoorneshwari is an icon of family commitment. Such personal desires are called selfishness. We need to suffer for the mstakes we make. How does or can God help you out? We should build belief in ourselves. But our feelings generate naturally. And as against those feelings, his feelings also formed. Only one doubt is now ruling this situation. Wherever I sit or stand, wherever I am, it is taking the hell out of me. Something deep within is crying out that I can't live without him. Who do I confide this to? It is not something that one can confide. Had I "been a tad more patient, I would have dealt with this successfully, smoothly. But there sure were reasons for losing my patience. Why did he behave the way he did? Is it right on his part to be indifferent in front of the world to some one he loved and at the same time to be soft to someone else? Is love limited only to the body? If he hasn't respected me, all it means is that his love is just deception and fraud. Where is the heart except in the body? Are two different kinds of justices, one for the mind and another to the body, correct? Are all men like this? I don't understand! One can't agree this way or that! Whatever this is, we need to live on. One should suffer the spin-offs of what one has done!*

Ushe, who had sat thinking of savouring and enjoying the wondrous delights of nature, was filled only with thoughts of Gopal. She slid down to earthly reality only when the car driver came back and stood before her. It was four thirty in the evening. "Madam! Shall we leave?" he said. "I am done with my *darshana* of God and my meal." Ushe then came down and called out her younger sisters. It might be night when they would reach Dharmasthala. Even if it was, they could stay somewhere, they decided, and have a sanctified sight of, or *darshana,* of God in the morning before leaving for home. Ushe told the sisters as much before asking them to answer any pressing nature calls.

****

On the morrow, they had the hair on the heads of the kids sheared before having a sanctified sight of the Lord. Ushe was surprised to see the vimmy zest and vervy bustle that her sisters bristled with. *I don't see such enthusiasm in me!, she told herself. I don't know whether there is God or not, will He do me any good? Yet I stand and bow before Him, joining my palms against my chest in devotional salutation. I believe. I might lose that belief again. It is as if I have fallen into a ditch, and am wallowing there without any support. I need to shore myself up myself. Somehow this two edged dilemma and depression do not leave me. Even as I see sisters enjoying bathing their kids in the Netravathi river dunking their legs in the river, my thoughts are on something else. Even when we stand before God, their thoughts are different from mine. But we need to adjust. Relationships acquiesce.*

The sisters went out for buying some things and when they didn't return even till six, Ushe got anxious. She sent the driver away to find and fetch them. She paid the hotel bill, got the luggage out before sitting waiting. She got angry with the sisters. They went out shopping whenever they came on tours. They wasted time. She told herself she would give them a tongue lashing. But why? Why should she scold them? What if she didn't have any interest in shopping? Shouldn't they have? 'Our elder sister got us here and she is taking us to task', *they would say?, wouldn't they?*

It was eight o' clock. And there was no trace of anyone. *Where do I go searching for them? Whay if I go out on a quest and they return, and our paths don't cross? We should have traversed half the distance by now. Why did they do this? What kind of a buying spree is theirs in an unknwn place like this? What is it that one gets here that one does not in Bengaluru?* She didn't have the car either. *What would the onlookers say if I sit waiting in the middle of a public street?* One or two passers-by did have an extended look at her, she felt. *What if the sisters had gone missing? Where is the driver looking fot them? Where are they?*

She began to feel hungry. Ushe helped herself to a cup of tea from a tea stall closeby. She thought she should face anything with her chin up. She looked forward to their arrival with patient concern. There were signs of rains, which further distressed her. Rains in Malenadu would mean unrelenting endless rains. In these parts, it doesn't rain, it pours and pours for an eternity! A thick group of cumulous clouds hovered above on this dark Dharmastala night. There was thunder and it did rain for a while before it thankfully stopped with winds gusting across. She covered herself with her saree end, and narrowing her eyes, looked for anyone that might turn up. Hungry and fatigued, she closed her eyes, as though she had forgotten everything worldly. She must have sat like that for an extended while.

When sisters came round and called, "Akka! Akka!" she startled before she woke up. The sisters had thought she might give them a piece of her mind, but not even a cheep did she utter.

"Shall we leave? Is everything that you wanted to do over?" she asked.

"Let us eat our meals here in Dharmastala before leaving. Not in a hotel, akka!"

The driver agreed, and it seemed right to Ushe as well. It was nine in the night when they reached the temple. It was time to shut down. His Holiness Veerendra Hegde and the sponsors of the all-important lamp-waving ceremony for the deity of *mahamangalaarthi* were present. As there were not many people around, Ushe and her family trained their eyes on the idol of God right till the burning lamp-waving ceremony got over. Then they saw the door of the sanctum sanctorum being closed, and with a nameless feeling of satisfaction, they walked over to the dining hall before eating bellyfuls of the temple meal, and ambling over toward the car.

"Shall we leave?" asked Ushe.

"*Akka*! It feels sick and weary to think of going back to Bengaluru! Shall we go to Mantralaya?"

Taking a look at each other's faces, Ushe and the car driver broke into a hearty laughing bout.

"Why, *akka*! Why are you laughing? If not you, who else can we ask?"

Ushe felt a touch bad.

"Is it possible to go to Mantralaya from Dharmasthala now?" She explained to them. "Do you know how long it would take to get to that burning oven of a town from this cool hilly Malenadu? Do we have a helicopter for us to fly? We will go there some other time, Okay? We will visit a place on each vacation your kids get. We are tired now. Don't you want your husbands? If we delay going to Bengaluru, your husbands will move the court against me! Shall we leave then? Are you ready? Did you have the kids pee?"

Leaving Dharmastala at eleven in the night, they reached Bengaluru by eight in the morning. The sisters had their bath, their breakfast at their elder sister's place and after the midday meal, they stood ready to leave for their places. The realisation that after her sisters departed, she would be all alone hit her, and Ushe began to weep rather loudly. It was the first time that they had seen their elder sister weep like she was doing.

"Why, *akka*?" they tried to solace their elder sister." Why get emotional like this? We both will visit you twice a week, okay?" Ushe then bought them some new clothes and driving the car herself, dropped them at their homes.

As soon as she got home, she put the soiled clothes away for washing. She had brought a picture each of Goddesses Sharadamma and Annapoorneshwari. She wiped them clean and vacating a niche in the kitchen, placed them there. She had so far neither a picture of God at home nor was she visitng temples. That she had now all of a sudden brought home a picture of God told her that there was some change in her. She phoned Gopal at his office.

"He has gone on leave on medical grounds," said the voice at the other end before ending with a question. "Who are you?"

She disconnected the call.

There were still three days left of her leave. She weighed in to herself on the mistake she had herself made. If the woman who has loved without marrying gets spited, seeing the man chatting, laughing merrily away and moving with some other woman, as if she is the legally wedded wife, or more than the legally wedded wife, what if the legally married woman comes to know of her husband's dalliances outside marriage?

Did I carry myself like I did with the person who explored and enjoyed my love in such intimate ways? This makes me a partner in the conspiracy of the Home Minister! If I reveal my big mistake with anyone, I could be subject to some big punishment. She sought to suppress her indiscretion that corroded her so it didn't surface even onto her outer awareness. She had realized only now that it was her mistake. When we make a mistake, at the emotionally charged moment we feel what we are doing is indeed right. If te body ails, we can correct it with medicine. But if the mind ails and gets awry, what could one do? It is not an ordinary ailment for us to find a solution on our own. Why did I think the way i thought? Doubt makes us make such gigantic mistakes. In the endthe mind acquires an irrepressible power to get our own dear and near ones into trouble. If this happens in some other's life, we look at it from outside. How does my soul prove to itself that I didin't amk amsitake just because the outer world didn't get to know what happened in my life. When we make a msitake that we like making, we don't want to act false to out own sensibility and often end up certainly making that mistake.

Ushe get up and when she called Gopal's mobile, the answer at the other end was, "The phone is under repair. Call after some time!"

This happened quite a few times. *I should ask him to pardon me. He should pardon me. My mind is craving to engage with him like before. But is all that possible now? The event of that day, the opposite reaction that I came up with and the unspeakable mistake kill your personality. Yet I need to come clean with him. It is he who has to pardon. It is his privilege and right. But how to tell him and when? For how many days do I keep it under wraps and stew in it? If i can't contact him on the mobile, shall I go to his place and tell him? He could be at home, if his wife has gone away to her college, I could go there and tell him directly? Shall I? What if this puts me in a spot? I should be the cause of any disaster this could cause.* But her desireto tell him every thing intensified. *What if his wife is around? I could say something explaining my visit. I should carry a book and making as if to give that to him, should talk and come back. What could be done beyond this? i am not able not to do that. How would the fire inside abate? Satisfaction of one's conscience is as important as one's honour. If it is true that even after those incidents of that day my love for him remains, does it mean that the insult and pain that I experienced that day are being treated as false by love? Where has that fury vanished? Having chased him down even when he went through tense and anxious moments, have my anger and resentments melted when he is hospitalised? The moment I learnt that he had sufferred a heart attack I have set aside my decision of vengeance and am sinking away with feelings of guilt. Only I need to pay for the insult done to me, and not anybody else. How would I otherwise get my peace of mind? In case I prefer a complaint of atrocity on a dalit, that would call for an enquiry. I would then be poking open the cinders covered with ash myself. Then people would see our bond as immoral and would frown not just on me, but on him as well. They would say I did this deliberately. Or they would put me in the dock saying this is politics and that I did it at the instance of the minister. When man is visited by a calamity, 'I' would come first, even if there is the other person who is someone you love so very honestly and intensely. Atleast for now i have been totally rejected.*

Even after all this, I need only him! Brushing aside my ego and self-respect, my inner self is rooting only for him. Although my rebellion, the feeling that he is my teacher and my feelings of fury because of wounded and injured love have been rising irresitibly in me, they have been dented and blunted. It is the call of love all over! It is the reign of love. This is not me. I am an official of the Dalit Welfare Commission. But more than the issue of caste, it is a social problem that is the cumber. Now it is a health issue. What can be done now? Who slapped me? Was it the person who loved me? Or the person who taught me in the class? or a fraudster ? Or a vile jerk who would misuse me and discard me? Who should I think positively of and who to condemn? How and how?

It was two o' clock in the night. But sleep stayed away. Ushe sashayed over to the kitchen, downed a glass of water before coming back and lying down. The self same thought haunted and bugged her, putting her mind off the track. She took out two sleeping pills and swallowed them. She felt drowsy but along with it came the feeling of cold and feverishness. Even if she crouched as he lay the cold feeling wouldn't go away. Since she hadn't eaten well for some days this was natural. But the situation could also have made for the unhealthy feeling. She felt some turmoil inside her belly. More than anything else it was the turmoil in the mind. She nodded off somewhere around four in the morning.

She felt heavy and her head seemed to whirl in the morning. She did some self-medication. Did she develop high B.P or something? Whatever it may be, she thought of getting it checked up. It didn't strike her that it was four months since she had had her last period. Woman's periods may stop anytime after forty years it seems. But Ushe had had her normal periods till the last four months. Even if they were not very regular, she wouldn't have bothered because she knew at that age, periods wouldn't be very regular. Even when she had physical union with Gopal, she hadn't bothered because both were well past the reproductive age.

She was a tad obstinate about some things. She deliberately exhausted herself doing a host of things right since the morning. Fatigue increased, and at about three in the afternoon when she was to take her meal, she felt so exhausted that she felt like throwing up. The maidservant would come and do her chores and go back in the morning. She ate and put the plate away in the sink in the kitchen. There was no possibility of anybody visiting her after that. Only on Sundays would her sisters visit her. She didn't expect anybody. What would she do? It was difficult, she felt, driving alone. Dr Bharathi working in the Malleshwaram Nursing Home was a good doctor. She slept off thinking of going to her even if by auto. She drifted off to sleep. Yet a discontentment simmered deep within.

****

A token was handed over to her at the Nursing Home as soon as she entered it. This was because she had already called the Nursing Home about her visit. Ushe showed the card to the nurse and after that was shown to the doctor, she was ushered in. Examining her, Dr Bharathi asked, "What is your age?" When she said "forty seven", the doctor raised her eyebrows in surprise. When the doctor asked, "How many children?", Ushe nodded denial. The doctor showed her the bathroom, asking her to give her urine sample for a pathology test. "Why the urine test, madam?" asked a bewildered Ushe.

"Don't get anxious?" replied the doctor. "You have waited this long. Your wait has borne fruit now!"

Ushe didn't figure it out.

Thinking that further probing would rile the physician, she nonetheless took the little bottle, walked into the bathroom, took the urine sample and gave it back to the physician. The doctor called the lab technician.

"You wait outside! I will call you."

An anxiety started forming in one of the corners of her mind.

What the doctor was trying to say was not clear. *What would the words, 'Your wait has borne fruit now' mean? Why should they do this urine test? Was it to test sugar levels? If that is the case, was I waiting for this disease for so long? All this is common at the age of forty seven or forty eight. Where is the question of waiting for it? If it is the sugar-disease, I know what to do. Why should I wait for her advice and prescription? I can do any therapy except taking pills. Maybe I have developed it, eating as I have, loads of the sweet dish of kesari baath!*

She paced the corridor of the clinic, as these thoughts paced a corridor of her mind.

Doctors are like this. A little illness, they make a mountain of it! Her cud-chewing session elongated. *Prescribing a lot of medicines, they let drugs batter and bruise your body. Let me leave! Don't want either this disease or their medicines.*

She came down the steps of the Nursing Home. She found no autos there at that time. It was going to be ten minutes to seven. Day was declining. Even as Ushe's desire to clear the place sharpened, the availability of autorickshaws nosedived. Just then, standing at the entrance doorway of the clinic, a nurse called out to Ushe: "Madam! The doctor is calling you. Where are you going?"

As if caught, Ushe climbed up the steps and sat before the lady physician.

"Did you go out and why?" the physician began. "Take the report! Why didn't you meet a doctor even though it had been four months after your last period? Why this indifference!? Why? Don't you want children? If you don't, why did you not take any action about it? You say you are forty seven. It is not right or good not to take care."

Ushe didn't figure out what the doctor was trying to say. *I know when periods end for women, there would be a host of problems they need to cope with. But why is this doctor talking in such serious vein? Why is she talking as if I have done a crime?*

"What is it, madam!? What is the consequence of my not having my periods? Please explain clearly."

"Why don't you understand? It has been four months since you have had your last period. You are pregnant. You don't know? This is very surprising. I will write out some medicines for you. You should take them without fail. You should eat regularly. Don't neglect thinking you have gone old. I will do scanning tomorrow. Not today as the scanning section is busy today. You should take rest, Should not lift heavy objects. Reduce driving and riding. Eat more of vegetables and fruit. Eat however much you want. Drink some milk both in the mornings and nights. Okay. Come tomorrow again!"

Ushe felt as if a bolt of lightning had struck her.

She didn't rise from the chair. All she heard was 'You are four months pregnant." She heard nothing else. The word 'pregnant' itself was a shocker for her. It was as though the ground beneath her feet sank and she slid to the netherland. She felt like pissing again. How should she take this matter? It was totally unexpected. The awareness that she didn't want this awakened before the doctor. Although she felt as if she was unaware, there was no confusion whih could lead her to go searching for reasons. *I am not a little girl for me to scream that I got betrayed. If I say that I got cheated at this age everyone will laugh, clapping their hands.* She didn't expect such a situation. She now felt that she should have expected such a situation. She should have taken precautions. The doctors would ask a hundred questions if one is not married.

"Doctor! Is it possible to conceive at this age? Could we not abort it?"

"You seem to be educated. You would understand.. It has to do with the constitution of one's body. It is not that it shouldn't happen. But it is difficult to remove the foetus at this stage. So many people crave for children. You are healthy. We shouldn't abort without any sound reason. Whatever be the job you hold, no one should think it is difficult to raise children. Okay. You can if you so want consult other physicians. I have no objection."

Ushe quietly got up and walked out of the doctor's room. Not quite knowing what to do, she determined not to take drugs. She took an auto, and on reaching home, got into her room, and bolting it shut, simply sat on the bed, for a long while trying to think her way out of the impasse. It was already slush, and this latest development made it worse. The fact that she was pregnant had not hit her. *I am pregnant. and pregnancy without marriage would invite snickers. What shouldn't have happened because of me had happened.* At a time when an indiscretion of hers was fretting her to death, another shock had further sunk her. Not worrying about the hunger she was feeling, Ushe sat like that till twelve in the night. As the hunger became unbearable, she put some cooked rice on to her plate, and taking some curds from the fridge, she ate it in two minutes before drinking some water.

She felt a measure of comfort.

Amidst all the anxiety and soul-wrenching tension, she didn't know when she drifted into sleep. When dawn broke, she sat all over again like a ghost. She should find a way out, or maybe she should consult another lady physician, she told herself. She then made a rotti and ate. The hunger didn't quite assuage. Ragi flour had got over. She then made a rice rotti with some onion shreds in it and drank a cup of milk as the doctor had advised. She had to go to office from tomorrow. She decided to see a lady physician today. It was impossible to think constructively about the foetus in her. It had to be removed, which would make her feel easier in the mind. But what to do and who to ask were questions which had no facile answers.

She thought of asking Rohini, the clerk in her office if she knew of any good lady physician. She quickly took up the phone and looked for her number. It was the last day of her leave. She had to attend office tomorrow. She cursed herself for the plight she found herself in.

****

Chapter Twelve

As planned, the Divine Wedding Festivites of God Madhugiri Venkataramana Swamy happened on Sunday, the thirteenth day of the month of Karthika with all pomp and pageantry. Gracing the occasion was no less than the Chairman of the Kannada Development Authority. Everyone regardless of caste and creed had been invited. Pamphlets had been printed and distributed among the poor folk. Food had been cooked well. Everyone ate the same meal. There was no discrimination made between invitees, the household folk and the poor. The Chairman himself served the poor and destitute. No one denied this.

He welcomed everyone with open and warm arms. He was the same solemn man when offering worship to God. Sharade had distributed work to all on the previous day itself. Susheela and Savitri were to take care of cooking work. And her younger brothers had to welcome every visitor and guest. That their elder brother should not incur any bad name was the motto. Sangita asked Sahana to arrange for turmeric powder, vermilion powder, coconuts, fruits, flowers and betel leaves. The elder sister's words were as good as the Vedas. Sitamma had been brought in a car and made to sit on a chair. She felt delighted to see kids frolick and lark about. Yet a thorn kept pricking her. Srihari was not to be seen. No matter how bad and evil a son was, he was after all a son. Her eyes glistened with emotion. Wiping off tears, she was talking to every one with great pride and gusto.

On the one hand that her son occupied a high position made for pride. The absence of another son made for pain on the other. What to laugh for and what to weep for?! "O God! You yourself resolve this hardship!" she said as she joined her palms against her chest in salutation even as copious tears flowed down her cheeks. This heat of pain is like wrenching your guts. She chided herself for possibly worshipping God with poisonous flowers or something some day.

They placed the idol of God on the swing and swung it. Singing a full-throated praise of the Lord, and exulting that two eyes did not suffice to take in the fully and splendidly decorated God, people joined their palms against their chests in a profound salutation to God. Assuming that saying a few words to Rajgopal was it itself a matter of pride, everyone made it a point to exchange words with Gopal. It did cross Gopal's mind that no one broached the news telecast on TV. Yet the matter didn't fail to haunt and bug him. This was because Kalyan Singh the police inspector, Mallikarjuna Swamy his personal assistant, Chandrika, Rangaswamy and his wife and some more staff of his office had visited the hills, and frail and frayed, had visited the temple and had their meals there.

They talked to Gopal and his mother before departing.

Saraswathi felt dismayed to see the number of people rising beyond her wildest expectations. "Don't worry!" assured the cooks. "When we feel we are falling short in some item, with a particualr batch of eaters, we will cook the items." It happened exactly the same way. If the meal is open to the indigent, people will keep streaming in right till three in the afternoon. Gopal felt some undefinable satisfaction. The poor could be of any community. He had felt proud to have broken the discrimination indulged in by these priests. All the people observed this. But this was not the only place on earth. Such discrimination happened elsewhere as well. What to do about those places?

Sharade liked this too. Even though he was the eldest, Gopal used to ask Sharade for her opinion. She had a good pragmatic knowledge of life in those parts. Gopal never ignored his sister's advice. Saraswathi too began to behave like that. Saraswathi used to get angry with Sharade, feeling as she did that Sharade used to lord over others. Saraswathi now felt pity on her. What bossing over did she really engage in? The property was not hers. It was to be distributed among all. What profit were they getting, especially from this land and garden? Next to nothing. There was more loss than profit! Moreover she bore the burden of the younger sisters and brothers.

She taught music to some boys just to while away time. She never wore jewels. Only when she went to talk marriage matters would she wear the sacred marriage neck-string. After dressing up for weddings she would put on clothes to suit her role of the boss in the household at times and at times of the manservant. She used to get some food and some satisfying sleep. She knew only this house. She kept sellin parts of the property with the marriage of each younger sister. She sold off the small house in Madhugiri for one marriage and the part of the land behind the tank in Shambhonahalli for another. But she had sold them after getting the signatures of her younger and elder brothers. The income from the property and the money Gopal used to send would suffice to manage the household. She didn't have even one gold bangle. She sold off all her jewellery for the education of her brothers.

We don' know how, but she never was short in matters of treating visitors to the house with yummy and sumptuous food. "Ayyo! Why do I need jewels and clothes and stuff? Life is just this!" she would say. She was quite the opposite of Srihari in these matters. He hadn't been seen as yet. Sharade had come to the temple as simply as she had always been. She had also kept her younger sisters under her strict control. This was in fact the honour done to her for all the hardships she had endured all along.

It was five in the evening when they returned home after the Divine Wedding Festivities. As they entered the house, some visitor seemed to have come home. Mother and Sharade had come back first. The Gopal couple arrived slowly. Brothers and younger sisters had come on foot. There sounded some murmured talk as they entered.

"Are you all right?" It was Srihari who spoke up in the room in which Sitamma used to sleep. "Did you remember all of us now? Because there is trouble for you there, you have come here now!? Now you want younger brothers and sisters! You need God, pooje and people, everyone! Earlier you didn't need God. You didn't think younger brothers are jobless, you didn't think of the hardships your younger brothers have had to go through! You didn't think of trying for jobs for them, did you? Tell me! You looked after only your interests."

It was as if Srihari had taken up the broom standing in the nook, and thrashed Gopal and Gopal stood rattled. Gopal surveyed Sriahari from top to toe. *Srihari had pointed out what in fact was true, hadn't he? Would that mean I shouldn't have progressed from here? I have given it in writing that I didn't want any of father's property. Would that not be enough? Should I have stayed back here and looked after everything here? Yes, I could have stayed back and written what I wrote in the city. I was innTUmakuru. It has only been five years since I moved to Bengaluru. I can get younger brothers jobs. I thought I could not bear fully the responsibility of hosting them at Bengaluru. I could have rented a separate house for them. Somehow I didn't make up my mind. I am to blame somewhat, but who is he to berate me like he did? He could have done all this himself. He looked like a terrorist who had come to stab me!*

"*Ey*! Who are you to rebuke *anna*?" It was Sharade who took Srihari on as she came running. "He has looked after all of you, assuming the position of a father. You should have earned money and done what you are saying he should have done. You go out to effect the welfare of the village? You come once a week and ask mother for money for your drinking sessions. Are you not ashamed ? He is a man the land wants. How are you qualified to talk about him?"

Srihari then let rip.
"Who are you to ask me? Chuck away whatever I am to get. I won't come again! You have come from somewhere and have kept all property to yourself as if it is all yours! Partition the property first and then talk! I will not turn up here again."

Sitamma, who had been all this while listening in, came quietly out. Her frame was quaking. Her face had flushed crimson.

"Oh, you blithering sinner!" she laid into him too, her voice climbing steeply in pitch. "What has possessed you? You are scolding your own elder brother and sister the way you want. Go and earn some money, you jerk! You are talking about property without earning a paise. Come and earn the way she is doing. Aren't Shivaramu and Raghavendra earning? You don't have the good sense that they have. I give you a little because of the umbilical bond. And you go and fritter it away on booze. Why were you ever born to me, as my son?"

This further riled Srihari.

The words that he came up with now crossed all limits. "You are a great mother, aren't you?" he growled. "You gave birth to so many children so they became a burden to mother earth. You are now asking why I was born at all. You were the one who gave birth! Why did you? You conceived and gave birth to me to slake which itching lust of yours?"

This made everyone else there fly off the handle.

"Ey! scram, you scumbag!" they bellowed at him. "You are asking your own mother why she bore you? Cut out! God won't do you any good. She keeps anxiously waiting for you. She sees that someone serves food to you every night. You are swearing at such a woman. Get out! You don't deserve to be here."

Everyone held him by the arm and tried to jostle and push him.

"Leave me, you disgusting jerks! You are great people and I am the only one who is bad." Saying this and jerking himself free, he gave a long hard look at Gopal on his way past the huge front entrance hall.

The mother in Sitamma couldn't keep from saying, "Come, Srihari! You eat something. It is God's *prasada*."

The son didn't hear mother's words. Unable to contain the distress, she sagged down right there, hands on head.

"*Amma*! Why do you worry?" The other children consoled her, as they lifted her and sat her on the chair. "You be happy with the other children."

"Son! Don't let this distress you, okay? He has spoken like this when you returned home after a service to God. Don't get sick and weary. He is like that! The devil has possessed him! He speaks without any sense. There are bad children in this world. But there is no bad mother. The belly that gave birth to you gave birth to him as well. Why did this happen? It must be some God's curse on us."

Gopal had to solace mother. Otherwise her blood pressure might shoot up.

"Mother, why would I feel sick and weary? You are all here. You have showered on me so much love and happiness. This is all there is to life. Pain is a part of it. If it is happiness all the way, who would bear the pain part? One should be prepared to have both. We should not hold any one responsible. Whatever has come to my lot is mine. How could one say no to it? Don't worry! You are important for us. The pain is only because he spoke the words that he did to his own mother. That only he is separate from us means that he doesn't know the value of these relationships. Someone may be telling tales to him, poisoning his mind against us. That is tht reason he has come here only to speak like he did. Since everyone was here he went away. Let us see! Don't worry. I will make efforts to set him right till the time I am going to be here."

Saraswathi was alarmed by her husband's words. He was doing something he shouldn't be doing in some new-found enthusiasm, and was preparing to face another disaster, it seemed to her.

"Ri! Let us go back to Bengaluru. Maybe we are a burden to them here." she said, quietly stepping up and beginning to weep.

Others felt sick and weary by Saraswathi's words. Then Sharade took up the word. If she didn't speak no one else would know what to say.

"You can't take his words seriously. He makes a trip home once a week and returns after creating a scene. What will you achieve by reacting to it? Next to nothing! Annayya! It is my responsibility to see that no harm happens to you. No body knows when he will come back here. We should completely ignore such people. There would be one or two people in every household like him. As annayya said just now, we will try to bring him back on track. If he insists on distribution of property, let him take away whatever is due to him. let us not talk about it now. Get up all of you! Let us sing a song each drinking some steaming-hot coffee."

Everyone felt a load lighter.

They sat in a row on the floor mat, as if nothing serious had happened. These blasted Brahmins don't move the chariot without drinking coffee. Without coffee to drink, they sit with hands on heads, as if their lives have come to nought. "Annayya! You take a little sugar! Attige! You too! You see I drink without any sugar. That is why I am not pudgy. We shouldn't eat much sweets either."

195

Sharade's words took everyone somewhere else. "After talking about coffee and songs, she now talks about sugar and sweets!' Jayasimha took a hilarious dig at his elder sister.

"Sorry, fellow! I have work to attend to in the kitchen. I will sing first."

"Okay, okay! Who will be left here to listen to others if you sing first? You are besides a music teacher, madam!"

Raghavendra and Shivaramu got the old tabla and harmonium and sat down to perform. Everyone sat in a circle in the living hall, keeping some distance from one another. The tabla and the harmonium made their way to the middle. Gopal chaired the session. Sitamma sat by and watched. Since it was a Sunday, the sons-in-law of the household i.e the husbands of Savitri, Sahana, Sangeeta and Susheela, who had come for the Divine Wedding Festivities came back right at the time of the musical programme after doing a tour of Madhugiri town. Such squabbles were not new to them. But because Rajgopal was there, they didn't feel free to talk. They were all reasonably placed in life. Two of them had government jobs. Two were doing business. But both in knowledge and age-driven wisdom, Gopal was way ahead. And because they were younger, they couldn't behave with him with any freedom right since childhood. But Gopal received all with great affection. He asked Sharada to give them chairs. Sharade found it embarrassing to sing before all. She rose, and covering her bosom with the saree-end got them chairs.

Sharade had to cook in all for twenty two people of the household: Sitamma's eleven children, two daughters-in-law, four grandchildren, and four sons-in-law. Sharade felt in a hurry. What is it that I can cook for so many quickly? was her question. Sweet pongal had been given at the temple as *prasada*, the food item first offered to God and then distributed among devotees as a sign of the inferiority of devotees. That could be placed at the end of the plantain leaves they were eat from.

Walking into the kitchen Sharade surveyed the scene to see what vegetables were available. There wasn't much Tur dal. A meal wouldn't count as a meal without *saru* and *huLi*. She opened the back entrance door. At some distance from their house was the house of Sitaram, the teacher. His wife was Parvati. Parvati enjoyed great familiarity and freedom with

196

Sharade. He had also turned up for the meal given on the occasion of the Divine Wedding Festivities. She got half a seer of tur dal from her. She kept a *koladapple* on the oven for making *saaru*, and made coconut chutney and cooked four seers of rice. The music session was still on when she came out at nine after finishing cooking. Saraswathi had got up in the middle of the session and grated four coconuts. There was no dearth of coconut and rice. They had to buy provisions like tur dal and condiments. Getting some cucumbers from the backyard garden, she made the raw vegetable dish of *koosambari*.

It was ten in the night, but the number of singers increased rather than decreased. "Thank God, no one seems hungry", she told herself when suddenly she remembered that she hadn't lit the lamp in the homeshrine. She scampered to the homeshrine. But the wicklamp was indeed glowing. "I lit it," said Saraswathi. "I felt sick and weary somehow. I couldn't bear it, the way Srihari spoke to Gopal. So I thought there must be some deficiency on our part in ou devotion to God, and lit the lamp. I feel better now. Srihari's words are like a stabbing knife!"

"Let us wait for a few days, *attige*!" temporised Sharade. "We will decide one way or another. They are crying 'property, property!' Who will buy land now? Had it been near Madhugiri we could have turned it into saleable sites. We need to wait even for selling sites. Can we convert the garden, the paddy fields and the land behind the tank into sites? What to do? People talk without understanding things. Some bits of land we sold off for the marriage of younger sisters. And the land at Shambhonahalli and Akkirampura is not enough for giving away to one person. It would be more for one. Only He knows how to distriibute them. If he wants, he could go and build a house and do cultivation at Shambhonahalli and Akkirampura. Who'd object to that? How do we go about it if he asks us to sell everything and give him the proceeds? What if we are conned? That is why we are saying if elder brother is with us here, we can do it. My knowledge of these things is very little. It is my responsibility to see that he is never in any trouble. Those who talk don't do anything. It is only those silent ones who achieve something. You live in Bengaluru. Why are you feeling afraid? I don't have even the kind of knowldge that you have. Nor do I have the education that you have. Yet you see how I am livng! You should also try to live like this! You should put in words of courage and face situations without fear. How can we escape situations? Are only we committed to this? You be here and see what happens!"

These are the words that Sharade spoke to Saraswathi in the kitchen. But they didn't quite sail over to the living hall where the music concert was on. Although Gopal sat at the event, listening to his younger sisters sing, he was chewing the cud of the recent incidents, alternately forgetting the weary sickness that accompanied them in the music that was on and then recalling them. Disgust and amusement alternated. Besides, the pleasant company of mother soothed him. Srhari would come sometime, they said. So he could talk things over, he thought. *We could give him whatever he is asking for after talking it with younger brothers. Sharade, poor woman, doesn't understand. She only That the earth in which we sow seeds will yield something or the other, and will not leave us empty-handed is all she knows. She has done a lot of worldly transactions. But she knows that dividing property is not easy. She doesn't desire anything. I have also said I don't want anything. And what after all do we have by way of property? Who should we give that to? We should not du unjustly by other children. I should ask lawyer Shyamnath over and talk to him. I have in any case come over. Let me resolve this before returning.*

Around ten thirty children began to snore. All got up nnd readied for the night meal, laying out plantain leaves on the floor in the living hall to eat from. Narayan's wife also stood ready to serve. Meals were served. And everyone ate the meal of saaru, chutney and *koosambari* with great relish, an an involunatry "How yummy!" escaping their lips.

Sharade arranged for the sons-in-law to sleep in the rooms in which there were divans. Even before they arrived, she had prepared a room for just her elder brother and sister-in-law. The room had a study table and an almirah for storing clothes. The Gopal couple slept there. Sharade would sleep beside her mother, laying out a floor mat. The rest of the women slept in the living hall, laying out beds on the floor and chatting right till twelve o' clock about their family sorrows and joys and swearing at Srihari.

****

It was six in the morning.

Thinking that the *parijata* flowers would wither and fall away, Saraswathi had set the alarm clock for the wake up call, and accordingly, she got up

198

to pluck flowers. All those days she would pluck a basketful of *parijata*, *kanigale* flowers, bell-flowers and *kanakambara* and sitting by the home-shrine, thread them into strings before decorating each picture of God with it and giving a *kanakambara* string to Sadhana for her to fasten in her hair. This was her first routine of the day, a routine that satisfied her. Except for helping Sharade in the kitchen work she would have no other work. Some exchange of ideas and notes with mother-in-law in the afternoon. She walked with Sharade over to Goddess Maramma temple to fulfill the vow of offering Her a saree, the vow she had made for Gopal.

She felt easier in the mind.

The thought that she had only one more week left of her leave after which she had to leave for Bengaluru for work did make her sick and weary. There was also the anxiety of leaving behind her husband. *What if there was some serious trouble if Srihari came back and talked the way he did* was the anxiety.

Gopal had just recovered and come back from the hospital. They couldn't be there for ever. She did broach this with her mother-in-law. Mother-in-law was mentally a more solid woman.

"Look! Isn't mother, the one who gave birth to Gopal, alive and kicking in this house having heard those words of Srihari's?!" Sitamma injected some courage into Saraswathi. "Isn't Sharada who should have been in her husband's place come here for a morsel of food, and dedicated her life to this household? She sold off all jewels to educate Srihari. He now blurts out whatever comes to his tongue. Isn't she living? Your husband is my son, you woman! I also know that he has just been out of hospital. Don't worry! Nothing of the sort you fear will happen. We will resolve his problem. Sadhana's marriage will also be fixed in the meanwhile. The groom has been decided on. They will come next week for talks about the wedding. He will finish that and come to Bengaluru. Don't be scared. They are our children. It is a righteous crisis. What can we do?"

Since Sitamma sobbed away holding her daughter-in-law's hands, Saraswathi felt a measure of comfort. She asked Sharade to come with them in the car to Goravanahalli Devarayana Durga. "Ayyo! Who would be there with mother?" Sharade said by way of an affable, if animated, reply. "I will be here. You people go and see it. Here are all my Gods. I have no desires!"

It was Friday.

They went off first to Devarayana Durga carrying two coconuts, five kilogrammes of rice, jaggory, one saree, turmeric, vermilion, plantains, betel leaves and nuts. The site of God Devaraya Narsimha was a beautiful place, hemmed in by a picturesque hill range. Driving a car to such a place was a beautiful experience. And how would it be if they went on foot? The couple had an eyeful of the scenery before Saraswathi did a worship at both the temples dedicated to the Gods of Yoga Narasmha and Bhoga Narasimha. Sharade had got done two specially prepared garlands, threaded not just two flowers at a time, as is done for ordinary garlands, but three, four or five at a time, the *toomaale*, just for the Gods. Saraswathi handed these remarkably and delightfully bountiful and thick garlands to the priest, asking him to offer them to the God before putting five hundred rupees into the till in each temple. They lifted their joined palms at their chests in salutation to the Lord before giving away in the end one hundred rupees as the priest's fee.

Then they made their way to Goravanahalli. Whether one believed in God or not, the journey was for sure very exhilarating. Gopal had never embarked on a travel of this kind. It was the first time that he had travelled with Saraswathi on a trip to temples. There was some delight in this. One depending on the other, there was here, much more than love and lust, a bond that rose above these.

Ssaraswathi gave the saree-of-the-vow away, asking the priest to put it on the Goddess before she filled the lap with the material they had brought along, the ritual of placing in the Goddess's lap, rice, the piece of blouse, jaggory and stuff. They made the couple sit there before they served them a meal as God's *prasaada*. Gopal observed keenly the life of the people there, their mindsets, and the way things were being monitored and managed there. Many people would come there to offer coconuts, blouse pieces, sarees, jaggory and stuff in fulfillment of the vows made earlier to this God. There was therefore good income for this temple. There would be arrangement of meals on a daily basis. There was a temple trust as well. To call it the Laxmi temple was especially appropriate, Laxmi being the Goddess of Wealth. It is not wrong to fill the stomachs of the have-nots from resources of the haves. But the various methods of worshipping there amused Gopal. Different kinds of pooje for different people. There has been commercialisation of these poojes in Bengaluru.

After the meal, they went off to see the Teetha dam. Jayamangali river was a beautiful river of Koratagere taluk. Even now there was no dearth of water in Koratagere taluk like they had in Shira and Madhugiri. Because of this Jayamangali river, all villages and hoblis were well provided with water in Koratagere taluk. This was the reason paddy and sugarcane were the staple crops in Koratagere. They should go to Akkirampura some day, they thought. There was an ancient house of theirs there. Farmers had planted sugarcane in their fields there. One felt like eating sugarcane but what to do? Sugar should not crystallsie in blood, you see!

Teetha is a small village. People have made use of the dam to suit their way way of life. The dam was visible from the Goravanalli temple. They thought it was a beautiful scene. There was sufficient water in the reservoir. Both the neat little village and the dam looked as if they were painted. An old woman called Kamalamma had actually seen Goddess Laxmidevi it seems. It was the custom to give two black beads and four bangles to girls. The putative belief was that if they place them and one fistful of rice and one anna daily before God in their homes, the girls' marriages would come off. After their marriage was fixed they had to offer the rice and the money to Goddess Laxmidevi of Goravanahalli, filling Her lap.

Girls from Bengaluru and other states would travel to Goravanahalli, make a vow, taking the beads and when their marriages came off, return to fulfill their vows. We don't know what kind of belief was this. But it is proved that life is a function of such beliefs. But somethings happen inevitably. Believers believe that these happenings happen because of God's grace.

Be that as it may, this is a social and spiritual agreement. It is because of some such force that the good sense of doing good happens to people. They in fact do. This is also an optimistic inspiration to common people.

Having done every service to God Saraswathi sashayed toward the car. The car passed through Koratagere and zoomed toward Madhugiri. It pulled up before a little hotel in Korategere for coffee. Some acquiantances came over and talked to Gopal.

Seeing Gopal and her daughter-in-law from a distance, Sitamma thought to herself, how nice it would have been, had they had a child. Gopal's younger brothers and sisters had all had children. Because Gopal didn't have any progeny, he had said he didn't want any of his parental property. It was his greatness. He didn't speak one unnecessary word. A nugget of gold he was! He could have paid more attention to household affairs. But maybe because he thought every sibling would study well and shape their own lives, he kept away from home. But he had the same kind of affection for everyone. If God gives you something, He takes away something. He vouchshafed intellect and a good position, but didn't give Gopal children. It was he himself who took the responsibility of marrying Sharade off. His younger uncle showed the groom. Somehow his younger sister's life went awry. He felt sick and weary. Later it was she who looked after younger brothers and sisters.

There was no provision in law those days for a share of parental property for girls. But law had changed now. Sharade would say, "I don't want anything, mother! If someone gives me a morsel of food, that would do! I will work in their home." Those words would sting Sitamma. What could she do? She was fifty two when her husband shuffled off his mortal coil. Sadhana was then two years old. They didn't allow her to undergo a tubectomy operation. Five or six children would have done. There were two children born between Gopal and Sharade. They were yet tiny tots when they died because of dysentery. That was why there was a distance of nine years between Gopal and Sharade.

Sitamma's thoughts went every which way.
"Did you have a *darshana* of God? Did you have a comfortable trip?" she asked ingenuously as the couple walked over and sat by her. Sharade brought them some coffee and she also sat drinking the steaming brew.

Bringing up the topic of father's annual ceremony, Sharade submitted it was the following Monday. Gopal would come to Madhugiri every year for the yearly ritual. This was not a matter of belief. It was an honour done to the dead-and-gone father, setting aside a day in a year to his memory. If the methods were according to the shastras, doing the ceremony without having to deny others' beliefs was right, it seemed to Gopal. Since he was the eldest, he should do it with all seriousness, he thought. Younger brothers and sisters would also join him. Younger brothers who had undergone the thread-investiture ceremony would take part in it. The family members of the two younger uncles would also join. Food for about forty, forty five people would be arranged. Only Raghavendra, Shivaramu, and Jayasimha would go there for the yearly postdeath routines of grandpa and grandma. Something seemed to strike Gopal before it receded. *I came here to take some rest. But this week is the death ritual. For next week are slated the marriage-talks. And the week after are the talks about property distribution. Sharade has said I should be here till Sadhana's wedding. I should sort out something for Srihari. Where then do I get rest?*

Till Sadhana's wedding it would be three months since I came here. Saraswathi will go back the day after the death ritual. She has finished all her work relating to her vows. Younger uncle has asked me over for a day. When could go there, I don't know. If i don't go, he would think otherwise. I should ask my friends, Vinay kumar, lawyer Shyamanatha and writer Krishna murthy over for a day.

He then let his thoughts flow toward the current inevitability. *The money that I had brought here for expenses here has all ended. There is no money left for the annual ritual. What to do? I have over the years spent myself for the annual ceremony. Who do I ask now? Mine is not the kind of personality that asks people for money!* As if he remembered all at once, he told Sitamma to call the cooks, the respectable Mrutyunjaya Shastri to talk things over and to tell younger brothers as well! There were only three days left.

But would Sitamma forget such things? She wouldn't. She had already informed everyone. The cooks said they would come over the following morning. He could send word to younger uncle through Raghavendra. Provisions and other things needed for the annual ritual could be bought after cooks gave the list of things when they turned up on the morrow. On Sunday they could clean and *madi*-purify clothes. Cooking had to be done in the *madi*-purity mode. All younger brothers had to be provided new bottom-wear wrap-arounds, the *panche*s and low wooden stools, Brahmins had to be given panches and *muguta*s, and low wooden stools for them to sit on. Sharade would arrange all these with meticulous efficiency. She said Brahmins should be given generous priestly fee, the *dakshine* and she would usually offer them a pair of panches costing as much as two hundred rupees.

Elder brother never disagreed with his oldest younger sister, for he knew that there worked in her a correct humanitarian consciousness.

The annual ritual would cost them at least ten thousand rupees. What to do? Whom to ask for money, keeping my prestige and honour intact? Let me see! I have time till tomorrow. He remained silent without telling anyone about the problem he faced. No body would know. They would, only if he let it out. There was no ATM yet in Madhugiri. If you wanted cash, you had to travel to Bengaluru. Saraswathi could be handed a cheque and asked to go over to Madhugiri by bus. He didn't want to go to Bengaluru now. He wanted to go once for all. But money had to be organised for the annual ceremony. *It is okay, everything has an answer in life. If I don't open up myself now, I will become small. I should spend without talking about money at all,* he thought. *Only then will I have some value.*

Mallikarjuna swamy had already phoned twice, asking when Gopal was going back to office. He also wanted to go back now. The rest was enough. But he had told everyone there that he would stay back till Sadhana's wedding. If he left sooner, word would spread that he was shirking his responsibility. *I have in any case come. Let me experience everything that comes my way before returning to Bengaluru*, he said wordlessly to himself. *Ushe's phone call also came twice or thrice. I cut it myself. Nonsense! She phones now after doing what shouldn't have been done. I shouldn't hear a shred of her voice. What horrible words she spoke! Chee! Her memory is like a scorpion's sting!*

Sipping coffee, Gopal changed tack, talking now about who Sadhana's groom was, what he was doing and stuff. The boy, the son of Narasimha Shastry of Chikkapete, was from Tumakuru. He was an engineer. He was employed in Bengaluru. Having seen the girl, he had agreed to the marriage. His father, mother, elder sister and brother -in-law were all to come for the talks. What their terms and conditions were for the marriage was to be seen. He was going to be the only engineer son-in-law of the household. That was one reason why the liasion was not to be averted. Gopal and others were thinking of giving away whatever they demanded and effecting the wedding in a grand fashion. The groom's pary was asking the wedding to be held in Bengaluru. But who would stay in Bengaluru and organize the wedding? Moreover it would be more expensive in Bengaluru. You had to set aside more than a lakh as rent for the wedding hall. And then to add to that, the special treatment for the groom, clothes, meals, jewellery and stuff. What to do?

Gopal hadn't been told all this, maybe because there was no time to tell him all these details. There were yet no definite talks held. All that was known was that the boy had consented. Mother was saying all sorts of things today. *We don't have the money to spend as much as a wedding in Benagluru would imply. That meant that mother was expecting me to spend that much.* Saraswathi took a look at husband's face. After exchanging looks, Gopal lowered his head and set to thinking. He had neverever temporized about any household function. But how would he to cope with this?

"*Amma*! Did they directly ask you to get the wedding done at Bengaluru? Are you simply guessing?"

"Yes. The boy's father did, casually, ask. In case they insist, we should be prepared, shouldn't we? I know the expenses would be more."

"We will do exactly as we did for other girls." Sharade, who had kept silent so far, broke in. "We needn't rack our brains about it. It would suffice if we satisfy the groom's party. Don't listen to mother! If you speak, the groom's party will not counter it."

"What property do you plan to sell this time?"
"We should sell off some property. Where is the money otherwise, tell me!"

Sharade used to get their signatures before selling the property. Now Gopal was right before her. Saraswathi was in some turmoil for some reason. Hers was only one thought: even when they had refused their share in parental property, why were they dragging them into this? This disgusted her. *Money and property alone wouldn't be enough. Responsibility is important too. Sharade, poor woman, has shouldered this responsibility thus far. Since we are from Bengaluru she is putting Gopal upfront. It is enough if he comes to know his exact role in this. Let us do whatever we can. It seems Srihari, who had gone away that day, did came back and had his meals at home on two nights. I was in the room. He said he was not coming for the annual ritual, and that he would come home only after he is given whatever was due to him. One part of the property will go to him. What to do fro Shivaramu and Raghavendra? They don't even have jobs as yet. Would Jayasimha and Narayana not stake their claims? They would. In sum we should resolve this without squabbling. We should sit and talk to other younger brothers before talking to Srihari.*

The basic experiences of life are important to a liteartteur. Real life is his school. If he intends writing purely from imagination, naturalness will be a casualty. If I run away from thislfe I can never come back again. Even if I did, nobody would value me. This is not like the Kannada Development Authority. This is the site where I took birth. Life is very important. Life comes before writing. Let me afford justice to people who trust me. here Sharade, who studied only upto the tenth standard, has separated from her husband, has ome back here and played a life-givng, life-nourishing role for her other siblings. Lfe ahs taught her a lot of things. She says she has no practical knowledge of the world. She has managed household affairs for the last twenty five years, providing meaning to ten lives. Being highly educated, if we quail, we may have to hang our heads in shame. It is okay even if I have to shell out a couple of lakhs myself. Let me be here and sort this out.

Gopal handed the coffee cup back, as he gently patted Saraswathi's hand, the pat assuring her, "Don't get scared. Nothing will happen!"

The look in his eyes told her that he had arrived at some decision.

Except Savitri, every one had come for the annual ritual. As it was a Monday, it was a tad difficult for her to make it. Srihari didn't. Had he come, he would have had to come the previous day itself for the meal in the madi-purity mode. Mother wouldn't agree to people eating anywhere before they came for the ritual. And mother came to know about his tryst with Ushe, only God save him! She brags everywhere that her son is a nugget of gold. She would not let me cross the house threshold if she got to know that he loved a woman from a backward class. Let me hold this back right here. Let me not bring this up again.

Gopal felt worried the moment this thing came up. *The blasted thing comes up again and again even if I don't want it.*

Sharade had got provisions and stuff from a shop already. Special delights that father was fond of, *atirasa, aambode, puuri,* the sweet liquid dish of *payasa,* squeezed tur dal *huLi,* the thick bittergourd mush, jackfruit, plantain stalk sidedish, green gram *tovve* and plantain stalk *raayata* were cooked.

One had to have a huge belly for eating all these! She had herself got all things without talking to her elder brother. She had washed *panche*s and *mugutas* to be given to all her brothers before putting them out to dry the previous day itself. She, madi-pure herself, put out *panche*s for drying for those who were to sit for Brahmin duties. Gopal was not happy about this madi-purity and impurity stuff. But there was no rebellion. Sharade's also was the same stand. Whether she believed in such stuff or not, she didn't question herself. Somewhere in a corner of her mind, she was convinced that all this was false. Instead of all this elaborate meaninglessness, if one fed and clothed some old men and women, that would be worth it, she would tell herself. But mother would not let that happen, would she? Besides, there was this fear of cousins. They would complain that these people were jibbing at doing a simple annual ritual. But Sharade did everything with absolute efficiency and without skimping about anything.

The ritual by the living for the dead-and-gone father began well past twelve o' clock.

Women were all in the room. The five male children sat down for the ritual. Srihari didn't turn up. Younger Uncle asked where Srihari was. Sitamma glossed over it by taking a topical detour. Younger uncle went away saying he would come later. No one was listening to whatever mantras the priests were jabbering. Brahmins who had come for Brahminic duties were asked to stand in the courtyard and their feet washed with water that had been carried in the madi-purity mode, and a plantain leaf put upside down and some cowdung placed on it: these were actions one didn't quite figure out. But one thought haunted Gopal. That was: hadn't his younger brothers committed any sin? His affair with Ushe came back to haunt him, and everytime the priest offered the holy water to the gods as he jabbered 'prachanimite', Gopal felt as if his experience of every day that he spent with her was being pushed away along with the water. *Why is this happening*, he wondered. *Remembrance now when water is being pushed away for father! Why did father give birth to me like this! So many children are doing this for father! What if something happens to me? It has so happened that I don't have children. Even now my mind is in turmoil. Had Ushe been my wife, instead of Saraswathi, sperms would have bristled in me. I would have become a father.*

This is not a mistake of my father. But she is no longer on my scene now. She is as good as dead. The offering, the arghya that I give away now is for her. For her love, for her death. Ushe is dead. prachanimite...

"Sir, what are you thinking? Drink the water after tipping it thrice onto your cupped palm! Take this, make three balls of black sesame along with this cooked rice and place the balls on the copper plate. My hands are weak. I used to mix it myself. You do it now!"

Only priests would do this mixing. Others wouldn't know. The cooked rice was falling apart, and so it was difficult to make balls of it. The cooked rice needed to be soft to make balls for the manes. The priest gave the rice away to the cooks for them to boil it further to make it softer. Stirring it with some water and cooking it to a softer consistency took a quarter of an hour. It was thus three o'clock when the balls-for-the-manes were offered to the manes, holy water sipped and Brahmins were served meals. Gopal felt his head whirled because he was starving. It was Rajgopal who, laying out plantain leaves, served the brahmins to their hearts' content. He valued the whole exercise because of his love for his father. But apart from that it didn't make much sense. What sense did it make to make balls-of-the-manes for father, only when mixing black sesame with cooked rice? One ought to stop this practice. It was difficult moreover for Gopal to stay starving. The priests sang the praises of Rajagoal's politeness when things got over with the offering of food to the deity, the *naivedya* and the priests got paid their priestly fees. How big a personality he was! He did the postdeath ritual of his father with so much devotion! It was five o'clock when, after they left, people were served their meals.

Gopal was very tired. Bending down he rolled over a floor mat there. Everyone was alarmed. "Anna! anna!" cried the brothers and came rushing. Golp showed his hand to suggest there was nothng the matter and that he would be all right once he ate something. He then drank a tumbler of water. Things seemed to settle down once he quietly ate his meal. Younger uncle and his younger aunt and their children had turned up. Only two boys had showed up from Gopal's youngest uncle's family. Srihari didn't come. Sitamma kept looking toward the entrance door in the hope of seeing Srihari walk up. No matter how evil her son might be, it was natural for a mother to see to the food of her child. That was mother's heart. Since he didn't turn up, she ate her meal, sick and weary.

****

The phone rang at midnight. Anxiety spiralled in everybody. Sharade quietly walked up and answered the call. It was a call from the local police station. The Circle police Inspector was speaking.

"Madam! Is Srihari from your family?"
"Yes, Sir!"
"Can you all any male member?"
"Okay, Sir! There is my elder brother, Rajagopal."
"Oh, madam! Isn't he the chairman of the Kannada Development Authority?"
"Yes, Sir! What is the matter? You have called at this hour?"
"There is no need to panic. Please call him, I will talk to him."

Finding herself deep inside a curious combo of anxiety and alarm, Sharade felt impaled on the horns of the Hamletian dilemma of whether to tell elder brother or not to tell him. He was sleeping in the room. Sister-in-law had told Sharade not to tell him anything which caused panic. She was to leave for Bengaluru the following morning. What else is in store for us, wondered Sharade. Exhausted after the annual ritual, Gopal was into a sound sleep. The Inspector was saying he would like a man to speak to. Rustling over to the home-shrine, she lifted her joined palms to and against her chest in a devoted obeisance to God before bustling over to rap on the door of the room in which Gopal was sleeping. Gopal quickly came and opened the door. He seemed alarmed too. His heart skipped a beat when Sharade told him the call was from the Police Inspector. What was the matter? A call from the police station at the dead of night! Had any information come from Bengaluru? Had anybody else come here to cause terror here? Whatever it was, he had to face it.

Gopal took up the receiver before saying no more than the greeting of 'namaskaara!' He breathed a lot easier when the inspector said, "It is an honour and a pleasure to speak to a dignitary like you, Sir!" But what the cop went on with caused anxiety. "Sir, there was a political convention in Pavagada today. Some naxals pelted cars with stones with the intent to

209

trouble the legislators there. The police arrested some of them. One of the arrested boys was one Srihari from Madhugiri. On being interrogated, he took your name. I asked them to send him here without informing anyone. They are bringing him here in a jeep. You are a big man. You please come over now to the police station and advise your brother. If you identify him in writing, we will release him from custody."

As he put the phone back, Gopal signed to Sharade for a glass of water. *I haven't thus far stepped into a police station. What is my position and prestige? I have to go to the police station, that too at two in the night! What if somebody sees me? Srihari doesn't have the goodness of heart so I could talk to him, facing him. We should not wake up mother. Heart-broken she will weep her eyes out.* Saraswati noticed husband's plight. She intuitively understood her husband. But she couldn't speak. She was, besides, leaving for Bengaluru tomorrow. How could she leave husband behind? She grew scared about how he would react if a panic-causing condition was created. But she couldn't speak out.

Gopal drove his car to the station along with Raghavendra and Sharade. The jeep carrying Srihari had already arrived from Pavagada when they reached the station. Srihari was there sitting. He must have copped a few punches. His jubba was torn. Gopal didn't speak. As Gopal entered the police station, the inspector got up and received Gopal, taking his joined palms up against his chest in respectful greeting. "The moment you stepped into the station is indeed a great moment of good fortune for us. That is my good fortune too." Gopal didn't react even now. Having seen Srihari, he asked the inspector for a sheet of paper. Having written the note identifying Srihari as his brother and signed and handed the the note to the inspector, he said, "I am grateful to you."

"Sir, I was your student at the college at Tumakuru. I remember every period of yours. I feel fulfilled having resolved a hassle of my teacher's. Don't say 'thanks.'" He pressed Gopal's hand to his eyes, a gesture, which touched Gopal's heart. Tears jerking out of his eyes, Gopal felt easier in the mind. He expressed his appreciation by patting Shanta kumar's back.

No one slept that night. No one woke up Sitamma. Sharade gave Srihari a fresh set of clothes. Blood had clotted on his body where the lashes had landed. Sharade applied neosporin ointment at those spots before handing him some pills. Before that she served him a meal. Gopal simply sat, his head bowed. He didn't know the language with which people swore at, and called people names. The only feeling he had was that he was his younger brother. He never ever spoke to him, opening up his heart and mind. All sat clammed up. Srihari was eating his meal, his head bowed. All women and Raghavedra and Shivaramu sat on beds, with their heads on knees.

Silence reigned in the living hall.

No one spoke. Which was why Sitamma didn't wake up. No one had the guts to take him on and rip him apart. If there is noise kicked up at the dead of night, people split open the silence and gather together. One's honour then goes for a toss. His meal eaten, Srihari rolled over on the cot in the living hall. Sharade didn't speak either. Humanitarianism! One must do this, she told herself as she covered him with a bedsheet.

"Annayya! Go sleep! It is four o' clock. You get up late tomorrow. It is okay! Attige! You also go sleep! You are leaving for Bengaluru tomorrow," said Sharade before going to sleep herself.

Saraswathi even now thought her husband could accompany her to Bengaluru. But she knew that that wasn't possible. It was no use talking. She would become a bad woman if she did. Feeling helpless regret about this, she went to bed, as did the others.

There is rebellion right at home. That too in my own home! Terror is not outside. I faced terror boldly, with my chin up so far. What an irony this is! Is it possible for me to correct him? I have given mother word. I should pave a way for him. We should sit together and talk first. Only later should we talk to him. We need to ask him what he wants. But will he talk to me, and listen to me? Nothing is possible if he is not ready to listen!

When did he develop this bond with Naxals? He must have joined the movement only recently. That is why he has been caught. The brothers are so different from each other! If the world lears he is a Naxalite it would look upon me differently, wouldn't it? I wanted to achieve something and show the world. Oh I had to fall into the debt of a former student, having had to go to the police station for the sake of my brother! I didn't pay enough attention to the growth of my brothers. This was my mistake. What is our choice? And nothing happens according to what we choose. We think something but what happens would be different. If everything pans out the way we want, there would be no pain. What affects and hurts us is what is left unexpressed, and not what is expressed.

I never knew about his Naxal connections! Didn't anybody in the household know? Let me try. If he wants to become good, we can think of relationships and property and stuff. If not, let the bond sever. Such people don't need homes and relationships! If it is not possible for me, let us see! What more can he ask for than his share of the property. If he wants that, he should behave like a good honorable family man. We can get him married. He might then stop knocking about like a vagabond. Let me speak to mother. Saraswathi is leaving for Bengaluru tomorrow. I should inject some courage into her. She would be alone there. She would be worrying about me.

Hordes of such thoughts pursued Gopal relentlessly the whole night before in the wee hours he drifted off to sleep. Something like this happened with the others as well.

****

Chapter Thirteen

Long before they got up the next rnorning, Srihari had sneaked off.

There was no trace of him for the next ten days. Everyone got anxious. But this,.i.e Srihari disappearing for extended periods, was not new. He was the bitter neem leaf amidst sweet jaggory blocks. Where to go scouting for him? They never bothered where he was. This also was a mistake. How did someone who didn't worry about how he had strayed join Naxalites? If he didn't land any job, he could have trusted the land the family owned and cultivated it, couldn't he? Did what he was doing behoove people like them? Whoever did it should be very principle-bound? If not, it would have no value. You would get only whacks!

It is true that people with a thinking consciousness like literatteurs and rebels support such movements. Pontiffs of mathas do tend to them. These rebels reject corruption and other dirt in politics. They don't trouble common people. It is terrorists who trouble society. There is even a subject called Naxalism. It rejects the system, based on principled theory. It doesn't do physical violence to any individual. The idea is that it ought to be a free force of resistance. It is true that such people learn skills to use arms. But there are also such people who do boldly resist the system but live in cushy air-conditioned houses and use swanky cars. They do help the poor and the destitute. But small-time Naxals get cheaply caught by the police. Such people become victims of Police bullets.

No one informed mother about Srihari's adventure. Since there was an important matter before the household, Srihari's incident receded to the

213

background. That was the issue of Sadhana' marriage. The groom's party had come to their place last Sunday for talks about the marriage. They were a cultured lot. Parents lived in Tumakuru. The groom's elder sister lived in Bengaluru. So the elder sister's house was the boy's residence for now. He could rent a separate house after the wedding. That was the current state of affairs. Although he had done an Engineering degree, Anantha kumar, the boy, was not for modernity in clothes and fashion etc. He was courteousness personified. He must be thirty two.

Everyone liked the liaison.

Rajgopal, Sharade, Jayasimha and Narayana sat for negotiations at the talks on behalf of the bride's side and the groom's parents, his elder sister and brother-in-law represented the groom. Sitamma sat as an observer. She spoke very sparingly these days when with strangers and outsiders. She used to freely mix earlier. But she would now be low-key, letting her eldest son and Sharade do the talking. That was because, without allowing others' words any room, their words carried, she thought, loads of authority and weight. Sharade sat at the talks, dressed like any other married woman, well deckedout, wearing the marriage badge of the neck-string, with lavish fresh flowers fastened in her hair on the head. She decked herself out like that so as not to arouse any suspicion about her separated status. Who would probe about her status after the wedding? Nobody would. If asked about her husband, she would temporise and say something evasive. If anyone probed about Srihari, she would be the first to reply. In sum if they could keep things under wraps till the wedding, it would be fine.

The lucky thing was that the groom's family was impressed by the decent, full and fulfilling life the bride's populous family gave the impression of leading. Who would come by such a groom's family? People sought a bride these days who has an Engineering degree. She should have a job, she. should be the parents' only daughter, she should be fair and svelte. They expected a whole lot of such things. But the present groom's party didn't expect or demand any of these. They did initially say the wedding be conducted in Bengaluru.

"We have married off so many girls in our household," Sharade explained. "We don't have the financial muscle to do the wedding in a city like Bengaluru. But if you want, we can do it in Tumakuru."

At this explanation, they trooped out for a huddle and when they came back, said the following, turning to Gopal: "Sir, You live in Bengaluru, don't you? You can try, can't you? Our relatives live in Bengaluru. You also save the bus charge. My son will also join you in this."

They didn't quite know what to say in reply.

We are saying that the expenditure would be more in Bengaluru. With all the kin of the household in Madhugiri, only I arranging the wedding in Bengaluru would be very difficult. Saraswathi wouldn't agree. A wedding would mean so many people would be travelling from here often. I can't say 'no' to them staying at my place in Bengaluru, can I? And when I am out and with only saraswathi staying at home, how would she alone manage their food etc? These are impossible things. Saraswathi can't adjust to them here the way she does at Madhugiri. She would always have a strand of dissatisfaction and disgruntlement. We should say something to the groom's party opposing holdin the wedding in Bengaluru.

"It is not that." Gopal said persuasively. "One point is expenditure. And the other is everyone of the household is here in Madhugiri and only I am in Bengaluru. It is not possible for me take any decision without their cooperation. I am these days always under the pressure of work. So the work of running about is done by my younger brothers. Right now I am not in a position to do such running about. We will for sure do it either in Madhugiri or Tumakuru."

Gopal felt it was okay by the time he finished speaking. That gave him a mite of comfort. But what followed Gopal didn't quite like.

"Sir!" It was the groom's father who spoke, giving it a whole new twist. "Who would run about when your own daughter is to be married? You say you are yet childless. Think of your younger sister as your own daughter! You can do some running about yourself like you per force do for your daughter!"

This didn't go down well with the bride's kin gathered there. They couldn't take any talk that found fault with elder brother's words. They exchanged looks. No word escaped anybody's mouth.

What an irony this is! Had I had a daughter, I had to do everything, right! But presently I am in the position of a chairman. This threat and intimidation have truly scared me. You have vim and verve when you have whatever you ought to have. The fact that you have something you shouldn't have must have dwarfed you. Sometimes the bond called marriage is questioning me. There is true love only in relationships other than marriage. A man loving a woman other than his wife and a wife loving a man other than her husband are both immoral but they appear right to them. Such thoughts see a life fuction like marriage as a chemical, social and biological agreement. The economical part comes first. Then comes the social, then the chemical and then the biological. This is my personal stand. But what to tell these people?

Mother who had kept silent all along took up the word now. Her affection for me and the idea that no one should insult me played their role in what she had to say.

"Look! You tell us to conduct the wedding at such and such a place." Sitamma spoke. "We will do it if we are able to. Otherwise, no. Let us not indulge in this business of the groom's party or the bride's party trampling the other. My son is the chairman of the Kannada Deveopment Authority. He has his own position and prestige. All these younger siblings of his are like his own children. You don't have the right to charge him with neglecting his duties. If you are okay with this, go ahead. Otherwise it is okay. If not you, there would be somebody else. My daughters have so far not put their foot down about marrying any particular boys. They have all married boys decided on by their elder brother and mother and are reasonably well in their husbands' places. They have never crossed the line set by their elder brother. He is saying it would be difficult to perform the wedding ceremonial in Bengaluru. You need to adjust a little. You ought not to pain others by being obstinate about some things."

Mother's words stilled the atmosphere. Mother had broken the stick into two unambiguous pieces. Sharade glared at mother. Jayasimha and Narayana kept signaling to mother that she should stay silent. The groom looked at his father. His mother stared down at the floor, wiping her face and hands with her hanky. Looking at his son, the groom's father walked out, signing to the son. The son and the son-in-law followed them. The son was advising the father. They saw the scene of the son-in-law simply listening.

Head bowed, Gopal mulled things with a 'Come what may, we will face it with our chins up!' kind of posture. Sharade rose and waked in, to brew some coffee. Narayana's wife went to help her. Some snacks had already been prepared. She gave away the tray of cups of coffee and glasses of juice for her to distribute. to the guests.

After a huddle of about ten minutes, the bridegroom's father walked in.

'Please pardon me, Sir!' he said apologetically. "I spoke something I should not have in a rush of blood. Please excuse me, *amma!* You do whatever suits you best! It would be better if it is done in Tumakuru. We expect about one thousand and five hundred people. There would be four hundred people for the 'respectful attention that bride's parents show the groom' ceremonial and the dinner in-honour-of-the-in-laws. Please perform the wedding meticulously. We will book the Wedding Hall ourselves. Whatever you give by way of the respectful-attentions-given-to-the-groom-by-the-bride's-party, the *varoopachaara*, is upto you. We will bring along with us the necklace with the marriage-badge in it, a pair of bangles and a pair of earstuds for the bride. The food should be good. Please do these!"

This was agreeable to everybody. Everyone agreed.

"Let us fix a good auspicious day and write out the wedding invite. By then we could decide on the day of the wedding. We should look for a day that suits the horoscopes of the boy and girl. We are in Tumakuru. We will make enquires and let you know."

Everyone was served the wheaten *poori*, the thick liquid dish of *saagu*, and the sweet saffron wheaten grit dish of *keesari baath*.

Sharade gave away to women vermillion powder, a blouse piece and a coconut, some betel leaves and nuts. Gopal handed over a coconut, betel leaves and nuts to male members of the visiting groom's party before putting his joined palms at his chest in a greeting of parting.

The groom's father sent the very next day the date when the wedding invite could be written out and a note saying 'There are two dates for the wedding in March. There still is three months' time.' There was time of one month for scripting the wedding invite. This was the important matter for now. Srihari's issue had receded to the backburner. But it stung you at times like the masked punch.

After the wedding talks, Srihari who had quietly sneaked in one night, ate his meal and slunk wordlessly off. He didn't even say where he was headed. Only Sharade had the courage to ask him. But even this courage had disappeared after the police station episode. She would serve him rice and te liquid dish of *huLi* after placing the eating plate on the floor. No word about what he would eat, how much and questions like whether it was enough etc. He would sleep the night and go off in the morning. Mother hadn't been informed about his Naxal connection and his being nabbed by the police and the midnight trip they had made to the police station. Had they done that, they could have mother drill some sense into him. Gopal and Sharade decided that they should tell Srihari if the police caught him over again, they would not be responsible.

But how to say this to him? There was no talk with him. It was the same pigheadedness. On one of those trips home he had told mother, "Give whatever is due to me in cash. or else, give me a house. I will sell it off." A weeping Sitamma informed this to Gopal.

"Don't take it seriously." Gopal told mother. "You keep quiet. We will drill some good sense into him."

But Gopal had an inner awareness of things. He thought he would sit with his younger brothers and discuss and dialogue. *Let us go to Shabhonahalli for a couple of days and to Akkirampura for a couple of days and understand the situation there. We could see what could be used for Srihari's problem and what to use for Sadhana's wedding. There is no other way, we need money for both. Sharade didn't like to sell the land. There were bits of land and the little housesin Madhuiri. She sold only them. The lands and gardens in Shambonahalli and Akkirampur are dependent on artificially arranged water. There is a drawwell and a borewell in Shambhonahalli whereas in Akkirmapura there are both tank water and borewell water. But if they had to be sold they needed to be sold holus bolus. Not piece meal. Sharade is very fond of the land behind the tank in Akkirampura. With the proceeds of each sugarcame harvest she had bought things for home, turning the house into an asset. Mother and the family who are looking after the lands in Shambhonahalli have developed a sentimental*

218

attachment to the property there. One couldn't talk about selling them off. In case we did, both pillars of strength of the household - Sitamma and Sharade - would thunder! What else to sell then?

Let me go to these lands and gardens first. We can ask Mangala to come over and look after mother those two days we would be out. Sadhana would be there. Raghavendra and Shivaramu would also be around. It woud be good if we could go over.

Gopal put this before Sitamma. Sitamma was delighted.

"Your younger aunt Bhagya is there in Akkirampura. Go see her!" Sitamma suggested, making for another piece of work to be done by Gopal.

Rajagopal felt a nameless joy.

He always felt thrilled at the prospect of going over to their lands and gardens. Sharade had grown some *ragi* behind the house here in Siddapura. She had got planted *avare, togari* pulses, some vegetables and some coconut saplings. She even went there at times for a stroll in the evenings. She also felt a frisson of joy running through her veins at the thought. If one went down the tank bund in Akkirampura, one ran into a little village called Baichapura. There adjacent to the garden was a little house. There was a farmer there too. His family lived there. Once in a week Sharade would, along with either Shiavaramu or Raghavenda, come to Koratagere, take a bus there and come to Akkirampura on the Gauribidanur road via Holavanahalli, amble down the tank bund and arrive at Baichapura, look at and review what had happened there before returning. Till she returned, either Sadhana or Raghavendra would look after mother. Initially she would take all dirty linen of the whole week in a basket, wash them at the tank and dry them before returning. Now she had seen to it that there was enough water to wash etc. The fatigue due to the age factor didn't allow her to slog like before.

She now sent younger brothers, Raghavendra and Shivaramu away on this trip once a week, which made her work lighter. This made her pay more attention to household affairs. What was it that was the source of her joy? Slogging like a devil at her, and leaning on, mother's place! That was all. Is there this kind of joy as well in this world? This was also the reason why Sharade meant even more than their own mother for her younger

219

brothers. Srihari also grew up this way. Maybe because of bad company or maybe because he was still jobless, a devil seemed to have possessed him. Sharade didn't have this attitude of divide-and-rule even for farmers. She had arranged all that was required for their lives. Their children were going to school too.

When he learnt that the landlord's family was going to come to Akkirampura, Shivappa, the tenant farmer there would clean up the place. Sharade at times did stay back there. There was an iron oven, the *kumati* there in addition to a firewood earthen oven. Sharade would cook food, kindling the firewood oven. She would brew coffee on the iron oven. She had a rope cot to sleep on. This summed up the facilities she had. She would tell people that this was what added up to one's zest for life.

Poems and stories light up our inner lives. Illiterate people should think lighting up one's life is a yoga in itself. That is their achievement. Sharade would, and did feel, hurt when people dubbed her a 'husband-deserter'. But she wouldn't brood over it. Forgetting it completely, she would have her head and chin up. She was toiling at that place just for a daily morsel of food. She was the favoured and dear elder sister and mother both to her other siblings.

Elder brother and younger sister both drove to Koratagere before, at the fork in Koratagere, they took the road to Gauribidanuru via Holavanahalli. It was not difficult for Gopal to drive. He drove the car effortlessly, no matter how zig zag the road was, as if it was a green bed, naming all the villages on the way, and exclaiming, "The smell of earth here is so very pleasant, isn't it, Sharu?". The car drove through Hulikunte, Holavanahalli, Somalapura, Bairanahalli before landing on the road on the raised bank of the tank, where all buses and cars parked. "There is a Venkataramana Swamy temple near here." Sharade piped up. "We will first go there." But Gopal wouldn't agree. "No... Let us go see what is happening in our garden. we have come here for two days. Let us attend to our work to facilitate things." The car drove toward Baichapura. It was a pleasure driving down from the tank bank. The rest of the road was a riot of delightfully colorful gardens, flowers, fence flowers, lolalotte creepers. Some of those flowers they couldn't name and the elegance of flowers one couldn't name is delightful.

There was a tree at a distance. There were no leaves at all on the tree. It teemed with saffron-coloured flowers. Amazed, Gopal stopped the car, saying, "Sharade! Come let us go see! Tree with only flowers. Oh which world are these flowers from?" As Gopal began walking by the tree, Sharade tailed him even as she shouted, "Annayya!. There are these country *jalaee* thorns. Don't go that side! There would be only worms and insects. You can see it from a distance. They are not that beautiful from near."

Gopal didn't listen to his younger sister. He observed from very near. That was how the tree was. By the time leaves shed, flowers bloom from its base. As Sharade said, Gopal said to himself wordlessly, seductiveness looks better from a distance. The flowers had thick petals. If you plucked these flowers they would stay fresh even for ten days. But no body would pluck them, no one would fasten them in the hair, no one used them for worship. After watching the spectacle of nature for a long while, a jaunty Gopal got on the car, as if happy with having discovered something and telling himself that he should have brought a camera along.

As the car pulled up by the home in the garden, Shivappa came sprinting and stood by the car. He knew Sharade well. He had only seen Gopal long back. He kept looking at Gopal. His wife emerged from their shanty at a distance. She had a child in her hands.

Sharade had brought some snacks, some fruit and other things. When she took them out of the boot, Shivanna stepped up, took them and put them in the house. Gopal had never seen this house of theirs. It was an ancient house of small short rafters. It had mud walls. Some of them had caved in. It had a living room and a cooking-room. The floor had been paved with black stones. It had an oven made from burnt earth, and a bathroom with an oven for hot water. There was a pile of firewood standing in a nook of the bathroom. Shivappa had swilled out the water-cauldron and filled it with water. Sharade had a phone connection done for the house. A phone would be handy in emergencies. The roof was made from bamboo sticks woven with thatch. In the middle was a window. There was a cot of ropes in the living room. Shivanna laid out the bed taken out from the car on the cot. He had mucked out and tidied the house the best he could. He, who had been gawking at Gopal so long, dashed in and brought up a pot of milk. Sharade took the two vessels she had brought, heated the milk in one of them before giving it away to Gopal in a huge tumbler, stirring some sugar into it.

"Why so much milk! Should I eat my meal or not?" asked Gopal. But Sharade prevailed over him. They ate up the chapattis and the side vegetable dish they had brought from Madhugiri, and took some rest before going on a tour of the garden. Land of ten acres which was buttressed by the tank. When Gopal saw the sugarcane fields, his mouth watered.

"I don't have the sugar disease." he requested Sharade. "I feel like drinking sugarcane juice. Let me drink!"

"Your wife will cane me if I let you drink sugarcane milk!" Sharade bantered.

Elder brother and sister walked up a long way, chatting in a light-hearted way like this. On that side paddy fields had been set out with border-ridges. Sharade's meticulous work stood out. She had got not only country manure, but chemical fertilizer as well. It was Shivappa who guided her in this. She would seek accounts from Shivappa on a regular basis. She had raised her younger brothers also in such a disciplined manner. Both walked like this on the field-ridge for a while and then off the ridge for a mile. They sighted a hut in the distance. When they got near, there was the sound of a sugarcane-press.

"*Annayya*! You talked of sugarcane, didn't you?" Sharade offered. "Come! You can drink some now!" She then asked him to sit on the date mat that had been laid out there before she walked in. A village boy brought two tumblers of sugacane juice. The sight from the date mat of the high heavens above and the yummy taste of the sugarcane juice below obscured every worldly pain.

To say that sitting on the floor mat he forgot the world, the terror threat and his duties would be false and self-deceptive. Those would always be right behind you. On the other side of the sugarcane mill by the boat of the flowing sugarcane juice was a wide huge metal vessel. They would put some coke and some lemon into it and bake it and when it turned into the consistency of jaggory, they would make balls of it, dry the balls before selling them at the weekly shandy. Or distribute to shops for them to sell. They really were hard-working and hardy people. They would really slog but the returns they would get were meagre compared to the back-breaking work they put in.

But the same thing would be sold at much higher rates in cities. City slickers wouldn't know how hard the villagers worked and the hardships they endured. Whatever it was, it was a beautiful lesson, and a satisfying experience for Gopal. It was six in the evening when they got back to the farm house. "Let's go see younger aunt," suggested Sharade. "We can come back at night and sleep here."

Younger aunt's was an ancient house. It had an arched entrance door. The moment the door was rapped, an old married woman walked quietly up and opened the door. Taking as she did after mother, she was without doubt mother's sister. She didn't go out often. They had seen her somewhere long back. She was a self-respecting woman. Her name was Bhagyamma. All her children were abroad. Saying that she would never leave Akkirampura, she has stayed put there. She had said no to children offering send her money. She lived her life without anybody's interference, earning some money, making wicks and happalas, send them out to Tumakur for sales, making husband's gratuity amount yield some interest. She was younger by two years than mother. Her back had hunched.

"Who is it?" she asked, but didn't seem to recognise Sharade from her voice. Sharade introduced herself. "O, Sharade!" she exclaimed. "Come on in! It has been a long time since I saw you. Is it Gopal? You people have come now to see your poor younger aunt. It seems you come to your fields often, but have you come here to see me?! You have come after so many years!. Come, Gopala! You have become a great man now!"

Bhagyamma touched him time and again.
"I saw on T.V. It made me sick and tired to see how the world behaves. Even though you are so distant, I made out that it was you, fellow! Don't worry, God is great! He doesn't do any bad to good people."

Gopal didn't say anything by way of a reaction. He felt warm somewhere deep inside. The face seemed to shrink.

223

Bhagyamma went in before coming back with two huge brass tumblers of jaggory fruit juice. The beverage was dripping from her fingers. She must have squeezed jaggory with her hands. Yet one can't measure this affection in materialistic terms.

"We will be here tomorrow as well."

"Okay. Good. I would be happy. You come here for breakfast and lunch."

Sharade felt her work lessened!

Let's have some coffee at the farmhouse, come here for breakfast and go back. Annayya has said we would walk on the tank bank. We will come back for lunch and go back to see the film, Sant Tukaram *at the tent in Akkirampura.*

Nobody would recognise Gopal in the village. Gopal didn't go out much as in cities, towns and taluk places, people would recognise him. There would be no such situation either. This time he wanted to go out, like small children.

Yielding to Bhagyamma's love, they had their night meal at her place. She had cooked the sweet liquid dish of beaten-rice jaggory *paayasa*, wheaten sweetmeat balls, rice and *saaru*. It was quaintly yummy. Meals were served in special plate-like brass vessels, the *harivaaNa*s. And water was given in brass tumblers. Even when they said no, as younger aunt insisted lovingly on having more, they had to give in. After the night meal, they returned to the farmhouse, telling younger aunt they would come back the following day.

Sharade laid out a floor mat with a coir pillow for her head. She laid out the bed brought from Madhugiri on the cot, and asked him to sleep on it.

When they were on the point of sleeping, Gopal thought he saw something glistening near the kitchen door and a piece of firewood on the threshold. Gopal pointed to it as he posed, "What is it?" Something looking like a piece of white nylon saree seemed spread out near the threshold. Sharade startled. She had known what it was. Knowing as she did that her elder brother wouldn't know, she quietly walked to the store room and got a staff. The store room was at some distance from the bathroom. She came back so slowly and cageily that even her footfall was not audible. Coming back she moved back the kitchen door. A snake as long as some twenty feet slithered in the living hall, and seeing it Gopal screamed out of fear. Armed with the staff, Sharade moved hither and thither with the intent of catching it. The reptile evaded Sharade, sliding from the living room to the kitchen and back at the speed of lightning. Sharade tried to chase it down. But the limbless serpent went missing in the lumber room. The lumber room was full of bamboo baskets, sacks of fertilizers, spades, crowbars, pickaxes and stuff. This made for room for the snake to hide itself. Sharade bolted the lumber room shut, as she said, "Let the dawn break, I will see you!"

Gopal simply gawked, stunned and stumped. *Snakes, they say, unfold their hoods, sting and bite. Sharade is chasing it! I had never seen such a huge serpent. The Madhugiri house is good, No chance of a snake there!* Gopal was completely awed.

"Ayyo! You can't be scared because of such things! A snake is seen whenever and everytime I come here. Do I get scared? You see in the morning. I won't rest till I kill it."

"Does it stay put there? Won't it go elsewhere?"
"It may. It will move into the short small beams in the roof. You look! To these small rafters, they have joined pieces of wood that resemble a serpent.
It will be there. It won't do anything, don't worry!"

After saying what she did, Sharade fretted at saying what she did because those words themselves might scare her elder brother.

Gopal closed his eyes, telling Sharade not to switch off the lights. But sleep didn't come to him. The fear caused by the presence of a serpent made for anxiety in him. He spent the night staring at the short small beams on the roof all night long. The living hall and the store room had a common roof. Thinking that the serpent might come out to wreak vengeance on Sharade, Gopal kept his eyes open. It was as if the fear that he had felt when he got the letter of the murder threat had returned.

There was some sound at the dead of night and shouting, "*Sharii,* It is the serpent,.. get up!" Gopal took up the stick, hit the roof of the short rafters.

"Ey, Sleep, *anna!*" suggested Sharade laughing. "It does not come out like that!" She then got up and dusted the bed.

"We will leave for home tomorrow itself."

"You're speaking like this! What about Shivanna and his family? They live in such a hovel. It is not even like this house! Are they not living with dignity and courage? Where would they go, fearing the reptile? Even if they go to some other garden for work, there would be these limbless eyelidless slitherers there as well. Where would they go from there? That is, wherever you may go, there would be snakes, mongooses, frogs and other living beings. We beat them dead and live! Where on earth can we go, getting scared? And similarly is it possible to live, hacking down the forest, tell me! Only if these people slog do they get rice for a meal and jaggory for a sweet dish of payasa! Where should these animals live? They need to learn to live on in corn-fields, gardens, orchards and groves. I will beat it dead only if it enters our houses. I won't hit it if it is in the fields. You don't get scared! I want to show you a lot tomorrow! You may not come this side again! Let us go to the Anjaneya temple. Let us also go to God Venkataramana Swamy temple. We will walk on the tank bank. Let us go to the tube by the tank where water springs up. You will like it very much. Don't be afraid! Just sleep!"

So saying, she placed a picture of God Narasimha by him.

"Ey, take it away! I don't believe in such things."

"Ey! What did you say, you don't believe?! When your wife did pooje, vows and stuff, you didn't believe? You sleep now. You will get sleep now."

Gopal thought better of arguing with his sister. If she gets angry, it would be difficult, thought Gopal to himself. Sleep did come to him now.

In the morning, they concocted some coffee and drank the brew.

She called Shivanna and asked him to get a couple of men. Holding the stick in hand, she opened the store room. Pushing things one by one, she jogged things. There was no trace of the reptile. Every one entered the store room and began looking for the serpent. Gopal remembered the situation the other day when the dog squad searched for the bomb. They looked for a long time but the snake was not sighted. They continued the search with the belief that it wouldn't go out of the store room, unseen.

They paused in their quest just to recover their breaths. Sharade gave them a cup of coffee. Even as she downed coffee, Sharade kept looking at the storeroom. She spotted a basket kept upside down, attached to a log of wood and covering the wall. She saw, she thought, some shape through the holes in the basket. Asking everyone to keep silent, she focused on the shape. The mind and the eyes harmonise very fast. She signed to people to join the quest again.

She gave the basket a shake. There was no reply. Gopal too walked over. He also trained his eyes on the basket. After five minutes, the reptile crept up the basket and with head down tried to slither down and out. But hearing the noise, it quailed before it tried to coast back into the basket. She hit the basket rather forcefully, which was when the serpent spread its hood and started to crawl out. But Sharade didn't let it creep out. Gopal came out at this stage. Shivappa and company pinned down the snake, pressing its tail before they repeatedly hammered it on its head. Then they took it out into the living hall. It was as long as the living hall. The scales on its body resembling mirrors, its body glistened! They pushed it into the courtyard before they made a bonfire of small sticks, dry leaves and twigs and burnt it after squeezing a one-anna coin into its mouth. Sharade said a pit might be dug right there and it be buried.

Sitting under a jackfruit there, Gopal saw the serpent being burnt. He felt he had lost something. *Poor thing, they have killed the snake and were doing the death-rite to it! But this was the question of their daily existence. What if it bit them?*

Why should it enter their house? if it is outside houses, they are not killed, said Sharade. But even when they are found in fields, people do still kill them, because they fear they might bite someone.

As if some important event had passed, Gopal sat musing.

"Come, *anna*! Take your bath!" said Sharade, having heated water in the boiler vessel. Gopal saw only the shadow of the snake in the bathroom, behind the boiler lid, by the little water tank and at the pile of firewood stacked in the nook. Wherever he looked, he thought he saw the serpent slide away. He didn't close his eyes. Whatever he touched would turn into a snake. "Snake! Snake!" he would vociferate and Sharade would be amused, and she would laugh at the elder brother's hallucinatory propensities.

When they went down to the younger aunt's place for breakfast, Sharade broached the incident of the snake. "Ey! Why did you kill it?" The aunt said said rather thickly. "Why did you kill it? You won't have children if you kill serpents! You have become a boy, you see! There is an anthill by the God Anjaneya Swami temple in front of the village. Go tip some milk into it and join your palms at your chest in deference. The morbid blemish with a detrimental effect, the *doosha* that you have incurred by killing a snake will not touch you!"

Both elder brother and sister exchanged looks.

Maybe younger aunt doesn't know about us. It has been years since she met us. Maybe she has completely forgotten. It has been twenty five years since I returned to my mother's home. It is fifteen years since younger aunt stopped coming outdoors. She used to earlier. Only recently has she stopped. We don't know why she said what she did. Forget it! She is after all an elder. Maybe she doesn't know.

Two big plates of ragi vermicelli, *soosalu* made from jaggory and sesame, the sweet liquid dish of gasagase *payasa*, chutney, and tamarind mush. Gopal ate heartily, getting second helpings like children do. Younger aunt asked whether Sharade knew how to make ragi vermicelli. "I do make, but it is a tad difficult!" replied Sharade. Younger aunt's hospitality was something they would not forget in a while. *It was some debt that we must have been under, whch made us come all the way from Bengaluru to enjoy such food and your hospitality,* he sang the praises of her cooking skills. Having downed some jaggory coffee, the twosome left, saying they would come back for the midday meal.

As they walked along the raised bank of the tank, Gopal remembered the childhood days when they used to come there. After a long walk, they reached a village called Baichapura. It was a lovely little village. A man called Thimmegowda there knew Nanjunda Rao very well. Coming to know that they were his children, he took them home and gave them two portions of the plantain fruit-stalk. The smell of cowdung wash that permeated the house told them that there was some endless love in there.

"What are you doing? How many children do you have?"

When they told him that none of them had any, he exclaimed, "Poor fellows!" He enquired about Sitamma's health. Saying he owned a sugarcane mill, he handed them a huge earthen pot of sugarcane juice. Gopal drank as much as to split open his belly. He would say to himself that he would remember the day till his dying day.

They then walked back up the tank bank and, at the tank tube, let their feet loose in the water, chatted, their talk, their pains and woes flowing away along with the water that slipped away through their feet.

"*Annayya*! Is marriage and children our choice?"

"No, girl! Don't rack your brains about it! We should think that whatever life gives us is our choice. You are living your life pretty well. Don't have any regrets, not even as much as a sesame grain. I don't have children. Supposing I sit brooding and worrying about it, who would hand me children? No one would. *This is my lot, this is about all I am to get!*, we should tell ourselves! Let us not think about it now. Younger aunt told us about the anthill by the temple, didn't she? You believe in such things. Let us go there and do what she asked us to do. Let us value her words."

"*Annayya*! If we gift younger aunt atleast a saree, she would feel happy!" Sharade suggested. "Let us drive to Koratagere after the meal and buy her a saree that she can wear."

Gopal would never say anything at variance with her sister's words. He nodded agreement. The matter Sharade came up with next was serious.

"This garden and the fields are all valuable. We can't sell them. I don't want to. There is more profit in these lands than in the ones at Madhugiri and Siddapura. Even if Raghavendra and Shivaramu don't land government jobs, they could cultivate these lands. That should do for their livelihood."

This is precisely why Sharade has brought me here. That is all right. But what to do about Srihari? We should give him a livelihood, Gopal said to himself before he told Sharade, "What to give Srihari, *amma*? We should do something about him also, right?"

"Why talk about that now? We will think about it later, Come along!"

They polished off the plantain fruit-stalk portions that the respectable Thimmegowda had given them. Gopal was computing to himself the possible expenditure for his sister's wedding. A wedding in Tumakuru would mean atleast five lakh rupees. *I could take a loan of three lakhs on my fixed deposits. We should not sell anything.* He was arguing to himself all the time that they could ask Srihari to cultivate some garden here. But till a decision was reached, he couldn't say anything for sure. Suppoisngit didn't pan out the way one wanted it to?

Th twosome came to younger aunt's place, washing their soiled legs. They had parked the car by younger aunt's house. Bhagyamma had cooked the sweet dish of *obbattu*, kosambari, a vegetable side dish, saaru and chitranna. she served them with all her heart on plantain leaves spread on the floor.

"*Chikkamma*!" Gopal effused. "Whenever I come to Madhugiri from now on, I will for sure come here. I like your cooking."

After their meal, Sharade served a meal to Bhagyamma before washing dishes for her. Saying they would come back for coffee, they left for Koratagere for buying the aunt a saree. They also bought some fruit and stuff and handed them to Aunt before they lifted their joined palms up and against their chests in farewell greeting. Bhagyamma was overwhelmed. That was because her husband, who had migrated to America along with her children three years back, had never come that side. They were testing her self-respect. Sharade thought of inviting her to their own home.

"Chikkamma! Why don't you come over for good to your elder sister's home? We are all there, you see."

"I won't come anywhere, leaving Akkirampura. I like this village and this house a great deal. There is this ancient God Venkataramana Swamy temple here."

Gopal and Sharade went over to the temple and paid their homage to the Lord by offering coconuts and plantains. They also walked over to the Hanumantha temple outside the village and offered milk to the anthill there. She had taken some milk from her aunt. Telling the aunt she would return the container the next time she came that side, she put it away in the car.

Gopal had told Shivanna in the morning to ask the film tent owner to get some good chairs for the two of them to watch the film Santa Tukaram in his cinema tent in the evening. He had also told Shivanna that they would pay if needed.

It indeed was arranged like that. Gopal had thought the village folk should not recognise him. But the tent owner had heard that Gopal was the son of Nanjunda Rao. He was one of the heavyweights of the land. He had got good chairs from his own house, thinking it was his good fortune that such people were visitng his cinema hall. He welcomed them with warm open arms. Even though he insisted that he wouldn't take any money, Gopal gave Shivanna the money to buy tickets.

The ten cinema hall was much like how Gopal had seen before. All around was white cloth. and behind was a tarpaulin cover. The projector ws situated at the back. There was no problem sitting and watching film there. But everyone was watching only them. Some came to know and some didn't. They talked in whispers. But Gopal and Sharade didn't look at anyone. Not did they talk to anyone.

Santa Tukaram was an old Kannada film. Father liked it a hell of a lot. Gopal liked the innocent acting done by Dr. Rajkumar. The film ended. The proprietor had arranged a bunch of bananas and a basket of guavas. He gave them away to them, saying, "Take these, Sir! It is our good fortune someone like you has graced out theatre today." He also did the farewell gesture of goodwill of giving away betel leaves and nuts. He had the fruits kept in the car.

The very next morning the elder brother-sister duo drove back home to Madhugiri as if they descended to earthly reality from a magical world. They related everything to Sitamma, their mother. Sitamma also felt like seeing her younger sister at Akkirampura. But her legs were not fully functional. She couldn't stir outdoors. And even at home she didn't move a lot. If she went to others' houses, it would be even more difficult. Where would she pee and poop there? Who would collect her discard and chuck away? Here at home somebody, especially Sharade, would do that.

Rajagopal narrated the story of the serpent and the way Sharade went about putting it to death. That was in itself a miracle for him. This was not the first time that Sitamma had heard about Sharade killing a snake. Here in the garden at Siddapura, a snake got trapped under the motor in the electricity room with the result the motor was not on for a long time. Roping in a servant like she did at Akkirampura, Sharade asked him to lift the motor before tactfully inducing the reptile to come out, and beating it dead. But this had come about about six, seven years ago. Such killing they say would amount to a morbid blemish with a detrimental effect, the *doosha* or improper conduct or offence. Especially women flee when they see these limbless slitherers. But Sharade didn't rest till she got a stick and beat it dead. God might have got furious because of this, Sitamma would think. But she wouldn't speak it out because Sharade might take umbrage. *Those creepy crawlers must be dunces for them to get caught like they do!*, she would fret inside her.

The moment her slder sister came home, Sadhana caught hold of some story book, leaving the cooking work and stuff to Sharade. That Sitamma swore at her didn't touch her eardrums. "When you go to your husband's place, Sharade will come there to cook for you and your husband!" she said sarcastically. "Till you get married, be in the kitchen learning some cooking, girl! If you sit holding a book, your husband will run here to eat, that's all!"

These words of Sitamma's flew away in the wind. Mangala came along and gave everyone some coffee. "I will cook breakfast. Shall I go home after that?" she asked her sister-in-law. Sharade didn't look upon Mangale, her younger brother's wife as the Other. Planning to bring in a girl from a poor family as Narayana's bride, she had accordingly chosen a girl from a poor family for Narayana. Yet Narayana had hived off.

"Wait! I will cook. You can eat before leaving."
"No, Children will come back from school. I have to go cook there."

Sharade understood Mangala's words.
"Okay!", she breathed before giving away the plantain and guava fruits she had been gifted in Akkirampura to be given to her children. "I have also brought sheep milk. You can take a bath and eat your breakfast before leaving. I will then brew some tea with sheep milk. Tea with sheep milk would be very tasty. You can drink it before leaving."

Sadhana, who had been sitting reading, scampered up and began devouring the fruits one by one. In the meanwhile Raghavendra, who stepped in, said, "What is this, *akka*? Should a girl who is about to marry merely sit consuming fruits? What about fruits for us?"

Sharade, who wanted to give Raghavendra some fruit, saw the huge pile of plantain peels by Sadhana. Sadhana simply sat, blinking wordlessly. *Where are these peels from amd where were the fruits for her to eat,* Sharade wondered even as she searched for the fruits. The fruits were there, right beside Sadhana!

"Ey, You thief! You are upfront for eating and when it comes to work, you back off!" She then gave some fruits to Raghavendra.

After everyone had his breakfast, the smell of tea with sheep milk in it spread around the house. Gopal also liked its taste. He related everything about Akkirampura to mother. No matter how he described the happenings at Akkirampura, his experience there beggared description. Sitamma felt specially satisfied that they had presented her sister a saree. *Her husband and children have gone and settled abroad. And this old woman says she would never leave her village! What if something untoward happens!*

"Look, Sharu!" Sitamma warned Sharade. "Whenever you go there in future, go talk to younger aunt. She might take ill anytime. What if she does? Who will look after her? Let us shore her up in her last moments."

This sounded right to Sharade as well. Gopal wouldn't interfere in such things. His first priority now was the Srihari issue. *We don't know what he would say to our proposal. Let him come, we should sit for talks. But I should consult mu friend and lawyer Shyamanatha first of all about how to hand down the share to only one person. Or ask him about what could be given to whom and accordingly apportion shares of the property and do the registration. Let him enjoy as per the will as it exists now. Or let it be. Whenever they want they would enjoy thir share. I should sek the lawyer's opinion. It is going to be a problem in the days to come, if not now. It is better we should take precaution right now.*

As Gopal went on thinking each stand of the issue of inheritance separately, he felt easier in the mind. Otherwise life feels heavy snd difficult.

Somehow if this issue and Sadhana's wedding happen without any hassle, that would suffice. I could by that time occupy my position. Mallikarjuna Swamy has already called so many times. "Come, Sir!" he had said assuring him. "There is no fear now. Everything is going on smoothly. You can do your work. Your dignity and prestige have only increased rather than decreased because of these dogs!"

Gopal felt shored up now. Ushe's thoughts had disappeared from his noddle. But her memories did haunt him sometimes. This was an internal desire. Once that desire was fulfilled, it was difficult to forget that face, erase that memory. Why did she behave that way the other day? What kind of women are these! Just because somebody talked to somebody, would it be immorality? Would it be discourtesy? Should she insult him like that when he behaved wth familiarity and freedom because the one he loved came back? What demeaning position she gave him!

This train of thoughts was cut off right there. She came as a cumber to the natural movements of his nerves... *thoo*...

Gopal got up and went out to wash his dirty clothes of two days. Ever since he came to Madhugiri, he was washing his own clothes. Everyone did the same here. Earlier, Sharade was washing everyone's clothes. She was ageing. Boys were all growing. They did whatever was their work. There was a maidservant to do routine household chores. Her name was Laxmi. Sharade did things having to do with mother. Sadhana would do that when Sharade wasn't around. Seeing all this self-help work ethos, Gopal started helping himself with washing his own clothes and such other jobs.

He asked all his younger brothers to come over next Sunday. There was not much point in saying they were all asked. Narayana visited the house to see mother and Jayasimha came over daily from Tumakuru. They could come to some decision. They could talk to Srihari the following week. They should take out all documents from Sharade relating to lands, gardens and orchards and irrigation facilties etc. No one had staked his/her claim to anything except Srihari. There was now law that even women had a legitimate claim to parental property. But it was also true that for the wedding of every girl an expenditure of three to four lakhs had been incurred. If they now distributed the property among male members,

Sharade and mother, one wouldn't get even that much. Girls wouldn't even stake their claim. But according to law, they had to get it in writing from girls that they wouldn't stake a claim.

These were the thoughts whirling through Gopal's head.

****

Chapter Fourteen

Except Srihari, all the members of the household met on Sunday. Sharade and Mangala were also there. Gopal knew that his younger brothers were no longer young. Narayana had two children. He was now forty three. Jayasimha was thirty four. He was the one to be married off now. After Sadhana's wedding was his turn. After that came Shivaramu and Raghavendra. None lacked worldly knowledge. In fact their knowledge of the real world was far higher than Gopal's. There is a huge difference between textbookish knowledge and the practical real world knowledge that one needs for the struggle of life in the world. In matters of money, wealth and property, everyone becomes knowledgeable because it is a matter of one's rights.

Gopal talked to everyone with great ingenuity and affection. He laid out the problem before his younger brothers in every minute detail.

"One is the issue of the wedding. We need money for that. But there seems no need to sell any property for it. But Srihari has said he should be given his share of the property. Whatever his share is, if we give it over to him now, we won't have any problems in the future. None of you will disagree with me or mother. Tell me your suggestions. What shall we give him? Shall we sell a part of the land here? Or we can ask him to cultivate a part of the garden there, staying there. In that case we can think of the distribution of the property later. You tell me. Whatever you say will hold. I don't have much knowledge. I don't want anything. I have given this in writing. So has Sharade. After your say, I will ask the girls. If they insist on their share, we will have to compute how much Srihari will get and give it to him. Tell me what we need to do?"

Nobody spoke for an extended while.

Nobody had ever talked about their claim to property. Elder sister had looked after everything so far. *Let her do*, they had thought, *whatever she deems fit. After her, whatever comes our way would be ours.* The law now said girls were also entitled to parental property. But there was no question of the question popping up now. They were all fine now with no schisms or differences. They figured elder brother was trying to induce a new awareness. But they were not ones to speak a word against their elder brother.

"*Annayya*! Who is staking any claim to property now? No one!" Narayana broke in, weighing in on Gopal's submission. "In case you feel something must be sold for the wedding, it is up to you. We will sign whatever you want us to sign. Don't jib! If some money remains, you give it to Srihari and wash off your hands. Whatever remains after all this, give us! Let us not talk about it as long as mother is around."

These words of Narayana's seemed fine. But what could be done? If one assumed that they should not sell any property, they could conduct the wedding. What to give him, if Srihari said he wanted neither the land nor the garden but wanted only hard cash? Sharade unrolled for her younger brothers what Gopal had in mind: "The gardens at Shambhoonahalli and Akkirampura are good. If we show interest in selling on our own, they will sell for lower rates. If we cultivate them longer, we can enjoy the yield. We can arrange some money for the wedding. Elder brother wants us all to decide on something about Srihari to tell Srihari accordingly. Tell us what to do."

The elder among the younger brothers, Narayana was a man of moderate restrained, cool-and-collected thinking. He put forward a suggestion. But Srihari might not agree to that. The suggestion was that Srihari could have a room built by the Shambhoonahalli fields, stay there, cultivating the fields. If he could revive and develop the land well, they could hand down the fields to him as his share of parental property, and that they couldn't hand the property over right now.

"Huun! Would he go cultivate fields having done an M.A?" Sharade said expressing her skepticism. "If he was interested in such a thing, why would he go to the police station to get kicks?"

Sitamma, who had been listening in, was surprised by the mention of Srihari getting kicked at the police station. "What is it?" she asked. "When did it happen? My son, I thought, was a drunk who did some mischief. But what did he do that he had to go to the police station? Tell me! You people are hiding something from me!"
Sharade bit her tongue, fretting about why she said what she had.

Everyone solaced Sitamma saying, "She said something which was not meant for him, *amma*!" However evil a son might be, how would a mother hide her son's mistakes and indisretions? Sitting wordlessly, Gopal watched Sitamma. If something untoward happened to their sons, mothers wouldn't tolerate. And if some injustice was done, how would she? But what Narayana said was true. That was the answer to the idea that selling should not be done. What then to do? To get him to agree was the thing to be done now.

"Look!' Gopal drew everyone's attention. "I will tell him all that you people said. That he could cultivate the field either in Akkirampura or Shambhoonahalli and we will write them out later in his name."

Sharade, who had been silent till then, took up the word.
"*Annayya*! Don't tell him about the fields at Akkirampura. The land there is more. It is more valuable as well. If you do that, you would be writing for a single person what should be distributed among three."

"*Akkayya*! Let him settle down somewhere! Later when we divide the property, we could parcel out the inheritance equally."

"Ey! You people thnk only in limited ways. Why don't you take a long-distance view? Elder brother is now saying, 'Wherever he now cultivates land, he will get it for good later'. Will he not say, "Write it out in my name right now!"? He would. He won't let go the opportunity. Then there will be squabbles and fights. Should we not pave some way for Shivaramu and Raghavendra? We can't hand over everything to him alone, can we? You think and tell us!"

Narayana and Jayasimha now sat, their heads bowed. They didn't know what to say.

They began thinking about the same thing now. Nothing was impossible. But they didn't know what he would agree to. *Let him also be like us,* they thought. *Why should we treat him on a special footing? He didn't support the weddings etc of girls in the family. He is now staking his claim to his share. Why should we accede?* They were thinking they shouldn't give any reply to elder brother's words. But they couldn't disrespect their brother either.

Jayasimha himself then took up the word.

"*Annayya*! Let him, if he wants, cultivate the lands and gardens in Shambhonahalli. Let him stay there. It is upto him. It would be okay even if he stays here like us. But let us not tell him that this or that piece of property is going to be his permanently. Let us say, 'As long as mother is around, we will not take up this matter.'"

All these words collectively shaped some decision.

"But *will he agree or not* is the question. Is there a rule that those who have done an M.A should not work in the fields? Why shouldn't they? In fact they could do it even more meaningfully. But for people who turn meaning into meaninglessness everything is a travesty of meaning. Let that also happen! I will ask him to turn up on Saturday. You all also show up that day. It is not easy to talk to him."

Everyone agreed to Gopal's drift of thinking.

Sharade had cooked for everyone. All sat together on the floor and took their meals. But the feeling was it wasn't particularly sound decision. It wasn't necessary to meet a lawyer for this. They could meet a lawyer when they did the actual dividing up sometime in the future. One wouldn't know what law would be like then.

Gopal washed his hand before sitting in the living hall, his face and mien rather solemn. When Sitamma said, "Come over and sit by me!", he ambled across and sat by her. He felt better and easier in the mind.

On the other side arrangements went on briskly about writing out the wedding invites of Sadhana's wedding. Gopala travelled to Tumakuru with

Jayasimha and bought a ring, a new shirt, and pant. He arranged for some money with Narayana promising him that Saraswathi would carry money when she came back from Bengaluru.

"Don't you bother, *annayya*! You are doing all this for the household. You can repay me at leisure."

Thinking that that was the honour due to his position, he spent quite a bit from his own pocket. He talked to cooks and decided on a meal for hundred people. It was to be a meal of tur dal *obbaTTu*. He told Cook Shamanna that the dishes should be really tasty. Madhugiri was well known for its cuisine. Gopal asked his younger brothers to fasten mango leaf festoons on top of house doors. He assigned the job of tidying up and decorating the house to Sharade, Sadhana, and Mangala. He brought home younger aunt so as to give Mother Company. Bhagyamma was not keen on coming. But Sharade and Gopal prevailed upon her to come. Bhagyamma, who hadn't stirred out of Akkirampura for years, hugged Sitamma, her elder sister before bursting into a loud and extended bout of weeping when she saw her. It was nearly fifteen years since they had seen each other. They noted with regret that they had at last met when their legs were giving way. The two of them didn't emerge out of the room.

Coconuts had been felled and the boughs detached and chucked away in the courtyard. Shivaramu stashed them away in the store room before mucking out the courtyard, aided by servants.

The scripting-the-wedding invite ceremonial came about in a simple fashion at home. There were twenty people from the groom's side. The gathering was dominated by people from Madhugiri. Members of the younger uncle's and the younger younger uncle's households, of neighbouring houses and some Brahmins turned up. In all hundred twenty people ate the meal.

The groom's party had brought the bride a Kanchi silk saree and a gold ring. Sangita decked out her sister with jewels. They had the groom slip the gold ring on to the bride's ring-finger. These practices didn't exist earlier. There was no question of boys and girls choosing to marry. In the bygone times, it was only on the wedding day that the bride and the groom used to get to see each other. There was then no question of getting the girl's opinion and letting her sit by the groom at the time of drafting the invite. There had been some change: slipping on the ring, holding hands, getting photographed together with others right at the time of the scripting of the wedding-invite, like at the wedding ceremony and so on.

Bhagyamma and Sitamma chatted about such things in slow dilatory detail. After the writing out, the bride and the groom bent down and touched the feet of elders, seeking their blessings. Sharade and Mangala gave away vermillion powder, turmeric powder, bangles, and coconut, betel nuts and leaves as a farewell goodwill gesture to all the married women assembled there. When the visitors stood ready to leave praising the dishes, they were also given betel and nuts as a farewell goodwill gesture.

A good part of the task was over. The crucial thing now was to sort out Srihari's problem. All sisters had converged. Saraswathi had also turned up at the wedding invite-writing ceremony. It was these sisters all the way after the groom's party left. Srihari hadn't shown up on the day of writing out the wedding-invite. But he did come at night enquiered about the event with his mother. He hadn't been informed, he said. "Where would you be for us to inform you?" asked Sitamma back, a conciliatory tone in her voice.
"In sum you people have learnt to do things without me," he cribbed.
"Go eat your meal! It is an *Obbattu* meal! Sharade will serve you. You speak to elder brother after that. He was waiting only for you. He will forge a path for you"

Sitamma whisked the hair on Srihari's head in an affectionate gesture. His lips had blackened and the face had turned wretched and glowless because of smoking and drinking. Sitamma was alarmed seeing the wales, the marks of blows on his hands, jubba and pyjama.

"What is this? Who bashed you up? Why do you get whacked by others? There is work, Son, at home. And we have land to work on and earn our keep. Why do you expose yourself to others' assaults? Don't fill your mother with fiery cinders, Son?! Learn how to live, staying right here!"
Sitamma paused because Bhagyamma stepped in. "Come, Bhagi!" she welcomed her sister, wiping away the tears and having her sit by her.

"She is Bhagi, your younger aunt, fellow!"

Srihari walked out after saying no more than "How are you, Chikkamma?"

Everyone was ribbing Sadhana, the wedding girl in the living hall. Gopal and Saraswathi were into some kind of dialogue in the room. Calling Srihari for his meal, Sharade laid out a plantain leaf on the floor in the Middle Room for him to eat from before serving him his meal. None of them spoke. In the living hall were Jayasimha and Narayana, snoring.

The moment they saw Srihari, all the women paused in their talk to stare at Srihari. The last time they had seen him was when he had come from the police station. Fear, anxiety and disgust about him had dropped anchor in them. They didn't care even to greet him with, "How are you?" After a brief lull, they resumed their talk as he sashayed into the Middle Room. People who are ushered into the world from the same womb find heavenly bliss or wish to find heavenly bliss chatting about mundane things like that costume, this food, those jewels, *saaru*, rice, garbage, soiled vessels, loans, work, salary, the new, the old. They relax, with one's head on the other's lap, one's leg intertwined in another's legs, find the great nectar of life, savouring squabbling, fighting and kicking up a noise. They reveal life's great truths, hide life's great truths during such times. They learn lessons. And teach lessons. They let the woman digest and realize the importance of woman in the household before sending her off with just a dab of the auspicious vermillion powder. This is life. Money has no value, compared with the bonds of elder brother, elder sister and younger brother and sister.

Since it was an auspicious occasion, Sharade gave away vermilion powder, betel leaves and nuts and a piece of silk blouse to her younger sisters. She handed some vermilion powder to younger aunt as well. Those who had to travel long distances stayed back the night. Younger sisters, who lived in Madhugiri and Tumakuru, left.

Narayana woke up and when he asked Mangala to get ready to leave, Srihari asked him where Gopal was, adding that he wanted to speak to him. Narayan signed toward the room in which Gopal was sleeping.
"Iwill come in the night. Tell him!" Srihari submitted before leaving. But he never turned up that night.

Narayana, was to leave for his home in Madhugiri didn't leave. He sent away Mangala and his children. Except Susheela and Sangita, every other woman had left. Placing chairs in the huge front entrance hall, Jayasimha and Narayana waited along with Gopal for Srihari till ten in the night. There was no trace of Srihari. Since leaves had been laid out for their meals, they sat looking hopefully toward the entrance door. As Sharade was tired, she didn't speak. Jayasimha went with Bhagyamma to Koratagere and had her get on the bus to Akkirampura. There might also have been the fear that Bhagyamma might get to know the family's inner secrets if she stayed overnight. Everyone in the family held the view that if there was something happening, it should be happily shared with the offer of a meal or something. But after the job was done, no one should be allowed to poke their noses in the family's affairs.

Since Srihari didn't show up, everyone slept off.

Had he come, things would have been smooth and felicitous. As he didn't, anxiety increased. If he had come when everyone was around, there would be no such anxiety. What if he came when no one was there? It would have been difficult for Gopal to negotiate. Gopal wouldn't know what to do if he spoke a tad boorishly, abrasively. It wasn't possible for him to talk, descending down to Srihari's level. Even now if he closed his eyes, it would seem as if Srihari's murderous eyes bored into him. Gopal wouldn't figure out what Srihari spoke.

Gopal turned sides as he lay on the bed.

He seemed out of sorts when Saraswathi left in the morning for Bengaluru. She said, "Come away as soon as possible," as she left. Shivaramu dropped sister-in-law at the bus stand on his Hero Honda motorbike. Waking up in the wee hours, Sharade had prepared for her chapathis and avare pulse *usli*.

****

Chapter Fifteen

Maybe the moment when the wedding-invite writing ceremonial took place was not auspicious. Sharade fed some water to Sitamma and wiped the mouth. A physician came and did a clinical examination but having done it, chose not to say anything. Sharade gave him an intent look. He handed her a paper slip, saying, "Get these medicines and injection vials." He kept saying something to the nurse there. Writing out whatever the physician told her, she walked out to bring them.

Sending Sharade home, Gopal took up the responsibility of staying back at the hospital. He took the paper slip from Sharade and brought all the medicines. Sitamma had been admitted to the Manipal Heart Care Centre at Tumakuru. Food was being supplied from Sahana's Tumakuru house to the care-givers at the hospital. Sharade and Gopal stayed put at the hospital. Mangala and Sadhana looked after the house at Madhugiri. Although Sitamma was conscious, she gawked at the proceedngs without speaking a word. She rapidly drfted to sleep moments after she was administered some drip medicine. Reading the ECG report, the physician merely said, "Nothing can be said now."

Gopal was as shocked as if the heavens had fallen on him. He could neither laugh nor weep. His eyes would now glisten with emotion as he realised life had become so very tough. The end seemed to be in sight of a mother who felt deeply for him. What woud be his lot if she breathed her last. This of course was natural but it could have been avoided for sometime. So much stink raised, that too at home, for a word of the moment. *Srihari dented my honout at home,* he lamented to himself. *What kind of younger sisters and younger brothers! And what kind of life is this!*

I had found fulfillment only in position, respect and honour. Now even that has been dented. It is difficult to get back what one has lost.

No matter how he sat hiding his face, pain simmered and boiled inside. He had come to Madhugiri to be relieved from the rather hostile atmosphere there in Bengaluru. But the situation here was barely better. *Why on earth did he come to earth after me? Why are all others one kind and only he different?,* Gopal wondered.

Srihari, who didn't come on the night of the wedding invite-writing ceremonial, turned up the next morning, only to confront Gopal with, "What did you decide?" Gopal never expected that he would be confronted like he had been. Fortunately Narayana hadn't as yet left for home. Jayasimha had left for Tumakuru. Gopal didn't have a ready answer for Srihari's rather unconscionable poser. Narayana stepped up and had Srihari sit, handing him a cup of steaming coffee, saying a soft and soothing, "Srihari, sit! We will sit and talk at leisure."

Walking in, Gopal brought Sharade along. Saraswathi had left. Susheela and Sangita were preparing to leave. Having cooked breakfast, Sharade was wiping her hands on her saree-end. Raghavendra and Shivaramu were in their room. Both of them rushed out at Srihari's high-pitched words. To begin with, Sharade and Narayana informed Srihari of the decision taken last Sunday.

Srihari sat wordless for a while before he took up the word.

"Is this elder brother's decision? Did all of you arrive at it, gathering together here?"

With Gopal not knowing what to say, Narayana spoke.

"We have all talked and arrived at this decision, fellow! How would *annayya* alone know, tell me!"

Now Gopal tried to take up the word.

"I don't know much about these things, Srihari! We all discussed this. I have already given in writing that I don't want any property. All this belongs to all of you. Do I have children? I have nothing to do with this."

"I don't want hear this story. That is your problem."

"What do you want? Why don't you take charge of the Shambhonahalli garden, get a room built for you there, and cultivate it. You can get married and lead your family life. We will write it in your name later. Isn't that okay?"

"That might be okay for you. You people should have called me when you gathered to discuss this. How can you take a decision without me? Who did this conspiracy?"

"How can you now say "You should have called me" when you never turned up at home? You went off that day and it is only today that you have turned up. You, who came home from the police station, went away in the morning without even informing us. What was the urgent work you had? Do you know what the police inspector asked us? Why did you join the Naxals again after you were warned against it? You should be here, sorting it out in a peaceable way, shouldn't you? Aren't these people all here? Why did you tread a different path?"

"Don't ask such questions! You have never turned up here to find out about us and you have come now? I never went to them after that day, but they didn't leave me! They would be after us because they have told us some confidential things. We would be far and away because if we are here, it would spell trouble for you people. We would be in some hotel somewhere in Bengaluru."

Deep inside Gopal was on the boil.

But what could he do? There was no telling whether what Srihari was saying was true or false. Gopal set to thinking. He felt there was no use talking when he realized that it was a fire that burned, spreading fierce heat rather than a lamp that glowed, shedding light. He signed to Narayana to get talking.

"What do I tell him, *anna*? He should understand himself," he said to Gopal before turning to Srihari and saying, "Nobody would come to know if you stay at Shambhonahalli. You be there all by yourself, cultivating the fields and the garden there."

"No. I don't know the work of the fields and the gardens. I don't want to be here. Hand over the money to me, selling whatever comes as my share of the property. I will go away for good."

Sitamma, who had been listening in so far, now dived into the conversation.

"Where would they get the money from? There is besides sister's wedding coming up."

Srihari grew more aggressive. It was only mother who would stand all he had to offer.

"You are there, quite the woman suiting their thinking," he howled. "You harp on girls, and girls, and give the boys coconut shells to go around begging alms in! If you don't want to give, say "no." Don't discriminate! What kind of a mother are you?! The story would have been completely different, had you had for all us the kind of affection you have for your eldest son."

Gopal was riled. He had always thought one shouldn't talk demeaningly about one's mother.

"Ey!" he menaced, hardboiling Srihari on his tongue. "Bark what you want! We will give you that. Don't belittle mother! All children are the same for any mother. Do you know with what kind of hardships she has raised all of us?"

"That is how you feel, because she has raised you to this position."

Sharade intervened now.

"Why do you talk like this, Sri? I have pawned and sold all my jewels for your education. It is only now that the household has reached a good position. Why did you become what you have become? You should have grown more intelligent and landed a good job."

"This woman has sold some sundry little things, and she always talks as if she has done some supreme sacrifice of her whole life! I will chuck away at you whatever you have spent for me out of the money that is due to me."

Gopal solaced her, seeing Sharade's eyes brim over with tears.

"Look!" he advised Srihari, still keeping his cool. "If you blurt whatever comes to your mind without any respect for anyone, no one would care for you. We should find you a path, give you some responsibility at some point of time, we thought. That is why we are asking you to look after the Shambhoonahalli fields and garden, and get married and that would really support you. And you will have given a life to a girl. That is our thinking. We can't do more than this."

"How is it that you speak as if this is the only thing possible? I am not asking you to part with your earnings, damn it! I am claiming my father's property. Who are you to take a decision about it?"

Sitamma flew off the handle.

"Srihari! Srihari! Ey, you sinner! He is your elder brother, you fellow! Don't talk like that! Without children of his own, he has treated you people like his own children. Rein in you rtongue!"

Gopal felt deeply hurt, sick and weary. It would dent his honour if he spoke more, he thought and so fell silent. In the end Narayana tried to persuade him puttting forward Gopal's argument.

"You can sell the same garden and hand me the money, can't you?"

"All our gardens are in great shape. If we volunteer to sell, they won't fetch good money. There are other children to take care of. We can't sell it just for your sake. Don't Shivaramu and Raghavendra need support, tell me!"

"Sell this house! Or hand me half of it! I will repair it and sell it off."

Everyone was stunned. Selling the house!

No one could even think of it! It was like the vital life that held their bodies together for all including Sitamma. No matter who went where, when they returned, it was the house which sheltered them like a mother. All eyes became burning fire. Their minds flamed.

"You want us to sell the house, don't you? Take it!" Sitamma thundered as she stepped up with a stick to bash Srihari. Her legs quaked. Narayana and Sharade came rushing, held her before seating her on the chair. Sharade ran in and getting some water, fed her.

A situation where Gopal had to involve himself, and speak taking a stand, had arisen. If he didn't, the situation would spin out of control. No matter what, he had to face it, and say something. Sitamma had never reacted as ferociously as she had now. She would shout only when something related to the house came up. Mother's wedding had taken place in this very

248

house. She had entered the house as a daughter-in-law when she was barely fourteen. She had shared her life's pleasures and pains with the pillars of this hallowed house. She had broken into sweats working for it. She had endured unbelievable hardships for the children. What would she feel when someone came up with word of selling it!

"Look!' Gopal warned him. "Don't talk of the house! This is the house which people have lived so very well in. As long as it is ours, people will continue to live and live well here. What do you think we will get if we sell it now? Peanuts! No one will come forward to buy such an ancient house situated on the outskirts of this village. You buy it yourself!"

"Why would I ask you if I have the money to buy?"

"Look, there is no use talking this way. It is important to take some decison now. I can't say anything more."

"Why say that? Sell the house! Or give me half the house! I will sell it for myself."

"Let us not talk about the house, Srihari! There is no need of any more talk either! Besides there is Sadhana's wedding. If you are okay with staying in Shambhonahalli and cultivating the garden there, it is okay! Or else we need not talk."

"How is it not possible?" Srihari flung off, rebutting his elder brother. "I will see! I will bring my lawyer. You are not the only big man who can take a decision. You are done doing politics there. You have come here now to do politics, haven't you?"

"Hold your tongue tight before talking. I don't want anything, do you understand? I agreed to do this job for you people at mother's instance. If you want to stay at the Shambhonahalli garden and cultivate it, do it! Otherwise clear off!"

Flying off the handle, Srihari menaced at Gopal. Narayana ran up and held him. There yet sluiced out of his mouth swear words and four-letter words.

"He is talking as if it is all his own!" Srihari sniffed. "This is sham! Let me!"

He rushed, making his way, grabbed and tore Gopal's shirt before socking him on his cheek. Before another blow landed on Gopal's cheek, everyone ran up and separated the two fighting fisticuffing brothers. They dragged Srihari away. Srihari's were hunky arms. Narayana couldn't hold him on his own. Raghavendra, Shivaramu and Sadhana joined forces in this mission of holding Srihari back. Sharade slapped him smack on his cheeks.

"You scumbag!" she pouted even as he gave him a full-blooded kick. "If you are seen anywhere in these parts, I will nab you and hand you over to the police. You mother-fucker! It was he who got who should have been in jail released from police custody and you are doing this to a god-like man? The next time you turn up, asking for property, I will whack you with my chappals. This is the garden I have cultivated with my sweat. Who told you? Did father grow this coconut grove? It is I who has cultivated it into this shape. You are staking your claim on it?"

"Annayya!" Shiavaramu and Raghavendra called Gopal giving him a shirt to wear. "Take this!" Gopal sat, head bowed, like a child whose innocence had been injured. They put the shirt on him. Gopal seemed unhinged. *These are children I have dandled wth my own hands and played with in my lap. And they are hungry to swallow me up! The murder threats I received never demeaned me like this! In fact my courage and self-confidence rose. But here my own younger brother socked me on the cheek. Is he really my younger brother?! Or is he somebody else in my younger brother's mask? Everything has been fine so far. Why did he go to the extent of slapping me? Is it any conspiracy?*

Gopal's body shook. All his strength seemed to grind to a halt just for that! His whole body heated up by the time he recovered from the blows.

No one had paid no attention to Sitamma amidst all the din so far. When Srihari stepped forward to grab Gopal and bash him, Sitamma shouted, "Srihari! Srihari!..." before collapsing all in a heap by the pillar.

She never came to.
"Thoo..." Srihari spat before walking out.

All sprinted toward Sitamma. They sprinkled water on her. She didn't regain consciousness. "Anna!" somebody screamed. And Gopal, who had been laid low and was in the room, nursing his hurt and injuries, ran out, totally unsettled. It was Narayana who had shouted. "Mother! Mother!" Gopal called. But his mother never responded.

They quickly phoned up Jayaram, the family doctor. Dr Jayaram turned up and examined her. His face didn't evince any hope or promise. "Take her quickly to the Tumakuru Heart Care Centre." was all he said.

Gopal, Narayana and Sharade deposited her in the ambulance. Sharade made her brothers eat their breakfast fast. Raghavendra and Shivaramu told Sadhana to take care of the house, and phoning Mangala to tell her to come there along with her children in the evening, and that Narayana was still with them, went off and admitted Sitamma to the heart care centre.

Sitamma didn't respond to any treatment.

"There has been a huge shock. Recovery is going to be difficult. Let us see!" said the physician. Gopal turned still, pressing mother's legs. Why did this thing called 'yesterday' come at all? There was no solacing the bruised and battered mind. No food went down the system.

"Annayya! Don't take it to heart. He is a politician." Sharade tried to put Gopal at ease. "Don't you grieve because he behaved the way he did. If you lose heart, how do I cope?"

"Please pardon me, anna!" Narayana also chipped in. "I didn't have the strength to stop him. He brushed me aside and menaced toward you. I feel ashamed even now to beg your pardon."

Holding the hands of both Sharade and Narayana, Gopal wept his heart out. He wept like a child, forgetting it was a public place, a hospital.

*****

Chapter Sixteen

Ushe consulted every available doctor about aborting her child, but she found it was not easy at all to get it done. She was into the fifth month of pregnancy, the time when the foetus would be turning slowly into the form of a tot. The physician showed through a scan that abortion was not scientifically desirable at that phase of pregnancy. Somehow the mother's heart in her interior had come to naught. She crazily went about asking every doctor for an abortion without telling them that she wasn't married.

Hearing her desperate pleas, doctors told her, "You say you are as old as you say you are. Didn't you know that you need to go to a doctor when periods stop? Abortion is not possible now." They sent her off advising her to take care of her health.

It had been two weeks since this advice from the physician. With no results forthcoming from doctors, Ushe now resorted to eatables that helped break the foetus. This increased her belief in such things. She implemented whatever she had heard in her office and elsewhere about abortions. The words of her staffer Rohini and of peon Muniratna seemed credible. She ate papaya, black sesame *chiguLi* and a *nugge* greens dish. Muniratna had told her about some lickable, a lambative. She only elicited such information without creating any room for suspicion in their minds about who it was for and why she sought such information. She ate those up, but with no results for a long week. Ushe didn't know what would happen to her if the foetus died. She needed the physician's suggestion for everything. Dr Bharathi had asked her to show her the medicines before she left, but Ushe could show the medicines only if she had bought them, couldn't she?

It was already three weeks after four months. She felt some turmoil in her belly. If she felt hungry she would eat well. But she did feel very fatigued. She had begun to wear the loose upper wear of *chudi* because of the fear of the swell of her belly showing. One Sunday her younger sisters came home after having a word among themselves about making a trip to her place.

"akka! You have become so very pudgy! You look very pretty now. You were lean and lacklustre when we went on tour. How come this change?"

"Look!" Ushe glossed over things as she minced. "I am already 'pudgy' mean? What if I get bulky or dark? Come, come! You cook something yourselves. I am a tad tired."

She showed them the location of things in the kitchen and of those in the fridge. The sisters submitted they could buy some mutton and cook mutton curry. But Ushe declined. "I don't like such things. You have beans and brinjals there. You put a lot of tur dal and cook some sambar. Do a vegetable sidedish. You have some curds there. We can, if you so want, get some sweets. I could cook some *kesari baath* in the end. Okay?"

"You! What to say? You have become a veritable Brahmin woman! You are like that! Having eaten only rice and vegetables, they would also be swollen as you are."

Ushe didn't react to this remark.

Some thought began to sting her. *Did I become pudgy? That too, like brahmin women? What is this, Why did sisters put forward this comparison? Do they get to know I am pregnant? The clothes I wear at home are always loose. Does it look susupicious like that?* She shuffled across into the room and had a look in the mirror. *No, the pregnancy is not showing. Evn if she draws in breaths the belly doesn't draw back. It is okay now. How long will I be like this? I should take care not to see sisters for some days. I should somehow take out this gddann foetus. It is trampllng me. I shiver if I think of what could happen in th future. Why am I not taking the days ahead seriously? Is there this feeling of indifferene and neglect even now? Or is it obstinacy? Howewer much i tried, nothing has happened. I will come to know if I go to a doctor and get a scan.*

It was only Ushe's thoughts that were at work. Wordlessly she watched her sisters cook. Pangs of hunger increased. She had been these days feeling very hungry. The mother who plans to remove the child in her belly can't bear her hunger. Hunger pestered Ushe. No matter what and how much she ate, hunger wouldn't take leave of her. So there were so many edibles snd things to be cooked at home. So were milk and fruits. She was eating either for herself or the child in her womb. She was feeling hungry and she ate to preventively maintain her health, and to facilitate a possible spontaneous abortion. Who wouldn't get pudgy if one overate for so many different reasons? Everyone would!

She couldn't drive either. When she stretched her legs to press either the accelerator, the clutch or the brake, she couldn't summon enough strength. She couldn't even walk fast and with ease. If one wanted to keep one's swollen belly under wraps, one had to see all body parts were even. Things didn't pan out the way it was thought they would. The same headache. She had lessened thinking about Rajagopal. She had thought she would somehow remove the foetus from her body but this didn't quite work out. Or, if life inside had died by now, what would happen later?

Her sisters cooked a variety of dishes and they then woke up Ushe. *Is it a small thing for a forty seven year old woman to get pregnant? It isn't!*
The sisters didn't know about her pregnancy. When Ushe saw the cooked delights piled on the dining table, her hunger doubled. They all sat and ate together. Ushe was on the point of saying, "You all come like this every Sunday and cook me yummy dishes! I will eat a hearty meal for a day." But the awareness of her own baby-belly held her back. Seeing Ushe eat the dishes so very heartily, one of the sisters ejaculated, *"Akka*! Did you like it? Let us meet like this every Sunday, and cook and eat! You may also be bored being all alone." Ushe felt choked, the rice sticking in her throat. "No, Let us not do that!" she hastened to say, "You husbands will swear at me. You cook them yummy things. That is your duty." The sisters felt, her elder sister might have felt sick and tired. She wasn't married. How could they solace her with words? Searching for words, and not being successful in their search, they served their elder sister a full and hearty bellyful. After the meal they all laid out a floor mat there and when they stood ready to leave in the evening, they thought their elder sister would drop them at their homes in her car. But saying the car was not in a good condition, Ushe got them an auto and sent them off prepaying the auto man.

As soon as she stepped in, she phoned Dr Bharati's clinic and found out when the doctor was going to be there. The female physician was to come to the clinic at eight in the night. The doctor would say somehing or the other. She would ask why Ushe didn't turn up. Her problem was not going to be sorted without the doctor's help. She called the nursing home again to ask when the female physician would be available at the clinic the following day. 'The doctor is going to be on leave tomorrow!' came the answer from the other end. She decided to go to the doctor at eight. Throes of hunger again! She cooked and downed a couple of chapathis. She drank up the fruit juice that was in the fridge and took a walk. There was some space within her compound walls. This doesn't mean she was fully happy and deeply gruntled. More than emotional distress, hers was an experimental kind of hardship. This was what caused the anxiety. She had thought only if her experiment didn't pan out would she think of the future course. This explained her restrained behavior.

Or was it that she felt at peace just to flush away all anxiety? Or was it that her dignity would be dented if she behaved otherwise? One could win over one of these with tact. But the other had to do with the heart. One had to win over it, keeping the bond in tact throughout life. One had to live, keeping a suitable solution ready at every stage. One had to preserve the truth under the cover of or with the help of so many falsehoods. One had to per force boil with a fire one couldn't keep away. One should experience as much joy and happiness as falls to one's lot. One wouldn't like this muddle. She had lived all these days all alone. Why was this unwanted pregnancy, this child after her? If she thought coolly even now she would admit that she never thought she coud welcome the child keeping in mind Rajagopal or the innocent child that was going to be ushered in. It wasn't that it was a fraud. She knew she had a role in it.

She had herself requisitioned the last meeting she had with Gopal to lure him in her seductive spell of love. But she had kept even the memory from being anywhere near and as if there was no alternative thinking about it. A child without a marriage!? If she allowed the child to be born, what if somebody asked her about its antecedents? She felt scared even now. What if she grew even pudgier? Was there no difference between being pregnant and having a pudgy paunch? She had herself nabbed so many such cases and handed them over to law. She had travelled to many sites of atrocities on Dalit women, investigated, ran from police station to police station and secured justice. She hadn't buckled under any pressure. She had made the lives of so many women easy and felicitous. She had got some women, even if small, jobs, telling them if there was any exploitation to inform her. It was natural for her to work with the Home Minister in her official capacity. When there were serious problems, which needed the intervention of the Home Minister, she couldn't take a decision without consulting him. She nw didin't feel like getting justice, placing the blame at Gopal's door : she had to find an answer herself. This was because she was also to blame for the muddle she was in. The other thing was honour and prestige. But what could be done? She had to face whatever came her way.

****

"You have come alone? Is your husband in a burkha, not to be seen? You should not come alone like this, madam! There shuold be somebody with you when it is dark." said D Bharathi examining Ushe. Ushe felt very odd: what should she answer? If she told the truth, it would be a grave insult to her own self. But what lie could she tell? What kind of a situation she had found herself in? The person I loved also grew distant. I couldn't tell the physician about my plight. How could she search for the husband that didn't exist? Ushe drummed up some courage.

"He has gone shopping. He will turn up when I leave. He feels embarrassed that I have become pregnant at this age."

"He then is fifty three or fifty four, isn't he?"

"Yes, doctor! I don't want this. When we grow old, who will raise it, educate it etc? We also need to have the energy to do it, right? Supposing something happens to us, would the child not become an orphan at such a young age? Please suggest a way out of this!"

Dr Bharati laughed a loud hearty laughter. She didn't know what to say. She couldn't make fun of her patients either. She would have to think before saying anything.

"Look, Ms Usha! We think of what you are saying if there are serious health issues when the woman is five months gone. You can see your own child yourself, I can show a scan. The child is very healthy. Why do you think of removing it? Your heart is really very hard and cruel. Remember no one lives trusting any body! So many kids wouldn't havc mothers when they are born. Or they wouldn't have fathers. Won't they live on? You shouldn't search for such reasons!"

The physician took Ushe near the scanner and focusing on the belly, showed her the image of the kid in the womb on a giant TV screen. Ushe could see the child: It had a bulky head, little hands and legs. The face wasn't quite visible. Breathing was normal. "Your child has grown better than we told you." The obstetrician submitted. "You should atleast now give up the idea of an abortion and think positively. Would anyone kill a child in the making without a sound reason? Don't you think you are sinning by thinking like that? Tke this! You need to take these medicines regularly. I have also indicated the date of delivery here. This has to be a caesarian section. Your womb would be feeble because of your age. It won't be a normal delivery. Okay, *namaskaara!*"

Dr Bharati would have many patients waiting to be attended to. So talking fast, she would dispose of patients as soon as possible. Ushe made as if to say something, but the obstetrician butted in to say, "Ms Usha! You are very healthy yourself! You be natural. No driving, neither cars, nor scooters. Take a lot of vegetables, fruits and milk! Don't skimp on food, fearing obesity. As I said, we will do a caesarian if it can't be an easy normal delivery. Relax! No tensions, Okay?"

Ushe felt tongue-tied.
She felt wretched and hopeless the moment it was said emphatically that there was no question of abortion. She felt darkness hemming in, feeling at a loss as to her next course of action. She had to solace herself, inject courage into herself. A new problem now loomed like a giant. But she was not one to lose heart. All at sea, a pensive Ushe simply sat on a chair outside for ten minutes. Like her, several pregnant women were there along with their husbands or sisters or brothers or mothers. Ushe's sorrow now welled up. There should have been someone with her as support. That she was an orphan bugged her. She wiped away the tears that trickled out. She should now leave for home. She rose, thinking autorickshaw men would ask for more fare as the day declined. She came down the steps of the clinic, her face and gait showing that something that shouldn't have happened had happened. She bought all the medicines that the physician had prescribed.

She bought some vegetables and fruits at Malleshwaram before hopping on an autorickshaw.

Even when she got back home, she was only thinking of something, without eating anything. Touching her belly again and again she brought tears into her eyes. She was really tension-free with the idea that she was going in any case to abort the child she was carrying. But the child, they were saying now, couldn't be removed. They also had laws to go by. They would not abort without any valid reason. Who could she confide this to? She had no one who would listen to her tale and feel delighted! If ever there was one, it was only Gopal! But he himself had gone away from her. There was a huge barrier now between him and her. She didn't know how this wall had come up. She was also to blame for it. The suspicion that he had done a fraud on her gave rise to a towering inferno in her before the crime she had committed turned out to be a huge miscalculated mistake. This devil, which had embedded in her inner reaches, needed to give up its ugliness and change to shed light on her and on her life. Since loving itself was real, one shouldn't suspect! But it was difficult now even to imagine the boiling volcano of fury that raged in her then. This was now showing her how cruel she was. It then would ride on her. One thing was the unpardonable indiscretion she had committed and the other was her pregnancy. No one would answer these! People would laugh if she told them about her state. She had come up with so many excuses when her colleagues asked her why she hadn't married. Imagine what they would think if her belly showed up!

They would naturally look askance!

She should wear her *chudi*s loose and cover up the belly, she told herself wordlessly. Could she digest this plight of hers as easily as one might think? She was going to have the child in the coming days. How could she hide the child?! There would then be a hundred questions seeking answers! Who would look after the child? She would have to weave a tapestry of lies to her sisters! What kind of circus one had to do for the child's survival! And what would she get after all? A lie in the office and a lie at home! But this was in fact the truth.

Ushe had laid down on the cot till one in the night without eating anything. She now felt intensely hungry. Freeing herself from anxious thoughts, she now quietly walked to the bathroom before coming back and helping herself to some rice and *saaru*, as she sat eating, some fear returned. In her whole life this was the frst time that she had eaten a meal at that unearthly hour. It was the solitude that had made her feel the fear. Pregnant women, they say, should have some companion. That was in fact one reason why she was alone. It was after four months of pregnancy that she had really thought about it. Today she had fully confirmed it. Was the fear about this? Where would the fear be real? If one looked at them, one by one, separately, there arose questions that ignited heat. Courage even ten times more than she in fact had now wouldn't be enough! Courage is necessary for work, but is not sufficient. One also needs cleverness and prudence. Even as she postponed the problem, the child in her would grow! The more she postponed, the more it would grow. She had to contend with two aggressive presences in her life: the father's and the son's.

It was two o' clock in the night.

Lying on the bed, Ushe laughed out loud and clear as she repeated for herself the expression: *father's aggressive presence and the son's*. Her raucous laughter split open the quiet of the night and was heard by the neighbours. She was surprised by her booming laughter herself. She felt a measure of comfort, having had the last midnight laugh at her situation, considering that a devil had ridden on her for so long. But she couldn't call the father husband! Nor their son 'son'! The two would become her secret bonds. And yet that was the truth. They were next to nothing to the external world. What an irony of circumstances! Above all, why should she assume the upcoming child would be a son? Where could she declare that the child would be her child while she couldn't own the person she loved so very much with all her heart, soul and body as her own husband?

It was an ambivalent situation.

One needed to instruct life. One needed to employ so many strategies. One needed to explain things to so many people. She tried to close her eyes and sleep, even in the topsy-turvy turmoil of her mind, thinking of the next day's work at the office. She, who had rolled on the bed in such a tempestuous state of mind right till four in the morning, drifted ever so slowly to sleep.

Holding a wreath of flowers in its tiny hands, a cuddly baby, crawling on all fours, ran wherever Ushe ran. Losing out in the end, Ushe herself took up the tot and the wreath before fondling the tiny tot. As the awareness that it was a dream crept up on Ushe, she woke up. Touching the belly over again, she checked for herself. The belly felt even pudgier. The tot one sees in a dream is not a figment of a dream, it becomes a reality! The day was not far off. This was for sure! How was that possible? If she remembered it, her heart would skip a beat. What all places could she run to for cover? Wherever she went, she would run into the same people. No one in her office had suspected her. No one had asked questions of a dubious nature. But they might have done it behind her back, who knew! There were reasons for Usha to think that way. Rohini her staffer did jab her a couple of times and look for some reaction. Attender Muniratna was a bosom friend of Rohini's. So there were whisperings between the two of them. Even being officers, women would be pries, creating room for gossip, idle talk and search for reasons for things they had no business probing... But Ushe had been an exception to this womanly norm. She had however kept her ears open to such talk after she became pregnant. Her present situation had made her do that. She had to work with them on a daily basis. She could take a transfer on promotion etc. But under the circumstances she could not go anywhere on transfer. She would require leave in the days ahead. She should enquire with her bosses whether she could go on leave for a year on medical grounds, she told herself. She could produce an affidavit, getting a doctor to write some other reason. She had so far been jibbing to apply for any kind of leave, and if she applied now for a year's leave all of a sudden, wouldn't people be surprised? They would. They might even show up at her home to see her! Yet was there any other way? No, there wasn't.

Whenever she distanced herself from anxiety, new paths began to appear.

She decided that, if taking out the baby was not an option, she could look for ways ahead after she was delivered of it. That it was her life came to the fore. Why should she not become a mother? She could spend the period of a couple of months of her nursing motherhood somewhere. She could then raise the child, declaring it was her adopted child. It would call her 'amma.' How delighting! After all this mumble-jumble cleared, only the two of them: she and the tiny tot! Who else could pry her with questions then?

All these thoughts of Ushe's were all preplans for the future. Nothing more. They were of course not final. But she would think these same thoughts time and again every day. She began to do the necessary preparations prior to applying for a year's medical leave, talking to her boss.

There seemed to be no hurdle in this regard. But she would have to be away for her younger sisters for a few months. She then had to put forward some reason and tell them she was going to some other town. They should not come to now that she had applied for leave for a few months before the date of delivery. They could come on Sundays if they so wanted. They would ask why she had asked for leave. Such thoughts would assail Ushe several times in a day. She could tell them the baby was her adopted child. Perhaps this matter of adoption might alarm her sisters.

They might have expected that their children could possibly get some share of their elder sister's earnings and property. With an adopted child being the heir to her property, they might, they might think, be deprived of that and so might distance themselves. How could she help such a contingency? This was the truth. Could she give away her earnings to some one other than her umbilical bond? These were all thoughts for the future.

What she needed to think about and solve right now was important. She should tell this somehow to Rajagopal, she told herself, and request him to be like before, as her lover. Before that, she should correct the mistake she had made. That was indeed the right thing to do. Her bond with him should be good and smooth. It had withered because only of her. Had she kept quiet, this would not have come about. If she came clean, unbosoming herself of everything, her love might yet rejuvenate. She didn't know what kind of bond this was, but she liked, needed and wanted it: that was, for sure. The child materializing in the world was now certain. Even if it was going to be an adopted child, Rajagopal was the father. This both he and she knew.

Wasn't this exploitation?

It was. Was it something that she did all by herself? No. She didn't find any answer to the question of why things were like they were. Where was failure? One would jib even at using the word, 'exploitation'. Every woman who loves and begets a child could not be a wife. *But why can't I,* Ushe posed to herself. *Why should not I ask this question?* But that was not possible. She was well past her marriageble age. Gopal was already sixty. Marriage at an age at which one should be dandling one's grandchildren was a further deathknell to one's honour. In case this was sweet news to Gopal, it was okay. But what if it turned out to be a shocker?! She should tell him in such a way that it didn't shock him. *Yes, that is the right thing to do,* Ushe concluded. *If, instead of talking on phone, I talk to him face to face, he might understand and appreciate what I am going to tell him. He ought to volunteer to marry me. If I build desires on my own, pain is guaranteed. What I should do and should not is not clear!*

He might pardon me if I request him with an explicit "Please pardon me!" Such a blunder has perhaps happened because of me, a slip that is graver than it appears. Now I am in the family way without a family! It wlll do if the idea that I am carryng his child makes for a feeling that would lead him to pardon me. Is it the case that things didn't happen the way I assumed, but he has deliberately developed a relationship, for example, with Mangala Deshpande to distance himself from me? One can't say such people don't exist. An illusion that is nowhere this thing called 'love' is what people fall for and achieve, a lure of the flesh, an infatuation. It is NOT love. Not that marriage need necesssarily have any meaning. This has been proved. It is not even that only the person who has borne a child is entitled to real love. We have seen many cases of people who have married many times and shammed love. It is a shame that a person like me who has had so much experience has been cheated. Ayyo Oh God! May such a thing not happen! That Gopal belongs to that league of people would poison the mind. That would be intolerable. What to tolerate then is not clear at all. But one certainty stands out and that is the child that is going to be born, whether the whole thing is fraud, deceipt, attraction, misuse or whatever. It is better to think about the child than about these other issues. This is the light that is visible for now. But doesn't the honest intense involved love that I carry and be delivered of, and raise have any value? If it doesn't, what is the meaning of value? Would he rejoice, agreeing that it is his own child? Or, would he marry me, considering that I was going to be the mother of his child. Further, what if some untoward thing happens? One should always be done thinking of negative things before one thinks of positivities. One should therefore be mentally prepared for both. Otherwise, things would exacerbate. But somewhere in one the nooks of my mind the belief that Rajagopal is not such a person has struck roots. The mind wants to believe that that is the right thing. If the culprit is the self, one feels good and at peace. If on the other hand the other is the one who has slipped, and not the self, he is the untrustworthy person, then the discomfort and turmoil that it causes might be to the extent of doing some harm to that person. Unable either to express the results of such a disaster or to experience them, it burns and burns fiercely. But how about keeping myself to myself, pass by the world and be myself to my own world? Life wins if I keep his love, indifference, insults, and complaints aside and lead a life of stilled consciousness with an attitude of sacrifice and indifference to the results of one's work. But then the love in the interior loses. Stilled consciousness should not be a fad of the moment. That ought to be the be-all and end-all, the essence and heart of one's way of living. It is only then that one can face and handle the ensuing struggle with courage and spunk. I should not develop even for a moment the feeling that he will some day own the child. One then stabilizes and solidifies. But this of course is easier said than done. One feels like slaughtering right now people who, having married once, love so many and pose as dignified persons. This being the case, where does one get this 'stilled consciousness' from?!

Tapping her own head once, Ushe pressed the calling bell. Muniratna the peon came running. "Tell the driver!" she said. "We need to go to Devanahalli. Some problem has cropped up there."

Ushe had of late was rather lacklustre in her official work because of a hassled personal life. Although not terribly hip, she dressed up, and made up okay. A loose dress worn so as not to show the part around the belly-button. There were three officers working under her. She would take up their isuues and problems investigate them heself, visiting the site of conflict and either solved them herself or handed them over to law-enforcing agencies.

She left, along with another official named Vinaya Kumar, for Devanahalli to investigate the murder of a Dalit woman. She commanded everyone's respect. She showed great intensity in her work ethic. Besides, her reach included the minister. She was reasonably good-looking as well. The question of why she hadn't married met with the stereotypically putative reply of family problems.

It was two o'clock in the afternoon when they got to Devanahalli. By the time they reached the spot, Mahadeviah the police inspector, a local official and the kin of the slaughtered woman were there waiting for them. The postmortem report said it was murder after a sexual assault. The man who did this was a local goonda who wielded considerable political influence in the area and who had sneaked off after the crime.

"Collect all available information from all possible sources," Ushe instructed the inspector. "Get his photograph and send it to all newpapers and nab him as soon as possible."

The poor and the Dalit elicited supreme neglect. By the time she left for Bengaluru after advising the inspector that he needed to take quick action and after consoling the bereaved family, it was eight in the night.

Asking the driver to turn left at Malleshvaram, she said, "Stop the car on the road next to Varalaxmi Nursng Home. I will be back in ten minutes." It was ten o' clock in the morning. Getting down from the car, Ushe walked over to Rajagopal's house. She was disappointed to see the compound gate locked. The neighbor, who stood in her compound, shuffled across to say, "They are not here. He was not keeping well. He must have gone to take rest. Who are you?"

"Just an acquaintance!" said Ushe laconically before walking over and getting into the car.

She couldn't walk normally, like before. There were just seven days before she was to go on leave. This put her at ease. It was only a temporary consolation of being relieved from one anxiety. But what would she do the whole of three months of her leave? Staying at home for such a long time without doing anything would be difficult. She should she thought buy some good books and music CDs. She should buy the things required for the kid sometime. Who would buy them for her? The disgust of taking leave for giving birth by stealth crystallised in her. But she had to now appreciate that only whatever fell to her lot was hers. She had better learn to enjoy it! This was the obsessive thought. After the delivery, she had to go out somewhere for three months. This was the current problem. She needed to tell the doctor. *Thoo... who wants hospital life?* she exclaimed to herself. She thought only about this whenever there was respite in the next three days. If she happened to wake up at the dead of night, the same thought would come back. And she would feel terrified. When one night she woke up around midnight, she switched on the lights, remembering something. She then looked for some telephone number, scouring so many files. She walked over to the kitchen, drank a glass of water, and returning, rested, sitting down on the sofa in the living hall. Around four thirty she took out a diary from the inner chest of the godrej almirah. Placing a finger on the page she intently looked at one particular number. There was written Sister Roja, Cochin, Kerala. Placing the diary on the table, she went to sleep totally at peace with herself. Sister Roja was in fact from Karnataka. She was a nurse in a hospital here. Her original name was Puttarangamma. When a patient tried to rape her, she slapped him on his cheek because of which he dropped dead. A court slapped on her, she was arrested. Ushe took up her case and shunting from police station to the court, she succeeded in unravelling the truth. The nurse had then married Joseph of Kerala origin and converted to Christianity. Rechristened Roja, she now lived in Cochin, working in a hospital there. Her husband was doing some business. Roja had a lot of respect, nay adoration, for Ushe. Only she looked like a leading light for Ushe now. Although she was not very rich she was reasonably off. Ushe should ask her how she could bear the responsibility of her nursing motherhood for three long months. Ushe did feel embarrassed to ask her but there was no other way.

The following day Ushe called Roja around eight o'clock. Roja's joy knew no bounds. Ushe related half her story to Roja and requested her help. Roja didn't initially say anything. She said she would get back to Ushe in two or three days after consulting her husband. Giving Roja her phone number an asking her to let her know as soon as possible, Ushe disconnected.

Along with the present undecodable situation Roja's was another. Ushe shrank, thinking that asking Roja was in itself a mistake. She enquired at other places to see if help was forthcoming. There was no way found for the next week. Ushe felt wretched. Roja's call did come one day, around ten in the night. Seeking Ushe's pardon, Roja said she took so long because her husband was away. "Please do come, madam! We have an upstairs room vacant where you can stay. We woud deem it our good fortune."

Ushe felt suddenly at ease and fortified. Paths make themselves. She could say she found the baby somewhere which she adopted when she returned to Bengaluru. She had to make arrangements to take care of it. This wasn't difficult in Bengaluru. There were so many day baby care centres in Bengaluru. But she wanted to inform this to Rajagopal. No matter how many times she called him, he didn't take the phone even once.

****

265

Chapter Seventeen

Every word that he was speaking seemed very heavy to Gopal who, eating the breakfast brought from home in the hospital, was discussing the possible future happenings. Sharade was also there. In fact it was she who had brought the breakfast from home. Everyone was almost expecting something disastrous to happen. A deep anxiety rode on their chests. They should go bring Srihari. He ought to see mother atleast during her last moments. What meaning did sonhood have if the son didn't do even that for mother? Gopal called Shivaramu and Raghavendra to say, "Bring him wherever he is! Let him see mother. No stink to be raised. He may see others as well. But mother is important for us now." By the time he ended saying this, his throat choked. Taking up the phone to call Saraswathi, he wiped his tears.

In the meantime he did get calls from Ushe, but he had promptly cut them off. He had in fact come away to stay away from her. *Why is she calling now*, Gopal wondered. *What tricks is she upto now? I should not give in or rack my brains.* Gopal felt his head heat up. He came into the room in which mother had been put up. She was on artificial respiration. Mother's half-open eyes seemed devoid of life. Pulling a chair close to mother, Gopal sat on it. Placing his hand on her hand, he sat watching her. The physician kept repeatedly visiting the ward to examine her. Narayana and Jayasimha stood outside, computing something, things like what would be the probable hospital expenditure, how much money to draw from the bank, whether to ask elder brother at all for money because he seemed in trouble, and he had said he didn't want any share in the property, and things like that. "Apply

266

immedialtely for leave, and come over! Mother is sinking," Gopal told Saraswathi. He disconnected, not leaving any room for her to even react. He walked back into the hospital ward, his mien rather solemn. The physician had arranged to shift Sitamma to the Intensive Care Unit. The body which had lived such a long full fulfilling life had curled up, shrunk and withered. Seeing nurses move the body, Gopal came over to help them do it.

But the physician wouldn't have it. "No, Sir," he suggested. "They will do it!" The physician himself helped the body onto the stretcher. The breath was weakening. It was felt they were taking her to the ICU for nothing. They felt they all should be with mother when she breathed her last. They were doubtful as to whether they would allow them inside the ICU.

"Sir, let her be here. Don't take her to the ICU," they requested the physician.

"No, it isn't that. If necessary, we will call you. One person can be with the patient in ICU. We have to make our efforts."

Narayana, Raghavendra came over and asked Gopal. It was learnt that shifting her to the ICU was indeed a matter for anxiety. Gopal felt oddly bad when Raghavendra walked up and told Gopal that Srihari was nowhere to be seen. *Where did he go even when mother, who bore him, is in her last stretch?* Gopal wondered in great concern. *He seems to get a meaning somewhere, a meaning he doesn't get here with us. He searches for it there and not here with his own mother, brothers and sisters.* Since Gopal didn't have much contact with him, he didn't have any authority over him. And they were grown up adults so that to advise them spanking or thrashing them was not possible. He had grown so much that he could even slap Gopal! If every one's life got smooth and happy, there was no end to one's joy. The lives the ten siblings led were not particularly rich. Each one's was different. But no one lived keeping relationships. A family would always have little squabbles and fights. But since they shared their parentage, some adjustment was of course necessary. But why did Srihari go the wrong way?

Rajagopal spent considerable time mulling mother, brothers and sisters. In the middle, the memory of Ushe would sneak its way through. Gopal effortfully pushed it into limbo. Remembering his teaching days with her, he did soften. Their relationship had revived in just under a year. To think about the way she thundered at him at the Kannada Authority! It was so very demeaning for him. What a bad moment it was for him! When he recalled it, he felt hurt, deeply outraged and belittled. Even if he didn't want her memory to come back, it would somehow squeeze its way through. *Why is it returning even in such a difficult situation,* Gopal asked himself. *Mother is on her death-bed. My heart is agitated, troubled and out of sync.*

Holding the little meal-bin in front of Gopal, Sharade said, "Eat!" But Gopal said no. Yet pressing him, Narayana and Sharade had him eat a couple of morsels. In their minds had collected into a deep pool the incident having to do with Srihari that had happened at home sometime back. Mother had paid with her life for the fact of Srihari socking elder brother on the cheeks. *What kind of love was this for her son!* they wondered. Srihari didn't earn such love. The affection that mother had developed for Gopal, who was in fact forever far away, in Bengaluru, was without parallel. Didn't she have this kind of attachment for other children? Even if a mother had ten children, her affection for all would be the same. But it would be a tad more for the eldest.

Sleep wouldn't come to Gopal in the hospital. Yet Gopal alone stayed back with mother. The rest went off to Sahana's house to sleep. Gopal logged a call from Ushe at eleven in the night, which Gopal disconnected immediately. *Why is she calling me continuously,* wondered Gopal. *What is there to talk? Everything is over and she has blackened my face. Fearing more trouble from her, I have stayed away from her. And yet what derisively loud laughter! She was so very soft and loving, but now her attitude has changed.*

It was six in the morning.

Sitamma shuffled off her mortal coil. Gopal grew very emotional. He, who had placed his head at her feet, didn't take it off. It was only then that the doctors came to know that he was the chairman of the Kannada Authority. A senior doctor came over and spoke words of reassurance. A bevy of nurses walked up to console Sharade.

Narayana didn't waste time in going on a phoning spree. All arrived at the house in Siddapura. They saw mother for the last time before they broke into an extended bout of heart-rending crying. The women had only recently come there for the wedding-invite-writing ceremonial. That they had come now to see her dead body was heart-wrenching. "Speak, *amma,* speak!" they wailed touching and feeling her ever so affectionately. Srihari swore at himself for causing her death by troubling her, talking about his share of the property and selling the house and stuff.

Gopal sat like a stone.

When the priest arrived, he got up and moved to organize mother's last journey on earth. "*Annayya! Annayya!*" Srihari called out, but Gopal didn't turn back to look. His eyes were a deep pool of tears. It was five in the evening when the six male children touched the funeral pyre wth fire.

"Inform the groom's party. There is no wedding for now!" declared Gopal as he stood ready to leave the following morning.

But the respectable Sitarama Shastri, the family priest remonstrated. "Sir! We need to take the mortal remains away for immersion tomorrow. It will be three days tomorrow since your mother died. You can't leave everything to your younger brothers! You stay back and complete everything before leaving! Doesn't your mother's soul need peace? Your mother had loads of affection for her eldest son!"

"That is right! You return after all this, *anna!*" chimed in Sharade, holding his hands in earnest supplication. Gopal's heart had dried up and hardened, and so had his eyes. He evinced interest in virtually nothing. Younger brother's deadly whack was mother's death-knell and death! It was an eye-opening lesson for Gopal. There were no words to speak. Saraswathi also walked up and put in words of reassurance.

The next morning they travelled to Talapurige to pick and choose mother's bony remnants. Picking up mother's burnt bones at the cremation site, Gopal turned incurably emotional. "These are mother's. These are the hands that took us up and with which she played with, and dandled, us. These are the legs that she spread us and bathed us on. These are the remains of mother's heart that hid her love for us. See this, Narayana! See!, Srihari! See! Jayasimha!" Showing the bony remains in the ashes like this to his siblings, he put them all in a copper water-vessel. He then turned to Srihari, "Take, touch and see! These are the bony remains. Your mother's remains, damn it! Is there a difference between *aasti*, property and *asti*, bony remains? See! Hold it! Tell me its price! Can we sell it? One can get anything in exchange for money. Could one get mother? Take! Bear it on your head!"

Elder brother was acting queer. "*Annayya*! Why are you getting so emotional? You weep! Weep your heart out! Why are you composing poetry in the graveyard? How deeply you loved mother! She yielded breath just because of the whack you got from him!" Hugging Gopal, everyone sobbed. Srihari also fell at Gopal's feet and sought his pardon. "*Annayya*! Please pardon me!" he begged Gopal even as he burst out weeping. "Or else, mother will call down curses on me!"

Keeping the metal vessel containing mother's mortal remains outside the house, they all bathed. Then they - all male children, uncle's son, and the priest - left for Srirangapattana for dispersal and disposal of the mortal remains. The priest had issued a strict commandment not to eat. Head bowed, Gopal sat with eyes closed. He had pressed the metal water-vessel that was in his lap to his chest in the spirit of preserving what was close to his own heart.

No one spoke. Having an offering of water done to the mortal remains at the river-confluence or the sangama area of the historic town of Srirangapattana, the priest declared the debt of life of the mother to this earth ended before letting the remains into the waters and saying, "Take in a sip of water three times!" Gopal didn't listen. He had the bony remains pressed to his chest.

Everything in this world is euphemeral, no one owning or controlling anything. Whatever has to happen has to happen. He whacked me. I felt the hurt. Mother died because I felt pain. This would be incorrect. But it is true to say that when Srihari hit me, mother felt as much hurt and humiliation as I did. That is what is meant by 'mother'. She is my mother. She played with me, loved me and stood in amazed delight at the way my being grew and evolved.

Shivaramu distributed the hot coffee he had brought from home in a flask. Since they were not to eat or drink in any hotel or public place, Sharade had concocted some coffee, stored it away in a flask right in the morning, and put the flask in the Srirangapattana-bound car. It was twelve o' clock when they got to Srirangapattana. Gopal didn't drink even coffee. He felt his head whirl as he got down from the car. "After the remains are dispersed in the waters, you may eat a meal in any Brahmin house if they want to serve you." Sharada had said. "Or else, you can head straight here, and eat after taking a bath". There were Brahmin families meant only to cook and serve people during the period of mourning after a death when normal life activities are suspended, the *sutaka*. Sharade had heard that such people cooked with a great sense of *madi*-purity. *Okay*, she told herself now without saying it. *At such times people feel really hungry. This being the case, fasting would be an ordeal. Besides, the priest would be unduly strict!*

"*Anna*! Look, you have a phone-call," said Shivaramu before handing the mobile over to Gopal. Everyone was walking on the sands of the river bank. Gopal took the device. He couldn't see the number in the darkness. The voice that said 'hello!' at the other end was Ushe's. Gopal didn't greet back with a 'hello!' But he slowed down. The others went ahead.

Gopal didn't want to speak at all. Yet he kept the mobile device close to his ears so as not give a different impression to his younger brothers. Ushe's voice was trembling. But since what had to be said, she thought, had to be said, she kept talking. She kept saying for about fifteen minutes that a slip of behavior that she had perpertrated wasn't quite a crime because she had done it for Gopal's love. Her words were ghee thrown to fuel a burning fire.

"If you say 'Pardon me!' how would the mouth open to do it?" Gopal lashed out in righteous but restrained rage. "Don't call me again. I am in deep distress. What you have told me just now is enough! You can't pardon your own self!"

Even as Gopal struck a discordant chord, Ushe kept saying she had some sweet news to share with him. Gopal's face grew murky even as it contorted. Rendered sick and tired by her words, he sagged down right there on a step. Ushe kept saying something. But Gopal felt darkness hemming him in from all directions. The words from the mobile were not heard. No matter what the matter was that she wanted to share, Gopal didn't feel like listening to anything. Such was the shock he had felt, which had made him downbeat. The pain, distress, fear, humiliation and insults he had experienced was all due to Ushe. That letter with the death threat, bomb scare, that intense love, the thirst in her body for him, his possible death were all of her making. What kind of pardon was she talking of? There might not be a lover of her kind in human history. Having forged a scheme in concert with the Home Minister to trap him, she was now talking of some sweet news. Sleazy words were waiting to come out! "You evil bitch!" he browbeat her. "Shut your trap! If you call me again, I will report to the police!" Such bawdy words must have come out of his mouth for the first time in his life. Although Gopal had let rip, she kept saying she had to share the joyous news.

"What more happy news can you have, you killer! Tell me if you can't stand even the fact that I still exist! I will yield breath here and now! Forget about listening to you, I will teach you the lesson of your life! You are threatening me? Are you a woman? You threaten me with death in a letter, with a bomb etc and you say you love me!? *Thoo...* I don't want to see your face or hear your voice! If you call me, ever again, you will be behind bars."

Younger brothers stood stunned, wondering why elder brother was yelling like he was. The copper water-pitcher of the mortal remains was still with Gopal. The mode of elder brother's words seemed strikingly odd to the others. *What is this? Elder brother never ever talked like this!*

They felt alarmed. How would a man thunder at the top of his lungs at a woman? He was talking of love and stuff. In the same breath he talked also of jail, killer, bomb, scheme, police, terror etc. What kind of words were these? Where was the place for such words in the encyclopaedia of the Kannada Authority? Was there?

Every one rushed to Gopal. Gopal didn't know what he was doing! He was quivering. His lips trilled as words fell out. The copper water-pitcher was also about to fall off. Srihari ran up to hold the water-vessel. Gopal wasn't yet aware of what was happening. His vitriolic attack was still on. "Go, you witch! Go tell the Home Minister or someone with whom you conspired to kill me the sweet news. You are now coming and giving me sweets after giving me poison to drink in the name of some beverage? If you speak one one more syllable, the police wll do you the honours. Tell me who else who conspired with. Nonsense! Keep the phone down, you home-wrecker!"

Gopal panted, not being aware of what he was speaking and without disconnecting the phone. He signed to Shivaramu that he wanted some water, and Shivaramu ran up and got him water in a glass, pouring the water that was in the bottle he got from the car. Gopal's hand was shivering so much that the water was spilling over from within the glass. Narayana sat by and fed him water. He took the cloth lying on his shoulder, the *shalya*, and fanned him. "*Anna*! What happened? What is all this? Give me the mobile! Look at it. Someody is still talking," Narayana said. "Some politics!" replied

272

Gopal. This Ushe must also have heard. She must have tried to hear it, and she must also have been equally shocked. Recovering, drinking some water, Gopal took the mobile before disconnecting it.

Words had hidden away. The breath of Gopal's body had lost its way, becoming miserably wretched. *How incredible that my Ushe who loved me wanted to kill me! A letter threatening my death! She, who was my own student!? Ayyo, you woman! How ruthlessly cruel you are!* Gopal's legs were walking like the devil's. There was no sky above, nor sands below. Before him were delusions called 'brothers.' A sword called 'love' loomed behind the back. Mother's mortal remains on the chest. Walking slowly and quietly, he caught up with his brothers. He should immerse mother in the waters. Only then will he get peace. Nothing else will remain in this world. *A sword behind my back, I said. This is something I have myself kept, loving it! It will never leave me!* It smelt around and poked into me only to do away with me!

Gopal came near the waters, holding tight the metal vessel containing mother's this-worldly remains. He was now thought-less. Everything was still. "Son!...," somebody seemed to call. Scared, Gopal turned to look. No one was visible. "Walk slowly!.." warned the voice. Gopal had hugged the vessel tight.

There was a flight of steps leading into the river. Green algae slime had spread on the steps below. If you stepped on those steps, you could slip and become part of the waters. The boatman who was thereabouts, warned him against going further, but, not quite hearing it, Gopal proceeded further and he felt the floor, and it was slippery.

The other male family members stood, surrounding Gopal. Gopal poured the bones into the waters before putting his joined palms against his chest in salutation and pressing the palms softly and reverentially to his eyes. His chest felt ponderous and weighty. The discomfort intensified. It was only darkness that he could see. He could see nothing!

"Take in water sips from your palms, Sir! Take an *uddarane*ful of water, take three such sips and come back without looking back!" instructed the priest. All the five men did the same before stepping right back. But Gopal, who had bent down to throw away the remains, didn't raise his back. As he took another step forward, he slipped into the lap of the water body as the current drew him in.

"*Anna! Anna,* Oh *Anna!*..." Heart-rending cries boomed.

All the five younger brothers scampered up. Things had spiraled out of control. The boatman grabbed Gopal by his hair before bringing him back ashore. The brothers cried their hearts out. Then the car was taken to the top of the flight of steps before Gopal was driven to Srivani hospital in Mysore. The physician there only went through the motions of examining him as Gopal had by then long breathed his last.

"You have come for mortal-remains immersion after losing your mother. Be bold!" The physician advised them as he patted their backs. "He has had a heart attack even before he fell into the waters. He was dead even before you brought him here. Drum up courage!" Coming to know that the deceased was the Chairman of the Kannada Authority, he regretted that he had come to his clinic during his last moments.

Thinking that destiny's last laugh had rapped on the door of the house in the form of Srihari, no one said anything to Srihari. Everyone's sorrow had collected in their chest as a holy temple. If they now took him to task, he could do something to his own self. So thinking they solaced him and brought him back home. "*Annayya! Annayya!*" they wept. "You have left us. Did you go away for good because you grew sick and weary?" But nobody came to know the real reason behind his abrupt death.

Whose was the phone call? What did they talk? Nobody asked such dubious questions.

But Narayana took up the mobile and saw the list of received calls. Who was it? Why did brother grow scared. Why did he get agitated because of the person's words? Had somebody threatened elder brother? One couldn't say that this was for sure. The person could have said some other thing and he might have been agitated by it. We can't deride anyone because we don't know what the person said. Or did the fact that he had been hungry since morning have its effect on the body?

Showing the number to Jayasimha, Narayana said tearfully, "See! Elder brother has been shocked when someone from this number phoned him. Shall we call the person and dig into this?"

"No. We shouldn't do it," replied Jayasimha. "We don't have our own person in our midst. What do we achieve, knowing the reason? In sum he has received one blow after another. We have our faultlines. What is the use, blaming others? You convey the news to every number except this one! Call home at once! They would all be waiting for us. We don't know how they will receive this shocking news. We can solace our own people first. Because someone did something, why should we investigate it? You think about how you will inform sister-in-law."

Mallikarjuna Swamy felt miserably wretched when they informed the Kannada Authority on phone about Gopal's demise as they drove from Mysuru to Madhugiri. He in turn told everyone in his office. Mallikarjuna Swamy called back to say, "Sir! He had his close friends in Kannada Bhavana. So many people need to see his mortal remains one last time. He is a Kannada heavyweight. Please keep the body here for half an hour before taking it to Madhugiri. It was his workplace. May his soul rest in peace!"

Narayana consulted Jayasimha. Jayasimha asked Narayana to ask Mallikarjuna Swamy to call back after five minutes. He asked him to ask Mallikarjuna Swamy to inform the media, both print and electronic. After telling Mallikarjun Swamy this, Narayana asked, "What do we do now?" Jayasimha grew pensive. His thoughts were on home. *How would they take this: the day before it was mother, and today it is elder brother! Does this odd event happen anywhere else? Why is it only in our home? Imagine how sister-in-law and Sharada the elder sister would react? Why did leave them all and go to Bengaluru? He shouldn't have gone for this chairmanship. His death is due only to that. This being the case, why should we keep the body there? No need. If anyone wants to see, they can come here to Madhugiri.*

Narayana told Mallikarjuna Swamy as much.

"There is a village called Siddapura near Madhugiri. Please come there! We are going to reach home rather late. Moreover we are all hungry. Elder brother has left us. People at home are anxious. We need to get home as quickly as possible. We can do the postdeath rites and honors tomorrow so you can come and see him. Our mother left us the day before. We have found it tough to face this double tragedy." So saying Narayana began to sob.

"Okay sir! I will inform those who are interested. Siddapura, did you say?"

"Yes, right. Siddapura. *Namaskaara*, please don't think otherwise."

That said, Narayana sat thinking, his hands on his cheek. Covering his face, Srihari sat by the driver. Gopal's dead body was in the other car on the backseat, on the laps of Raghavendra and Shivaramu. The two of them had the corpse on their lower limbs, unmindful of the hunger that bothered them. As it was Gopal's car, laying the body on the backseat wasn't a problem. No one spoke as the car sped through towns and villages. But Narayana, holding Gopal's mobile, did look for the call that came in the afternoon. Since Gopal had deleted her name, he had to look for the nameless number, which was a touch difficult. He chose one number of the call that had come at that particular time and called. Jayasimha sat, head bowed while Narayana listened in.

The voice at the other end held forth: "I know you have pardoned me. I have some delightful news for you. I don't now how you will take it. I am pregnant now, nearly six months gone. Three more months, our child is coming. Shall we forget the past and live like before?"

Narayana got curious and alarmed at the same time. He was impaled on the horns of whether to speak or not to speak. If he did speak in reponse, she might recognise the voice as not Gopal's and so stop speaking. So he kept wordless.

"Why, Mr Poet, are you silent?" the voice at the other end continued. "You haven't come out of your anger? Have some mercy on us, the poor! I did a mistake in an emotional moment. I am now seeking your pardon. I also assure you that it won't repeat over again. Please don't say 'no' ! I will give this child a glowing future. You look and rejoice! Why this silence? Has your health improved? Has the Kannada Authority work been boring? Nothing of this sort will ever happen again. Please come! I believe you will!"

Narayan undid the call. *We have no use for these words. They uproot trust and honour. Let us not touch this number again. We can't say that this is the cause of elder brother's heart attack either. She might be someone elder brother has nothing to do with. She might have spoken to the wrong number. She did mention the Authority. But she didn't say which Authority. But there is no doubt that the number is the same. One can't think of an affair etc in regard to elder brother. Elder brother came here to take rest. There was news in the papers that he faced a murder threat. Except that we don't know anything. But why did elder brother behave the way he did? Why did he grow scared? What was the shock due to?*

The string of thoughts that the call had set off raced, one piece of the string behind another. Speeding past Kunigal, the cars tangoed toward Tumakuru. The sun, the eye-of-heaven was seeking his westerly home, filling the heavens with a coppery red. No matter how fast the four-wheelers moved, it seemed slow! Wondering what lurked deep underneath the silence that reigned in the car, Narayana thought better of speaking and instead, chose to think about things that needed to happen. The same Siddapura, the same house, younger sisters and brothers, the same sister-in-law and the same life!

With the village approaching, his heart started palpitating, and he pressed his chest.

****

About the Author of this Translation

Prof P.P. Giridhar is a well-recognised translator of creative fiction in Kannada, a south Dravidian language. He may well be ranked among the best literary translators that ever breathed, along with a Gregory Rabassa!

He has a graduate degree in Education, postgraduate degrees in Linguistics and English literature and a Ph.D in Linguistics. Has shown great flair for literature and translation. This is his sixth English translation in print of a Kannada novel. His English translation(1998) of *Parasangada*

279

Gendethimma, Srikrishna Alanahally's novel earned him the American Kannadigas' special award, administered by the Karnataka Sahitya Akademi in 2000. He also won a Translation Grant in 2007-08 from the ICWT, University of California, Irvine, the only Asian to win the award that year. He has published abroad (in the USA, in Japan, in Spain, in Canada and in Singapore) on linguistic structure, on literature and the language of literature, and on translation as a phenomenon. He ran and edited for several years a translation journal called *Translation Today* and a website called www. *anukriti.net*. His website is giridharpp.weebly.com. A sample of his creative output: **a.** Discursive: Mao Naga Grammar, Angami Naga Grammar, Kannada Case Grammar, Angami-English-Hindi Dictionary. **b.** Literary Translation: Gendethimma, Vaishakha, Awadheshwari, The Inscrutable Mystery, The Bounds. His contrarian-sounding paper called Literary Art : An Interrogative Meditation, questioning the literary credentials of literary pieces like the much hyped Kannada novel titled **Sanskaara** was presented at an International Conference on Language, Linguistics and Literature organized by the Global Science and Technology Forum on June 8-9, 2015 in Singapore.

About the Author of the Original

Ms Kamala Narasimha is known to be a bold free-thinking novelist in Kannada. She is doing her PhD on the education of the disabled. **The Earth's Womb** was her first novel. It was an influential novel which also earned some critical acclaim. It is about a woman who develops insatiable love for her land, and thus puts her life on the line for it, remaining unmarried etc. Kamala had to face many pains and hardships in life which made her tough and strong. In her novels we see such female characters, who face life's irksome hassles and nettlesome challenges with great courage and self-assurance. Unbinding themselves they walk with a resolute tread toward the positive state of a totally explored human personality, contributing to themselves and to their environment. Kamala's creative fiction which has the stamp of originality and novelty met with some controversies which she countered successfully. Her creative output:

Novels: Bhugarbha 2007, Aposhana 2010, Haddu 2010

Poetry: Bellada Madu 2007

Short story: Shadyantra 2007, hangella kalicida jiivakke, santeyallondu haNate. 2013, ananta nii, anantanaada 2015

She is the secretary of Karnataka Women Writers' Association,

Tumakuru branch, and Director, Dowry Resistance Forum